ORIGINAL

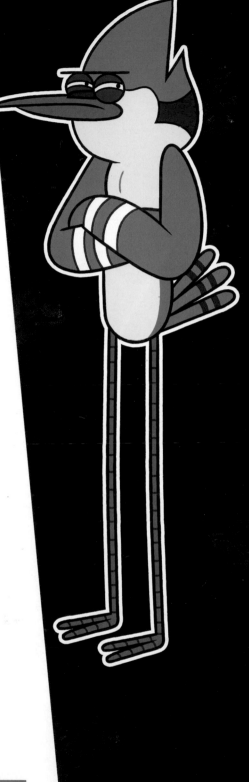

DESIGNER	**ASSISTANT EDITORS**	**EDITORS**
GRACE PARK	SOPHIE PHILIPS-ROBERTS & MARY GUMPORT	SIERRA HAHN SHANNON WATTERS & WHITNEY LEOPARD

WITH SPECIAL THANKS TO
MARISA MARIONAKIS, JANET NO, CURTIS LELASH, CONRAD MONTGOMERY, KELLY CREWS, RYAN SLATER AND THE WONDERFUL FOLKS AT CARTOON NETWORK.

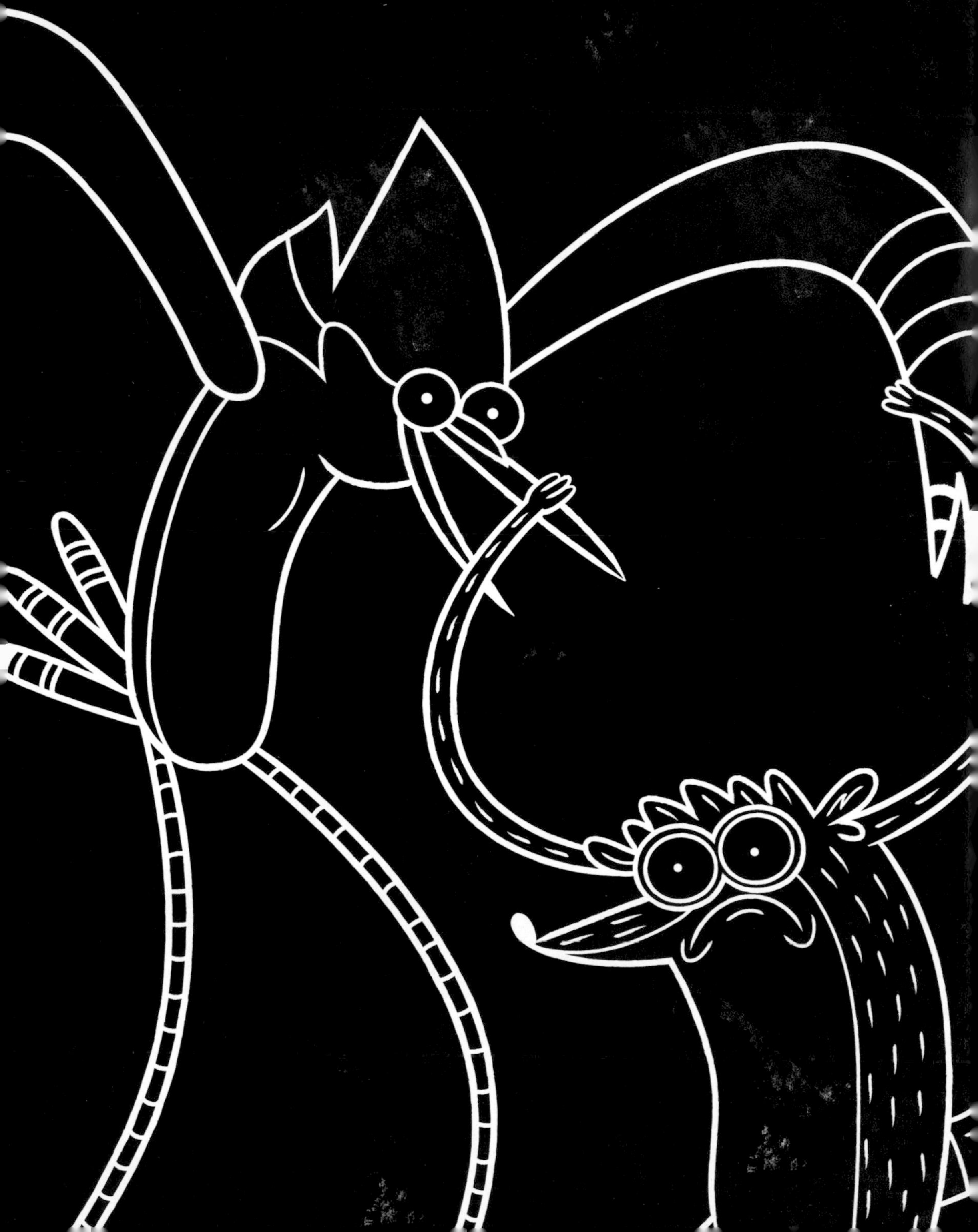

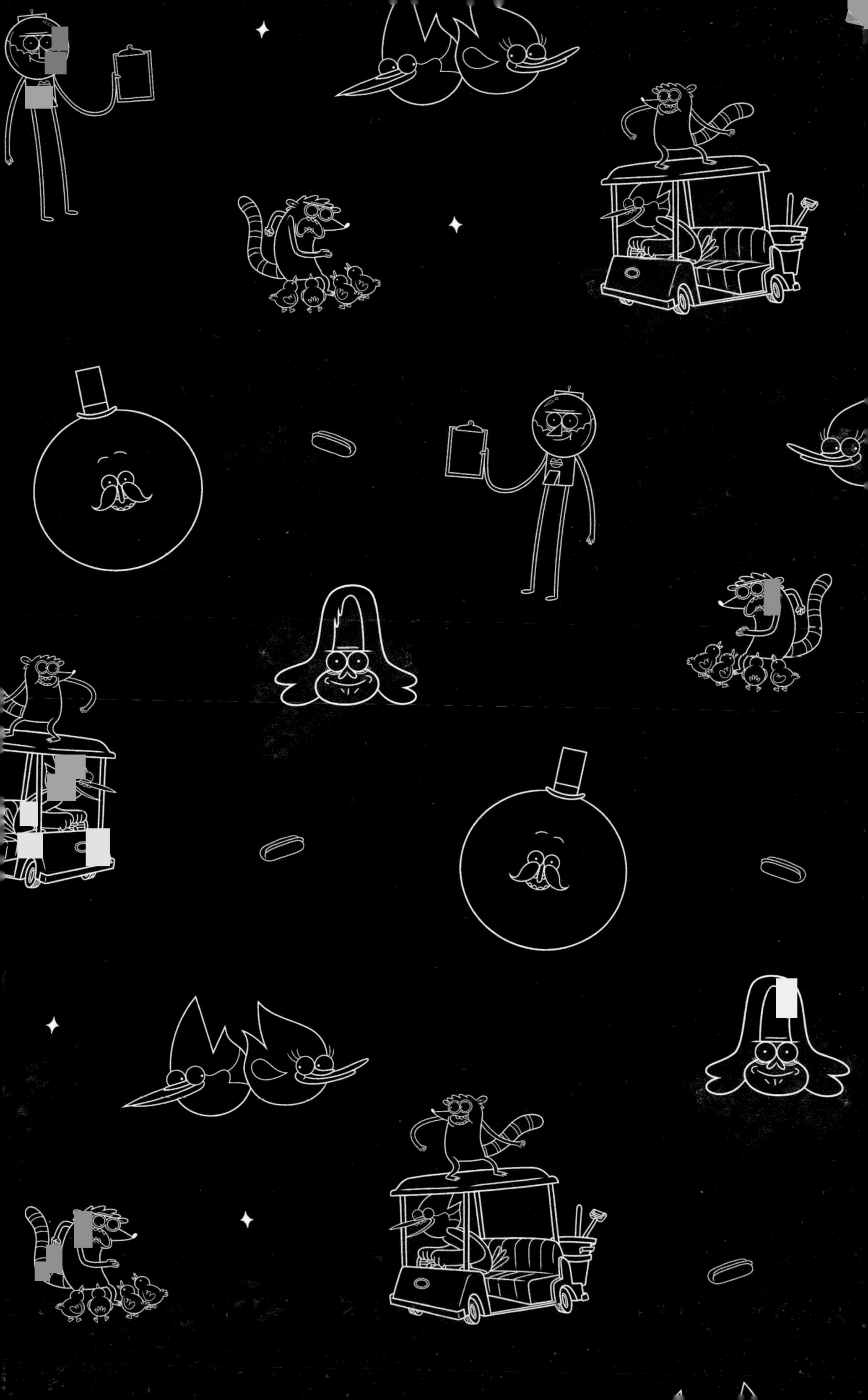

ROSS RICHIE CEO & Founder • MATT GAGNON Editor-in-Chief • FILIP SABLIK President of Publishing & Marketing • STEPHEN CHRISTY President of Development • LANCE KREITER VP of Licensing & Merchandising
PHIL BARBARO VP of Finance • ARUNE SINGH VP of Marketing • BRYCE CARLSON Managing Editor • MEL CAYLO Marketing Manager • SCOTT NEWMAN Production Design Manager
KATE HENNING Operations Manager • SIERRA HAHN Senior Editor • DAFNA PLEBAN Editor, Talent Development • SHANNON WATTERS Editor • ERIC HARBURN Editor • WHITNEY LEOPARD Editor • JASMINE AMIRI Editor
CHRIS ROSA Associate Editor • ALEX GALER Associate Editor • CAMERON CHITTOCK Associate Editor • MATTHEW LEVINE Assistant Editor • SOPHIE PHILIPS-ROBERTS Assistant Editor
JILLIAN CRAB Production Designer • MICHELLE ANKLEY Production Designer • KARA LEOPARD Production Designer • GRACE PARK Production Design Assistant • ELIZABETH LOUGHRIDGE Accounting Coordinator
STEPHANIE HOCUTT Social Media Coordinator • JOSÉ MEZA Event Coordinator • HOLLY AITCHISON Operations Assistant • MEGAN CHRISTOPHER Operations Assistant • MORGAN PERRY Direct Market Representative

REGULAR SHOW: Parks and Wreck, November 2017. Published by KaBOOM!, a division of Boom Entertainment, Inc. REGULAR SHOW, CARTOON NETWORK, the logos, and all related characters and elements are trademarks of and © Cartoon Network. (S17) Originally published in single magazine form as REGULAR SHOW 2014 ANNUAL No. 1, REGULAR SHOW 2015 SPECIAL No. 1, REGULAR SHOW 2017 SPECIAL No. 1. © Cartoon Network. (S17) All rights reserved. KaBOOM!™ and the KaBOOM! logo are trademarks of Boom Entertainment, Inc., registered in various countries and categories. All characters, events, and institutions depicted herein are fictional. Any similarity between any of the names, characters, persons, events, and/or institutions in this publication to actual names, characters, and persons, whether living or dead, events, and/or institutions is unintended and purely coincidental. KaBOOM! does not read or accept unsolicited submissions of ideas, stories, or artwork.

BOOM! Studios, 5670 Wilshire Boulevard, Suite 450, Los Angeles, CA 90036-5679. Printed in China. First Printing.

ISBN: 978-1-68415-042-7, eISBN: 978-1-61398-719-3

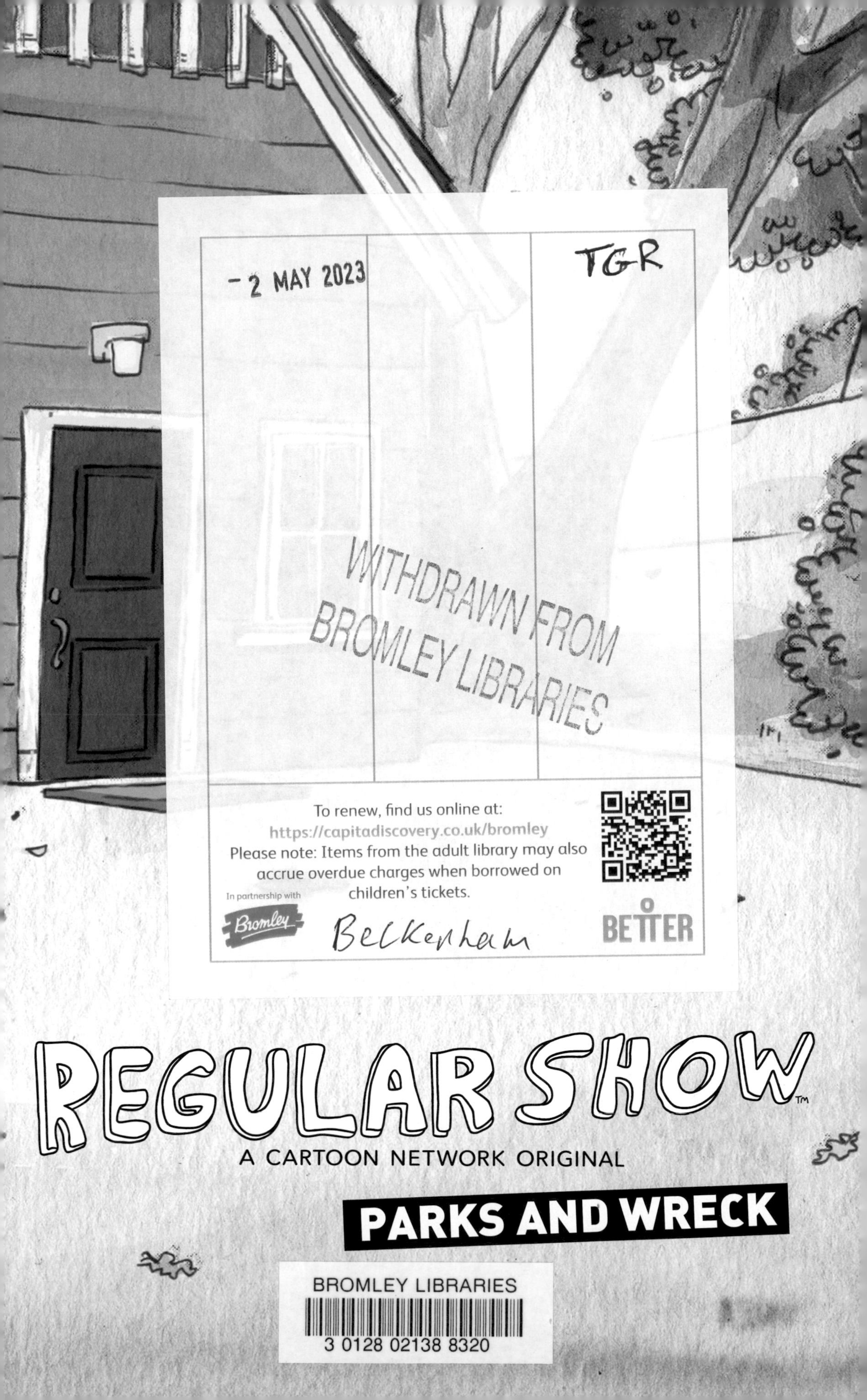

REGULAR SHOW™

A CARTOON NETWORK ORIGINAL

PARKS AND WRECK

REGULAR

A CARTOON NETWORK

CREATED BY JG QUINTEL

"SKY KICKS"

SCRIPT BY **KEVIN BURKHALTER**
ART BY **TESSA STONE**
LETTERS BY **COREY BREEN**

"WI-FI MADNESS"

SCRIPT BY **YUMI SAKUGAWA**
ART BY **ALLISON STREJLAU**
COLORS BY **LISA MOORE**

"VIDEO GAME GENIE"

SCRIPT BY **JIMMY GIEGERICH**
ART BY **MAD RUPERT**
COLORS BY **WHITNEY COGAR**

"MUSCLE SCOUTS"

BY **ANDY KLUTHE**

"SPRING EQUI-NOT"

BY **MOLLY OSTERTAG**

"FLIGHT FIGHT"

SCRIPT BY **KEVIN PANETTA**
ART BY **RIAN SYGH**
COLORS AND LETTERS BY **KATY FARINA**

"COUSIN GEOFF"

BY **KRISTINA NESS**
LETTERS BY **SHAWN ALDRIDGE**

"MELAN COLLIE"

SCRIPT BY **SHANNA MATUSZAK**
ART BY **DEREK CHARM**
LETTERS BY **JIM CAMPBELL**

"RE-BIRTHDAY"

SCRIPT BY **DEREK FRIDOLFS**
AND **PAMELA LOVAS**
ART BY **TERRY BLAS**
LETTERS BY **ED DUKESHIRE**

"GHOST GENESIS MECHA FIGHT"

SCRIPT AND ART BY **SARA GOETTER**
COLORS BY **JEN HICKMAN**
LETTERS BY **ED DUKESHIRE**

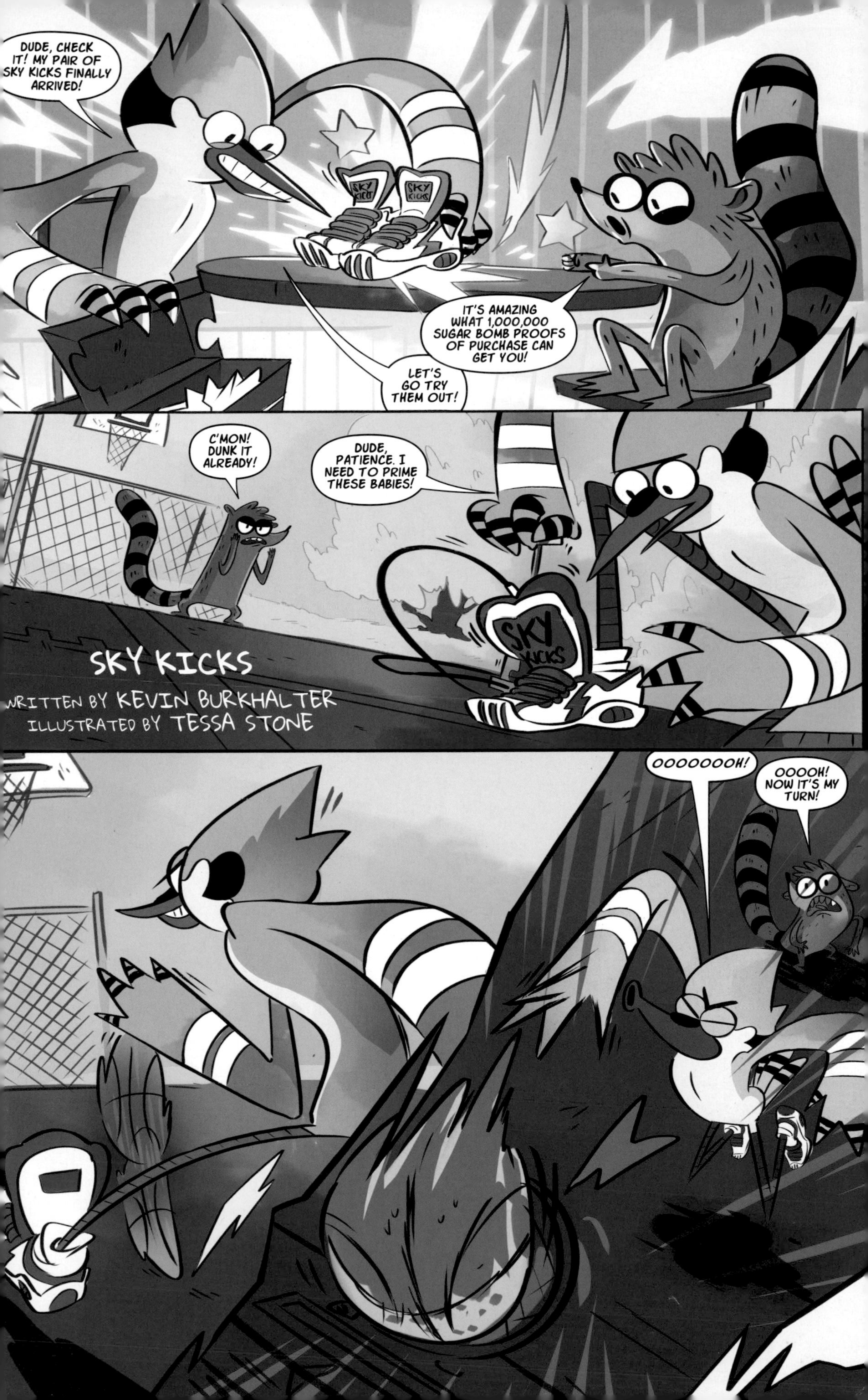
DUDE, CHECK IT! MY PAIR OF SKY KICKS FINALLY ARRIVED!
SKY KICKS
IT'S AMAZING WHAT 1,000,000 SUGAR BOMB PROOFS OF PURCHASE CAN GET YOU!
LET'S GO TRY THEM OUT!
C'MON! DUNK IT ALREADY!
DUDE, PATIENCE. I NEED TO PRIME THESE BABIES!
SKY KICKS
SKY KICKS
WRITTEN BY KEVIN BURKHALTER
ILLUSTRATED BY TESSA STONE
OOOOOOOH!
OOOOH! NOW IT'S MY TURN!

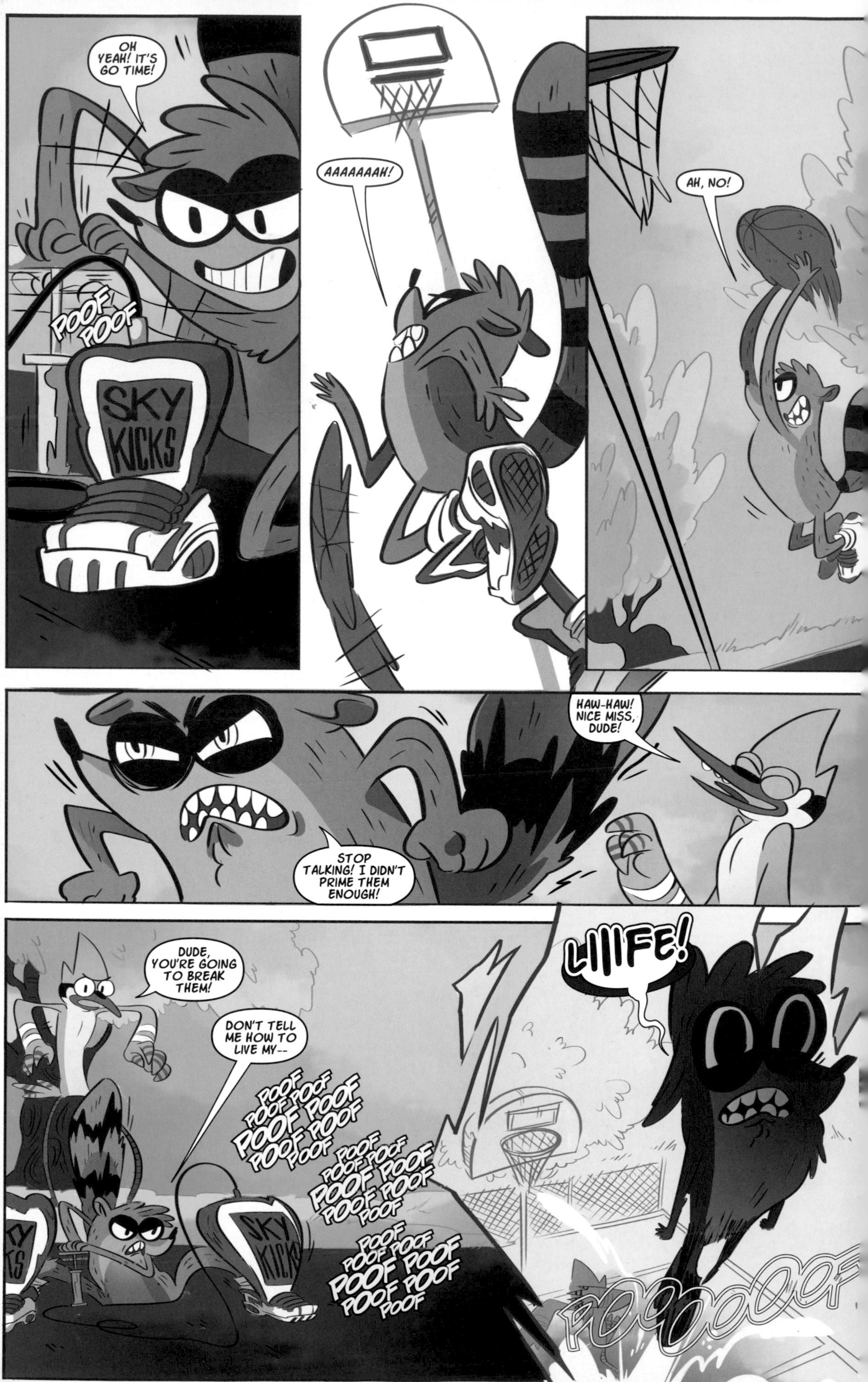
OH YEAH! IT'S GO TIME!
POOF POOF
SKY KICKS
AAAAAAAAH!
AH, NO!
HAW-HAW! NICE MISS, DUDE!
STOP TALKING! I DIDN'T PRIME THEM ENOUGH!
DUDE, YOU'RE GOING TO BREAK THEM!
DON'T TELL ME HOW TO LIVE MY--
POOF POOF POOF POOF POOF POOF POOF POOF
POOF POOF POOF POOF POOF POOF POOF POOF
POOF POOF POOF POOF POOF POOF POOF POOF
SKY KICKS
LIIIIFE!
POOOOOOOF

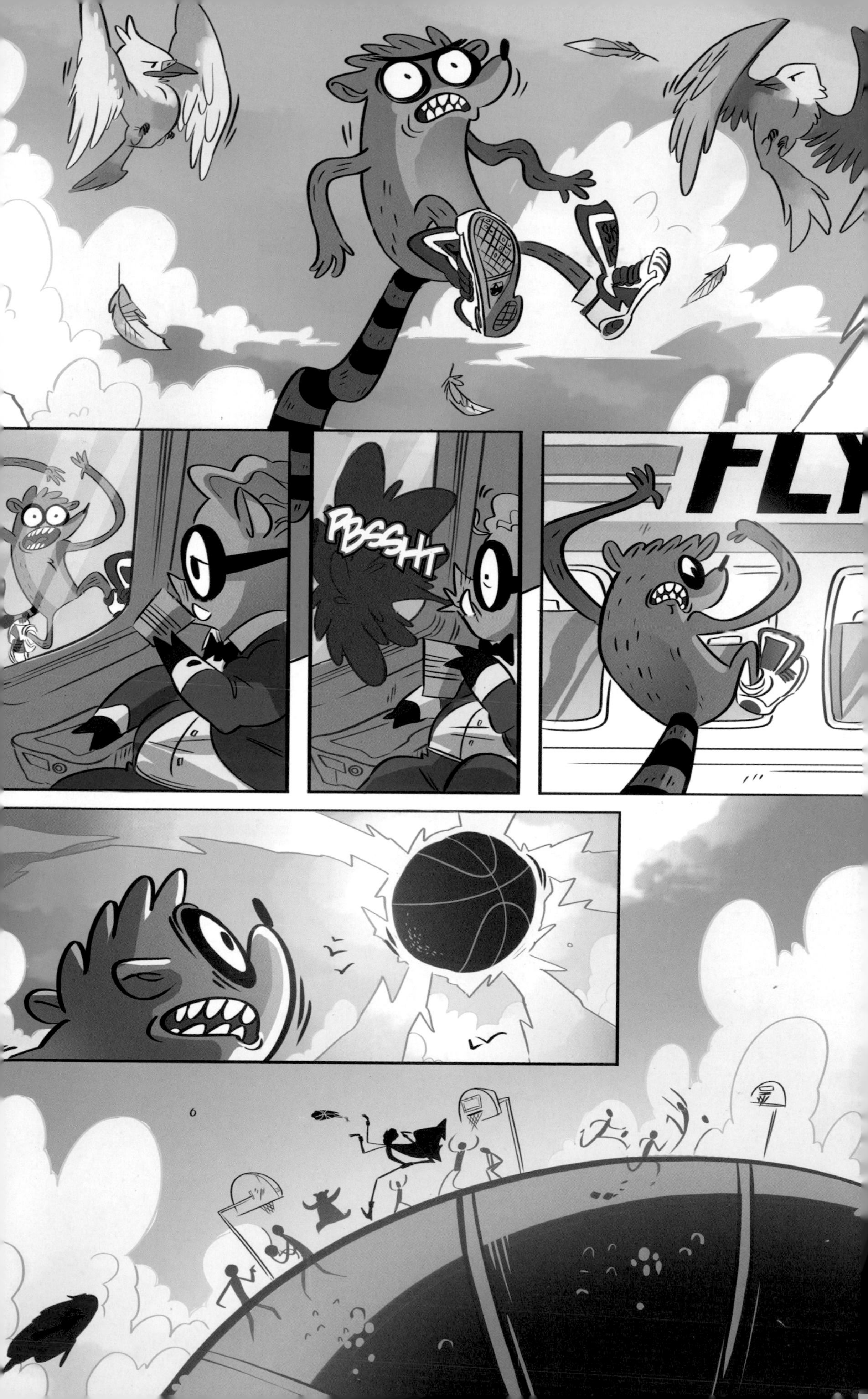
PBSSHT
FLY

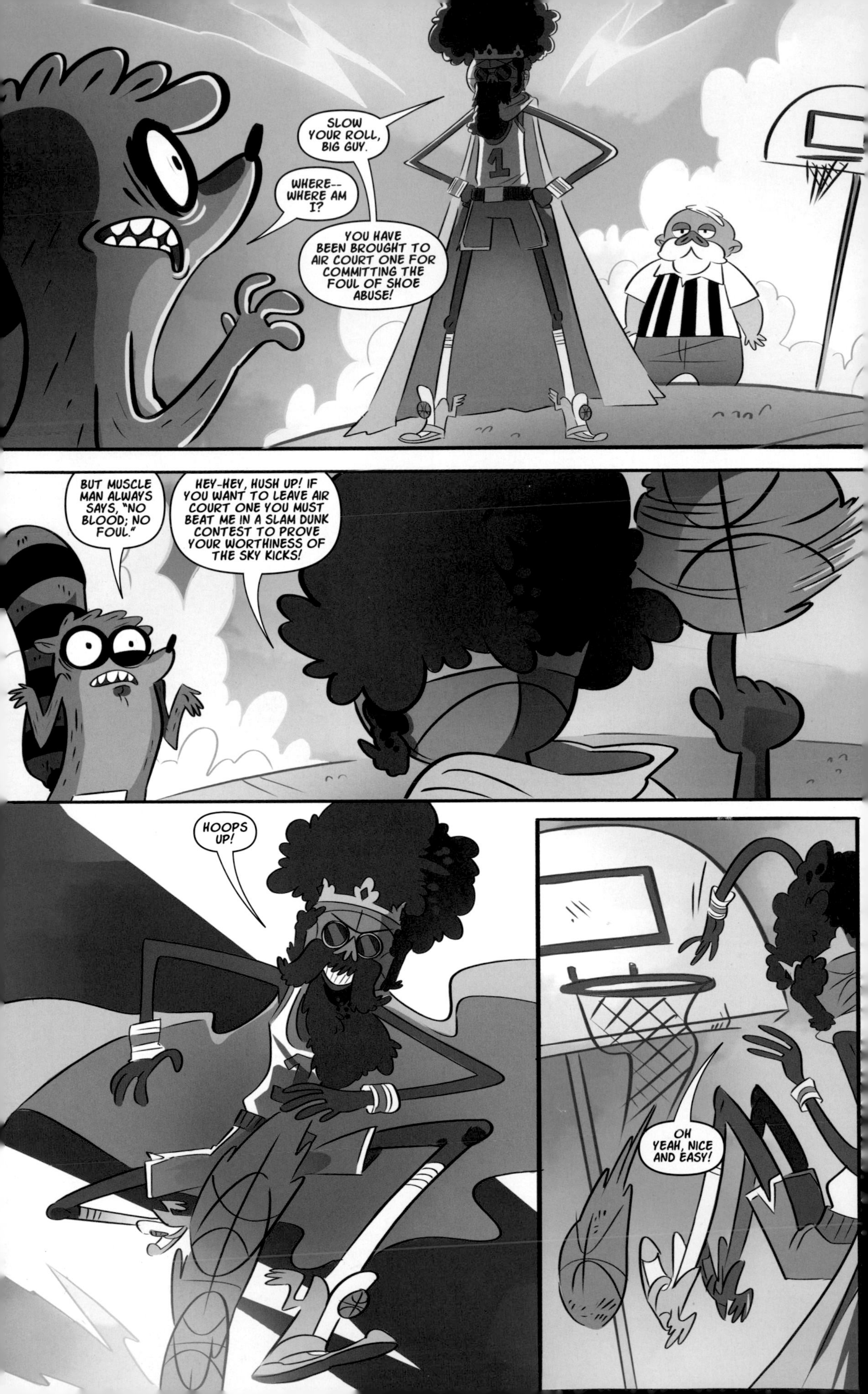
SLOW YOUR ROLL, BIG GUY.
WHERE-- WHERE AM I?
YOU HAVE BEEN BROUGHT TO AIR COURT ONE FOR COMMITTING THE FOUL OF SHOE ABUSE!
BUT MUSCLE MAN ALWAYS SAYS, "NO BLOOD; NO FOUL."
HEY-HEY, HUSH UP! IF YOU WANT TO LEAVE AIR COURT ONE YOU MUST BEAT ME IN A SLAM DUNK CONTEST TO PROVE YOUR WORTHINESS OF THE SKY KICKS!
HOOPS UP!
OH YEAH, NICE AND EASY!

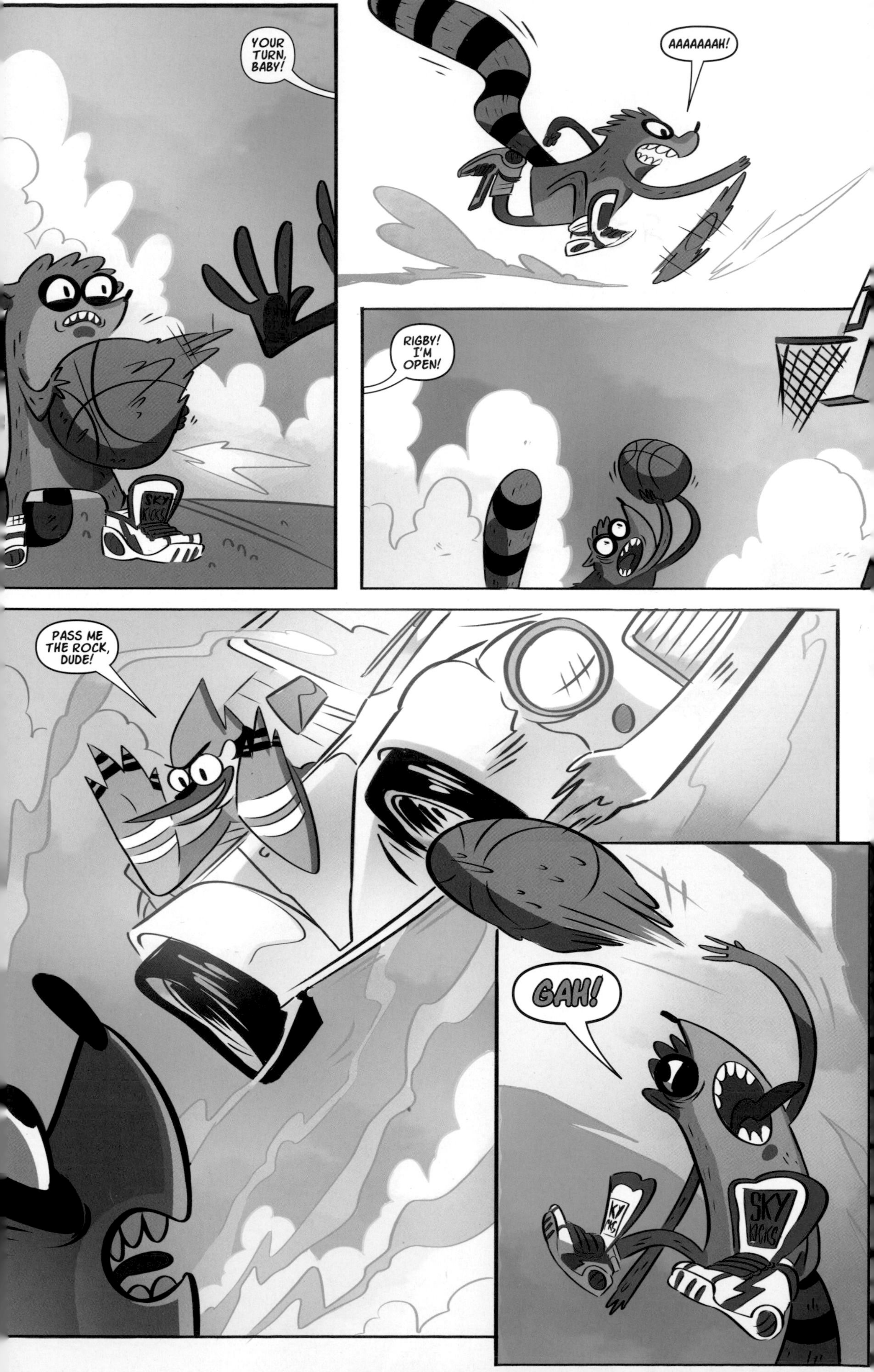
YOUR TURN, BABY!
AAAAAAAH!
RIGBY! I'M OPEN!
PASS ME THE ROCK, DUDE!
GAH!
SKY KICKS

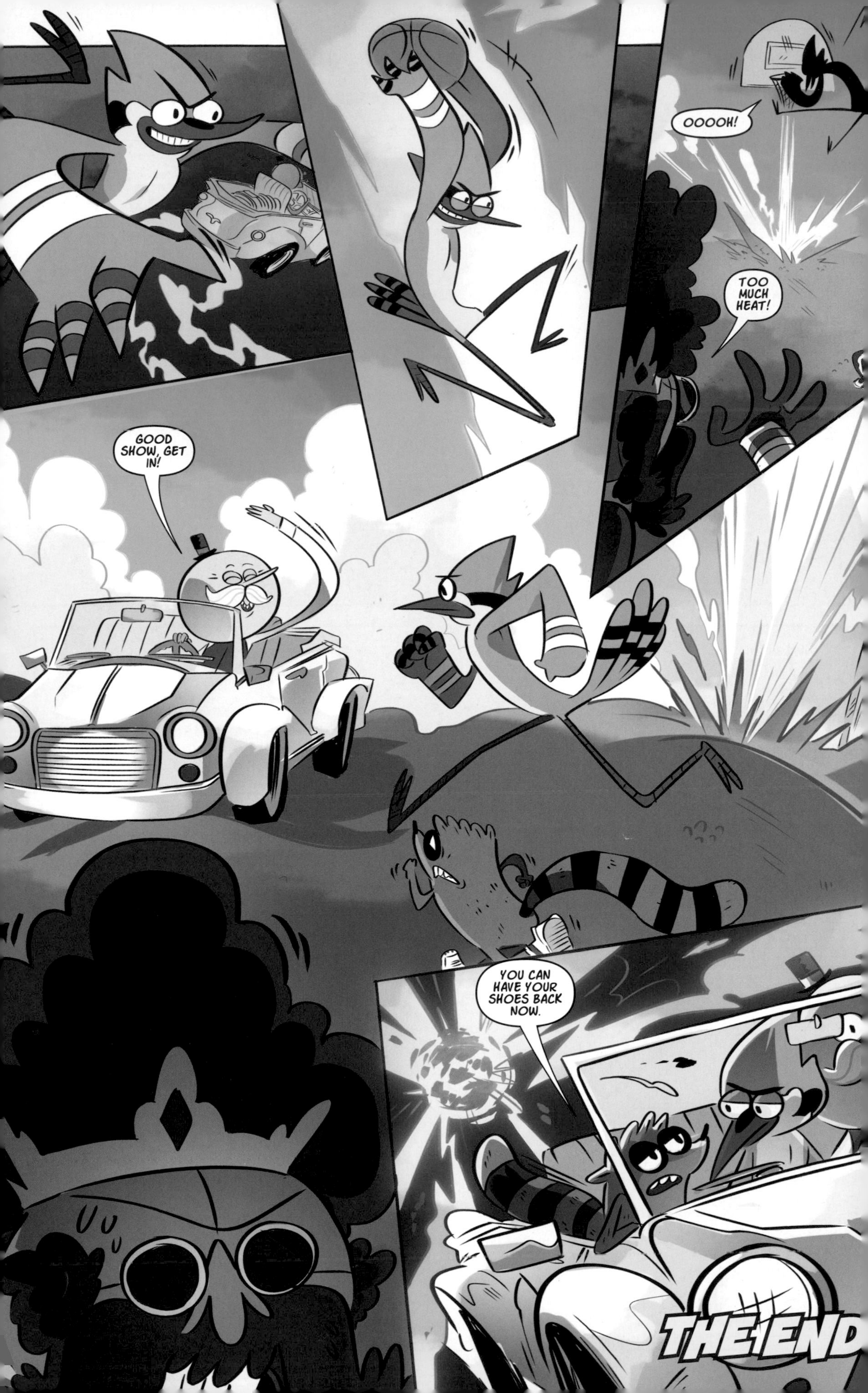
OOOOH!
TOO MUCH HEAT!
GOOD SHOW, GET IN!
YOU CAN HAVE YOUR SHOES BACK NOW.
THE END

WI-FI MADNESS

WRITTEN BY YUMI SAKUGAWA
ILLUSTRATED BY ALLISON STREJLAU

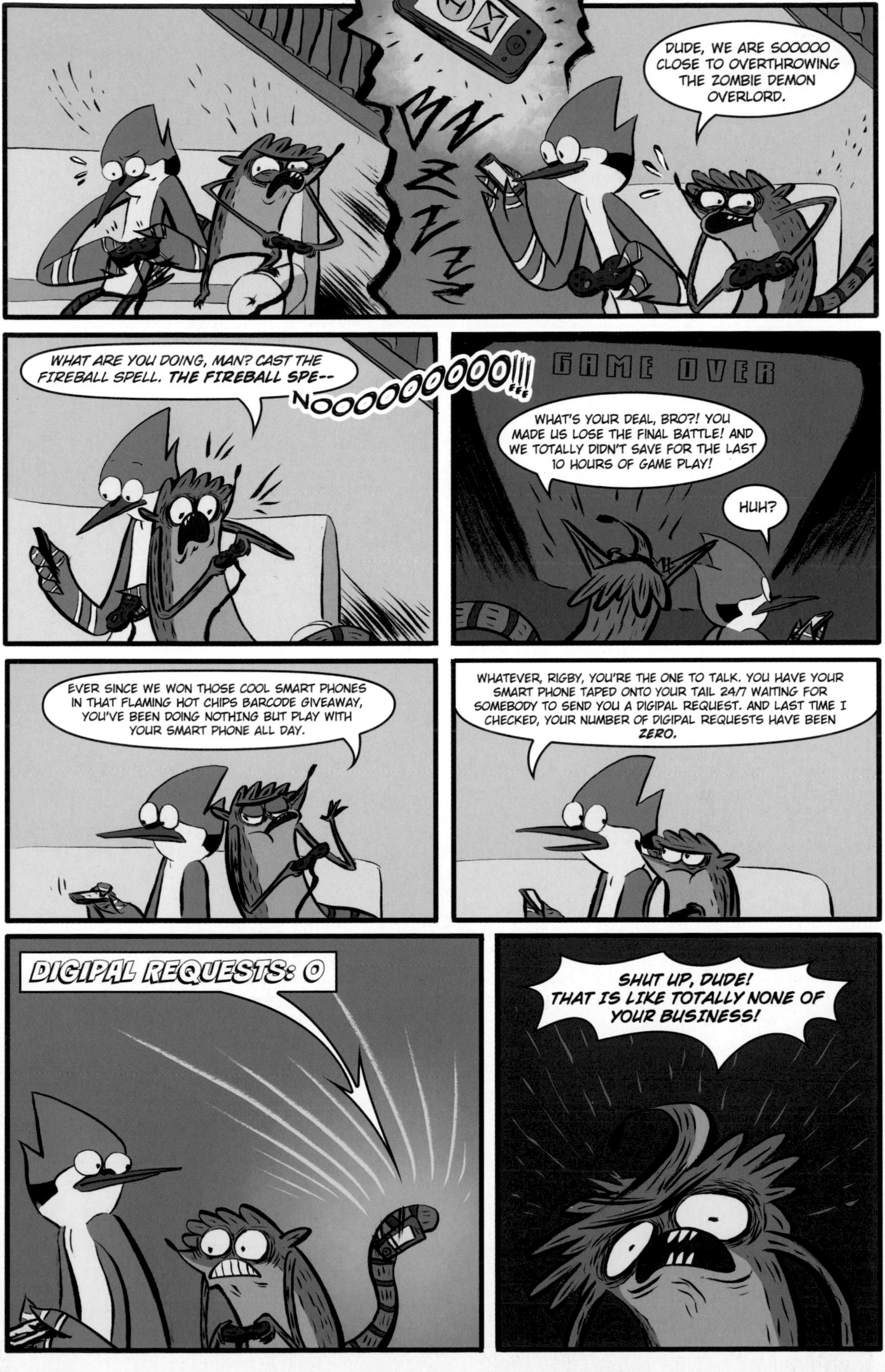
DUDE, WE ARE SOOOOO CLOSE TO OVERTHROWING THE ZOMBIE DEMON OVERLORD.
WHAT ARE YOU DOING, MAN? CAST THE FIREBALL SPELL. THE FIREBALL SPE--
NOOOOOOOOOOOO!!!!
GAME OVER
WHAT'S YOUR DEAL, BRO?! YOU MADE US LOSE THE FINAL BATTLE! AND WE TOTALLY DIDN'T SAVE FOR THE LAST 10 HOURS OF GAME PLAY!
HUH?
EVER SINCE WE WON THOSE COOL SMART PHONES IN THAT FLAMING HOT CHIPS BARCODE GIVEAWAY, YOU'VE BEEN DOING NOTHING BUT PLAY WITH YOUR SMART PHONE ALL DAY.
WHATEVER, RIGBY, YOU'RE THE ONE TO TALK. YOU HAVE YOUR SMART PHONE TAPED ONTO YOUR TAIL 24/7 WAITING FOR SOMEBODY TO SEND YOU A DIGIPAL REQUEST. AND LAST TIME I CHECKED, YOUR NUMBER OF DIGIPAL REQUESTS HAVE BEEN ZERO.
DIGIPAL REQUESTS: 0
SHUT UP, DUDE! THAT IS LIKE TOTALLY NONE OF YOUR BUSINESS!

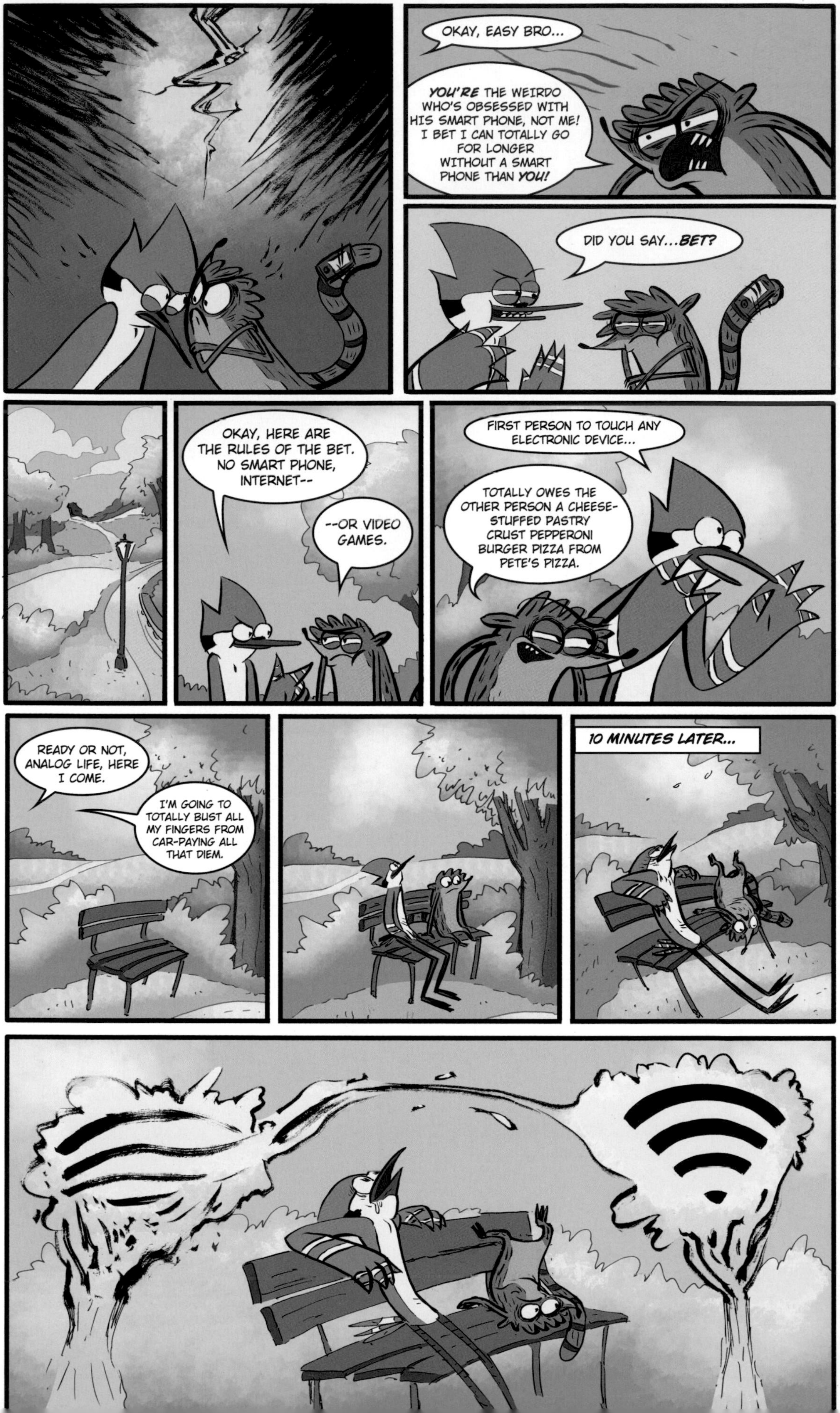
OKAY, EASY BRO...
YOU'RE THE WEIRDO WHO'S OBSESSED WITH HIS SMART PHONE, NOT ME! I BET I CAN TOTALLY GO FOR LONGER WITHOUT A SMART PHONE THAN YOU!
DID YOU SAY...BET?
OKAY, HERE ARE THE RULES OF THE BET. NO SMART PHONE, INTERNET--
--OR VIDEO GAMES.
FIRST PERSON TO TOUCH ANY ELECTRONIC DEVICE...
TOTALLY OWES THE OTHER PERSON A CHEESE-STUFFED PASTRY CRUST PEPPERONI BURGER PIZZA FROM PETE'S PIZZA.
READY OR NOT, ANALOG LIFE, HERE I COME.
I'M GOING TO TOTALLY BUST ALL MY FINGERS FROM CAR-PAYING ALL THAT DIEM.
10 MINUTES LATER...

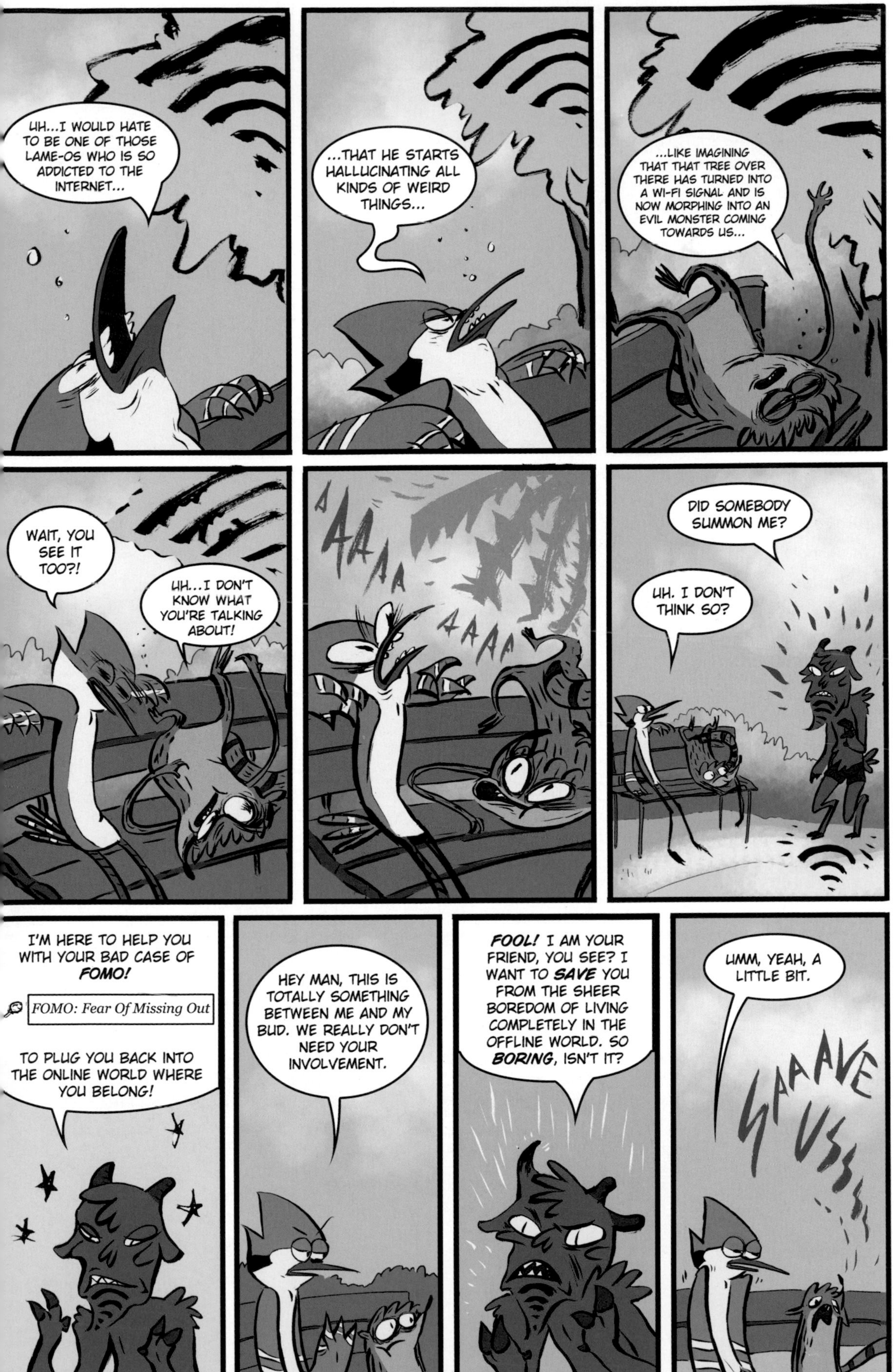
UH...I WOULD HATE TO BE ONE OF THOSE LAME-OS WHO IS SO ADDICTED TO THE INTERNET...
...THAT HE STARTS HALLUCINATING ALL KINDS OF WEIRD THINGS...
...LIKE IMAGINING THAT THAT TREE OVER THERE HAS TURNED INTO A WI-FI SIGNAL AND IS NOW MORPHING INTO AN EVIL MONSTER COMING TOWARDS US...
WAIT, YOU SEE IT TOO?!
UH...I DON'T KNOW WHAT YOU'RE TALKING ABOUT!
AAAAA AAAAA
DID SOMEBODY SUMMON ME?
UH. I DON'T THINK SO?
I'M HERE TO HELP YOU WITH YOUR BAD CASE OF FOMO!
FOMO: Fear Of Missing Out
TO PLUG YOU BACK INTO THE ONLINE WORLD WHERE YOU BELONG!
HEY MAN, THIS IS TOTALLY SOMETHING BETWEEN ME AND MY BUD. WE REALLY DON'T NEED YOUR INVOLVEMENT.
FOOL! I AM YOUR FRIEND, YOU SEE? I WANT TO SAVE YOU FROM THE SHEER BOREDOM OF LIVING COMPLETELY IN THE OFFLINE WORLD. SO BORING, ISN'T IT?
UMM, YEAH, A LITTLE BIT.
SAAAVE USSS

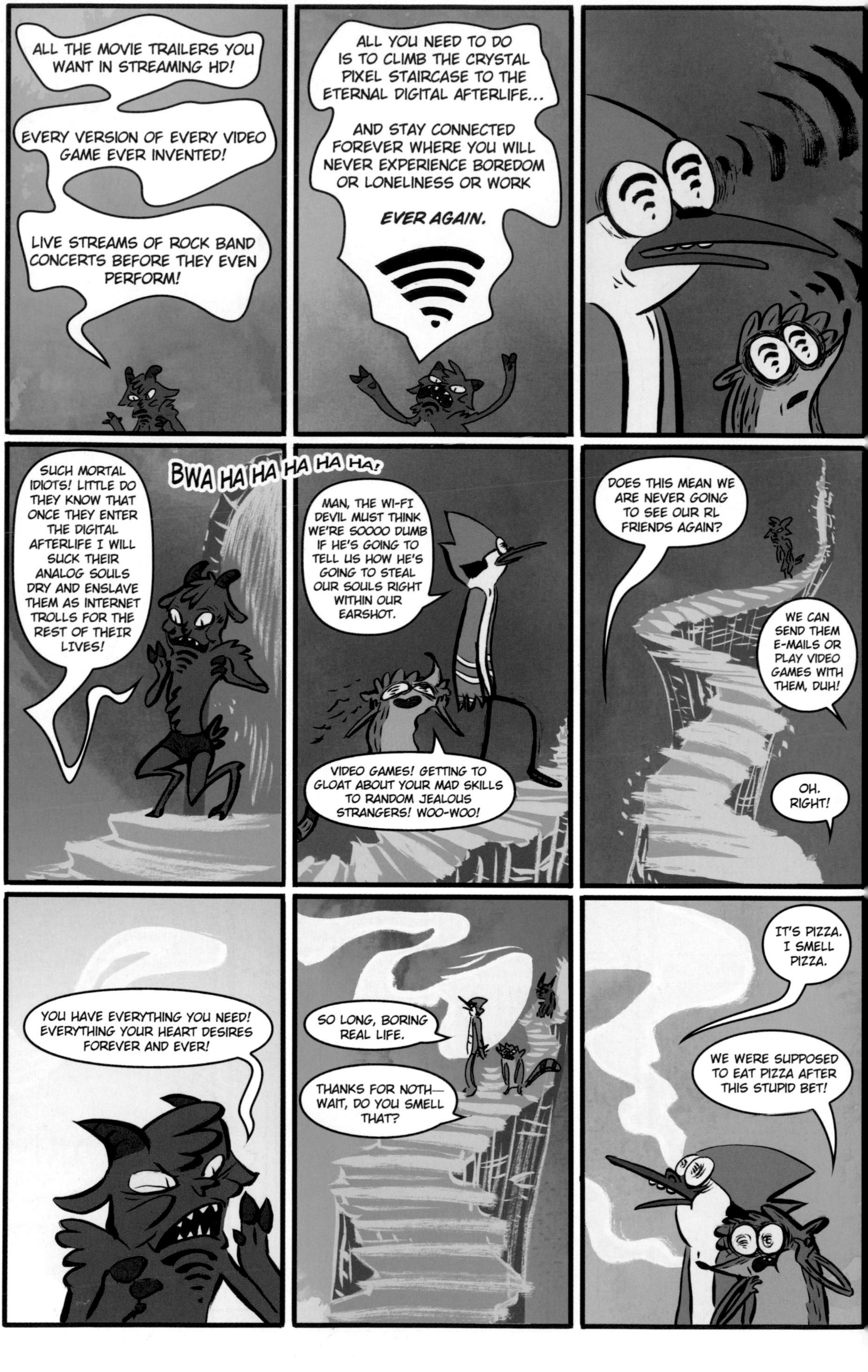
ALL THE MOVIE TRAILERS YOU WANT IN STREAMING HD!
EVERY VERSION OF EVERY VIDEO GAME EVER INVENTED!
LIVE STREAMS OF ROCK BAND CONCERTS BEFORE THEY EVEN PERFORM!
ALL YOU NEED TO DO IS TO CLIMB THE CRYSTAL PIXEL STAIRCASE TO THE ETERNAL DIGITAL AFTERLIFE...
AND STAY CONNECTED FOREVER WHERE YOU WILL NEVER EXPERIENCE BOREDOM OR LONELINESS OR WORK
EVER AGAIN.
SUCH MORTAL IDIOTS! LITTLE DO THEY KNOW THAT ONCE THEY ENTER THE DIGITAL AFTERLIFE I WILL SUCK THEIR ANALOG SOULS DRY AND ENSLAVE THEM AS INTERNET TROLLS FOR THE REST OF THEIR LIVES!
BWA HA HA HA HA HA!
MAN, THE WI-FI DEVIL MUST THINK WE'RE SOOOO DUMB IF HE'S GOING TO TELL US HOW HE'S GOING TO STEAL OUR SOULS RIGHT WITHIN OUR EARSHOT.
VIDEO GAMES! GETTING TO GLOAT ABOUT YOUR MAD SKILLS TO RANDOM JEALOUS STRANGERS! WOO-WOO!
DOES THIS MEAN WE ARE NEVER GOING TO SEE OUR RL FRIENDS AGAIN?
WE CAN SEND THEM E-MAILS OR PLAY VIDEO GAMES WITH THEM, DUH!
OH. RIGHT!
YOU HAVE EVERYTHING YOU NEED! EVERYTHING YOUR HEART DESIRES FOREVER AND EVER!
SO LONG, BORING REAL LIFE.
THANKS FOR NOTH— WAIT, DO YOU SMELL THAT?
IT'S PIZZA. I SMELL PIZZA.
WE WERE SUPPOSED TO EAT PIZZA AFTER THIS STUPID BET!

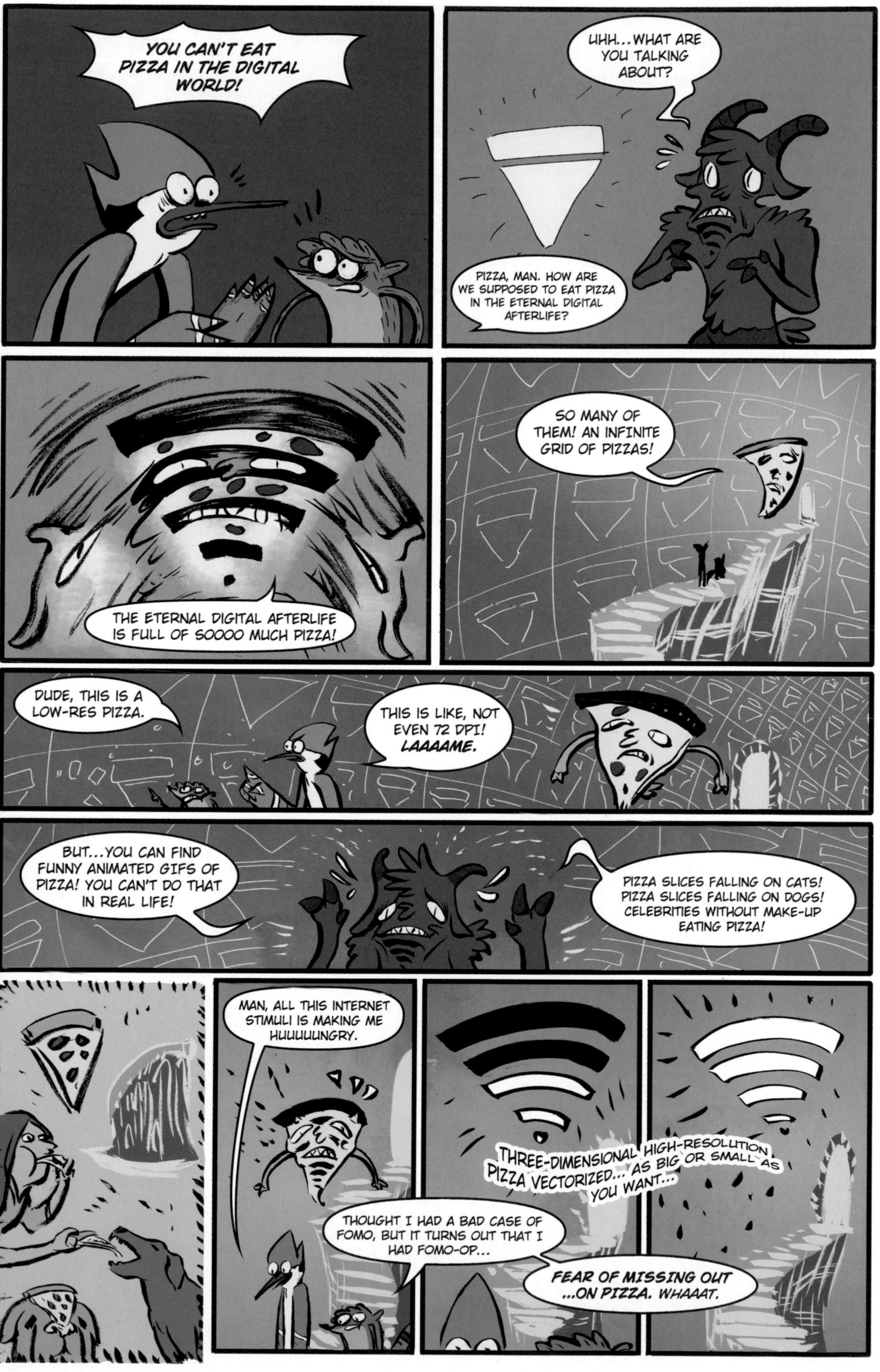
YOU CAN'T EAT PIZZA IN THE DIGITAL WORLD!
UHH...WHAT ARE YOU TALKING ABOUT?
PIZZA, MAN. HOW ARE WE SUPPOSED TO EAT PIZZA IN THE ETERNAL DIGITAL AFTERLIFE?
THE ETERNAL DIGITAL AFTERLIFE IS FULL OF SOOOO MUCH PIZZA!
SO MANY OF THEM! AN INFINITE GRID OF PIZZAS!
DUDE, THIS IS A LOW-RES PIZZA.
THIS IS LIKE, NOT EVEN 72 DPI! LAAAAME.
BUT...YOU CAN FIND FUNNY ANIMATED GIFS OF PIZZA! YOU CAN'T DO THAT IN REAL LIFE!
PIZZA SLICES FALLING ON CATS! PIZZA SLICES FALLING ON DOGS! CELEBRITIES WITHOUT MAKE-UP EATING PIZZA!
MAN, ALL THIS INTERNET STIMULI IS MAKING ME HUUUUUNGRY.
THREE-DIMENSIONAL HIGH-RESOLUTION PIZZA VECTORIZED... AS BIG OR SMALL AS YOU WANT...
THOUGHT I HAD A BAD CASE OF FOMO, BUT IT TURNS OUT THAT I HAD FOMO-OP...
FEAR OF MISSING OUT ...ON PIZZA. WHAAAT.

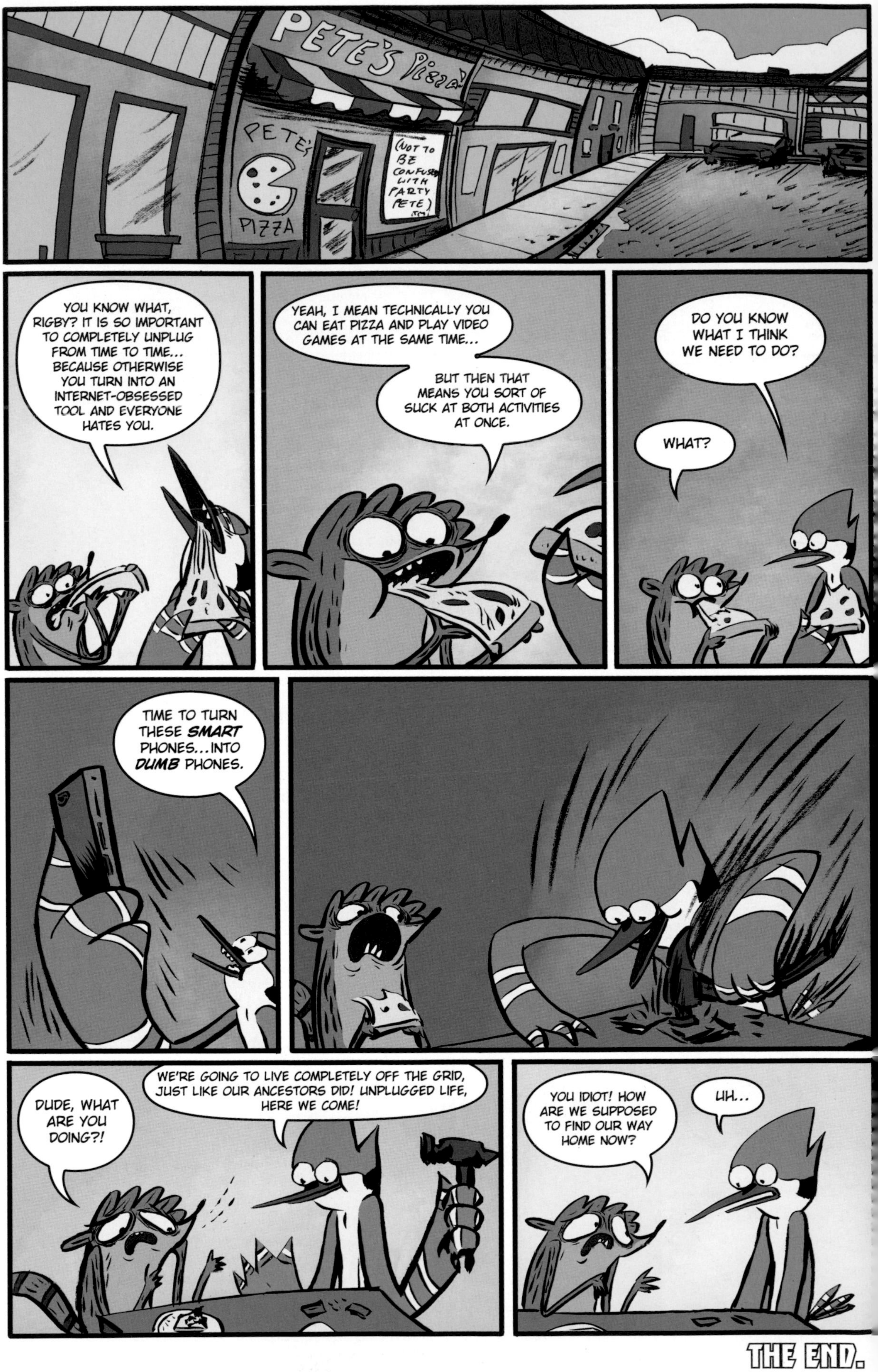
PETE'S PIZZA!
PETE'S
PIZZA
(NOT TO BE CONFUSED WITH PARTY PETE)
YOU KNOW WHAT, RIGBY? IT IS SO IMPORTANT TO COMPLETELY UNPLUG FROM TIME TO TIME... BECAUSE OTHERWISE YOU TURN INTO AN INTERNET-OBSESSED TOOL AND EVERYONE HATES YOU.
YEAH, I MEAN TECHNICALLY YOU CAN EAT PIZZA AND PLAY VIDEO GAMES AT THE SAME TIME...
BUT THEN THAT MEANS YOU SORT OF SUCK AT BOTH ACTIVITIES AT ONCE.
DO YOU KNOW WHAT I THINK WE NEED TO DO?
WHAT?
TIME TO TURN THESE ***SMART*** PHONES...INTO ***DUMB*** PHONES.
DUDE, WHAT ARE YOU DOING?!
WE'RE GOING TO LIVE COMPLETELY OFF THE GRID, JUST LIKE OUR ANCESTORS DID! UNPLUGGED LIFE, HERE WE COME!
YOU IDIOT! HOW ARE WE SUPPOSED TO FIND OUR WAY HOME NOW?
UH...
THE END.

VIDEO GAME GENIE

WRITTEN BY JIMMY GIEGERICH
ILLUSTRATED BY MAD RUPERT

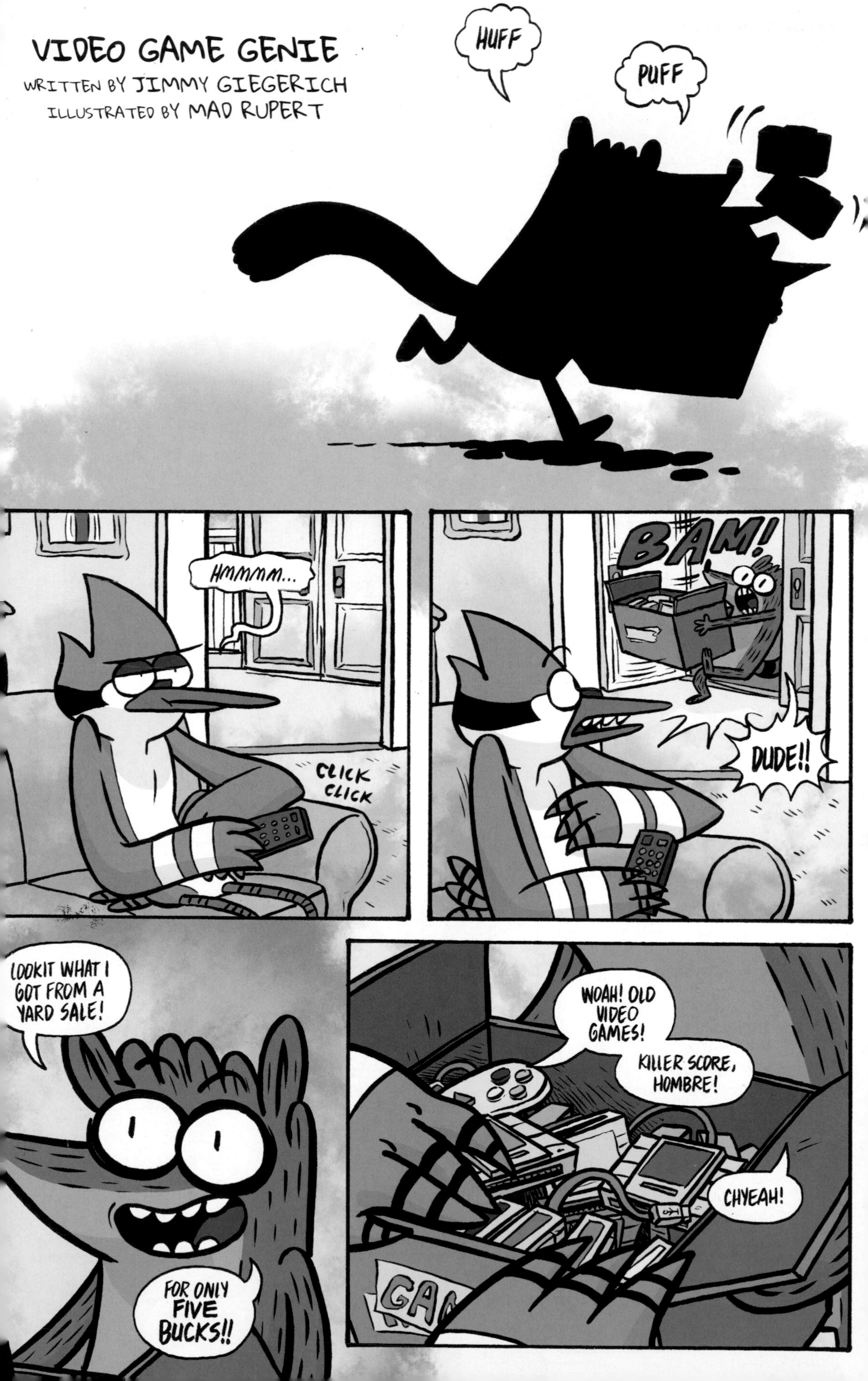
HUFF
PUFF
HMMMM...
CLICK CLICK
BAM!
DUDE!!
LOOKIT WHAT I GOT FROM A YARD SALE!
FOR ONLY FIVE BUCKS!!
WOAH! OLD VIDEO GAMES!
KILLER SCORE, HOMBRE!
CHYEAH!

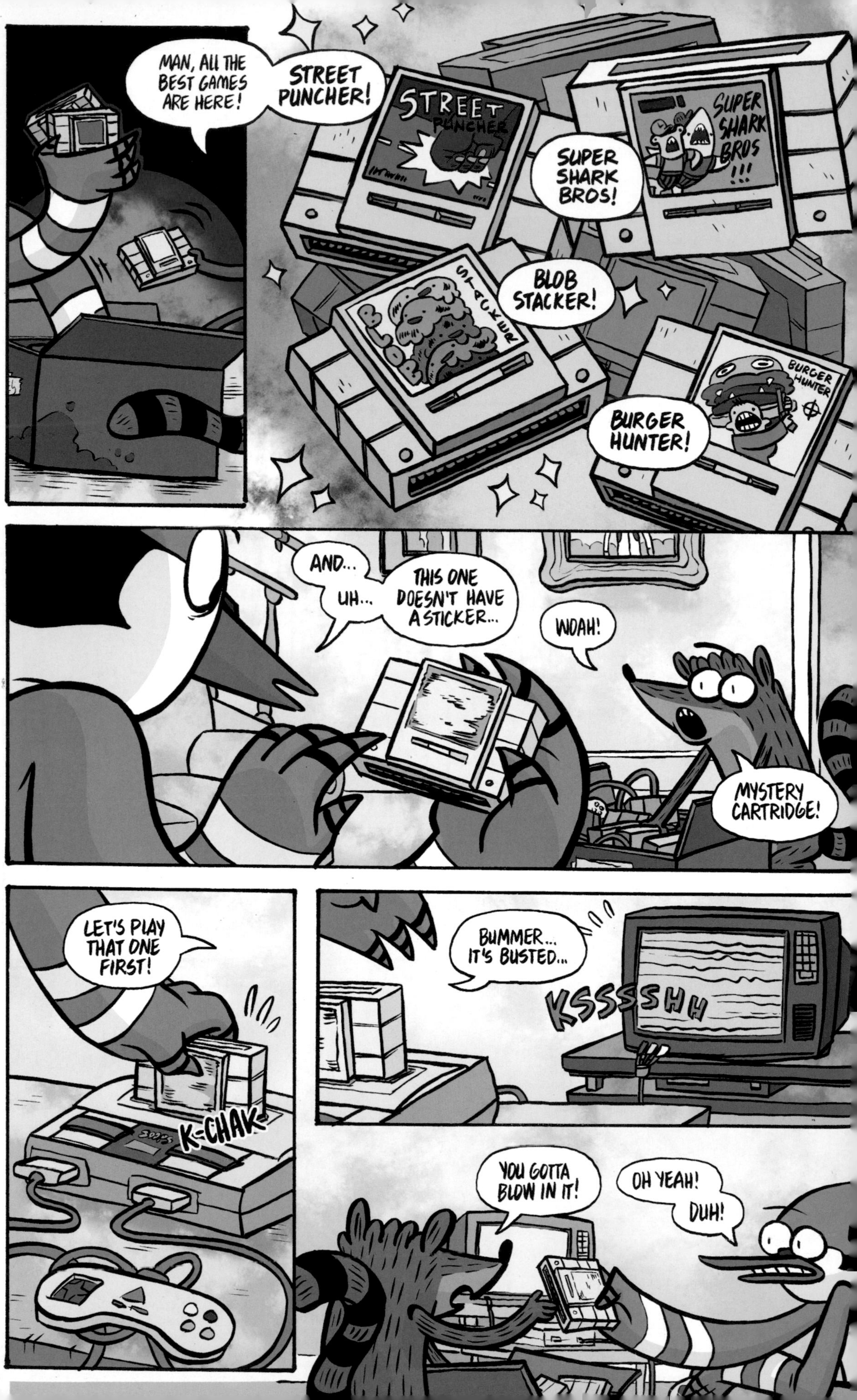

MAN, ALL THE BEST GAMES ARE HERE!
STREET PUNCHER!
STREET PUNCHER
SUPER SHARK BROS!
SUPER SHARK BROS!!!
BLOB STACKER!
BLOB STACKER
BURGER HUNTER!
BURGER HUNTER
AND...
UH...
THIS ONE DOESN'T HAVE A STICKER...
WOAH!
MYSTERY CARTRIDGE!
LET'S PLAY THAT ONE FIRST!
K-CHAK
BUMMER... IT'S BUSTED...
KSSSSHH
YOU GOTTA BLOW IN IT!
OH YEAH!
DUH!

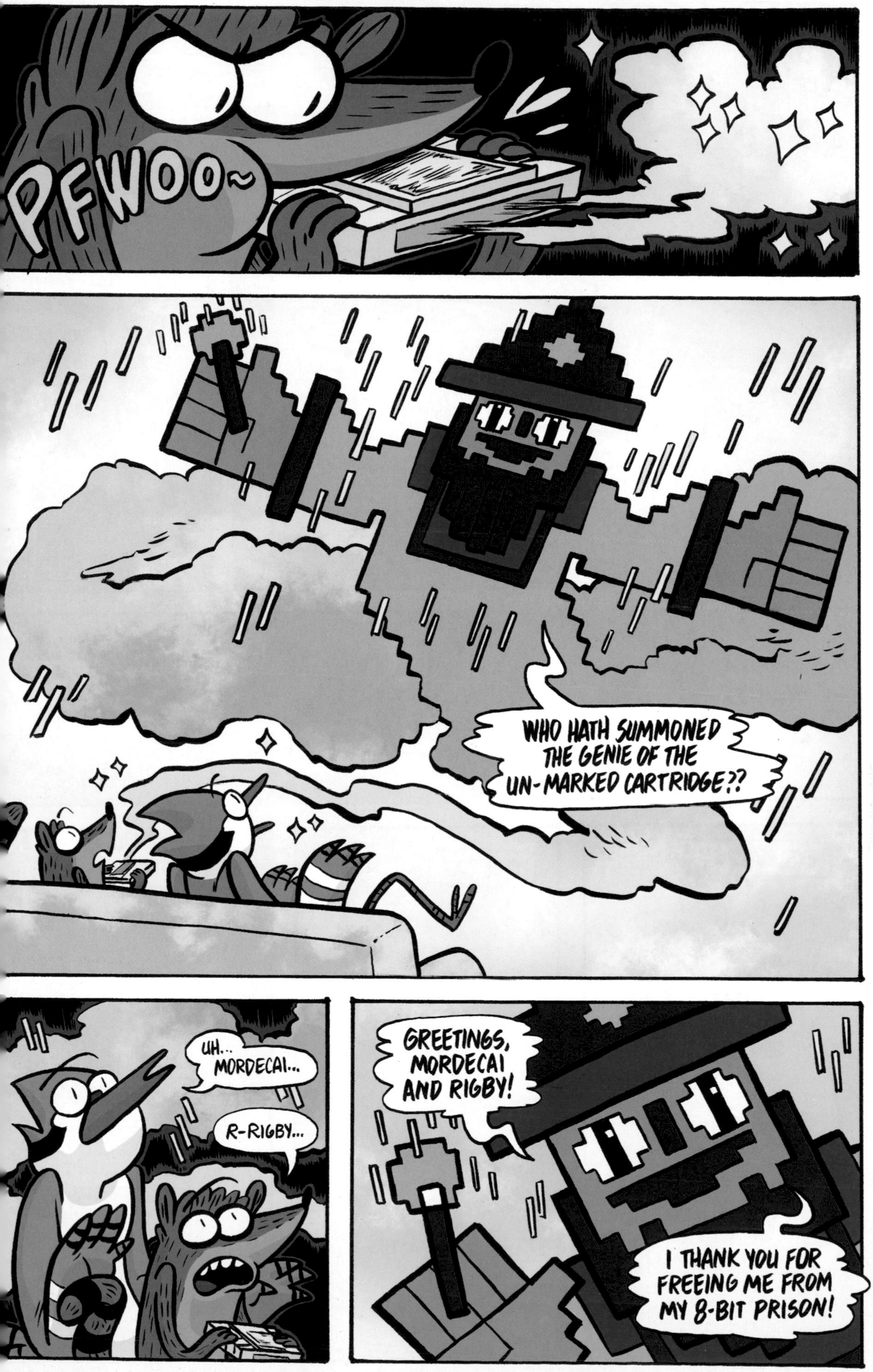
PFWOO~
WHO HATH SUMMONED THE GENIE OF THE UN-MARKED CARTRIDGE??
UH... MORDECAI...
R-RIGBY...
GREETINGS, MORDECAI AND RIGBY!
I THANK YOU FOR FREEING ME FROM MY 8-BIT PRISON!

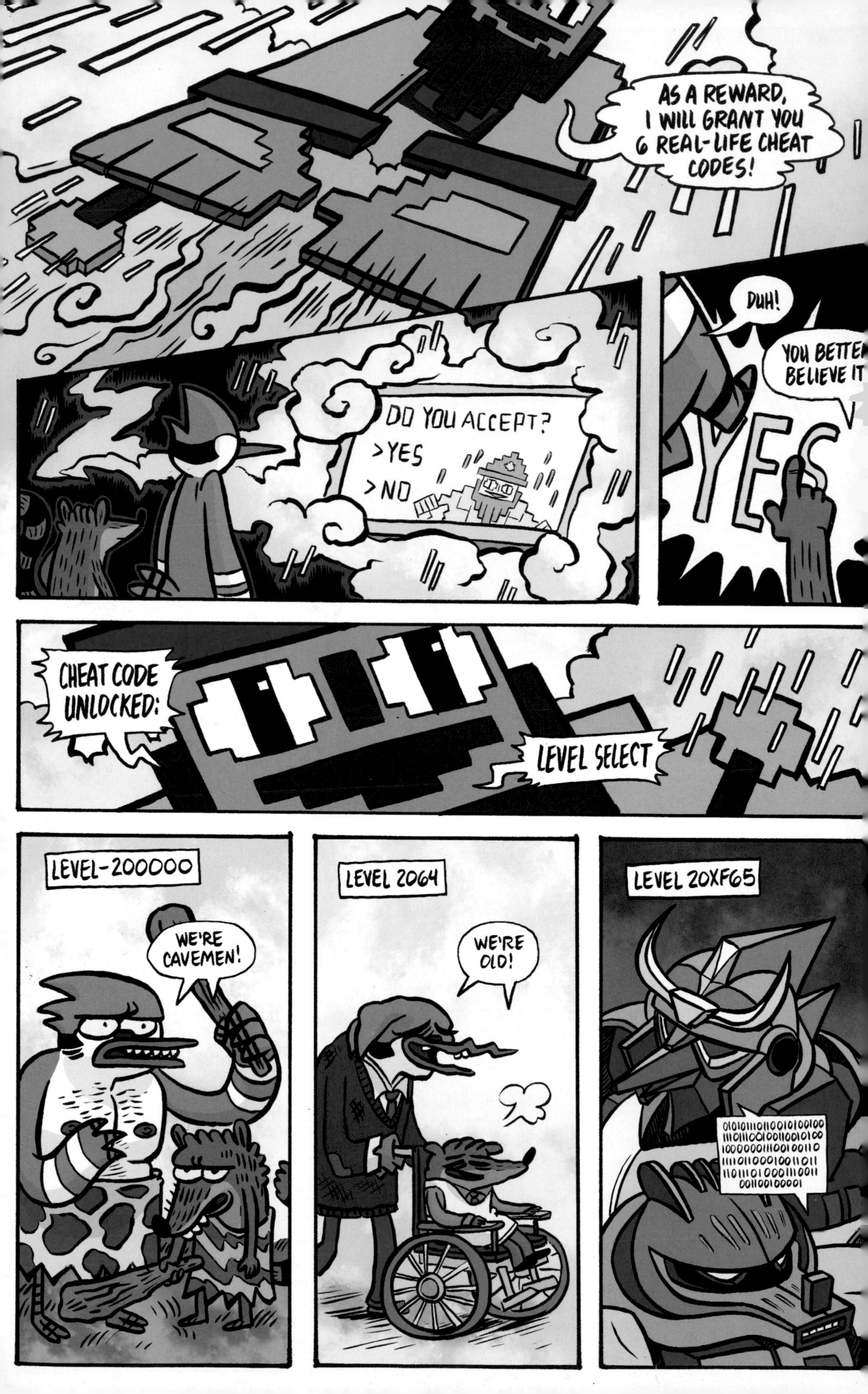
AS A REWARD, I WILL GRANT YOU 6 REAL-LIFE CHEAT CODES!
DO YOU ACCEPT?
>YES
>NO
DUH!
YOU BETTE BELIEVE IT
YES
CHEAT CODE UNLOCKED:
LEVEL SELECT
LEVEL-200000
WE'RE CAVEMEN!
LEVEL 2064
WE'RE OLD!
LEVEL 20XF65
010101110110010100100 111011100100110010100 1000000011100100110 111101100010011011 110111010001110011 001100100001

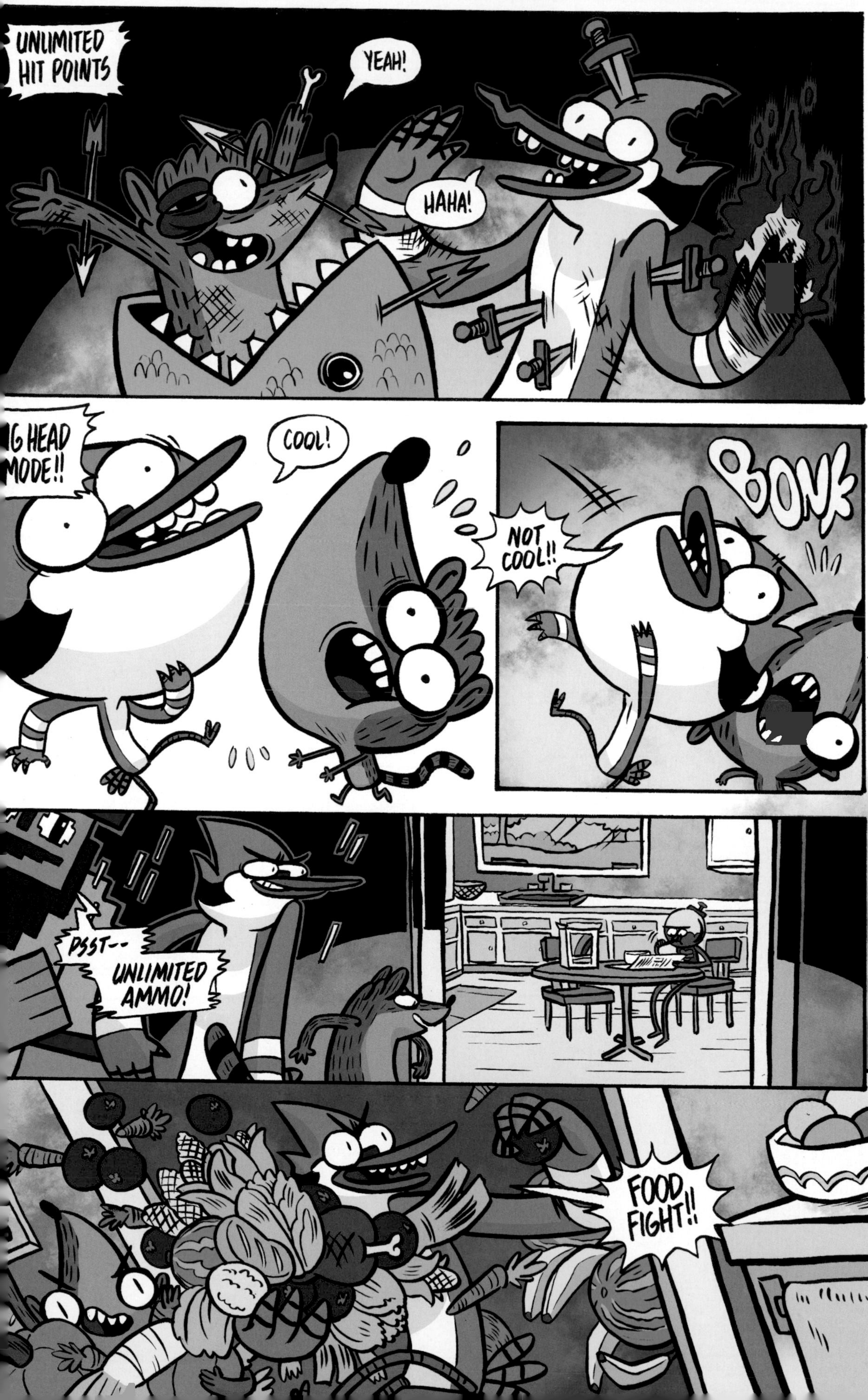
UNLIMITED HIT POINTS
YEAH!
HAHA!
G HEAD MODE!!
COOL!
NOT COOL!!
BONK
PSST--
UNLIMITED AMMO!
FOOD FIGHT!!

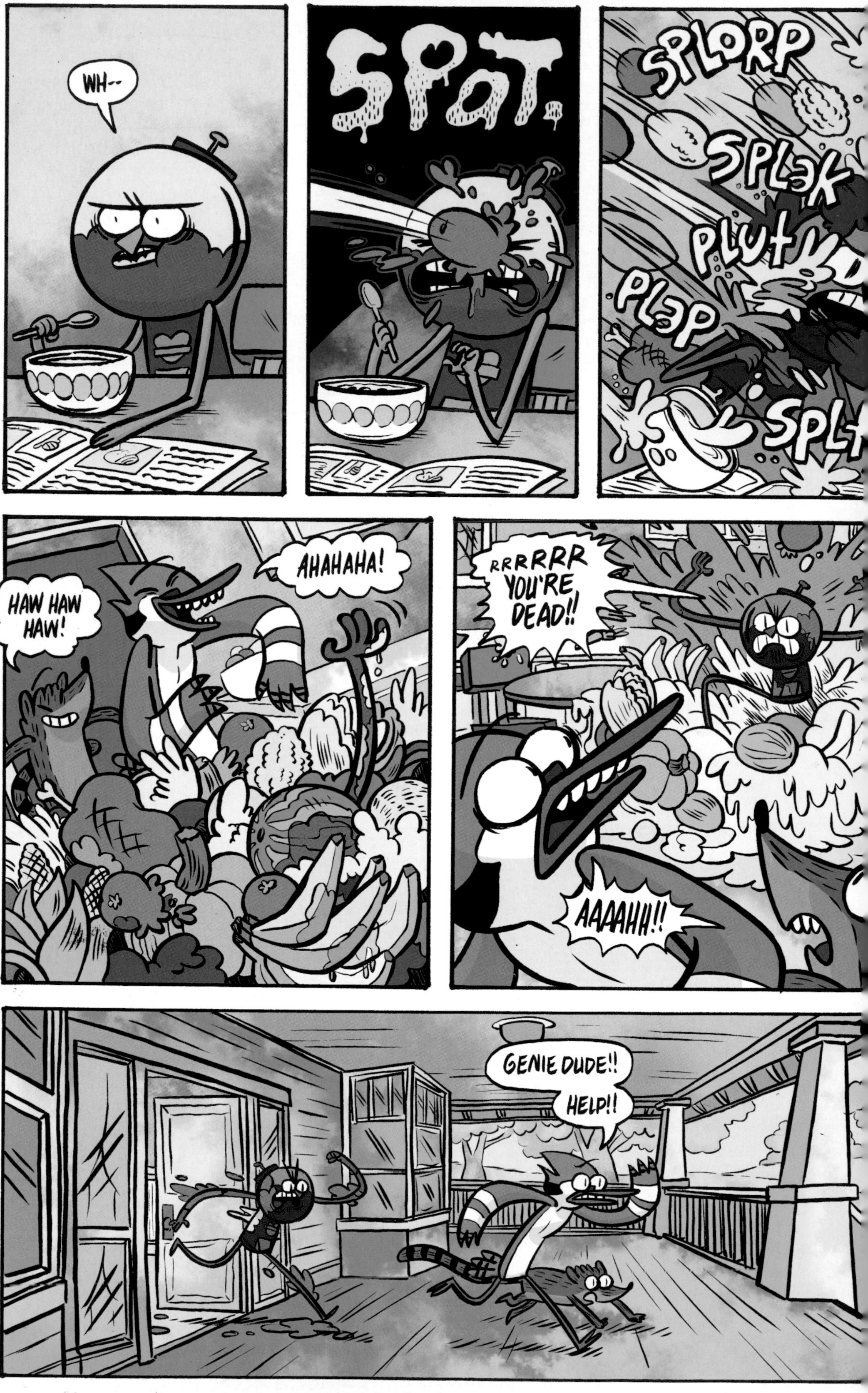
WH--
SPOT
SPLORP
SPLAK
PLUT
PLAP
SPLT
HAW HAW HAW!
AHAHAHA!
RRRRRR YOU'RE DEAD!!
AAAAHH!!
GENIE DUDE!!
HELP!!

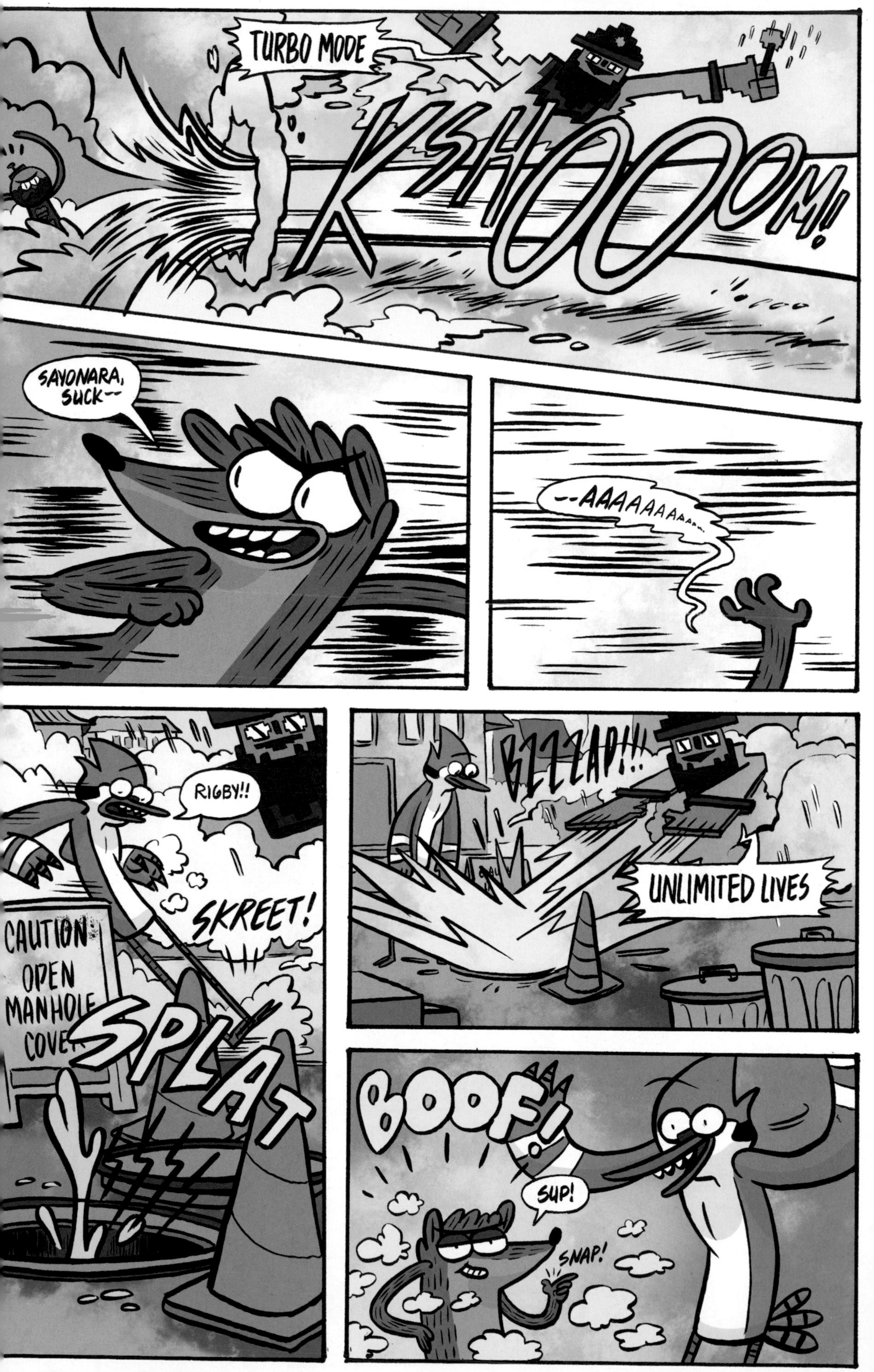
TURBO MODE
KSHOOOOM!
SAYONARA, SUCK--
--AAAAAAAAaa...
RIGBY!!
SKREET!
CAUTION OPEN MANHOLE COVE
SPLAT
BZZZAP!!!
UNLIMITED LIVES
BOOF!
SUP!
SNAP!

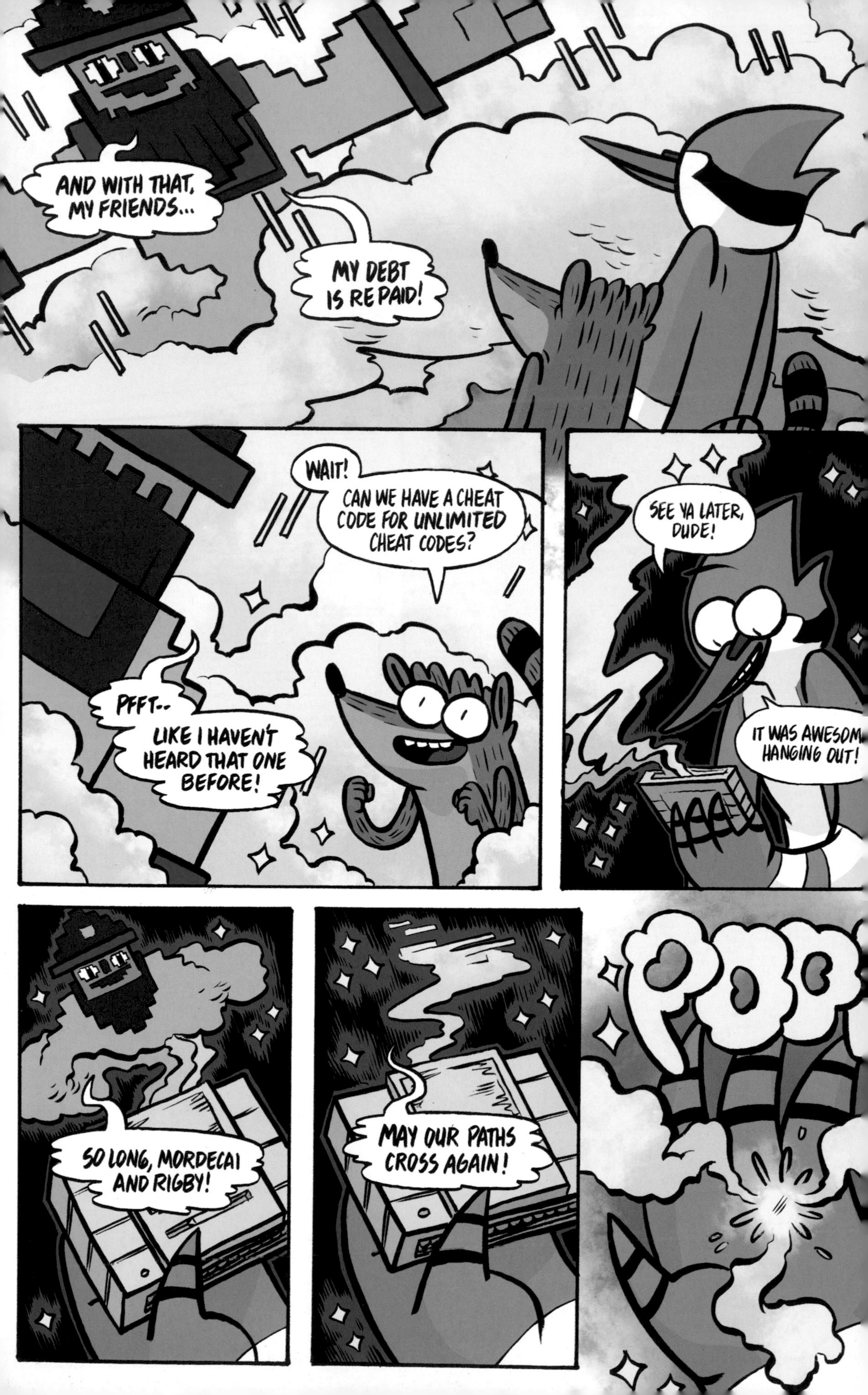
AND WITH THAT, MY FRIENDS...
MY DEBT IS REPAID!
WAIT!
CAN WE HAVE A CHEAT CODE FOR UNLIMITED CHEAT CODES?
PFFT..
LIKE I HAVEN'T HEARD THAT ONE BEFORE!
SEE YA LATER, DUDE!
IT WAS AWESOM HANGING OUT!
SO LONG, MORDECAI AND RIGBY!
MAY OUR PATHS CROSS AGAIN!
POP

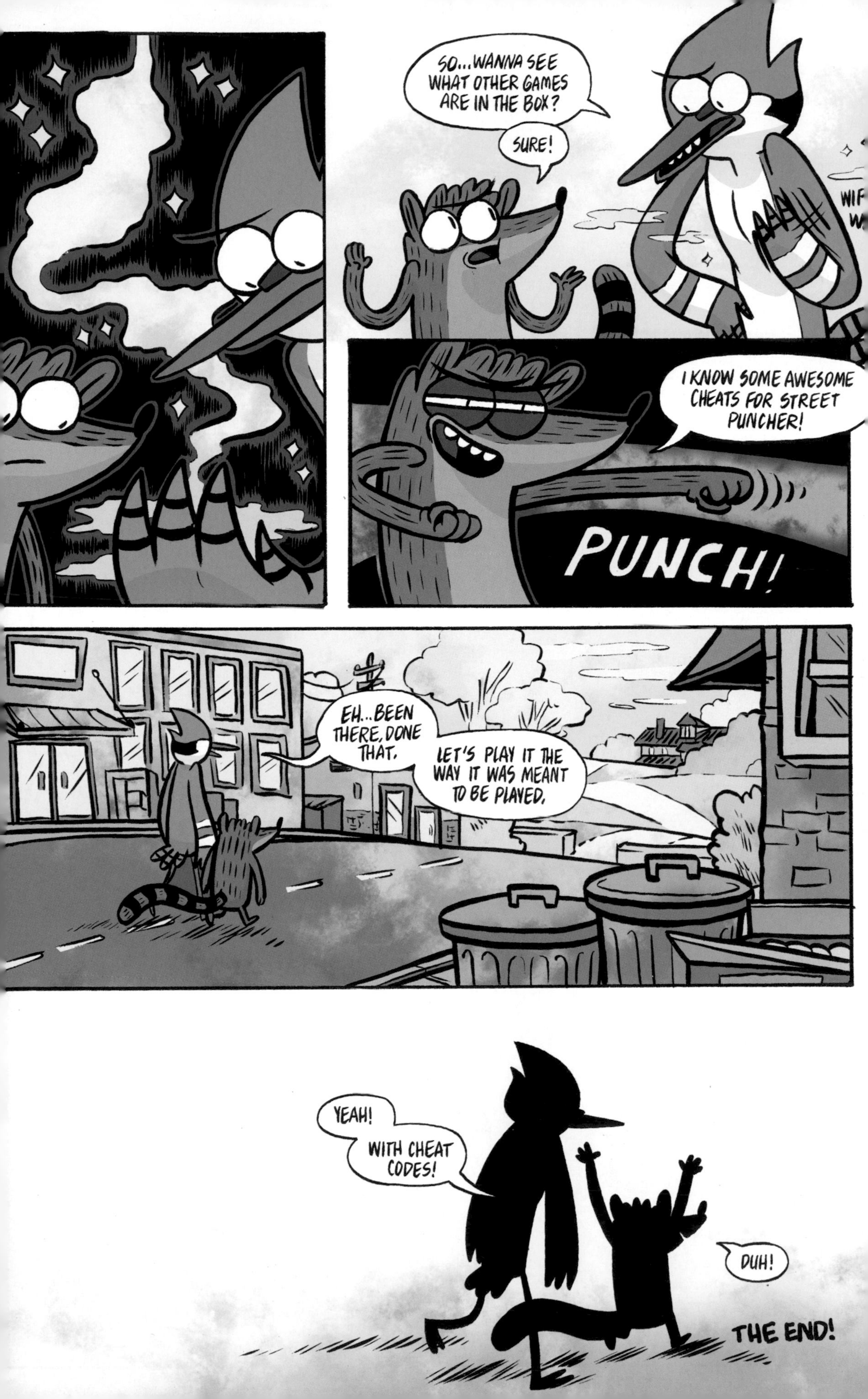
SO...WANNA SEE WHAT OTHER GAMES ARE IN THE BOX?
SURE!
I KNOW SOME AWESOME CHEATS FOR STREET PUNCHER!
PUNCH!
EH...BEEN THERE, DONE THAT.
LET'S PLAY IT THE WAY IT WAS MEANT TO BE PLAYED.
YEAH!
WITH CHEAT CODES!
DUH!
THE END!

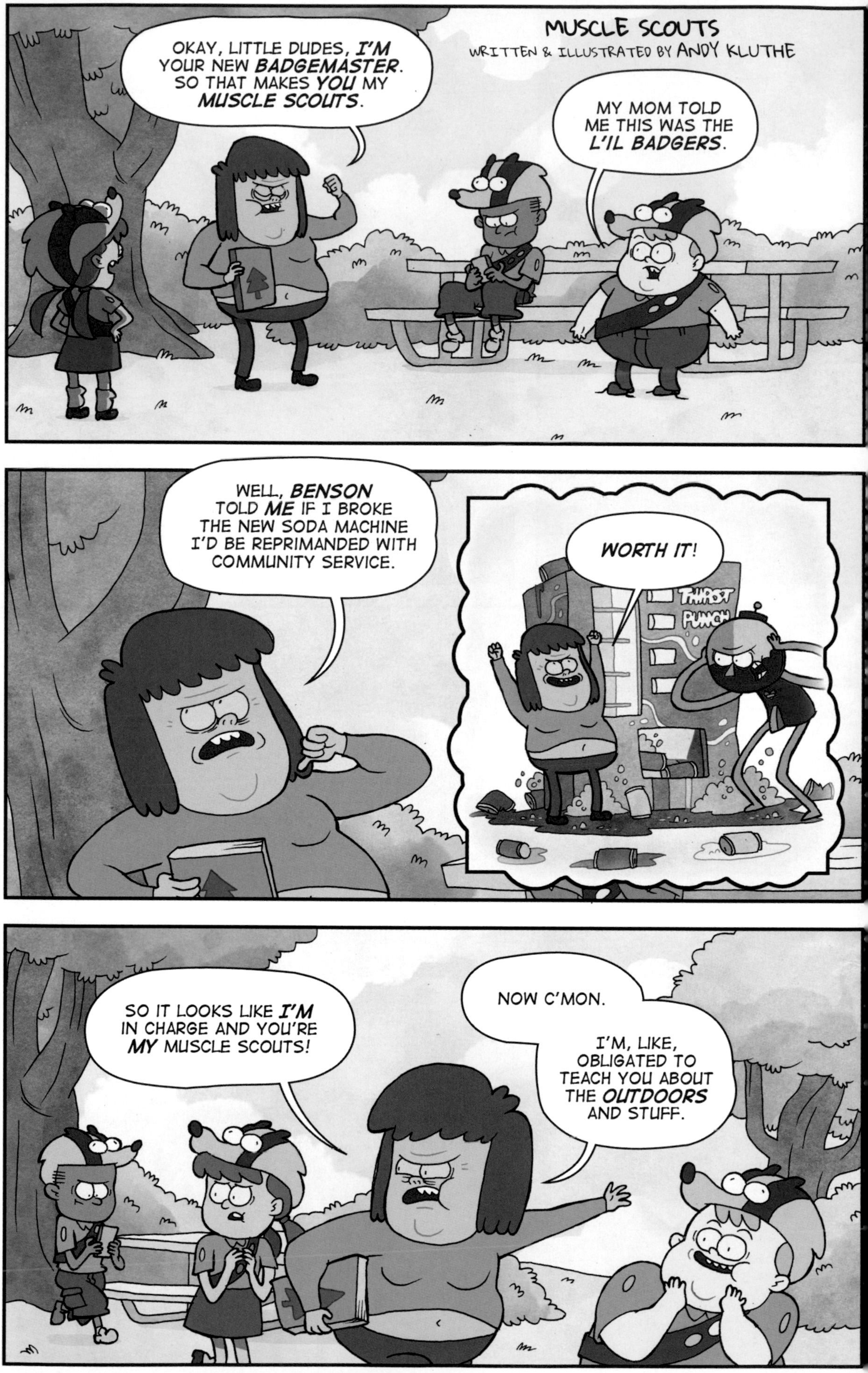
MUSCLE SCOUTS
WRITTEN & ILLUSTRATED BY ANDY KLUTHE
OKAY, LITTLE DUDES, I'M YOUR NEW BADGEMASTER. SO THAT MAKES YOU MY MUSCLE SCOUTS.
MY MOM TOLD ME THIS WAS THE L'IL BADGERS.
WELL, BENSON TOLD ME IF I BROKE THE NEW SODA MACHINE I'D BE REPRIMANDED WITH COMMUNITY SERVICE.
WORTH IT!
THIRST PUNCH
SO IT LOOKS LIKE I'M IN CHARGE AND YOU'RE MY MUSCLE SCOUTS!
NOW C'MON.
I'M, LIKE, OBLIGATED TO TEACH YOU ABOUT THE OUTDOORS AND STUFF.

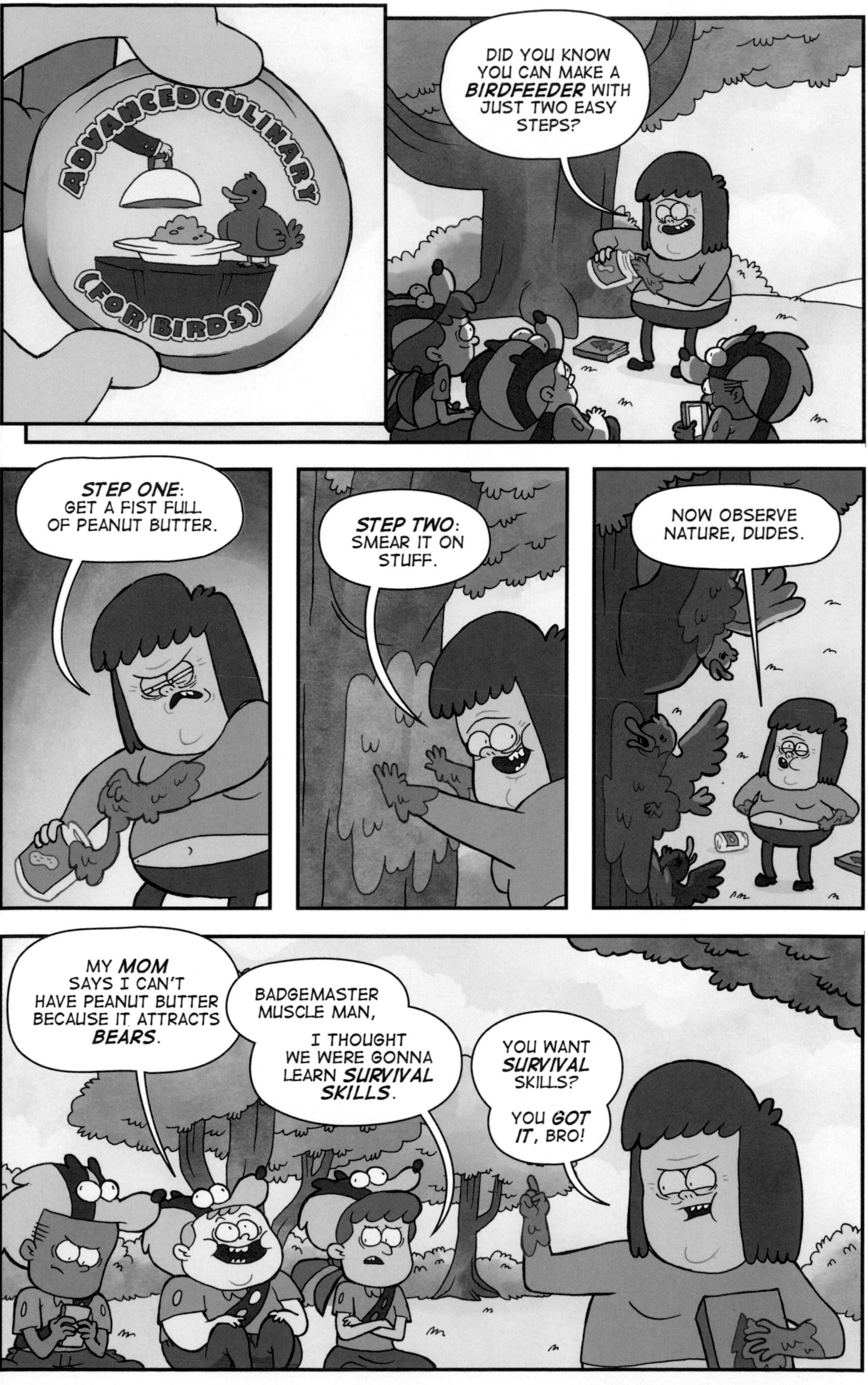
ADVANCED CULINARY (FOR BIRDS)
DID YOU KNOW YOU CAN MAKE A BIRDFEEDER WITH JUST TWO EASY STEPS?
STEP ONE: GET A FIST FULL OF PEANUT BUTTER.
STEP TWO: SMEAR IT ON STUFF.
NOW OBSERVE NATURE, DUDES.
MY MOM SAYS I CAN'T HAVE PEANUT BUTTER BECAUSE IT ATTRACTS BEARS.
BADGEMASTER MUSCLE MAN,
I THOUGHT WE WERE GONNA LEARN SURVIVAL SKILLS.
YOU WANT SURVIVAL SKILLS?
YOU GOT IT, BRO!

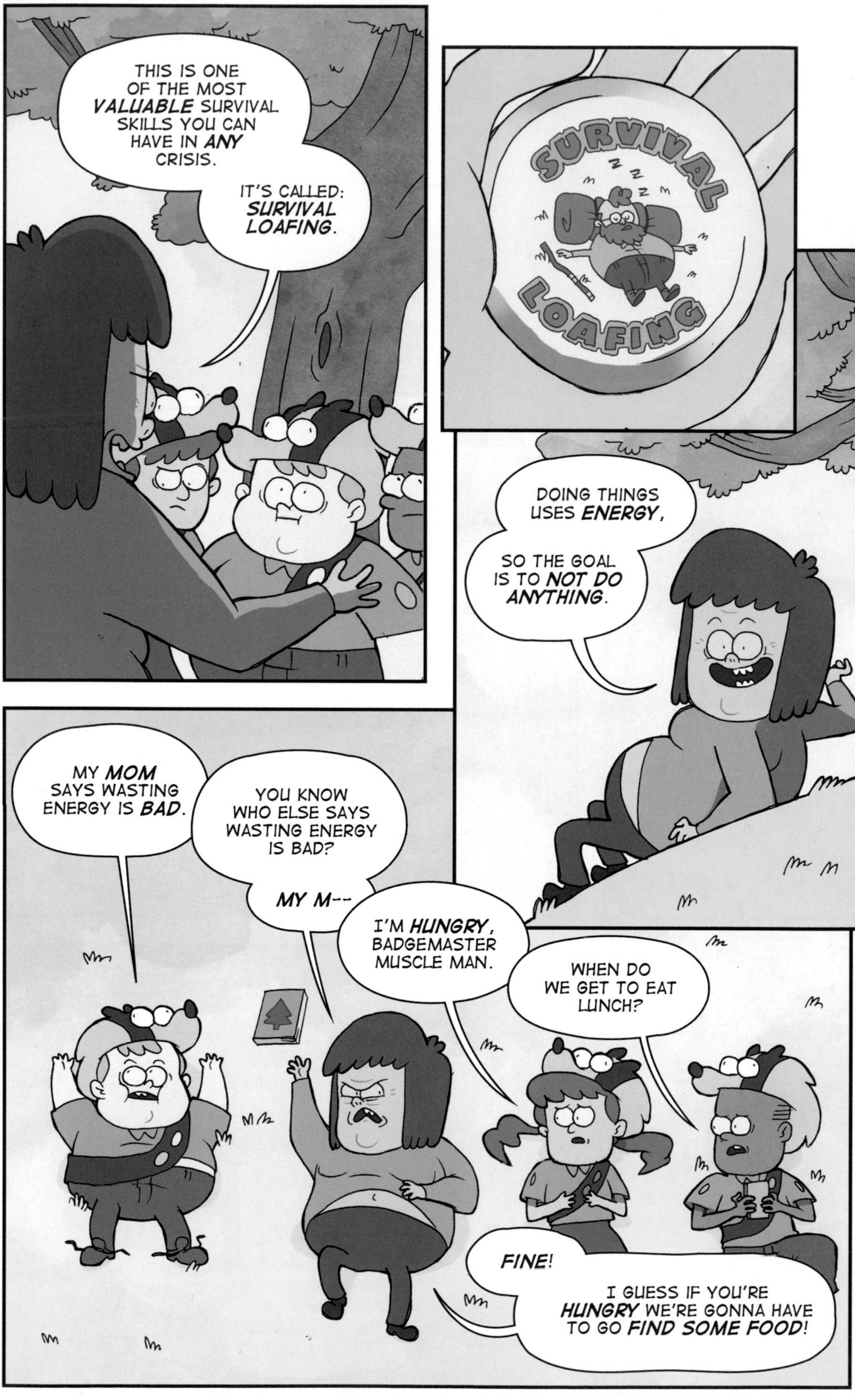
THIS IS ONE OF THE MOST VALUABLE SURVIVAL SKILLS YOU CAN HAVE IN ANY CRISIS.
IT'S CALLED: SURVIVAL LOAFING.
SURVIVAL LOAFING
DOING THINGS USES ENERGY,
SO THE GOAL IS TO NOT DO ANYTHING.
MY MOM SAYS WASTING ENERGY IS BAD.
YOU KNOW WHO ELSE SAYS WASTING ENERGY IS BAD?
MY M--
I'M HUNGRY, BADGEMASTER MUSCLE MAN.
WHEN DO WE GET TO EAT LUNCH?
FINE!
I GUESS IF YOU'RE HUNGRY WE'RE GONNA HAVE TO GO FIND SOME FOOD!

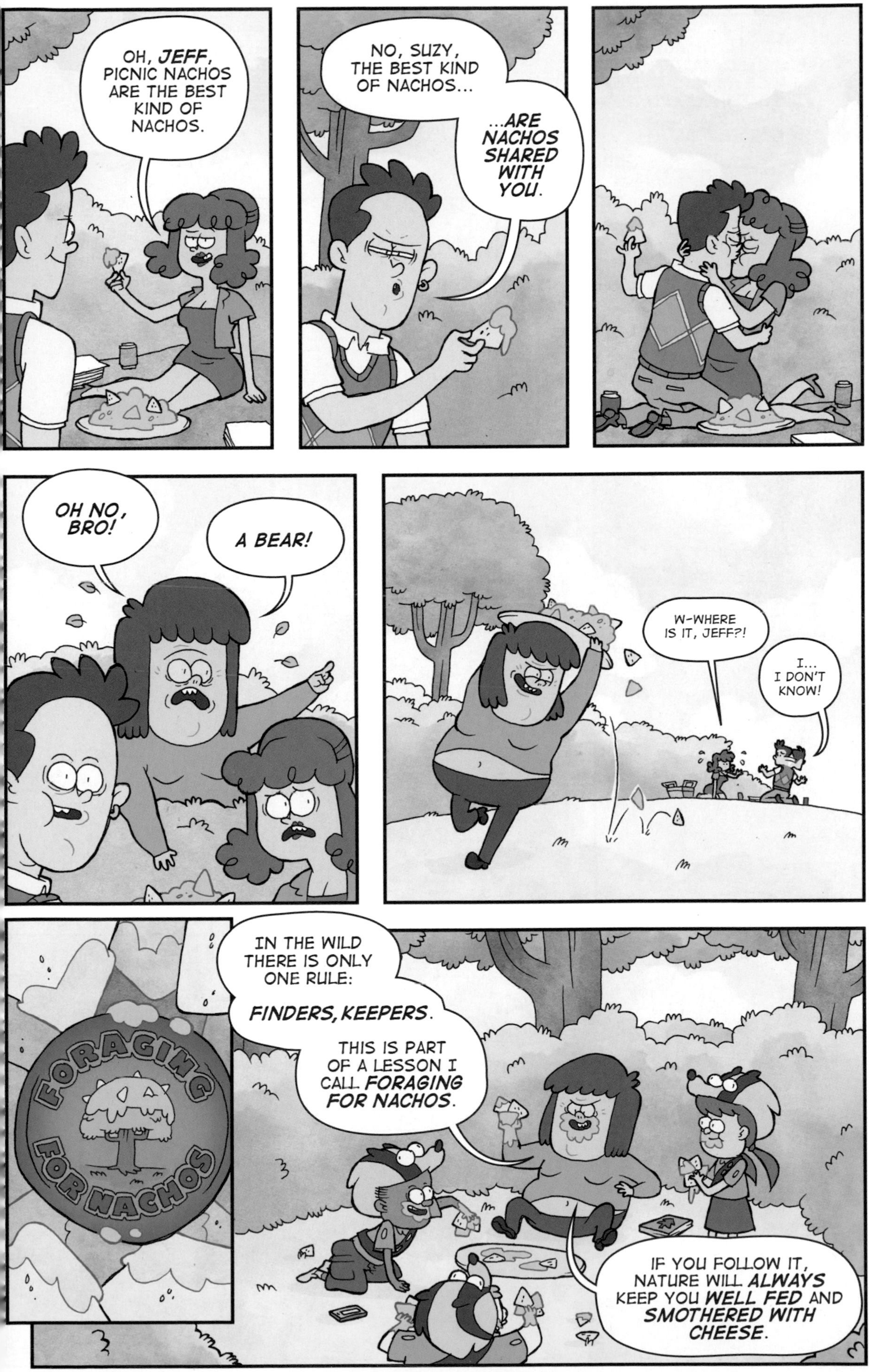
OH, JEFF, PICNIC NACHOS ARE THE BEST KIND OF NACHOS.
NO, SUZY, THE BEST KIND OF NACHOS...
...ARE NACHOS SHARED WITH YOU.
OH NO, BRO!
A BEAR!
W-WHERE IS IT, JEFF?!
I... I DON'T KNOW!
FORAGING FOR NACHOS
IN THE WILD THERE IS ONLY ONE RULE:
FINDERS, KEEPERS.
THIS IS PART OF A LESSON I CALL FORAGING FOR NACHOS.
IF YOU FOLLOW IT, NATURE WILL ALWAYS KEEP YOU WELL FED AND SMOTHERED WITH CHEESE.

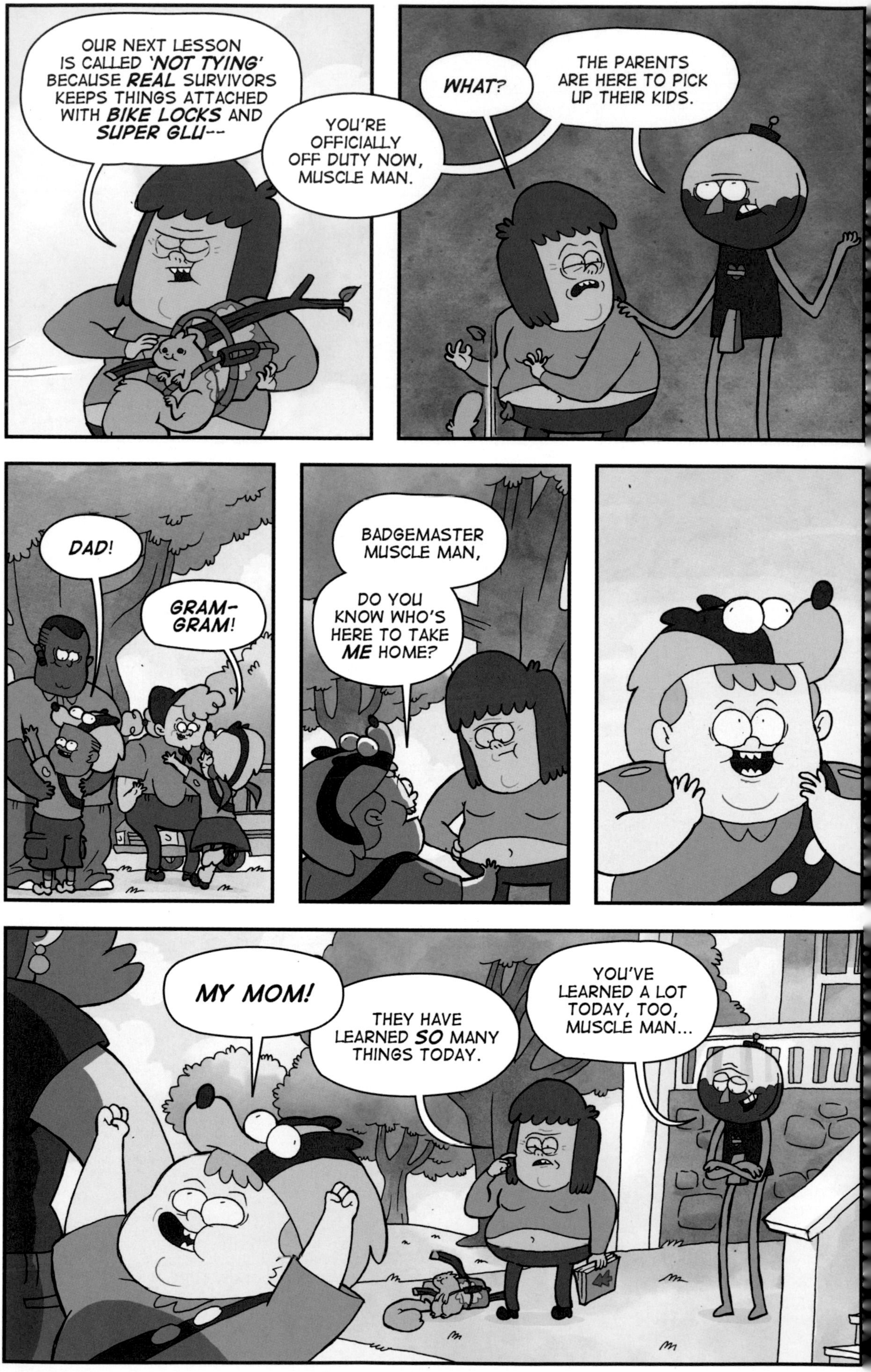

OUR NEXT LESSON IS CALLED 'NOT TYING' BECAUSE REAL SURVIVORS KEEPS THINGS ATTACHED WITH BIKE LOCKS AND SUPER GLU--
YOU'RE OFFICIALLY OFF DUTY NOW, MUSCLE MAN.
WHAT?
THE PARENTS ARE HERE TO PICK UP THEIR KIDS.
DAD!
GRAM-GRAM!
BADGEMASTER MUSCLE MAN,
DO YOU KNOW WHO'S HERE TO TAKE ME HOME?
MY MOM!
THEY HAVE LEARNED SO MANY THINGS TODAY.
YOU'VE LEARNED A LOT TODAY, TOO, MUSCLE MAN...

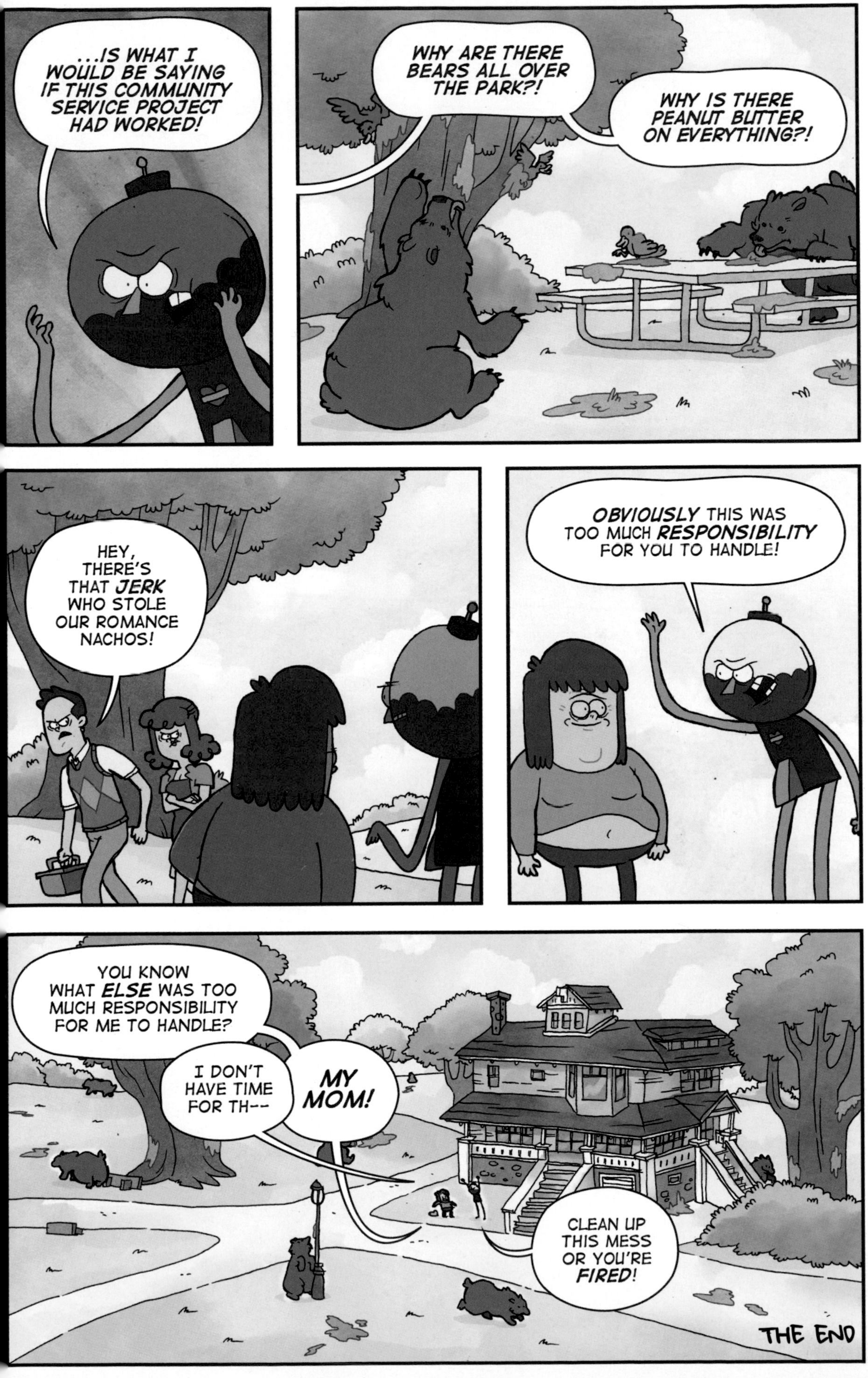
...IS WHAT I WOULD BE SAYING IF THIS COMMUNITY SERVICE PROJECT HAD WORKED!
WHY ARE THERE BEARS ALL OVER THE PARK?!
WHY IS THERE PEANUT BUTTER ON EVERYTHING?!
HEY, THERE'S THAT JERK WHO STOLE OUR ROMANCE NACHOS!
OBVIOUSLY THIS WAS TOO MUCH RESPONSIBILITY FOR YOU TO HANDLE!
YOU KNOW WHAT ELSE WAS TOO MUCH RESPONSIBILITY FOR ME TO HANDLE?
I DON'T HAVE TIME FOR TH--
MY MOM!
CLEAN UP THIS MESS OR YOU'RE FIRED!
THE END

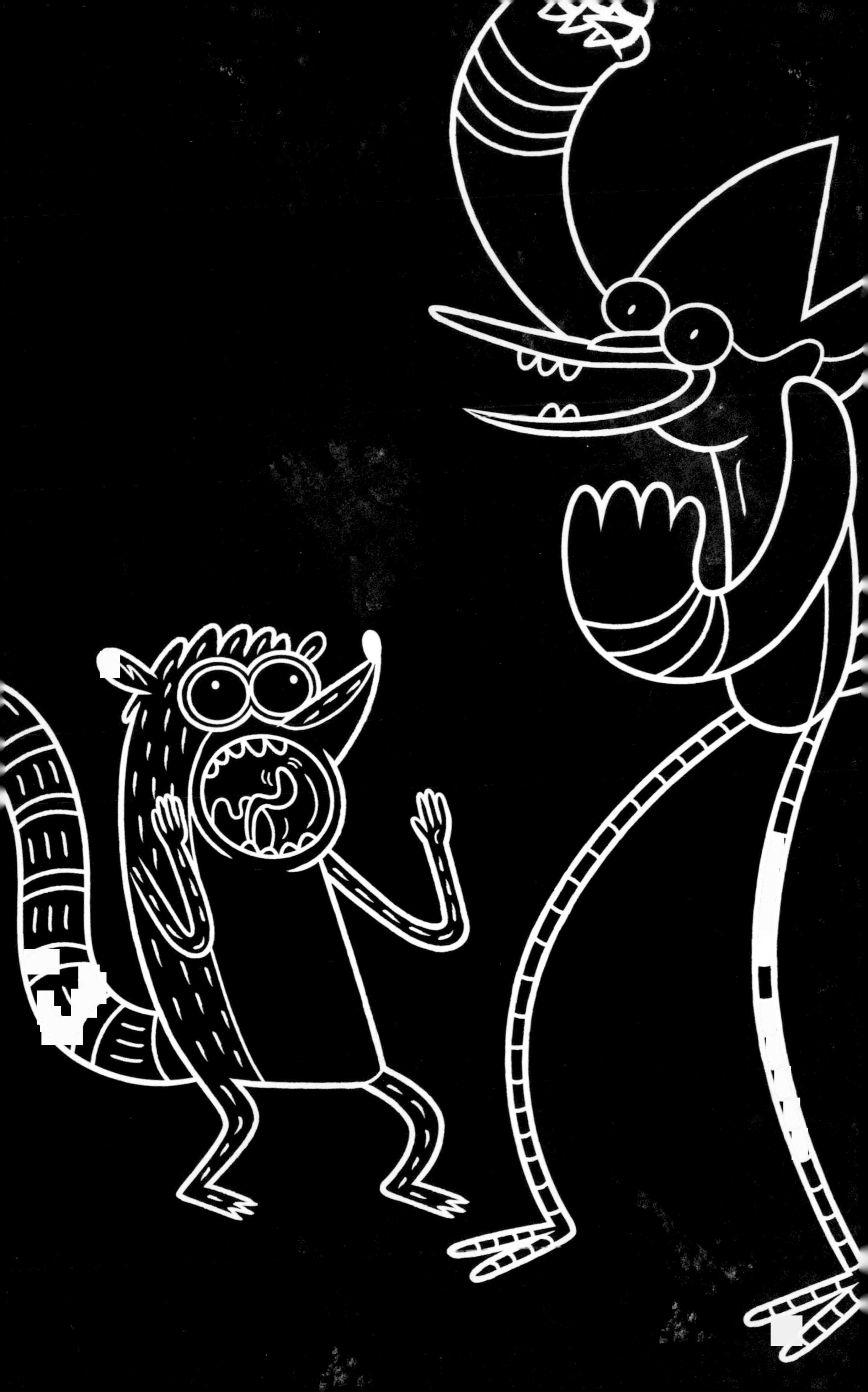

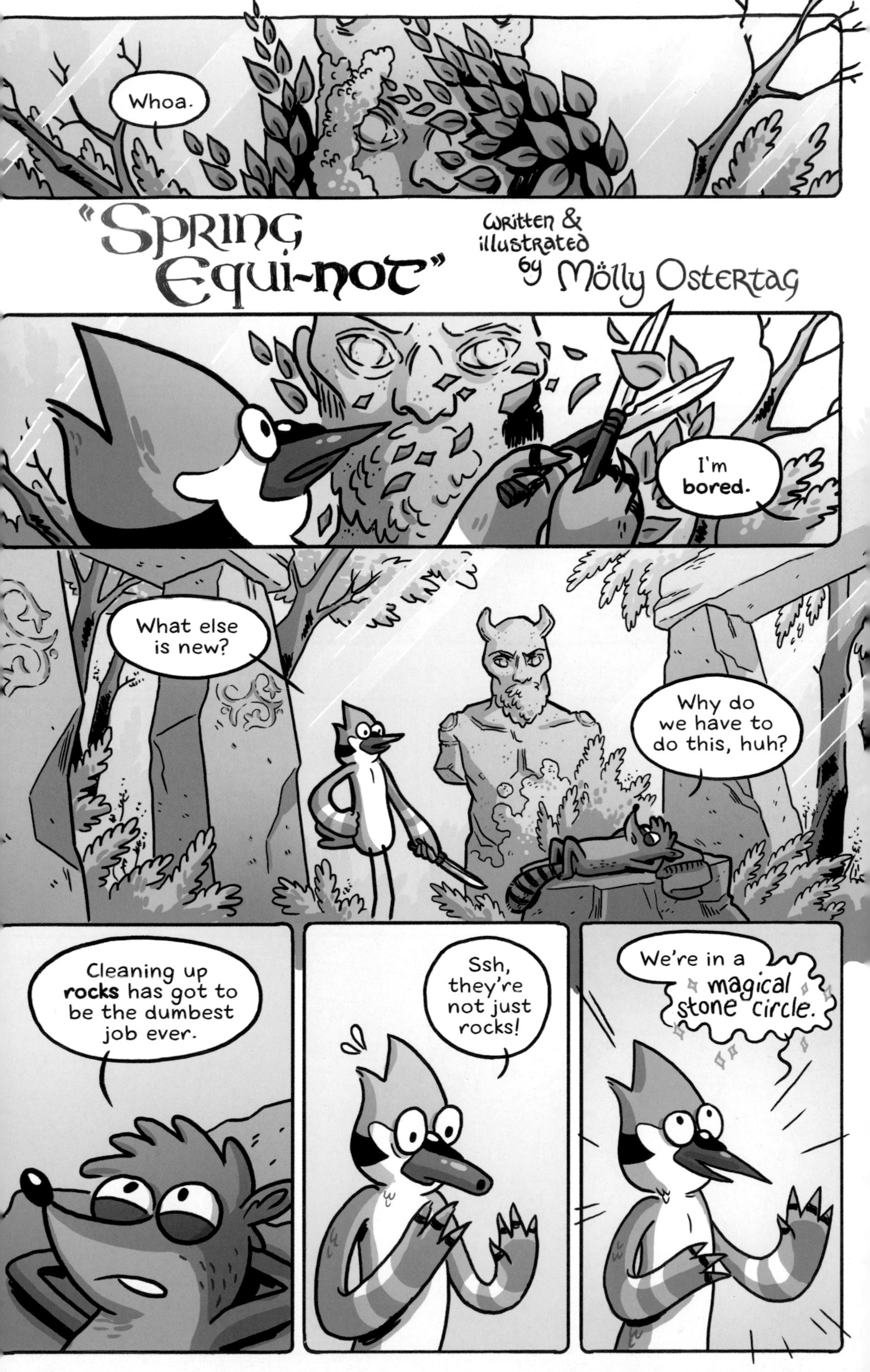
Whoa.
"Spring Equi-not"
Written & illustrated by Mölly Ostertag
I'm bored.
What else is new?
Why do we have to do this, huh?
Cleaning up rocks has got to be the dumbest job ever.
Ssh, they're not just rocks!
We're in a magical stone circle.

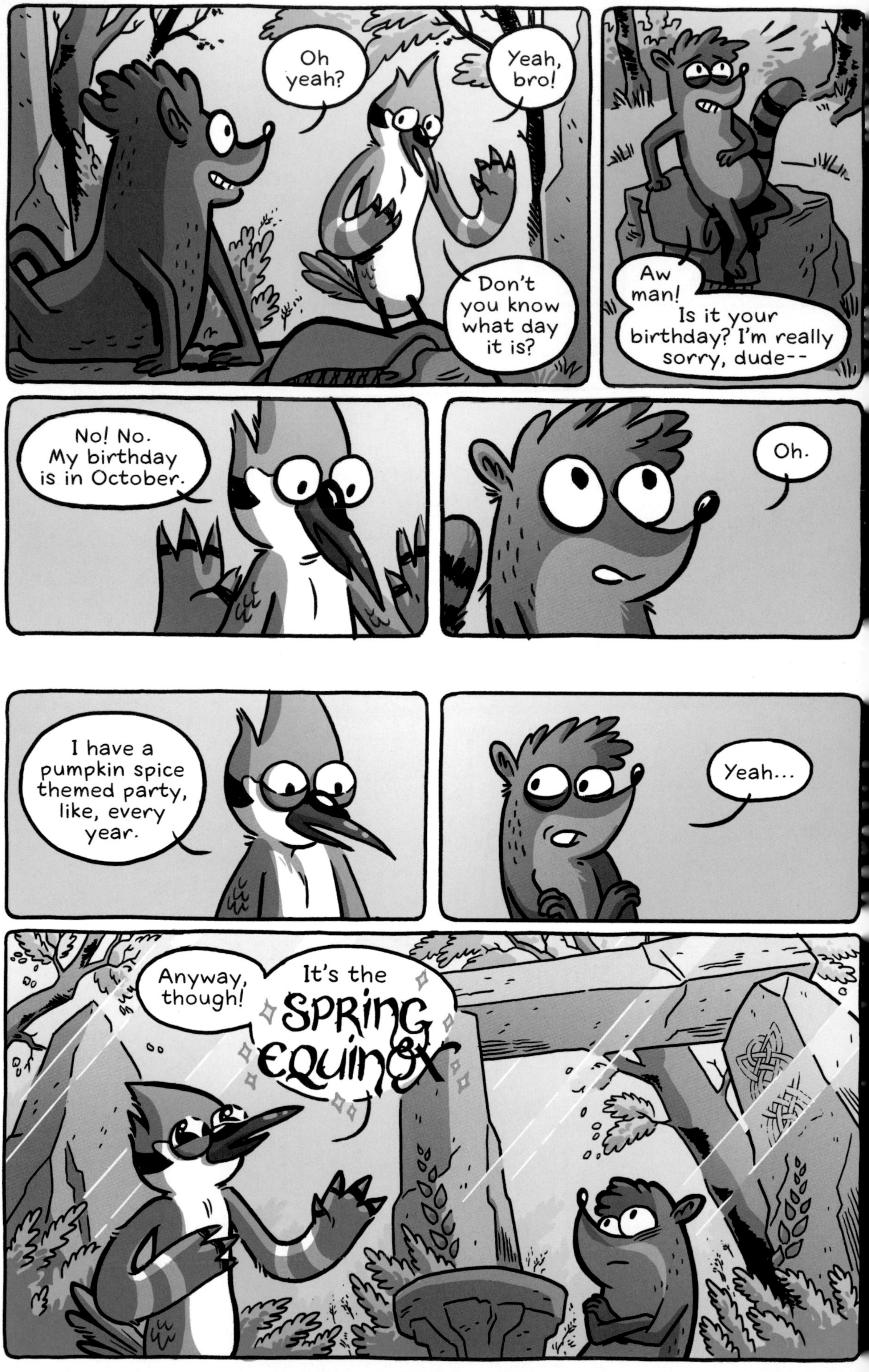
Oh yeah?
Yeah, bro!
Don't you know what day it is?
Aw man!
Is it your birthday? I'm really sorry, dude--
No! No. My birthday is in October.
Oh.
I have a pumpkin spice themed party, like, every year.
Yeah...
Anyway, though!
It's the SPRING EQUINOX

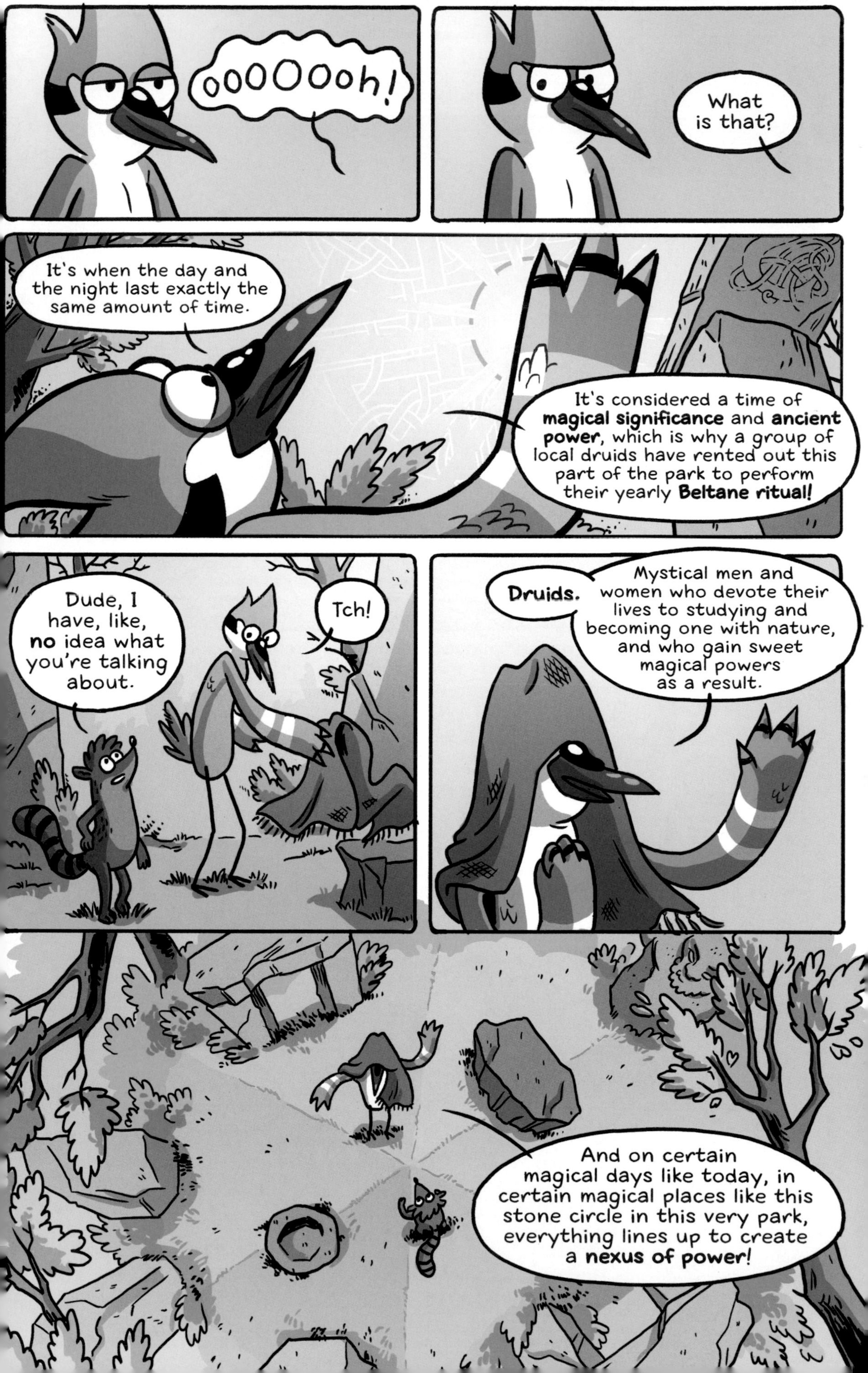

oooOooh!
What is that?
It's when the day and the night last exactly the same amount of time.
It's considered a time of **magical significance** and **ancient power**, which is why a group of local druids have rented out this part of the park to perform their yearly **Beltane ritual!**
Dude, I have, like, **no** idea what you're talking about.
Tch!
Druids.
Mystical men and women who devote their lives to studying and becoming one with nature, and who gain sweet magical powers as a result.
And on certain magical days like today, in certain magical places like this stone circle in this very park, everything lines up to create a **nexus of power**!

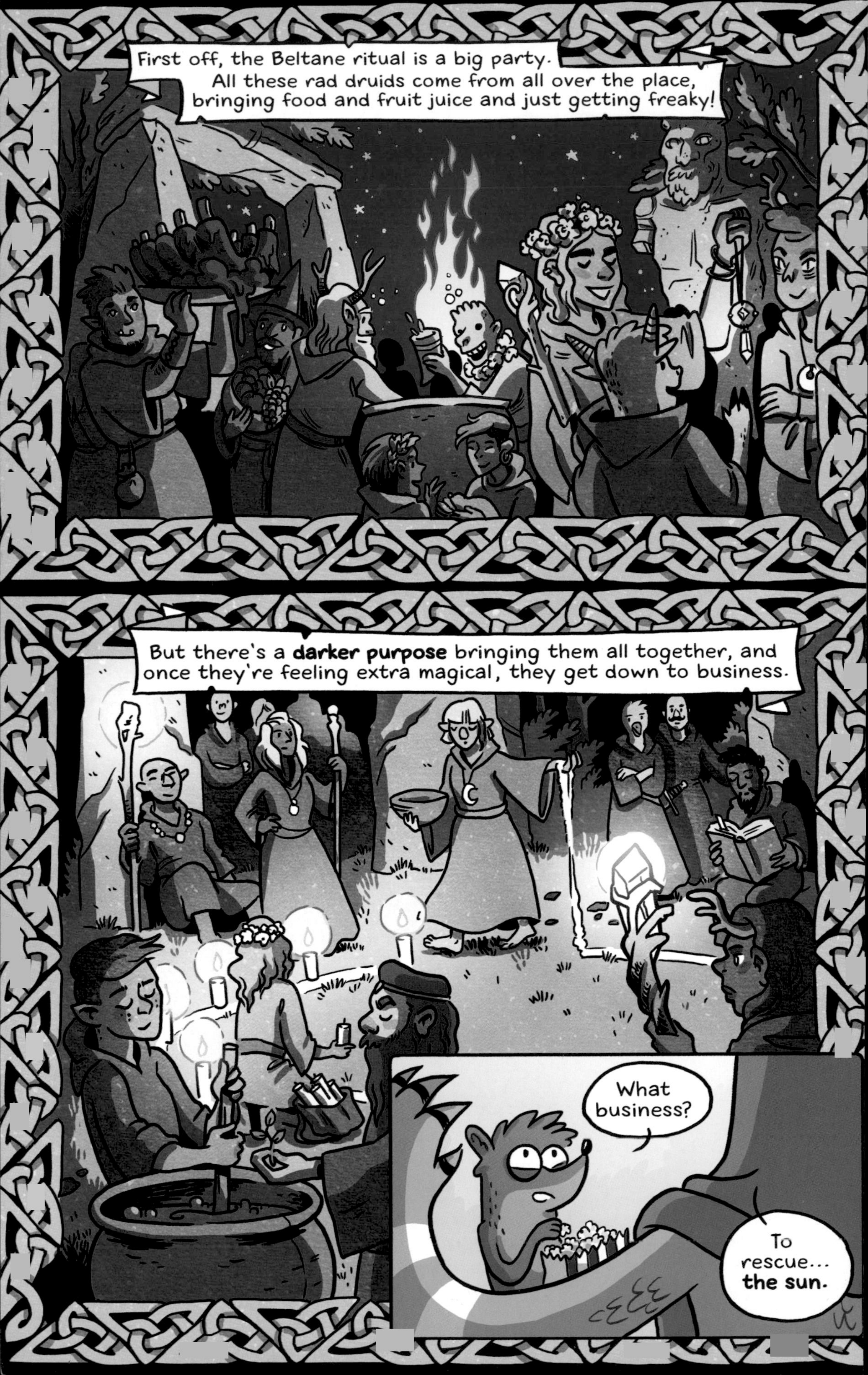
First off, the Beltane ritual is a big party.
All these rad druids come from all over the place, bringing food and fruit juice and just getting freaky!
But there's a **darker purpose** bringing them all together, and once they're feeling extra magical, they get down to business.
What business?
To rescue... **the sun.**

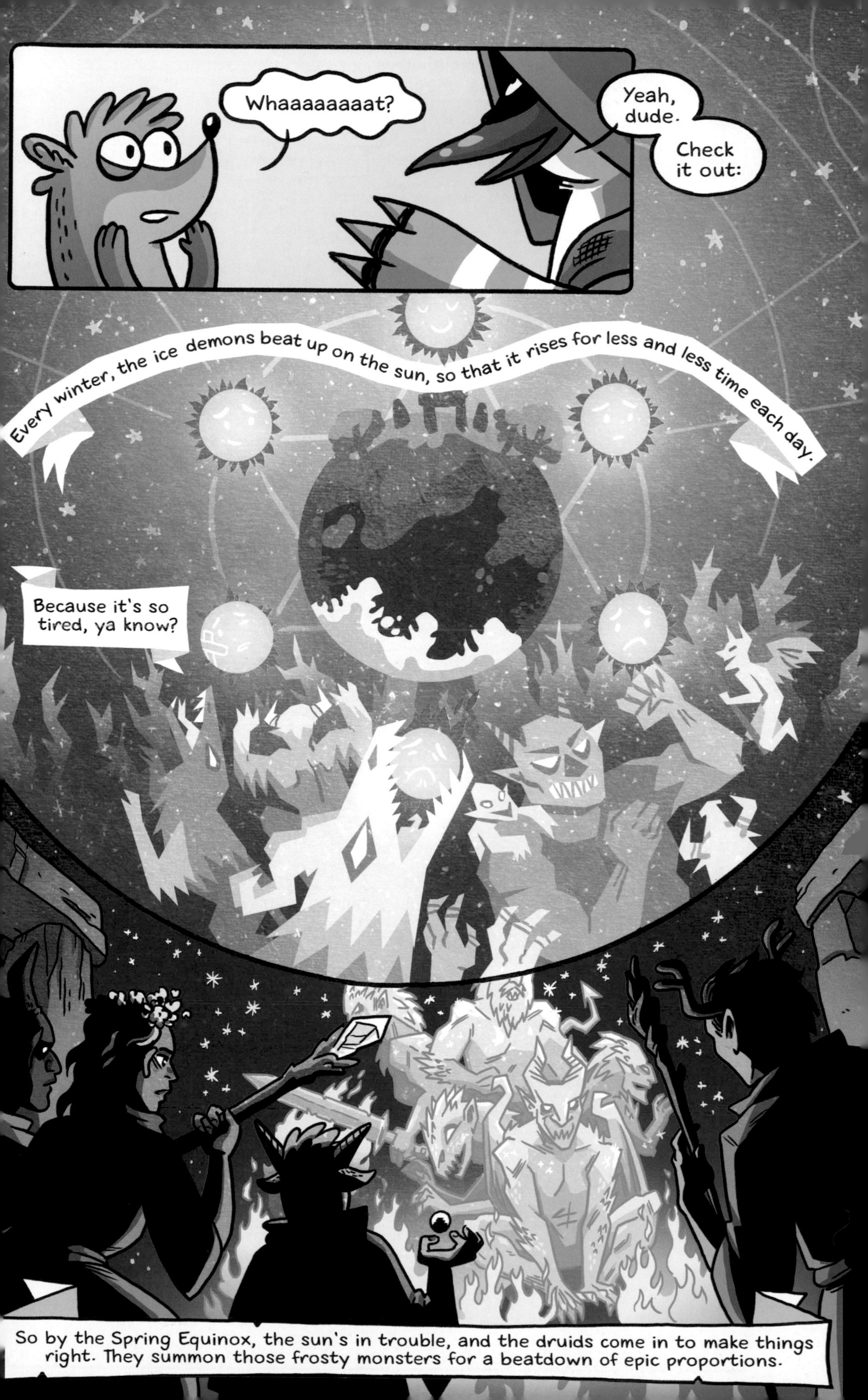
Whaaaaaaaat?
Yeah, dude.
Check it out:
Every winter, the ice demons beat up on the sun, so that it rises for less and less time each day.
Because it's so tired, ya know?
So by the Spring Equinox, the sun's in trouble, and the druids come in to make things right. They summon those frosty monsters for a beatdown of epic proportions.

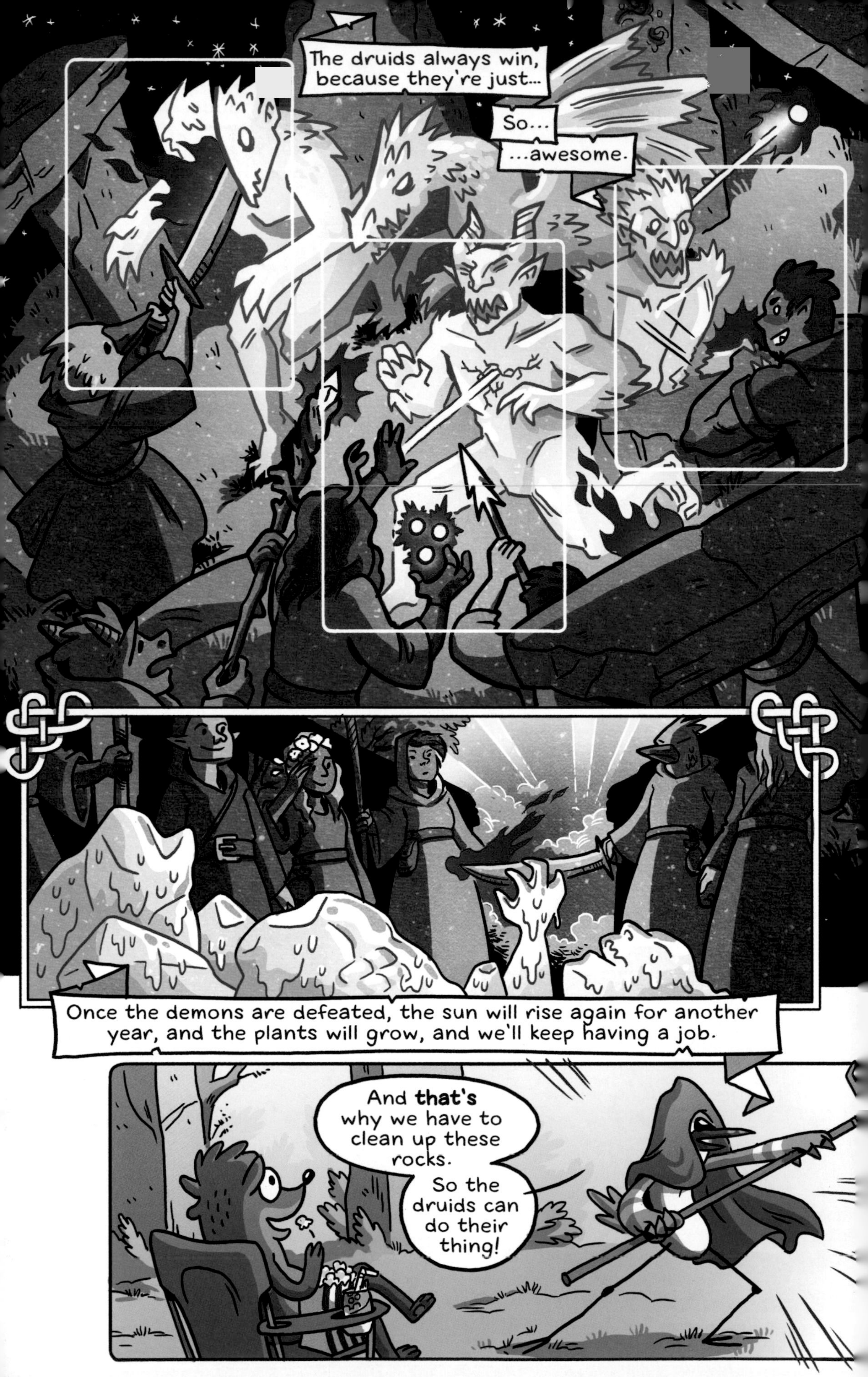
The druids always win, because they're just...
So...
...awesome.
Once the demons are defeated, the sun will rise again for another year, and the plants will grow, and we'll keep having a job.
And **that's** why we have to clean up these rocks.
So the druids can do their thing!

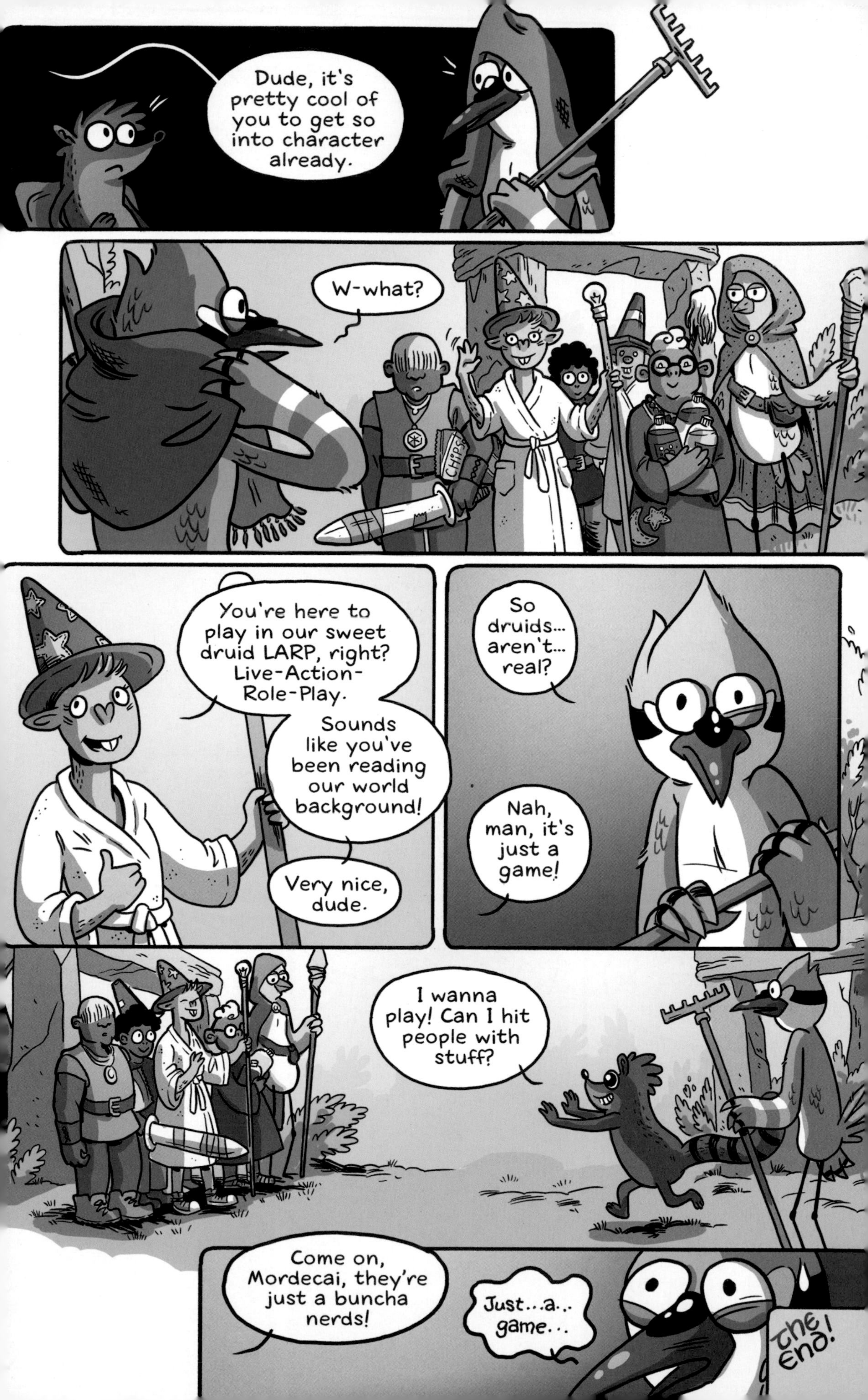
Dude, it's pretty cool of you to get so into character already.
W-what?
You're here to play in our sweet druid LARP, right? Live-Action-Role-Play.
Sounds like you've been reading our world background!
Very nice, dude.
So druids... aren't... real?
Nah, man, it's just a game!
CHIPS
I wanna play! Can I hit people with stuff?
Come on, Mordecai, they're just a buncha nerds!
Just...a...game...
The End!

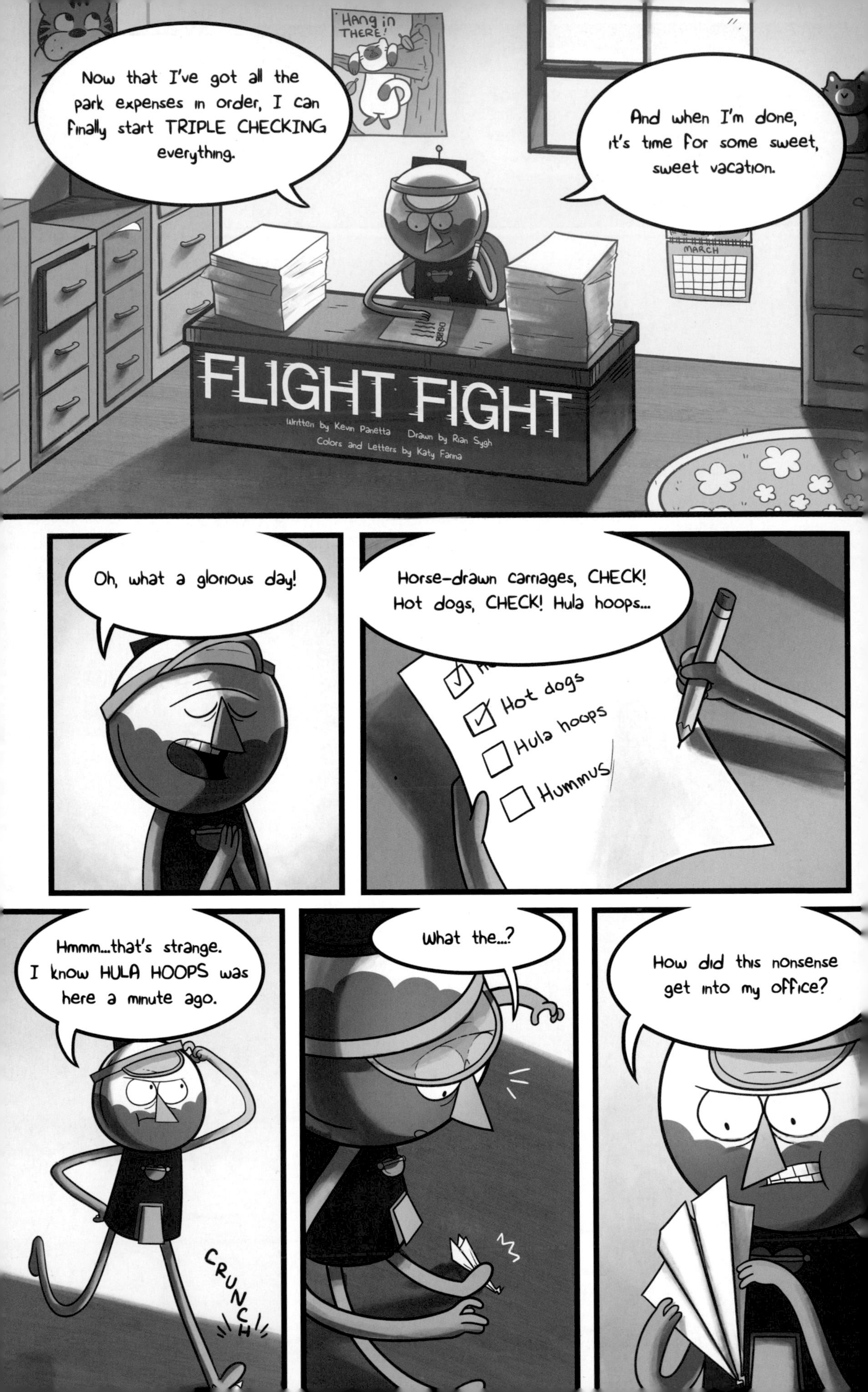
Hang in THERE!
Now that I've got all the park expenses in order, I can finally start TRIPLE CHECKING everything.
And when I'm done, it's time for some sweet, sweet vacation.
MARCH
FLIGHT FIGHT
Written by Kevin Panetta Drawn by Rian Sygh
Colors and Letters by Katy Farina
Oh, what a glorious day!
Horse-drawn carriages, CHECK! Hot dogs, CHECK! Hula hoops...
Hot dogs
Hula hoops
Hummus
Hmmm...that's strange. I know HULA HOOPS was here a minute ago.
CRUNCH
What the...?
How did this nonsense get into my office?

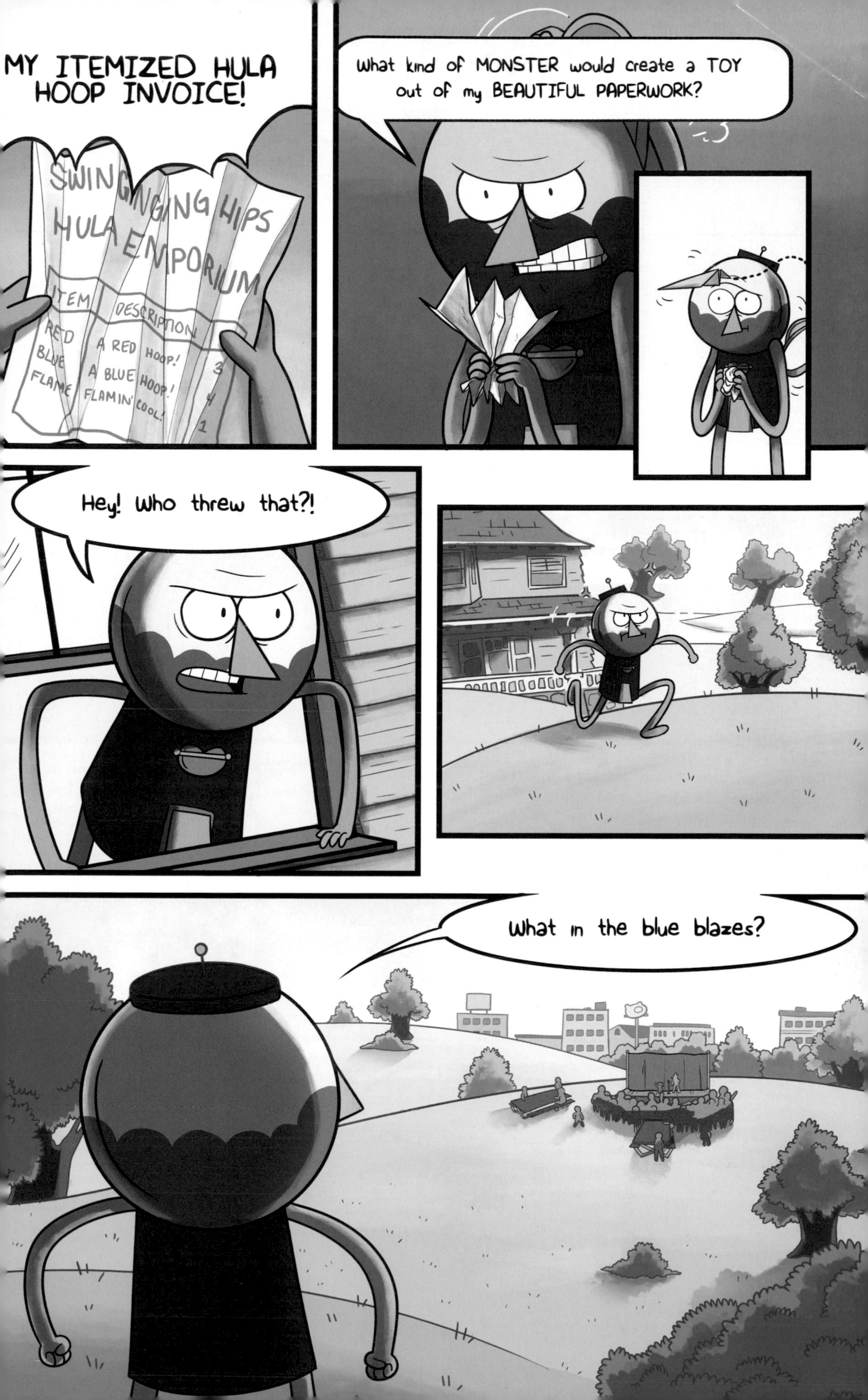
MY ITEMIZED HULA HOOP INVOICE!
SWINGING HIPS HULA EMPORIUM
ITEM
DESCRIPTION
RED
A RED HOOP!
BLUE
A BLUE HOOP!
FLAME
FLAMIN' COOL!
3
4
1
What kind of MONSTER would create a TOY out of my BEAUTIFUL PAPERWORK?
Hey! Who threw that?!
What in the blue blazes?

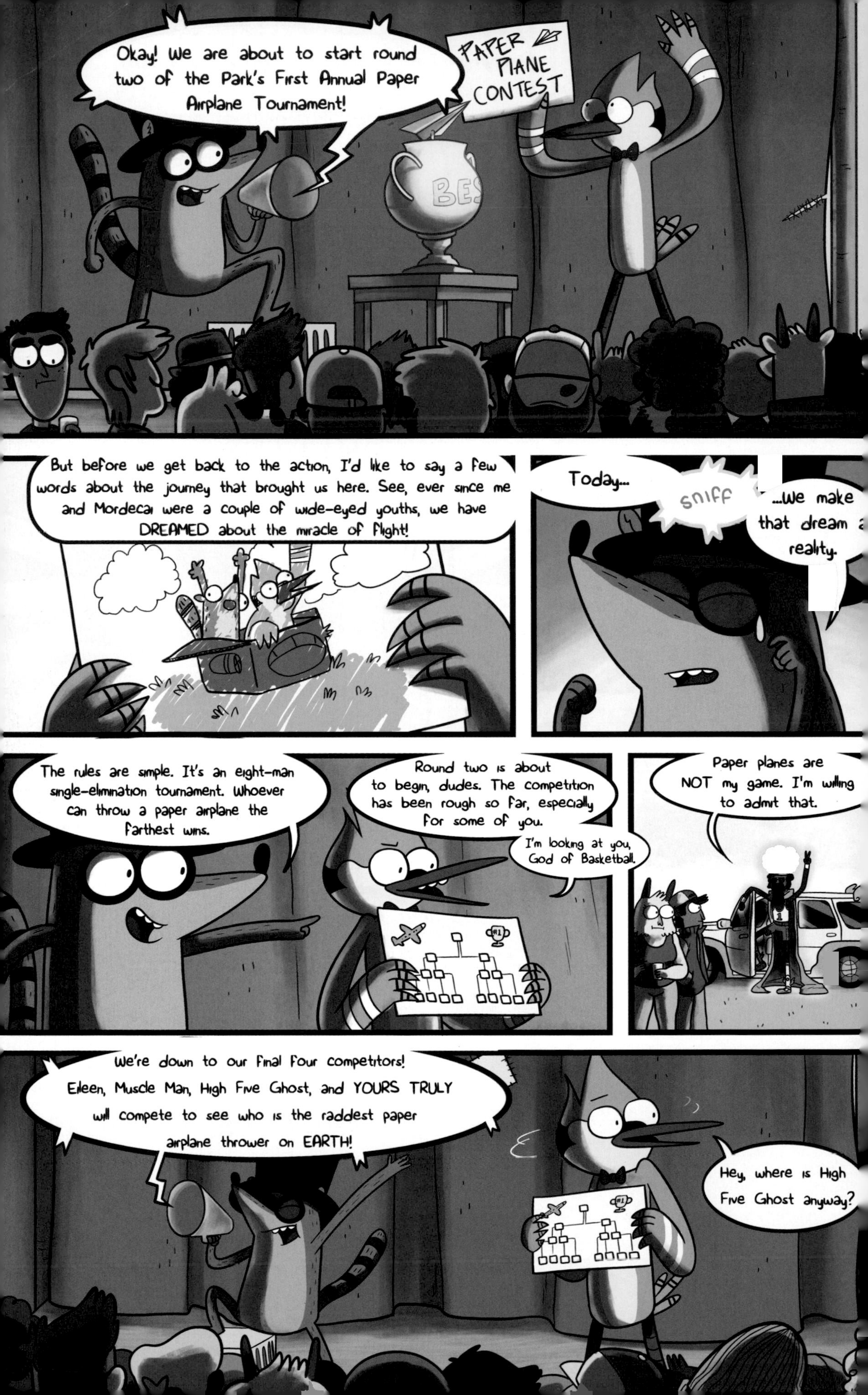
PAPER PLANE CONTEST
Okay! We are about to start round two of the Park's First Annual Paper Airplane Tournament!
BES
But before we get back to the action, I'd like to say a few words about the journey that brought us here. See, ever since me and Mordecai were a couple of wide-eyed youths, we have DREAMED about the miracle of flight!
Today...
sniff
...we make that dream a reality.
The rules are simple. It's an eight-man single-elimination tournament. Whoever can throw a paper airplane the farthest wins.
Round two is about to begin, dudes. The competition has been rough so far, especially for some of you.
I'm looking at you, God of Basketball.
Paper planes are NOT my game. I'm willing to admit that.
We're down to our final four competitors! Eileen, Muscle Man, High Five Ghost, and YOURS TRULY will compete to see who is the raddest paper airplane thrower on EARTH!
Hey, where is High Five Ghost anyway?

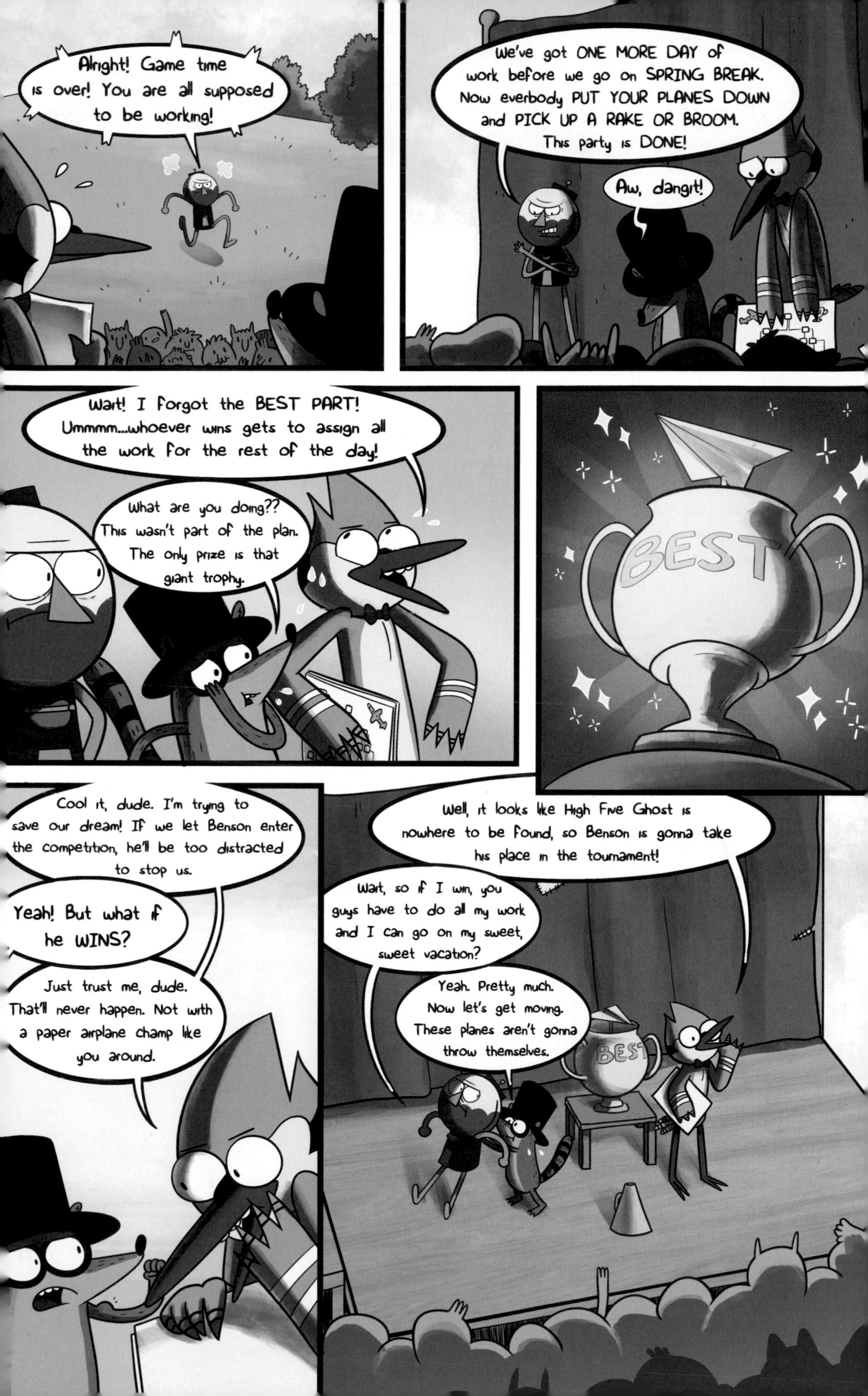
Alright! Game time is over! You are all supposed to be working!
We've got ONE MORE DAY of work before we go on SPRING BREAK. Now everbody PUT YOUR PLANES DOWN and PICK UP A RAKE OR BROOM. This party is DONE!
Aw, dangit!
Wait! I forgot the BEST PART! Ummmm...whoever wins gets to assign all the work for the rest of the day!
What are you doing?? This wasn't part of the plan. The only prize is that giant trophy.
BEST
Cool it, dude. I'm trying to save our dream! If we let Benson enter the competition, he'll be too distracted to stop us.
Yeah! But what if he WINS?
Just trust me, dude. That'll never happen. Not with a paper airplane champ like you around.
Well, it looks like High Five Ghost is nowhere to be found, so Benson is gonna take his place in the tournament!
Wait, so if I win, you guys have to do all my work and I can go on my sweet, sweet vacation?
Yeah. Pretty much. Now let's get moving. These planes aren't gonna throw themselves.
BEST

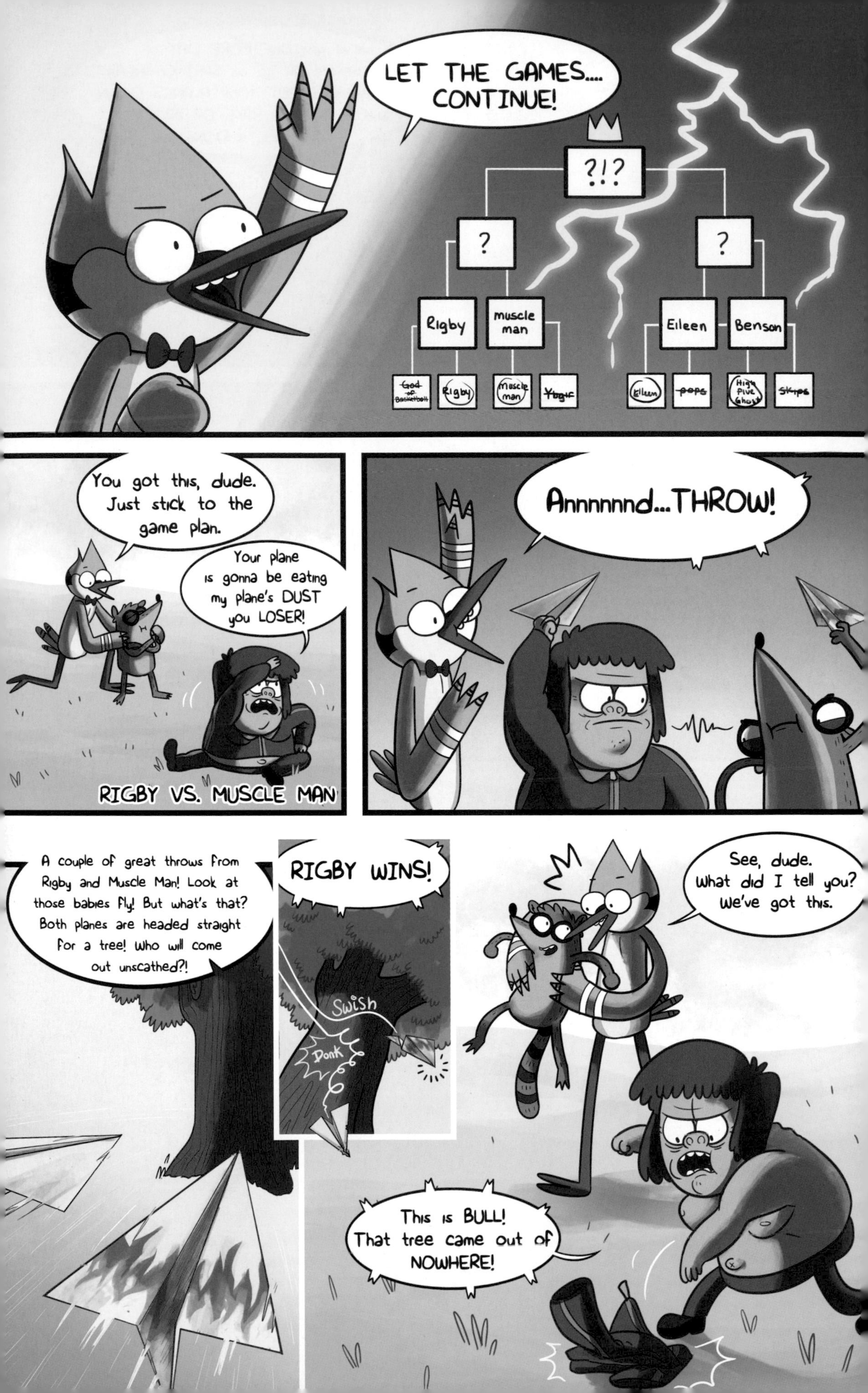
LET THE GAMES.... CONTINUE!
?!?
?
?
Rigby
muscle man
Eileen
Benson
God of Basketball
Rigby
Muscle man
Eileen
pops
High five Ghost
You got this, dude. Just stick to the game plan.
Your plane is gonna be eating my plane's DUST you LOSER!
RIGBY VS. MUSCLE MAN
Annnnnd...THROW!
A couple of great throws from Rigby and Muscle Man! Look at those babies fly! But what's that? Both planes are headed straight for a tree! Who will come out unscathed?!
RIGBY WINS!
Swish
Donk
See, dude. What did I tell you? We've got this.
This is BULL! That tree came out of NOWHERE!

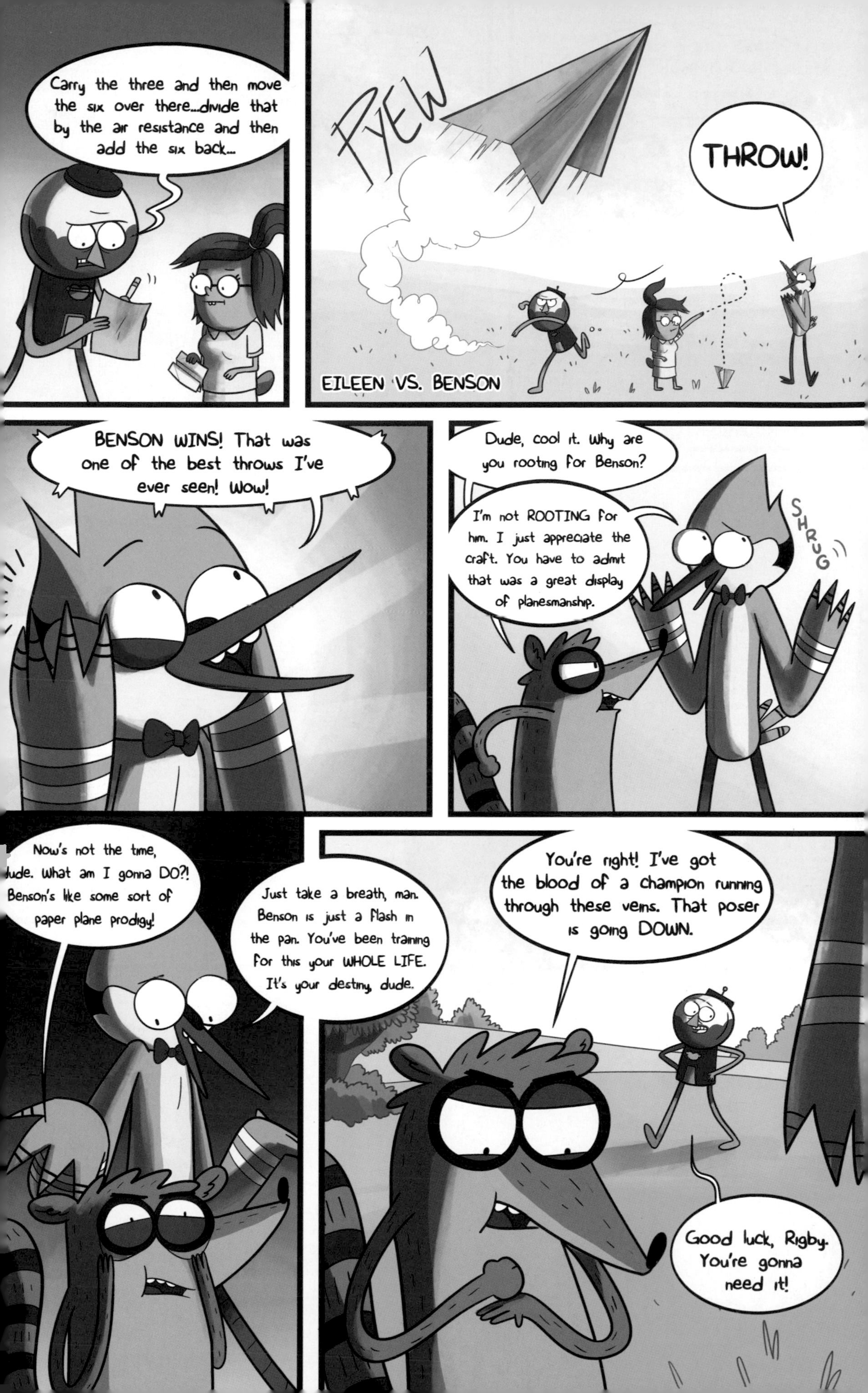
Carry the three and then move the six over there...divide that by the air resistance and then add the six back...
PYEW
THROW!
EILEEN VS. BENSON
BENSON WINS! That was one of the best throws I've ever seen! Wow!
Dude, cool it. Why are you rooting for Benson?
I'm not ROOTING for him. I just appreciate the craft. You have to admit that was a great display of planesmanship.
SHRUG
Now's not the time, dude. What am I gonna DO?! Benson's like some sort of paper plane prodigy!
Just take a breath, man. Benson is just a flash in the pan. You've been training for this your WHOLE LIFE. It's your destiny, dude.
You're right! I've got the blood of a champion running through these veins. That poser is going DOWN.
Good luck, Rigby. You're gonna need it!

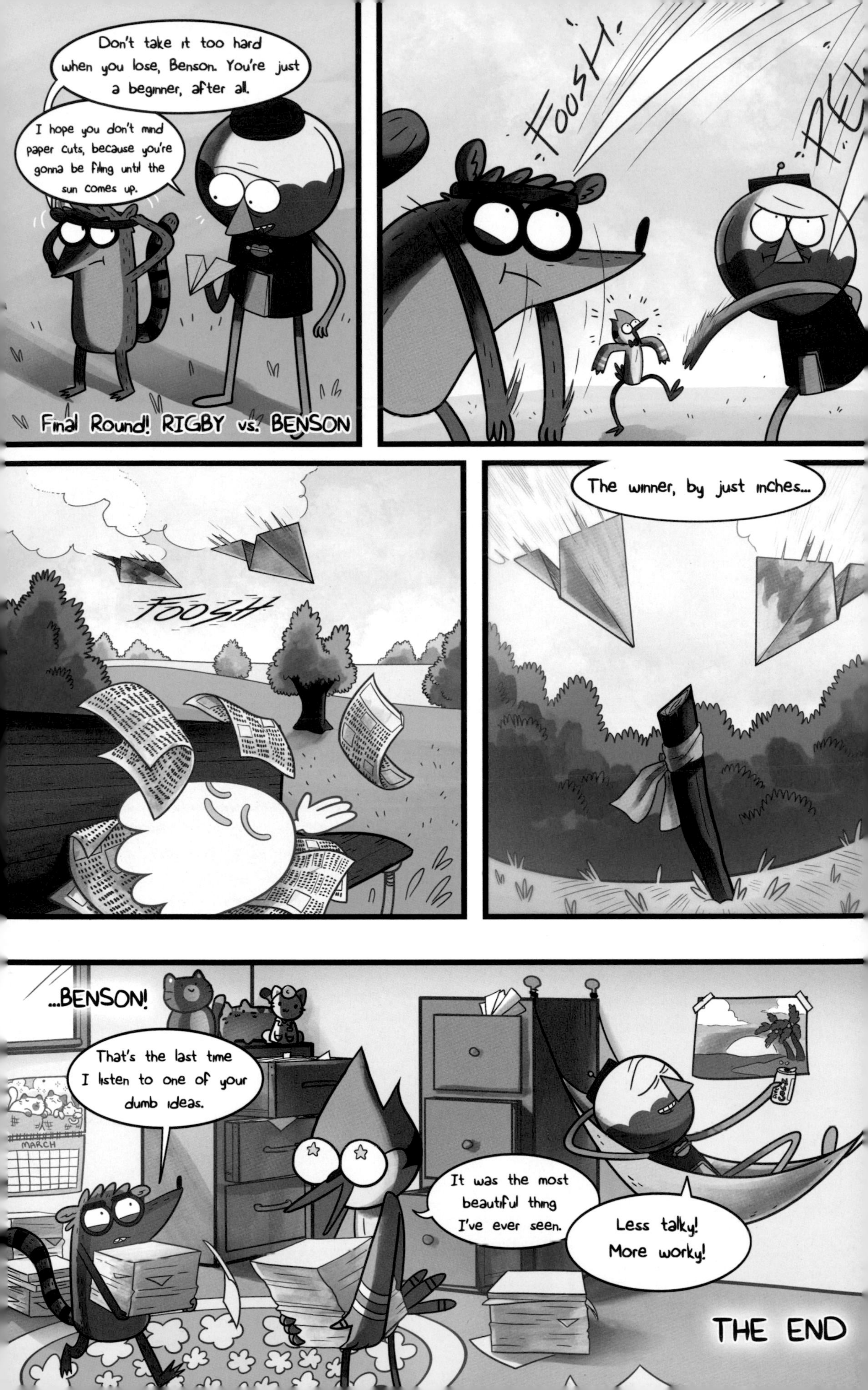
Don't take it too hard when you lose, Benson. You're just a beginner, after all.
I hope you don't mind paper cuts, because you're gonna be filing until the sun comes up.
Final Round! RIGBY vs. BENSON
FOOSH!
FOOSH
The winner, by just inches...
...BENSON!
That's the last time I listen to one of your dumb ideas.
MARCH
It was the most beautiful thing I've ever seen.
Less talky! More worky!
THE END

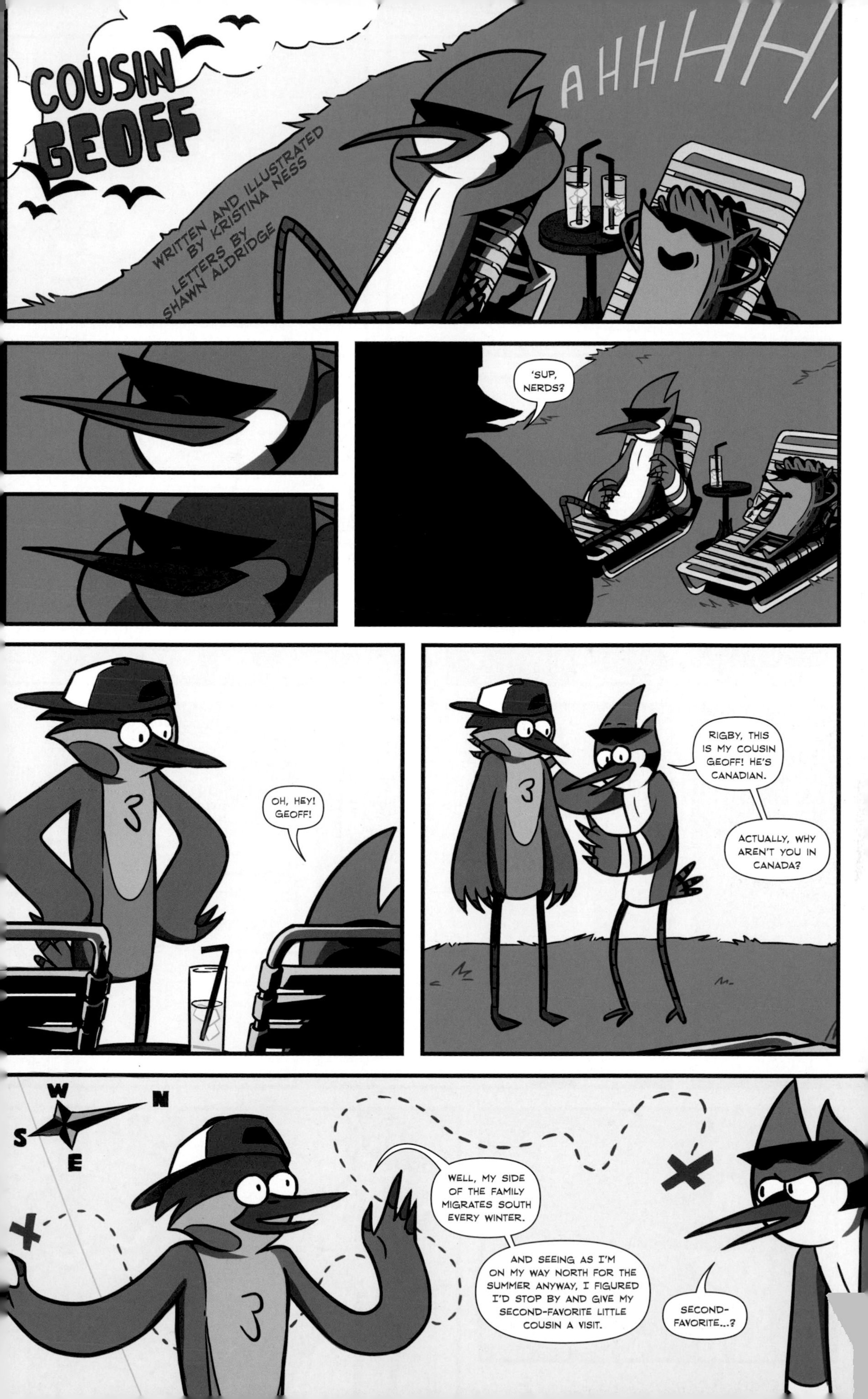
COUSIN GEOFF
WRITTEN AND ILLUSTRATED BY KRISTINA NESS
LETTERS BY SHAWN ALDRIDGE
AHHHHH
'SUP, NERDS?
OH, HEY! GEOFF!
RIGBY, THIS IS MY COUSIN GEOFF! HE'S CANADIAN.
ACTUALLY, WHY AREN'T YOU IN CANADA?
W
N
S
E
WELL, MY SIDE OF THE FAMILY MIGRATES SOUTH EVERY WINTER.
AND SEEING AS I'M ON MY WAY NORTH FOR THE SUMMER ANYWAY, I FIGURED I'D STOP BY AND GIVE MY SECOND-FAVORITE LITTLE COUSIN A VISIT.
SECOND-FAVORITE...?

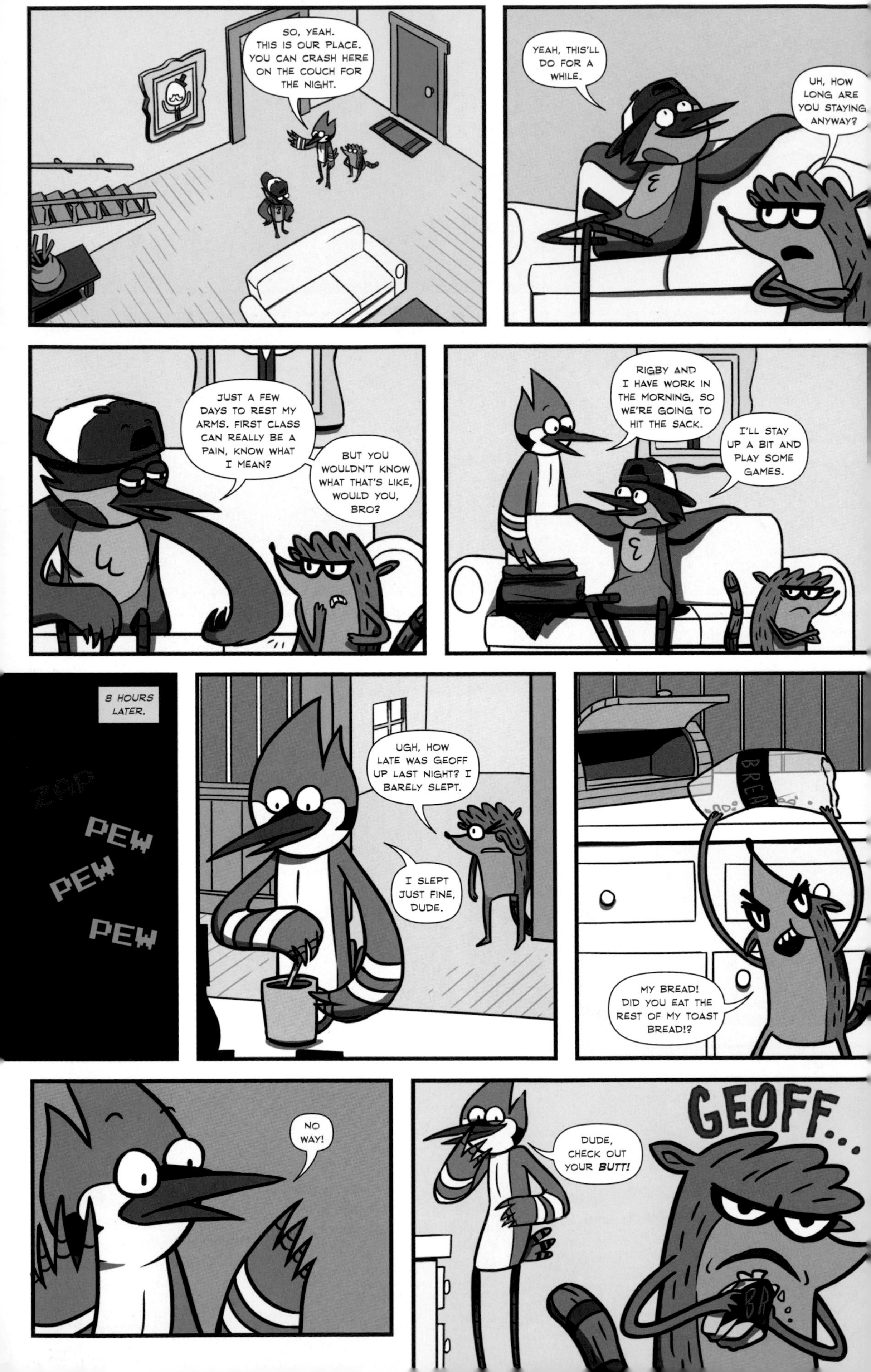
SO, YEAH. THIS IS OUR PLACE. YOU CAN CRASH HERE ON THE COUCH FOR THE NIGHT.
YEAH, THIS'LL DO FOR A WHILE.
UH, HOW LONG ARE YOU STAYING, ANYWAY?
JUST A FEW DAYS TO REST MY ARMS. FIRST CLASS CAN REALLY BE A PAIN, KNOW WHAT I MEAN?
BUT YOU WOULDN'T KNOW WHAT THAT'S LIKE, WOULD YOU, BRO?
RIGBY AND I HAVE WORK IN THE MORNING, SO WE'RE GOING TO HIT THE SACK.
I'LL STAY UP A BIT AND PLAY SOME GAMES.
8 HOURS LATER.
PEW
PEW
PEW
UGH, HOW LATE WAS GEOFF UP LAST NIGHT? I BARELY SLEPT.
I SLEPT JUST FINE, DUDE.
MY BREAD! DID YOU EAT THE REST OF MY TOAST BREAD!?
NO WAY!
DUDE, CHECK OUT YOUR BUTT!
GEOFF...

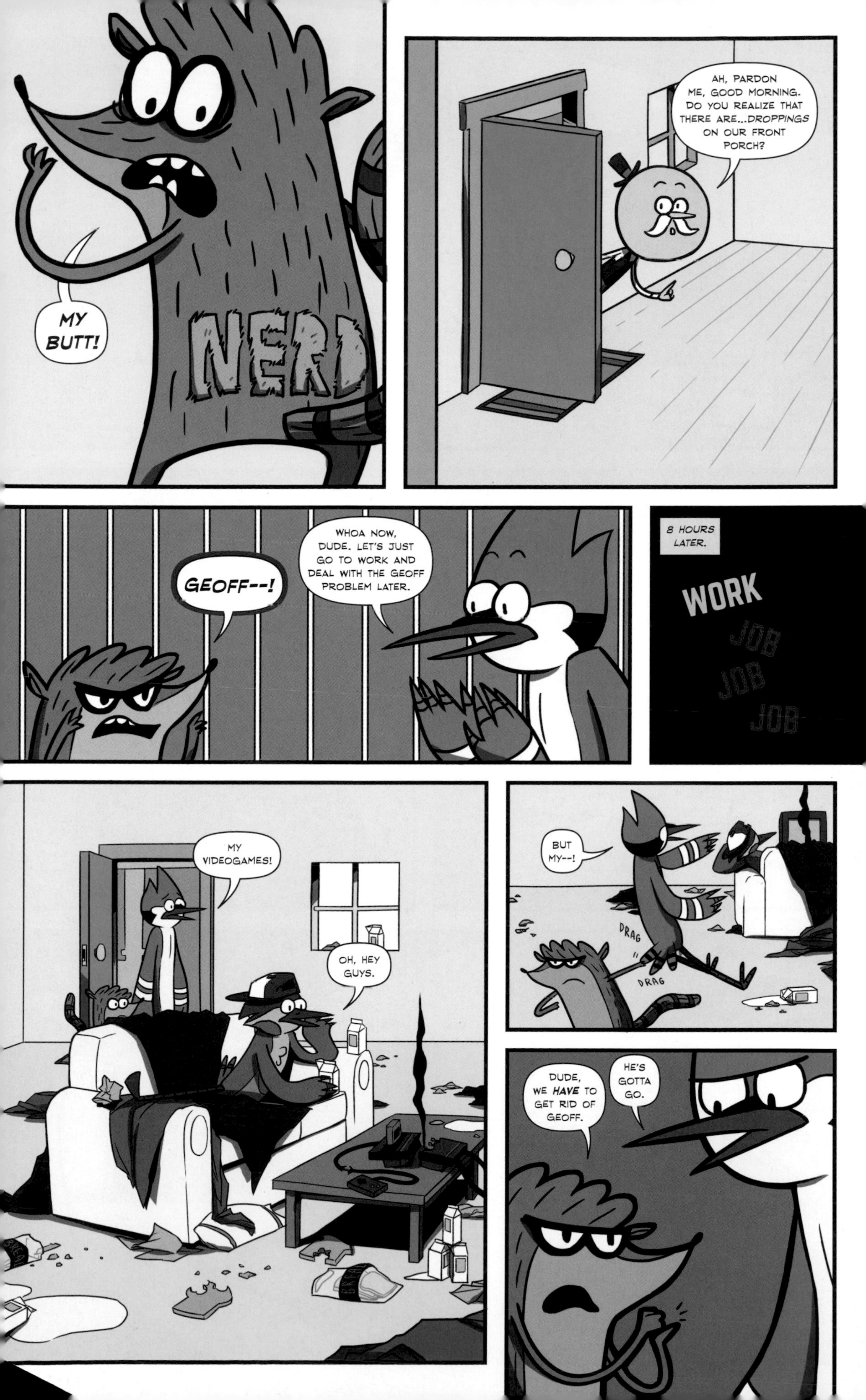
MY BUTT!
AH, PARDON ME, GOOD MORNING. DO YOU REALIZE THAT THERE ARE...DROPPINGS ON OUR FRONT PORCH?
GEOFF--!
WHOA NOW, DUDE. LET'S JUST GO TO WORK AND DEAL WITH THE GEOFF PROBLEM LATER.
8 HOURS LATER.
WORK
JOB
JOB
JOB
MY VIDEOGAMES!
OH, HEY GUYS.
BUT MY--!
DRAG
DRAG
DUDE, WE HAVE TO GET RID OF GEOFF.
HE'S GOTTA GO.

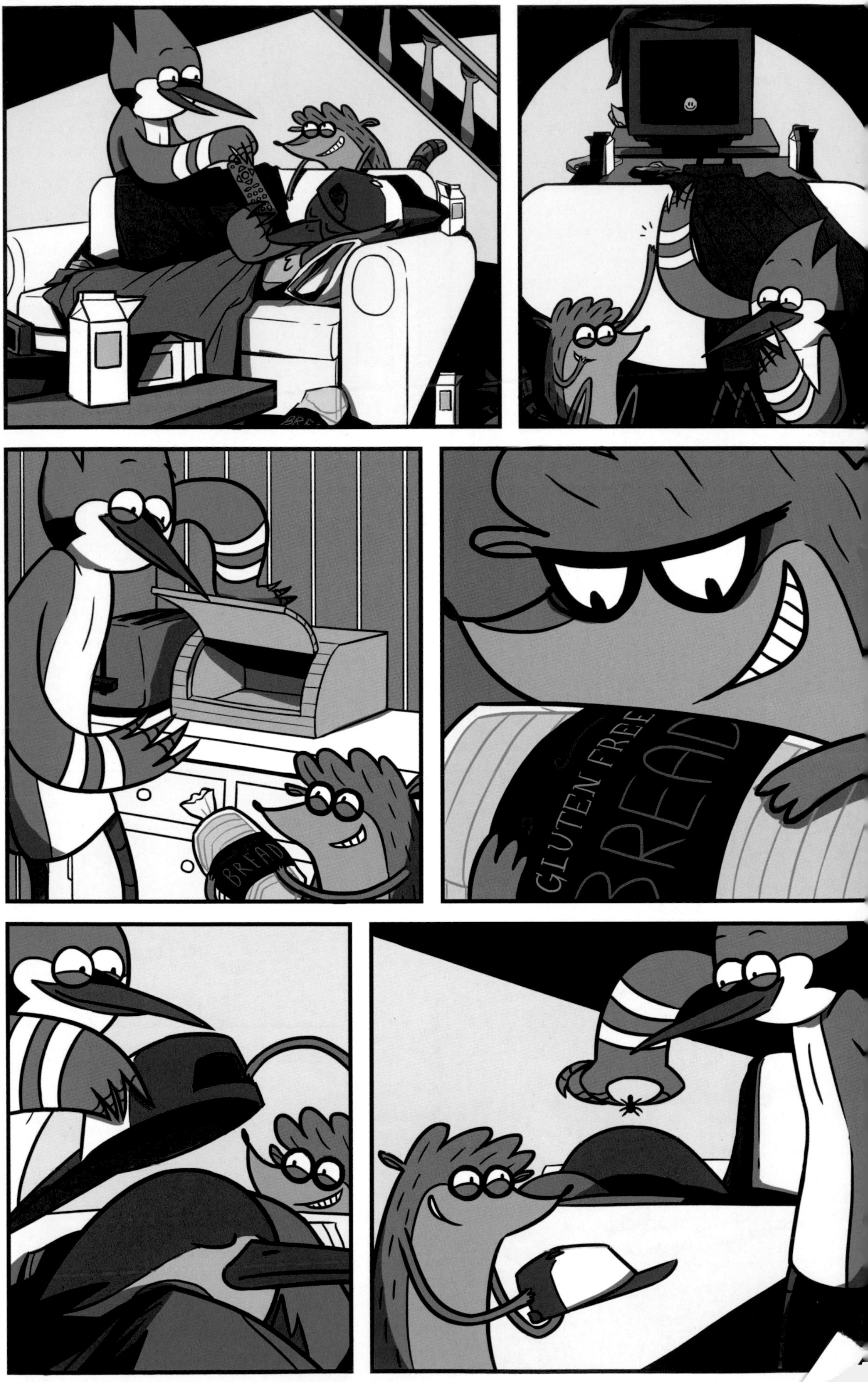
BREAD
GLUTEN FREE
BREAD

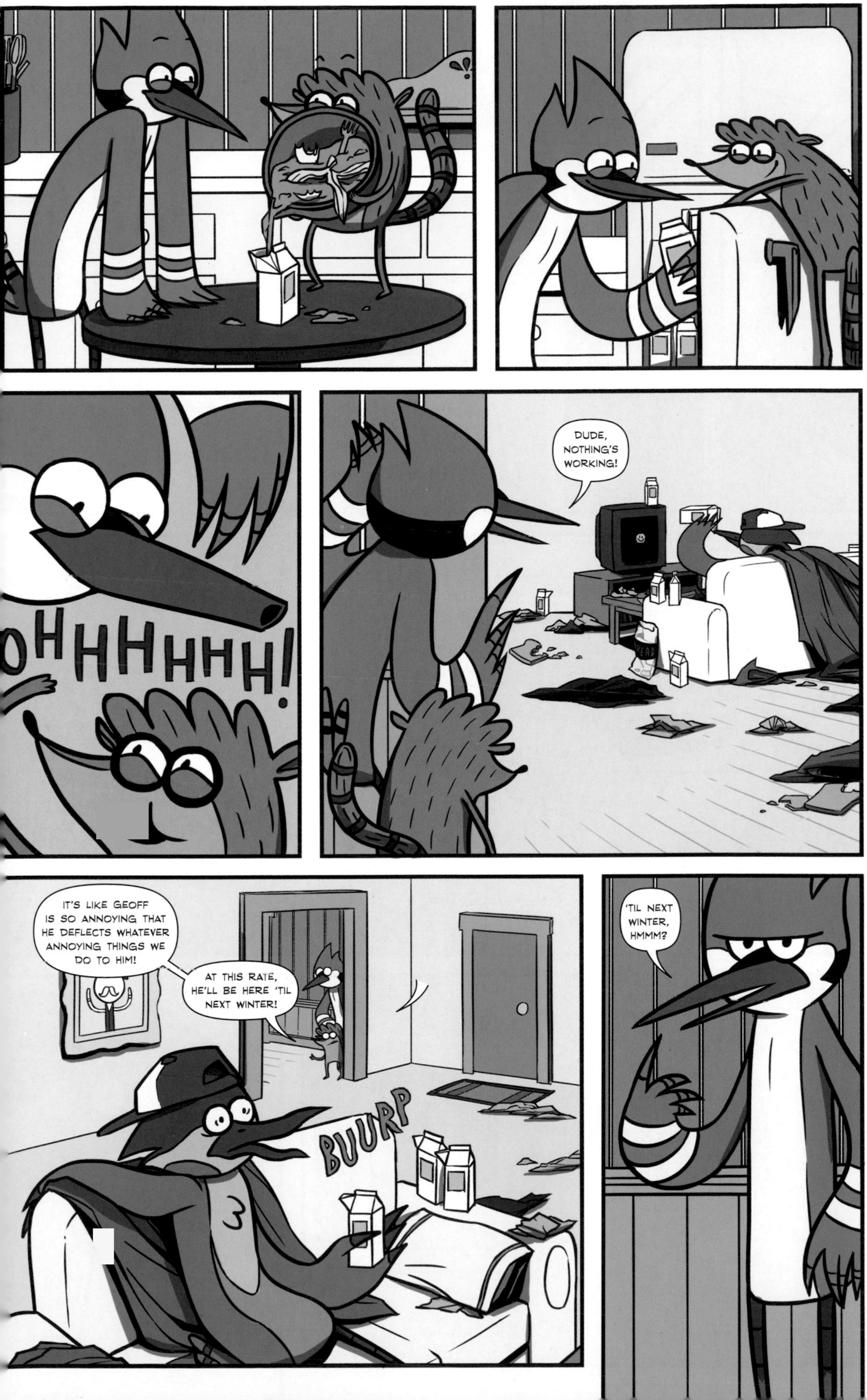
OHHHHHH!
DUDE, NOTHING'S WORKING!
IT'S LIKE GEOFF IS SO ANNOYING THAT HE DEFLECTS WHATEVER ANNOYING THINGS WE DO TO HIM!
AT THIS RATE, HE'LL BE HERE 'TIL NEXT WINTER!
BUURP
'TIL NEXT WINTER, HMMM?

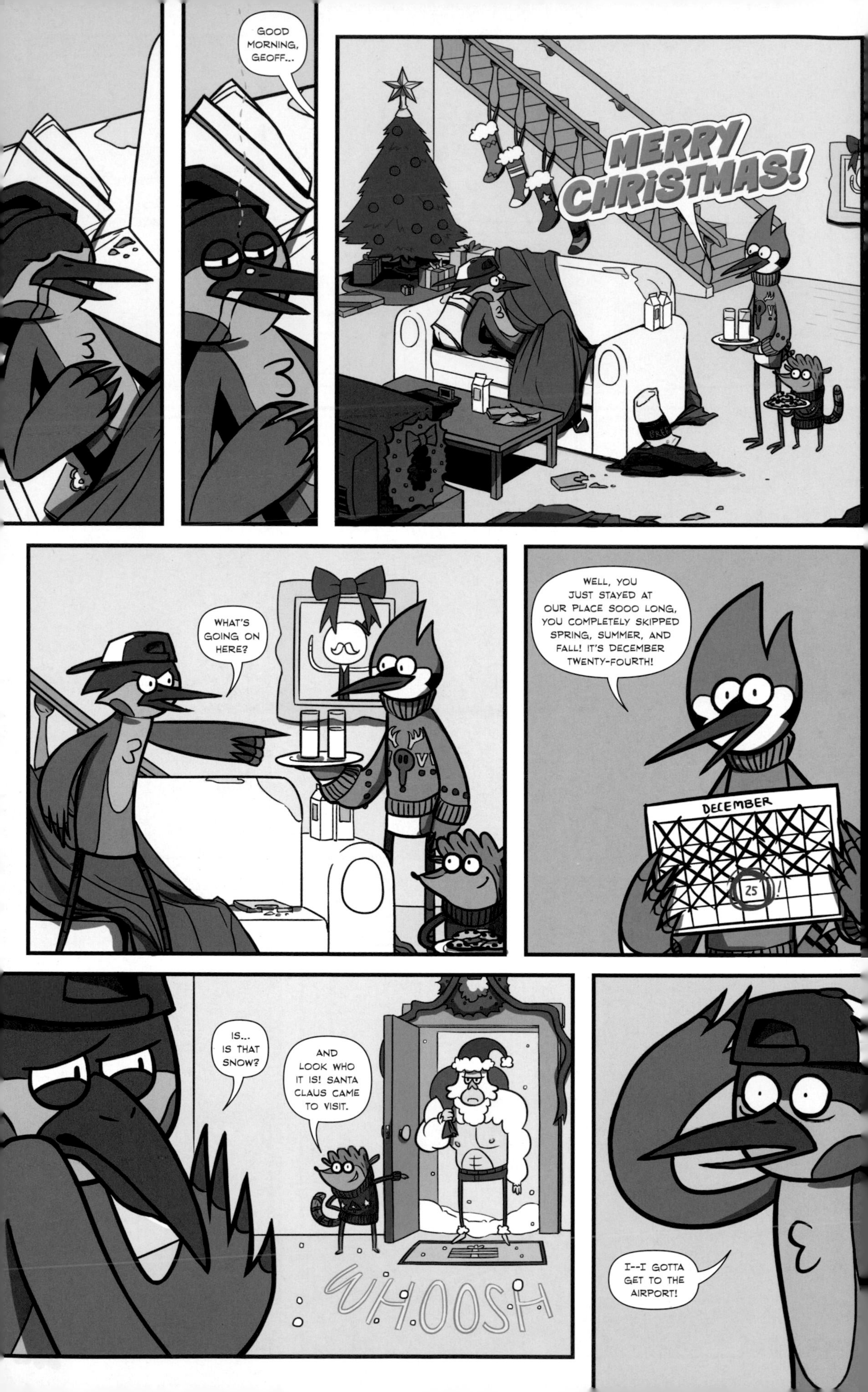
GOOD MORNING, GEOFF...
MERRY CHRISTMAS!
WHAT'S GOING ON HERE?
WELL, YOU JUST STAYED AT OUR PLACE SOOO LONG, YOU COMPLETELY SKIPPED SPRING, SUMMER, AND FALL! IT'S DECEMBER TWENTY-FOURTH!
DECEMBER
25
IS... IS THAT SNOW?
AND LOOK WHO IT IS! SANTA CLAUS CAME TO VISIT.
WHOOSH
I--I GOTTA GET TO THE AIRPORT!

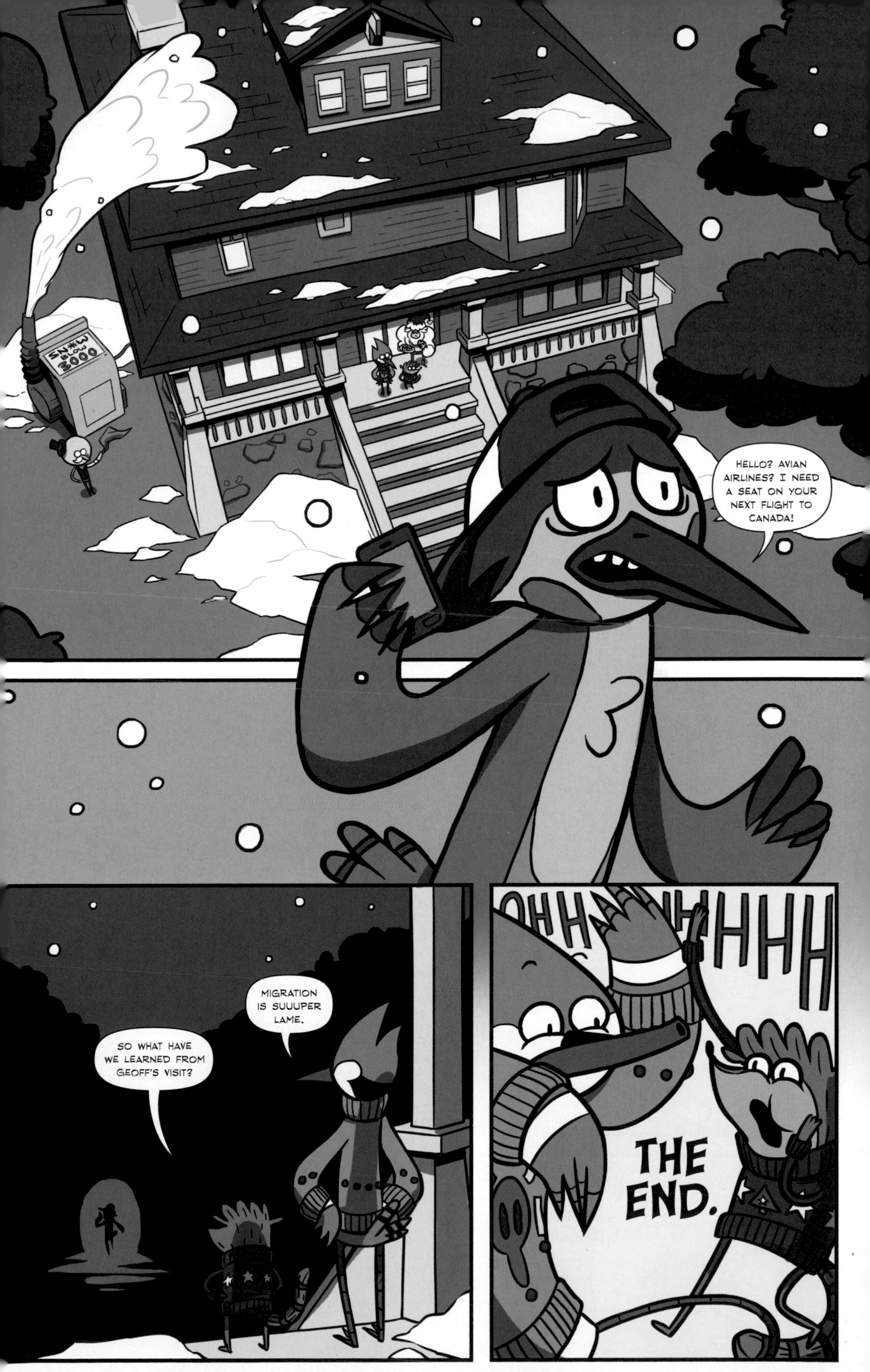
SN*W BLOW 3000
HELLO? AVIAN AIRLINES? I NEED A SEAT ON YOUR NEXT FLIGHT TO CANADA!
SO WHAT HAVE WE LEARNED FROM GEOFF'S VISIT?
MIGRATION IS SUUUPER LAME.
OHHHHHHHH
THE END.

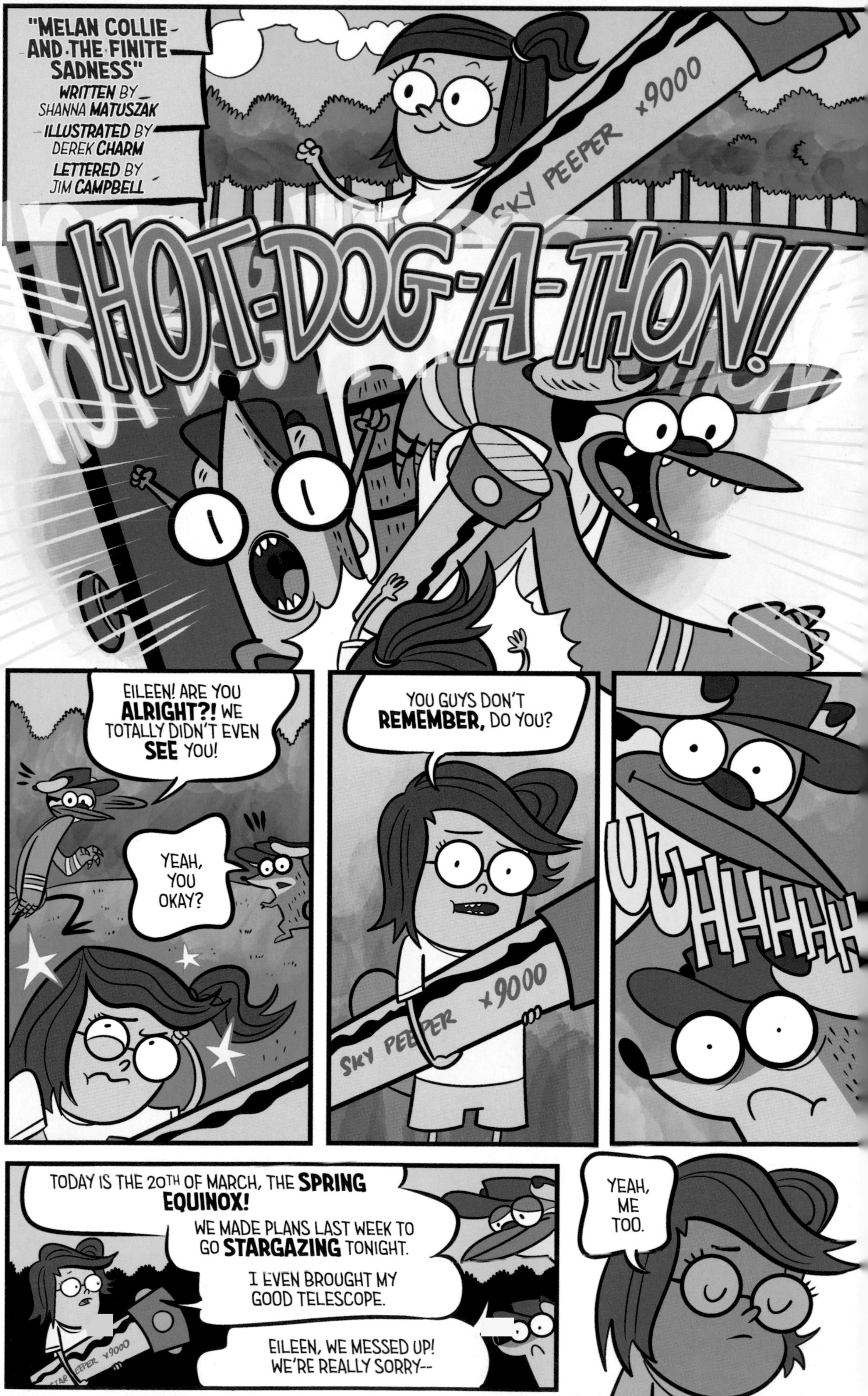
"MELAN COLLIE AND THE FINITE SADNESS"
WRITTEN BY SHANNA MATUSZAK
ILLUSTRATED BY DEREK CHARM
LETTERED BY JIM CAMPBELL
SKY PEEPER x9000
HOT-DOG-A-THON!
EILEEN! ARE YOU ALRIGHT?! WE TOTALLY DIDN'T EVEN SEE YOU!
YEAH, YOU OKAY?
YOU GUYS DON'T REMEMBER, DO YOU?
SKY PEEPER x9000
UUHHHHH
TODAY IS THE 20TH OF MARCH, THE SPRING EQUINOX!
WE MADE PLANS LAST WEEK TO GO STARGAZING TONIGHT.
I EVEN BROUGHT MY GOOD TELESCOPE.
EILEEN, WE MESSED UP! WE'RE REALLY SORRY--
YEAH, ME TOO.

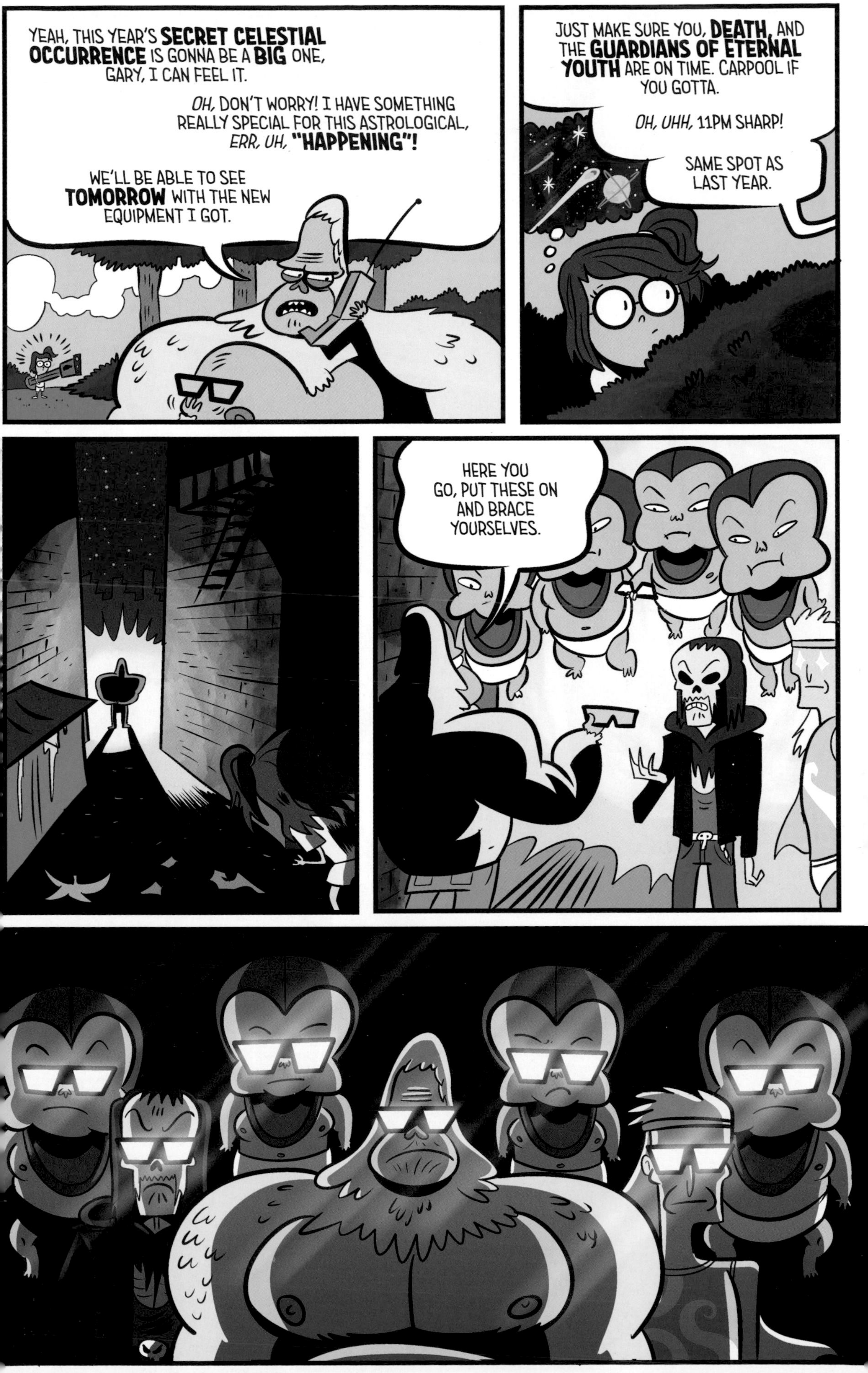
YEAH, THIS YEAR'S SECRET CELESTIAL OCCURRENCE IS GONNA BE A BIG ONE, GARY, I CAN FEEL IT.
OH, DON'T WORRY! I HAVE SOMETHING REALLY SPECIAL FOR THIS ASTROLOGICAL, ERR, UH, "HAPPENING"!
WE'LL BE ABLE TO SEE TOMORROW WITH THE NEW EQUIPMENT I GOT.
JUST MAKE SURE YOU, DEATH, AND THE GUARDIANS OF ETERNAL YOUTH ARE ON TIME. CARPOOL IF YOU GOTTA.
OH, UHH, 11PM SHARP!
SAME SPOT AS LAST YEAR.
HERE YOU GO, PUT THESE ON AND BRACE YOURSELVES.

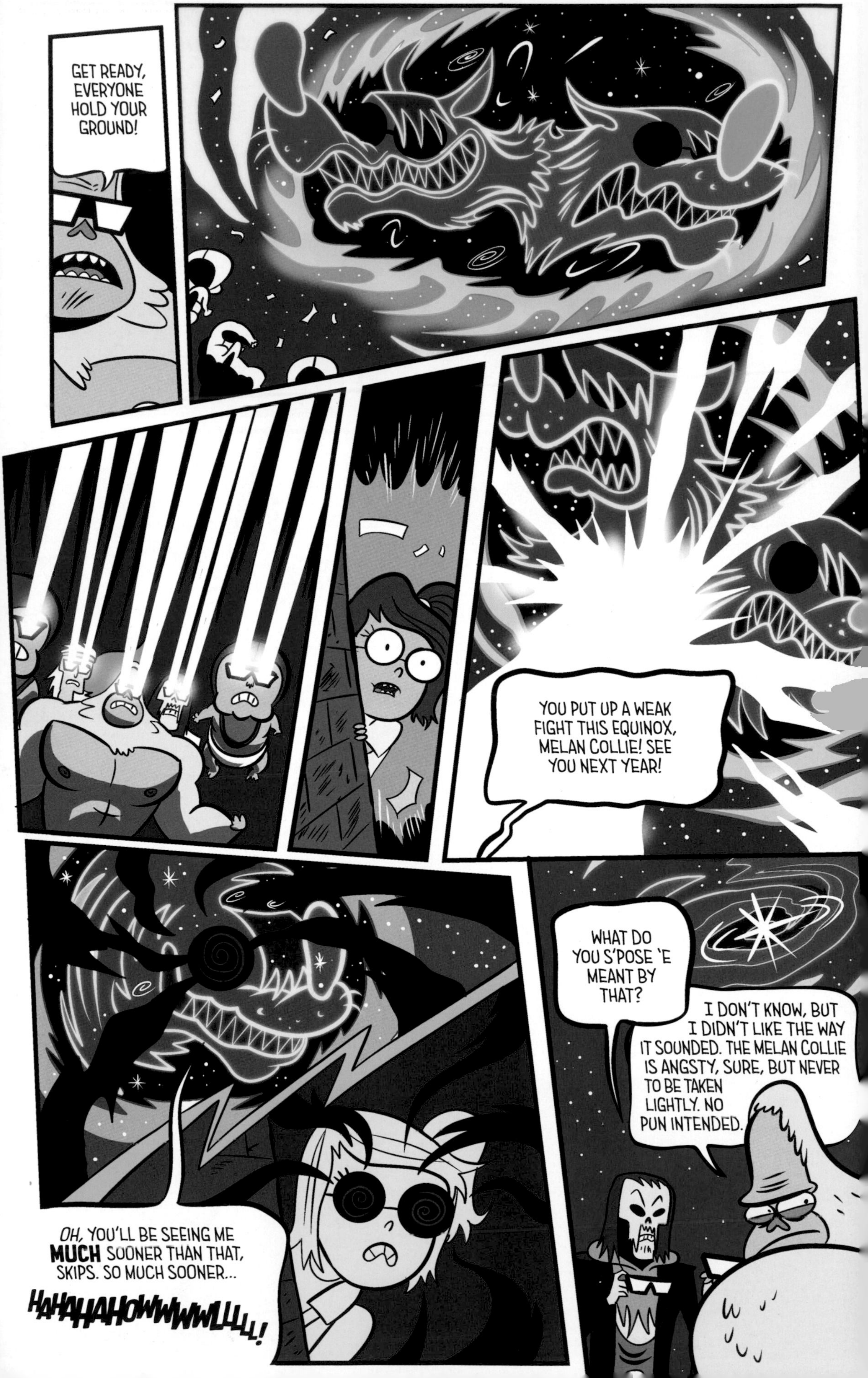
GET READY, EVERYONE HOLD YOUR GROUND!
YOU PUT UP A WEAK FIGHT THIS EQUINOX, MELAN COLLIE! SEE YOU NEXT YEAR!
OH, YOU'LL BE SEEING ME MUCH SOONER THAN THAT, SKIPS. SO MUCH SOONER...
HAHAHAHOWWWWLLLLL!
WHAT DO YOU S'POSE 'E MEANT BY THAT?
I DON'T KNOW, BUT I DIDN'T LIKE THE WAY IT SOUNDED. THE MELAN COLLIE IS ANGSTY, SURE, BUT NEVER TO BE TAKEN LIGHTLY. NO PUN INTENDED.

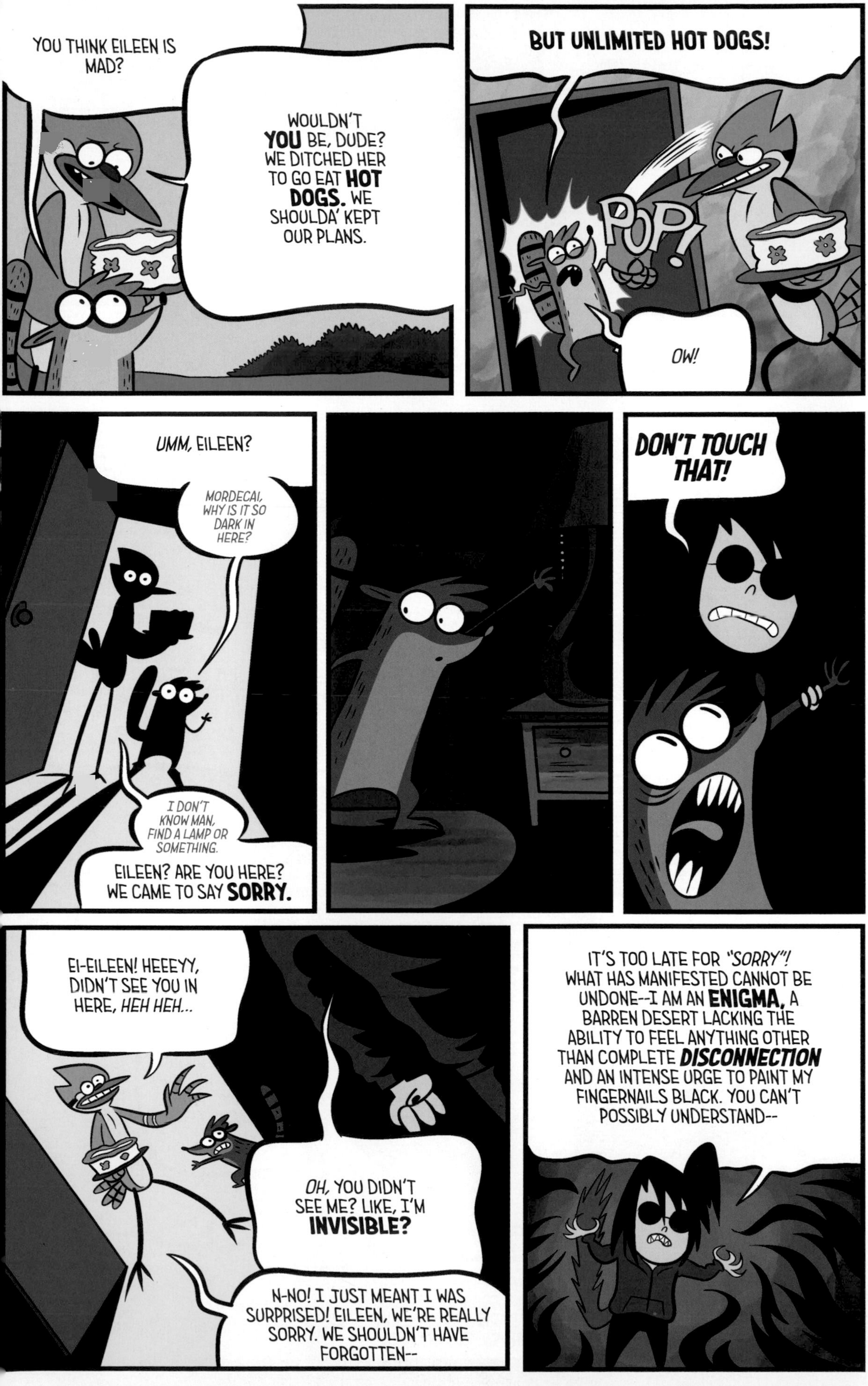
YOU THINK EILEEN IS MAD?
WOULDN'T YOU BE, DUDE? WE DITCHED HER TO GO EAT HOT DOGS. WE SHOULDA' KEPT OUR PLANS.
BUT UNLIMITED HOT DOGS!
POP!
OW!
UMM, EILEEN?
MORDECAI, WHY IS IT SO DARK IN HERE?
I DON'T KNOW MAN, FIND A LAMP OR SOMETHING.
EILEEN? ARE YOU HERE? WE CAME TO SAY SORRY.
DON'T TOUCH THAT!
EI-EILEEN! HEEEYY, DIDN'T SEE YOU IN HERE, HEH HEH...
OH, YOU DIDN'T SEE ME? LIKE, I'M INVISIBLE?
N-NO! I JUST MEANT I WAS SURPRISED! EILEEN, WE'RE REALLY SORRY. WE SHOULDN'T HAVE FORGOTTEN--
IT'S TOO LATE FOR "SORRY"! WHAT HAS MANIFESTED CANNOT BE UNDONE--I AM AN ENIGMA, A BARREN DESERT LACKING THE ABILITY TO FEEL ANYTHING OTHER THAN COMPLETE DISCONNECTION AND AN INTENSE URGE TO PAINT MY FINGERNAILS BLACK. YOU CAN'T POSSIBLY UNDERSTAND--

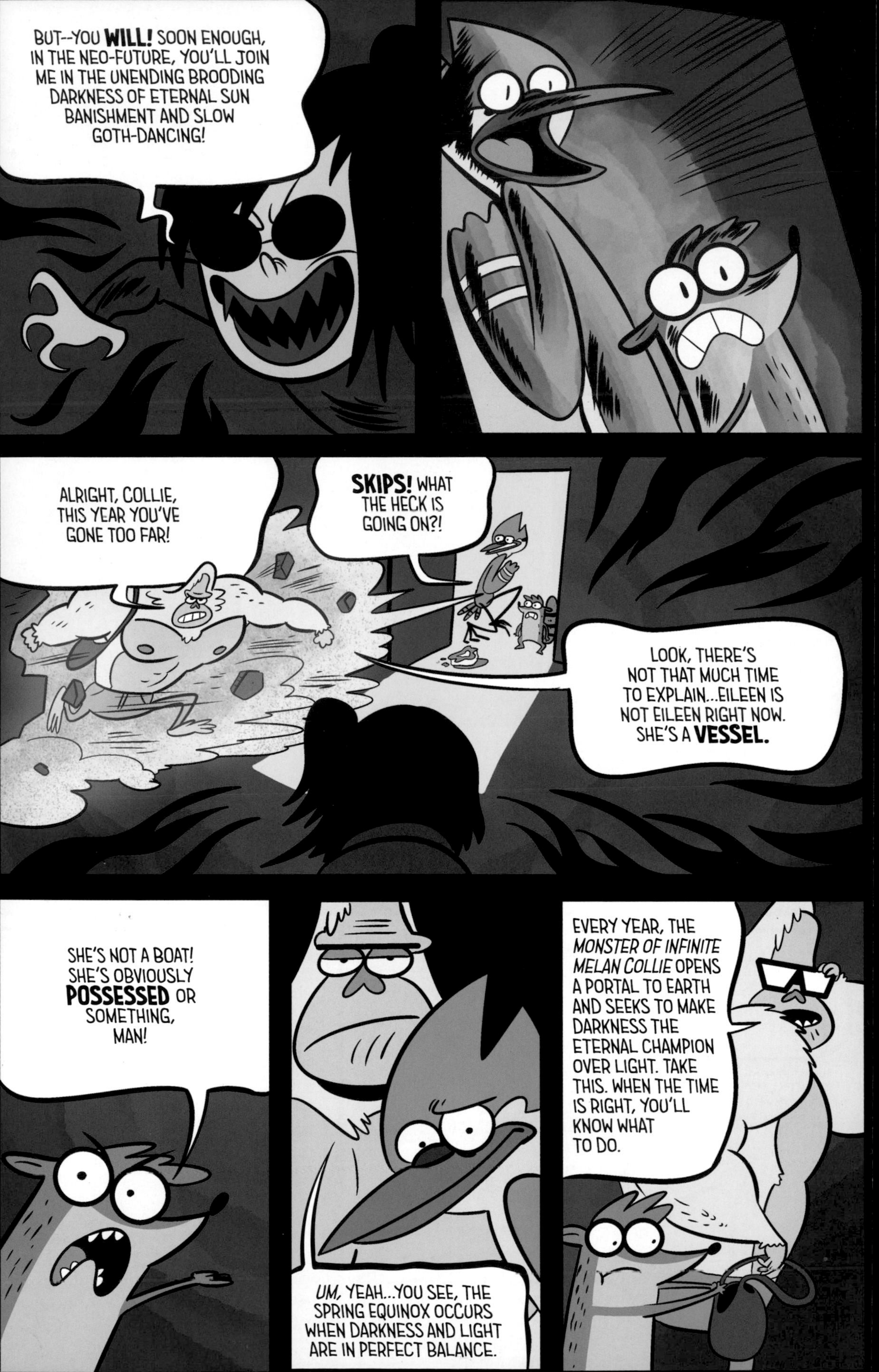
BUT--YOU **WILL!** SOON ENOUGH, IN THE NEO-FUTURE, YOU'LL JOIN ME IN THE UNENDING BROODING DARKNESS OF ETERNAL SUN BANISHMENT AND SLOW GOTH-DANCING!
ALRIGHT, COLLIE, THIS YEAR YOU'VE GONE TOO FAR!
SKIPS! WHAT THE HECK IS GOING ON?!
LOOK, THERE'S NOT THAT MUCH TIME TO EXPLAIN...EILEEN IS NOT EILEEN RIGHT NOW. SHE'S A **VESSEL.**
SHE'S NOT A BOAT! SHE'S OBVIOUSLY **POSSESSED** OR SOMETHING, MAN!
UM, YEAH...YOU SEE, THE SPRING EQUINOX OCCURS WHEN DARKNESS AND LIGHT ARE IN PERFECT BALANCE.
EVERY YEAR, THE *MONSTER OF INFINITE MELAN COLLIE* OPENS A PORTAL TO EARTH AND SEEKS TO MAKE DARKNESS THE ETERNAL CHAMPION OVER LIGHT. TAKE THIS. WHEN THE TIME IS RIGHT, YOU'LL KNOW WHAT TO DO.

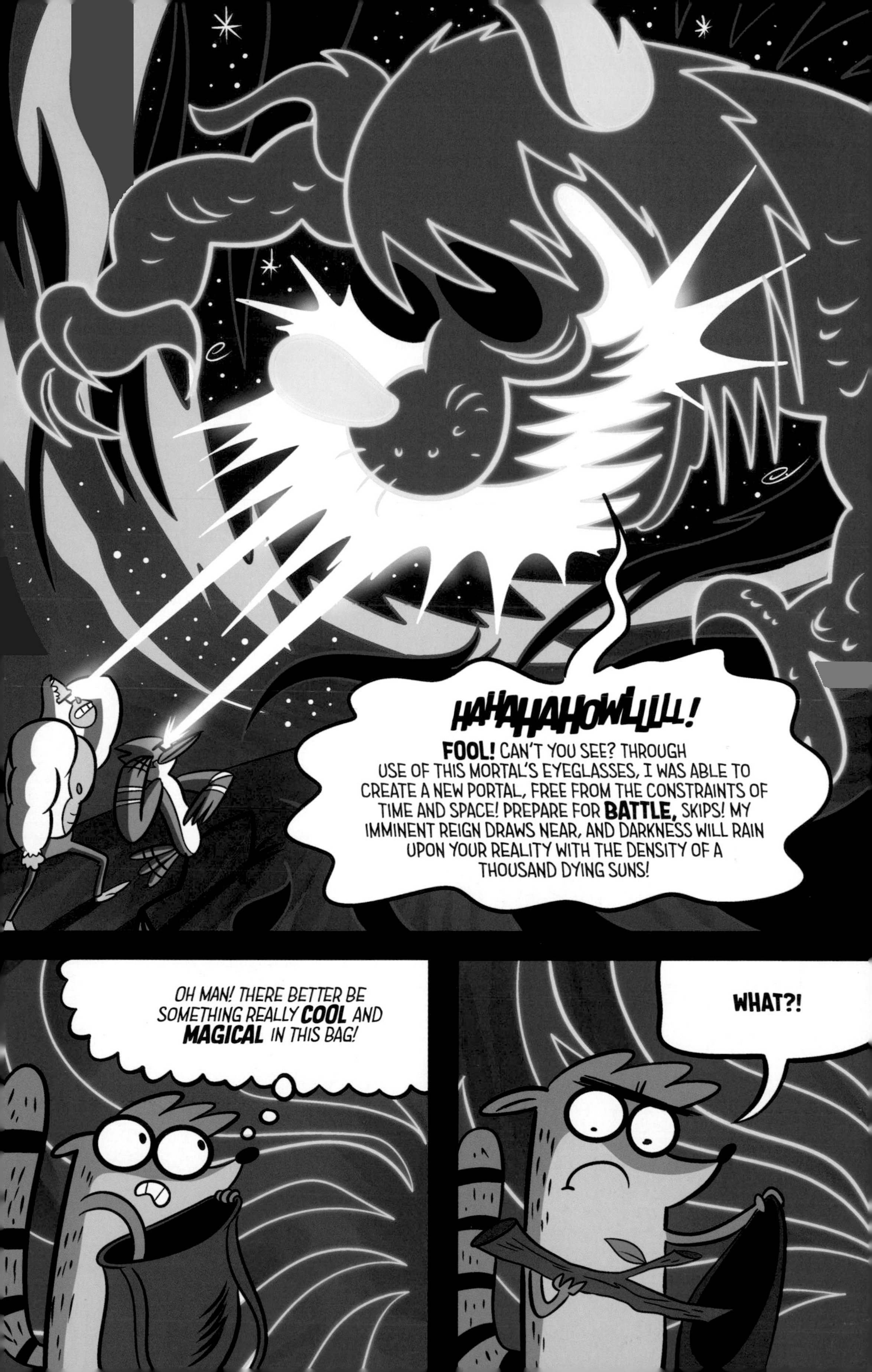
HAHAHAHOWLLLLL!
FOOL! CAN'T YOU SEE? THROUGH USE OF THIS MORTAL'S EYEGLASSES, I WAS ABLE TO CREATE A NEW PORTAL, FREE FROM THE CONSTRAINTS OF TIME AND SPACE! PREPARE FOR BATTLE, SKIPS! MY IMMINENT REIGN DRAWS NEAR, AND DARKNESS WILL RAIN UPON YOUR REALITY WITH THE DENSITY OF A THOUSAND DYING SUNS!
OH MAN! THERE BETTER BE SOMETHING REALLY COOL AND MAGICAL IN THIS BAG!
WHAT?!

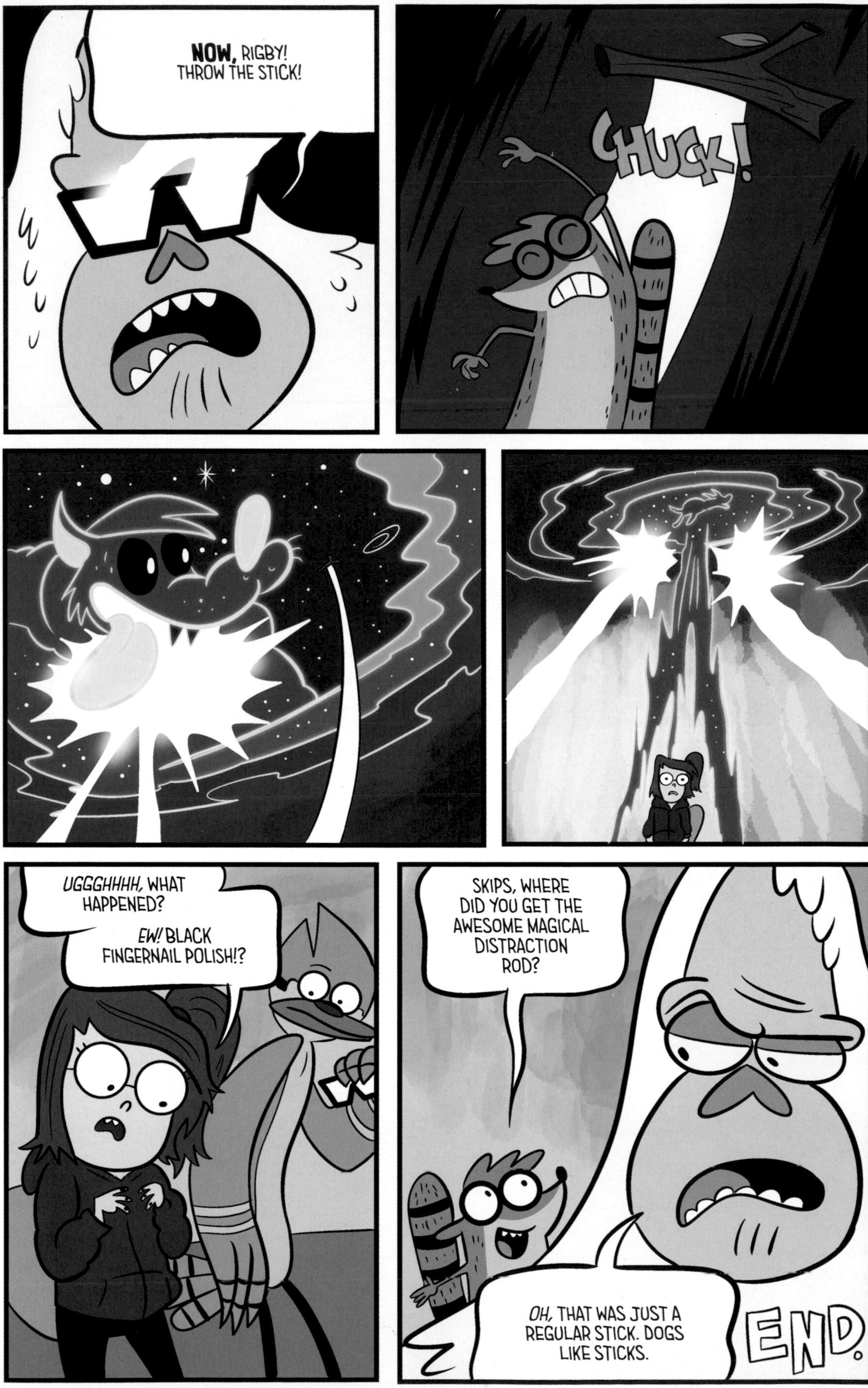
NOW, RIGBY! THROW THE STICK!
CHUCK!
UGGGHHHH, WHAT HAPPENED?
EW! BLACK FINGERNAIL POLISH!?
SKIPS, WHERE DID YOU GET THE AWESOME MAGICAL DISTRACTION ROD?
OH, THAT WAS JUST A REGULAR STICK. DOGS LIKE STICKS.
END.

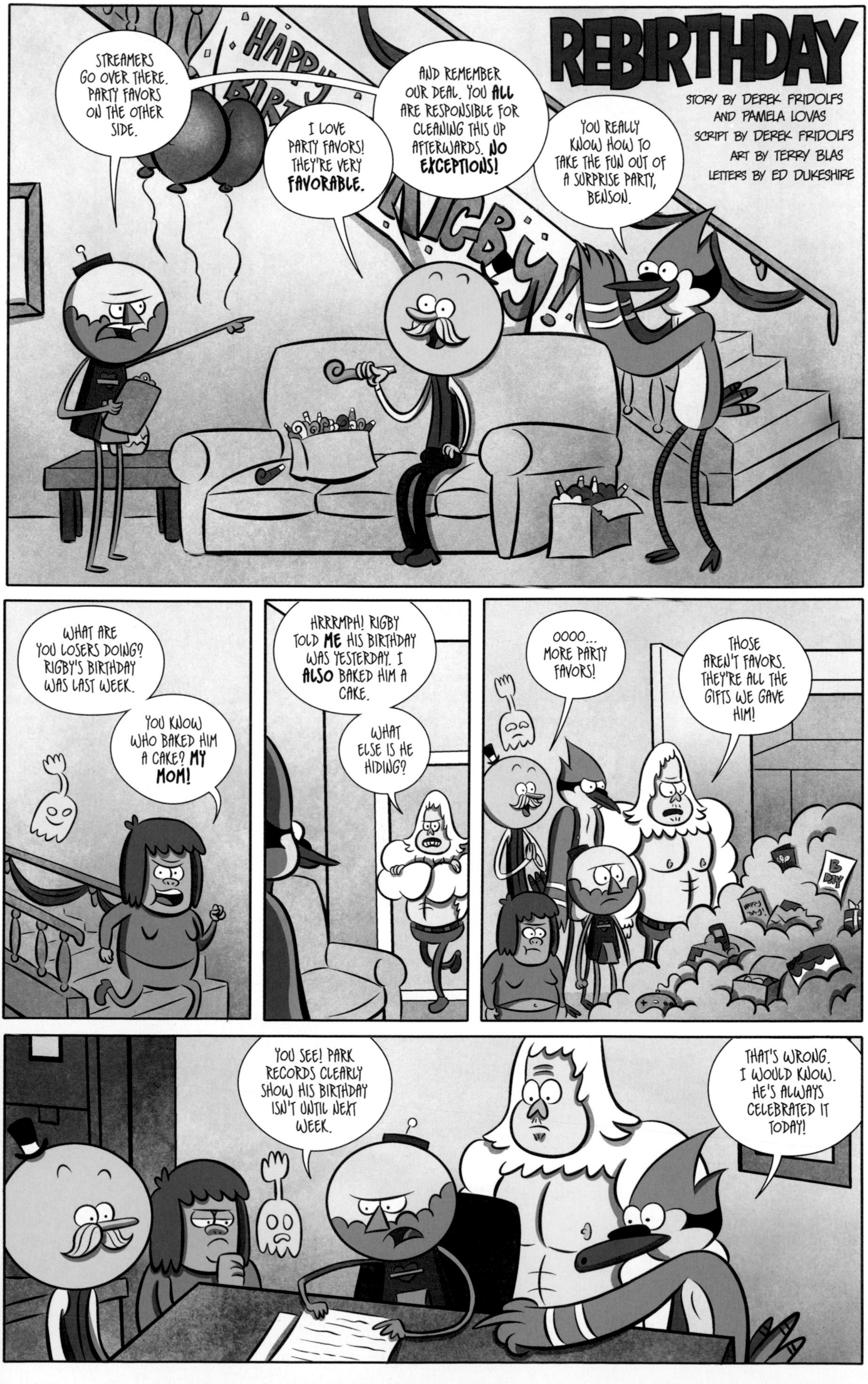
REBIRTHDAY
STORY BY DEREK FRIDOLFS AND PAMELA LOVAS
SCRIPT BY DEREK FRIDOLFS
ART BY TERRY BLAS
LETTERS BY ED DUKESHIRE
HAPPY BIRTHDAY RIGBY!
STREAMERS GO OVER THERE. PARTY FAVORS ON THE OTHER SIDE.
I LOVE PARTY FAVORS! THEY'RE VERY FAVORABLE.
AND REMEMBER OUR DEAL. YOU ALL ARE RESPONSIBLE FOR CLEANING THIS UP AFTERWARDS. NO EXCEPTIONS!
YOU REALLY KNOW HOW TO TAKE THE FUN OUT OF A SURPRISE PARTY, BENSON.
WHAT ARE YOU LOSERS DOING? RIGBY'S BIRTHDAY WAS LAST WEEK.
YOU KNOW WHO BAKED HIM A CAKE? MY MOM!
HRRRMPH! RIGBY TOLD ME HIS BIRTHDAY WAS YESTERDAY. I ALSO BAKED HIM A CAKE.
WHAT ELSE IS HE HIDING?
OOOO... MORE PARTY FAVORS!
THOSE AREN'T FAVORS. THEY'RE ALL THE GIFTS WE GAVE HIM!
YOU SEE! PARK RECORDS CLEARLY SHOW HIS BIRTHDAY ISN'T UNTIL NEXT WEEK.
THAT'S WRONG. I WOULD KNOW. HE'S ALWAYS CELEBRATED IT TODAY!

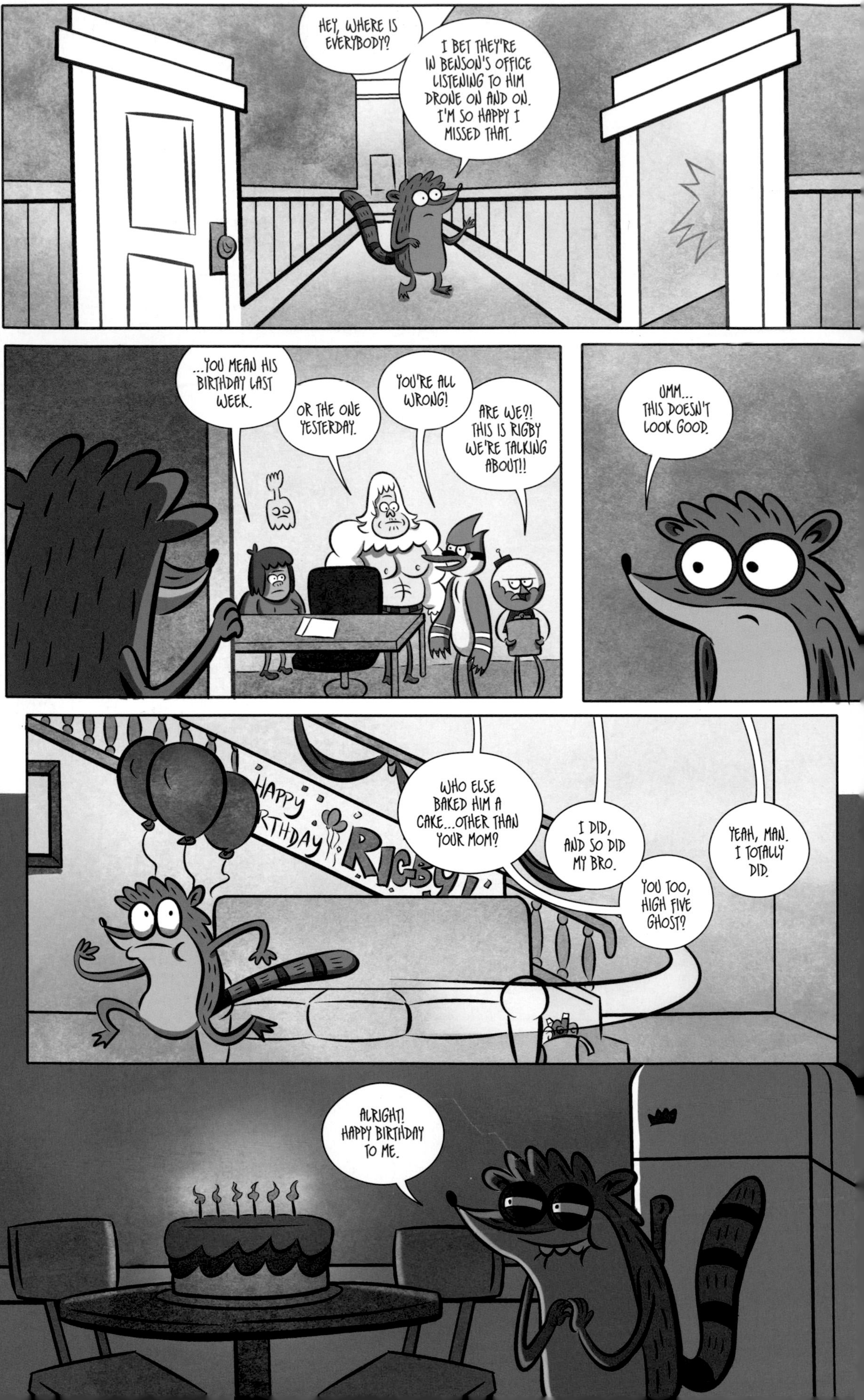
HEY, WHERE IS EVERYBODY?
I BET THEY'RE IN BENSON'S OFFICE LISTENING TO HIM DRONE ON AND ON. I'M SO HAPPY I MISSED THAT.
...YOU MEAN HIS BIRTHDAY LAST WEEK.
OR THE ONE YESTERDAY.
YOU'RE ALL WRONG!
ARE WE?! THIS IS RIGBY WE'RE TALKING ABOUT!!
UMM... THIS DOESN'T LOOK GOOD.
HAPPY BIRTHDAY RIGBY!
WHO ELSE BAKED HIM A CAKE...OTHER THAN YOUR MOM?
I DID, AND SO DID MY BRO.
YOU TOO, HIGH FIVE GHOST?
YEAH, MAN. I TOTALLY DID.
ALRIGHT! HAPPY BIRTHDAY TO ME.

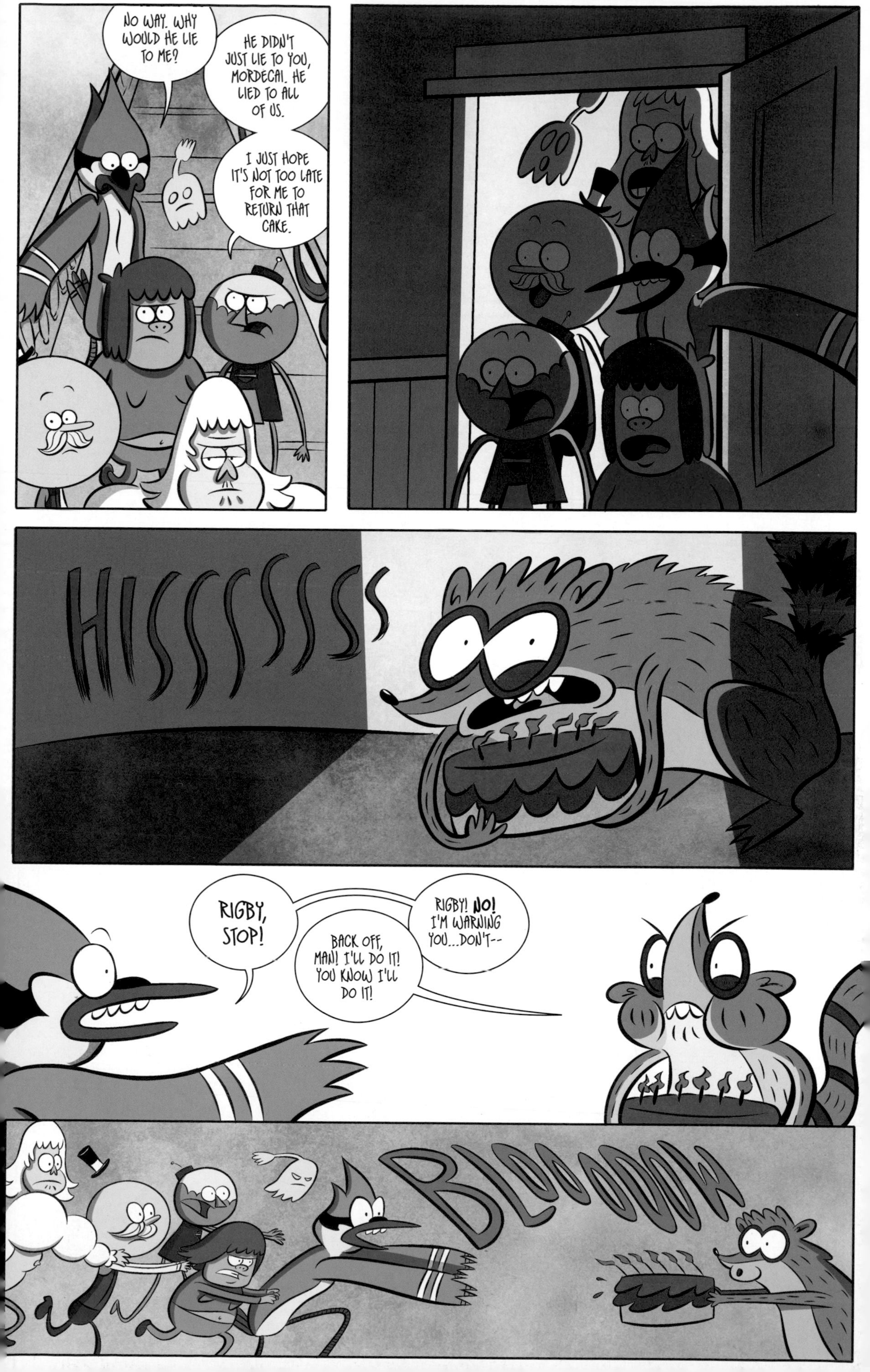
NO WAY. WHY WOULD HE LIE TO ME?
HE DIDN'T JUST LIE TO YOU, MORDECAI. HE LIED TO ALL OF US.
I JUST HOPE IT'S NOT TOO LATE FOR ME TO RETURN THAT CAKE.
HISSSSSSS
RIGBY, STOP!
RIGBY! NO! I'M WARNING YOU...DON'T--
BACK OFF, MAN! I'LL DO IT! YOU KNOW I'LL DO IT!
BLOOOOOAA
AAAAAAAA

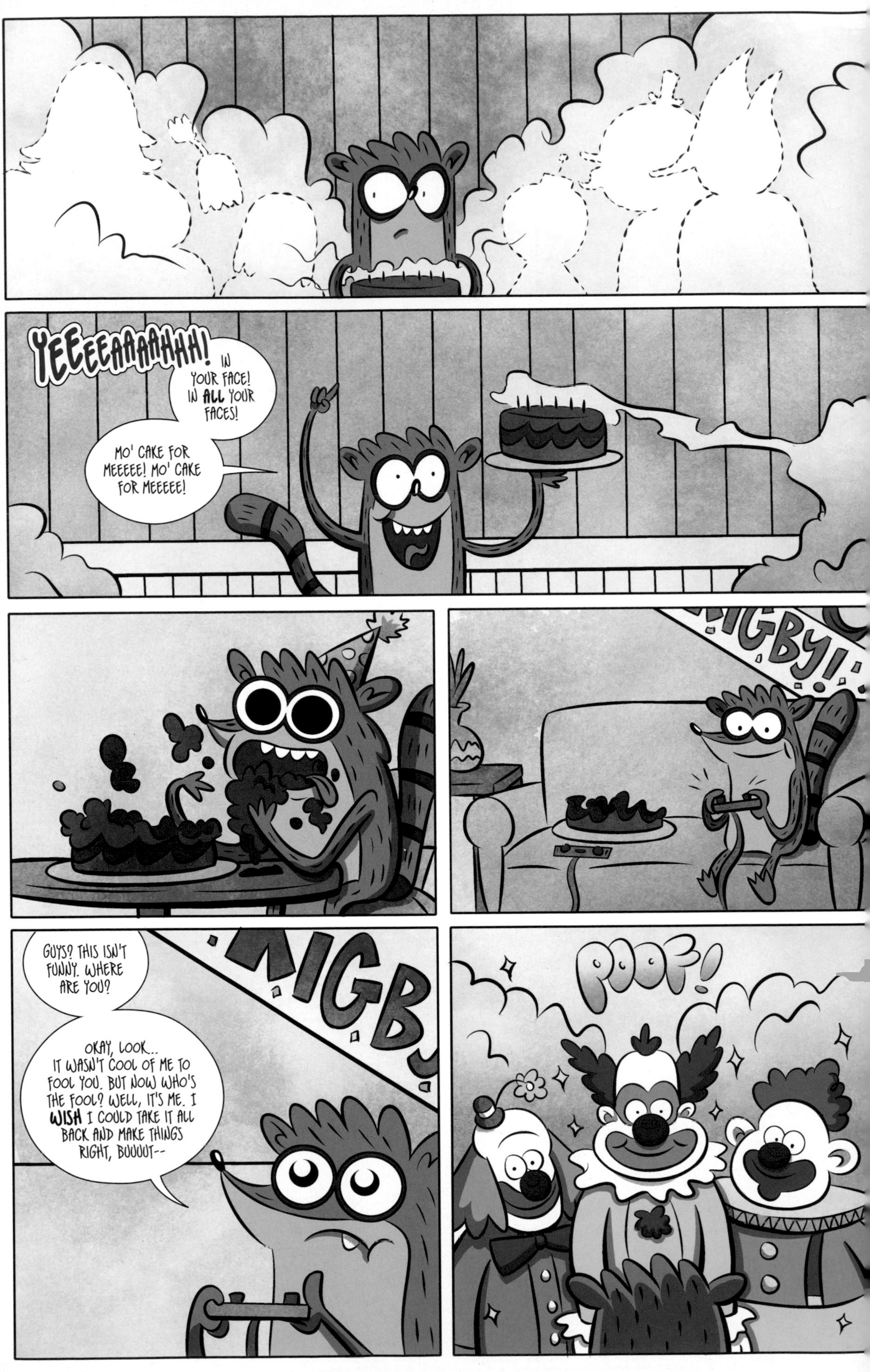
YEEEEAAAAHHH!
IN YOUR FACE! IN ALL YOUR FACES!
MO' CAKE FOR MEEEEE! MO' CAKE FOR MEEEEE!
IGBY!
GUYS? THIS ISN'T FUNNY. WHERE ARE YOU?
OKAY, LOOK... IT WASN'T COOL OF ME TO FOOL YOU. BUT NOW WHO'S THE FOOL? WELL, IT'S ME. I WISH I COULD TAKE IT ALL BACK AND MAKE THINGS RIGHT, BUUUUT--
IGB
POOF!

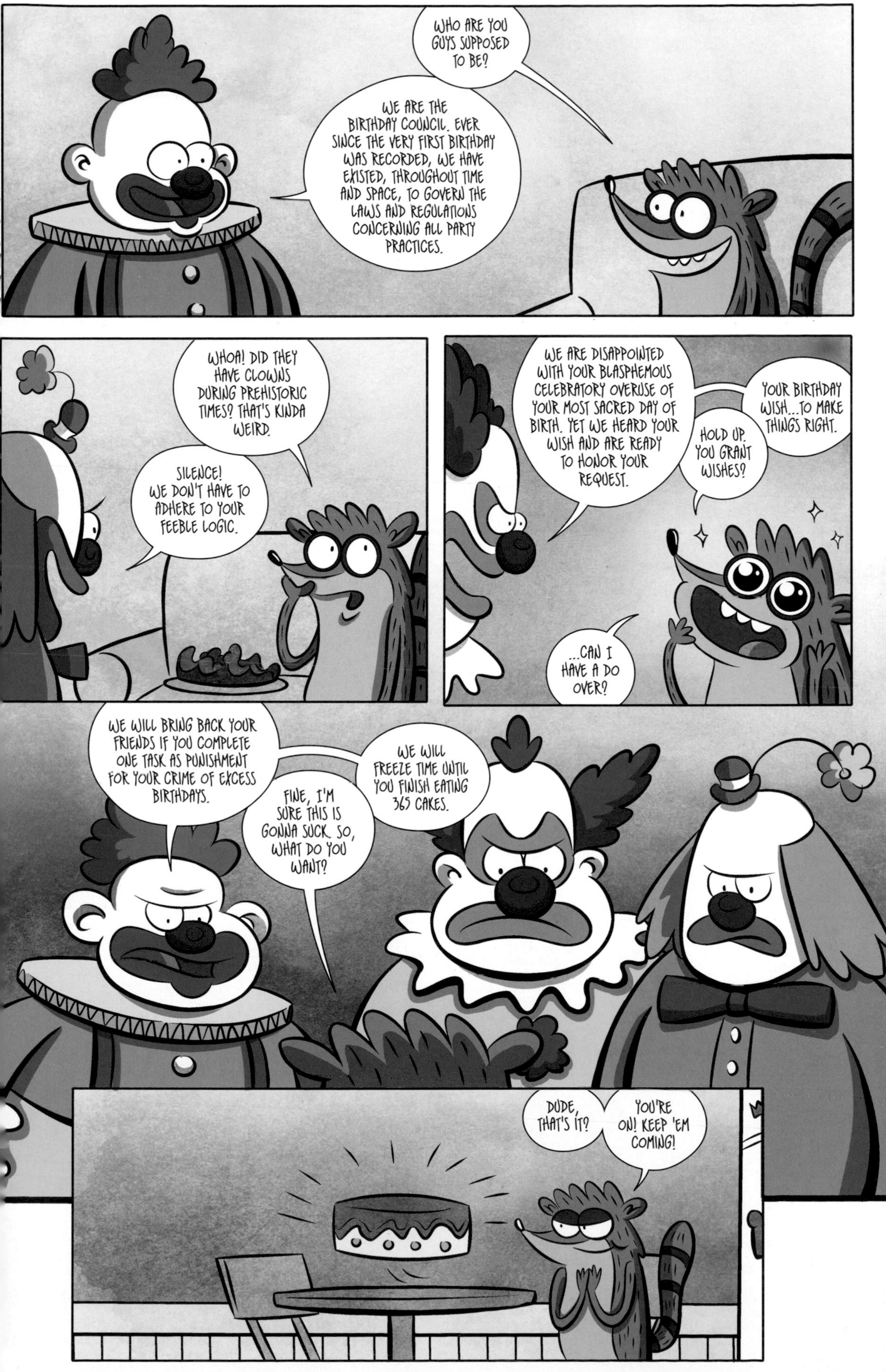
WHO ARE YOU GUYS SUPPOSED TO BE?
WE ARE THE BIRTHDAY COUNCIL. EVER SINCE THE VERY FIRST BIRTHDAY WAS RECORDED, WE HAVE EXISTED, THROUGHOUT TIME AND SPACE, TO GOVERN THE LAWS AND REGULATIONS CONCERNING ALL PARTY PRACTICES.
WHOA! DID THEY HAVE CLOWNS DURING PREHISTORIC TIMES? THAT'S KINDA WEIRD.
SILENCE! WE DON'T HAVE TO ADHERE TO YOUR FEEBLE LOGIC.
WE ARE DISAPPOINTED WITH YOUR BLASPHEMOUS CELEBRATORY OVERUSE OF YOUR MOST SACRED DAY OF BIRTH. YET WE HEARD YOUR WISH AND ARE READY TO HONOR YOUR REQUEST.
YOUR BIRTHDAY WISH...TO MAKE THINGS RIGHT.
HOLD UP. YOU GRANT WISHES?
...CAN I HAVE A DO OVER?
WE WILL BRING BACK YOUR FRIENDS IF YOU COMPLETE ONE TASK AS PUNISHMENT FOR YOUR CRIME OF EXCESS BIRTHDAYS.
FINE, I'M SURE THIS IS GONNA SUCK. SO, WHAT DO YOU WANT?
WE WILL FREEZE TIME UNTIL YOU FINISH EATING 365 CAKES.
DUDE, THAT'S IT?
YOU'RE ON! KEEP 'EM COMING!

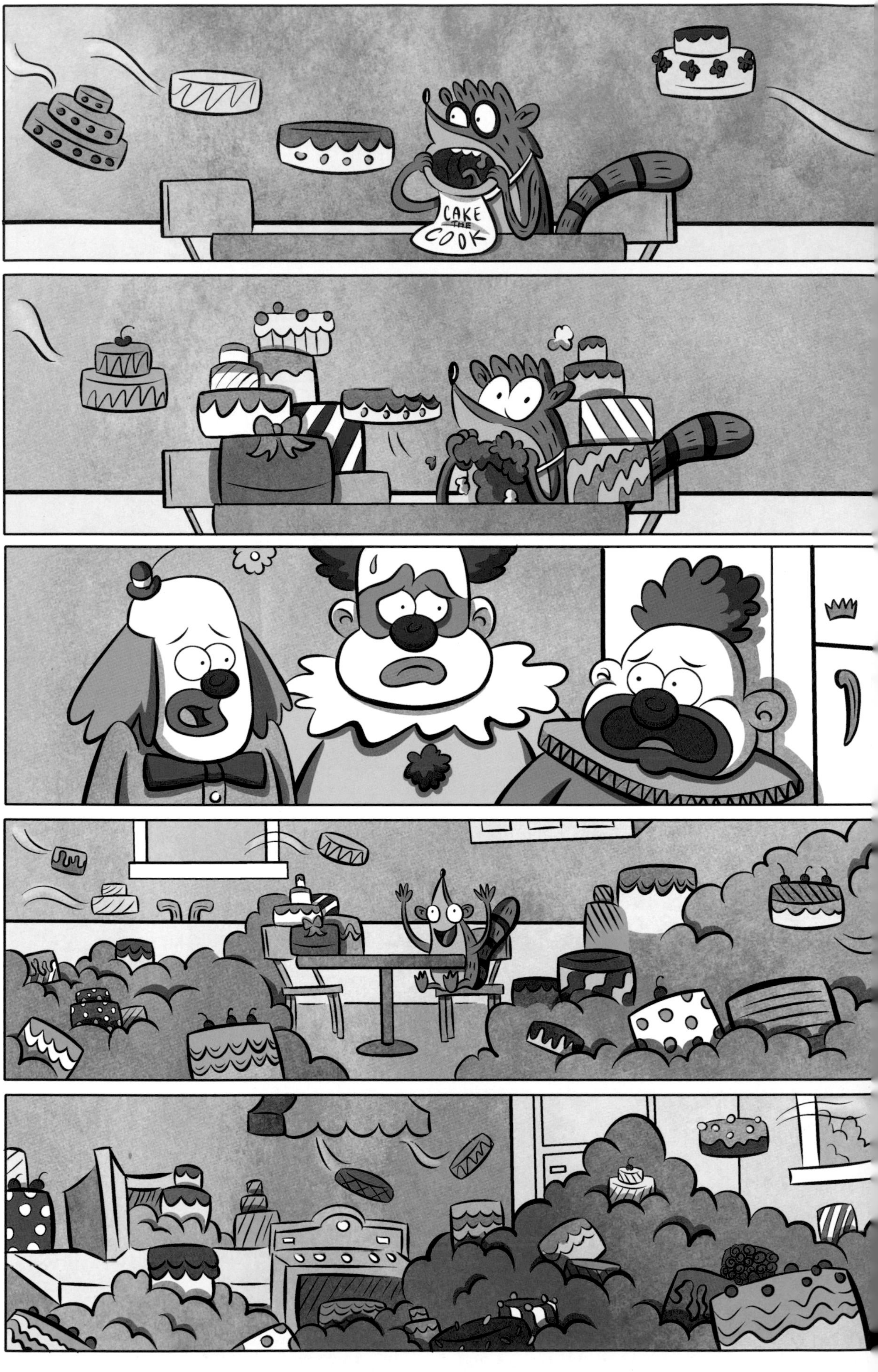
CAKE THE COOK

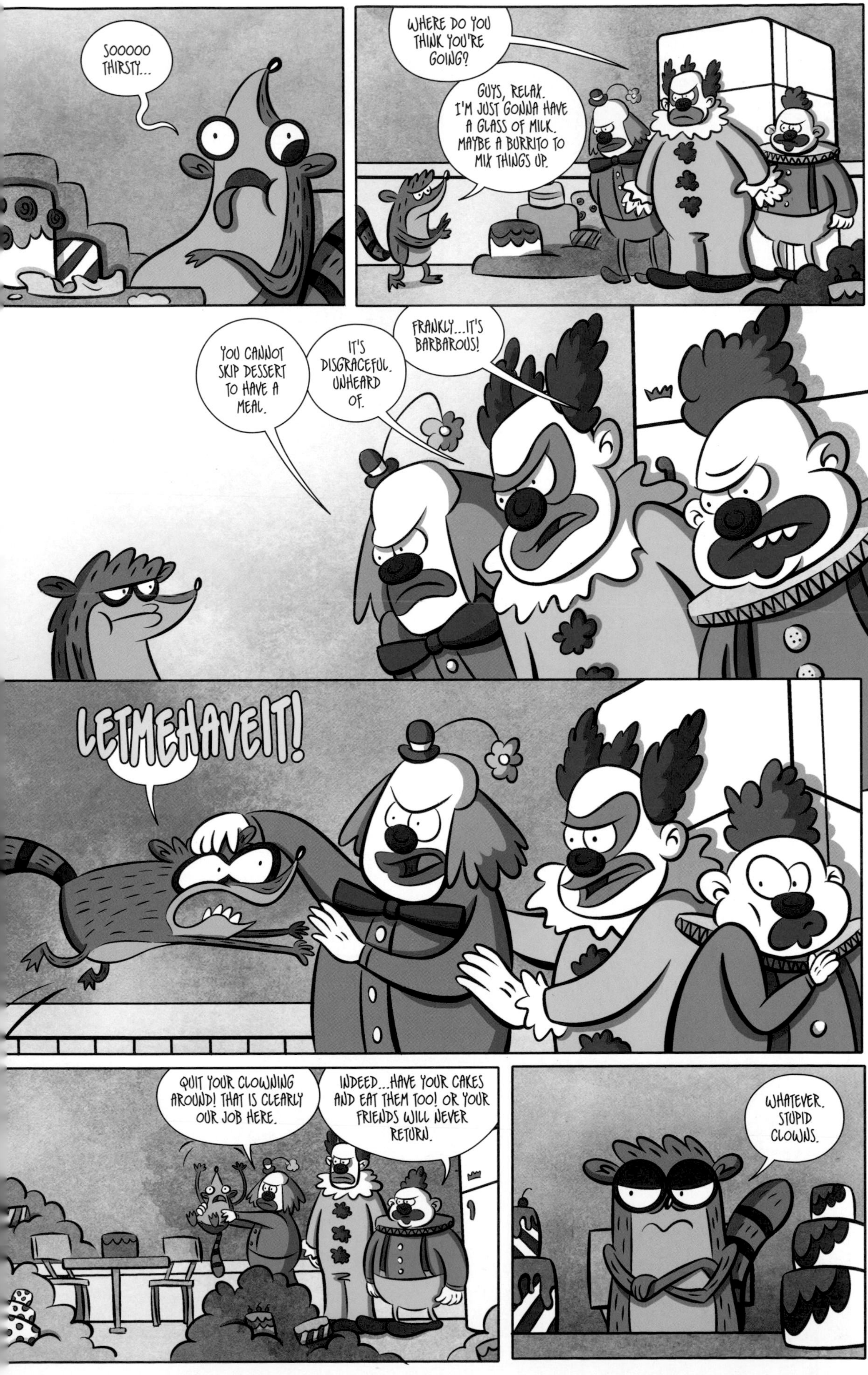
SOOOOO THIRSTY...
WHERE DO YOU THINK YOU'RE GOING?
GUYS, RELAX. I'M JUST GONNA HAVE A GLASS OF MILK. MAYBE A BURRITO TO MIX THINGS UP.
YOU CANNOT SKIP DESSERT TO HAVE A MEAL.
IT'S DISGRACEFUL. UNHEARD OF.
FRANKLY...IT'S BARBAROUS!
LETMEHAVEIT!
QUIT YOUR CLOWNING AROUND! THAT IS CLEARLY OUR JOB HERE.
INDEED...HAVE YOUR CAKES AND EAT THEM TOO! OR YOUR FRIENDS WILL NEVER RETURN.
WHATEVER. STUPID CLOWNS.

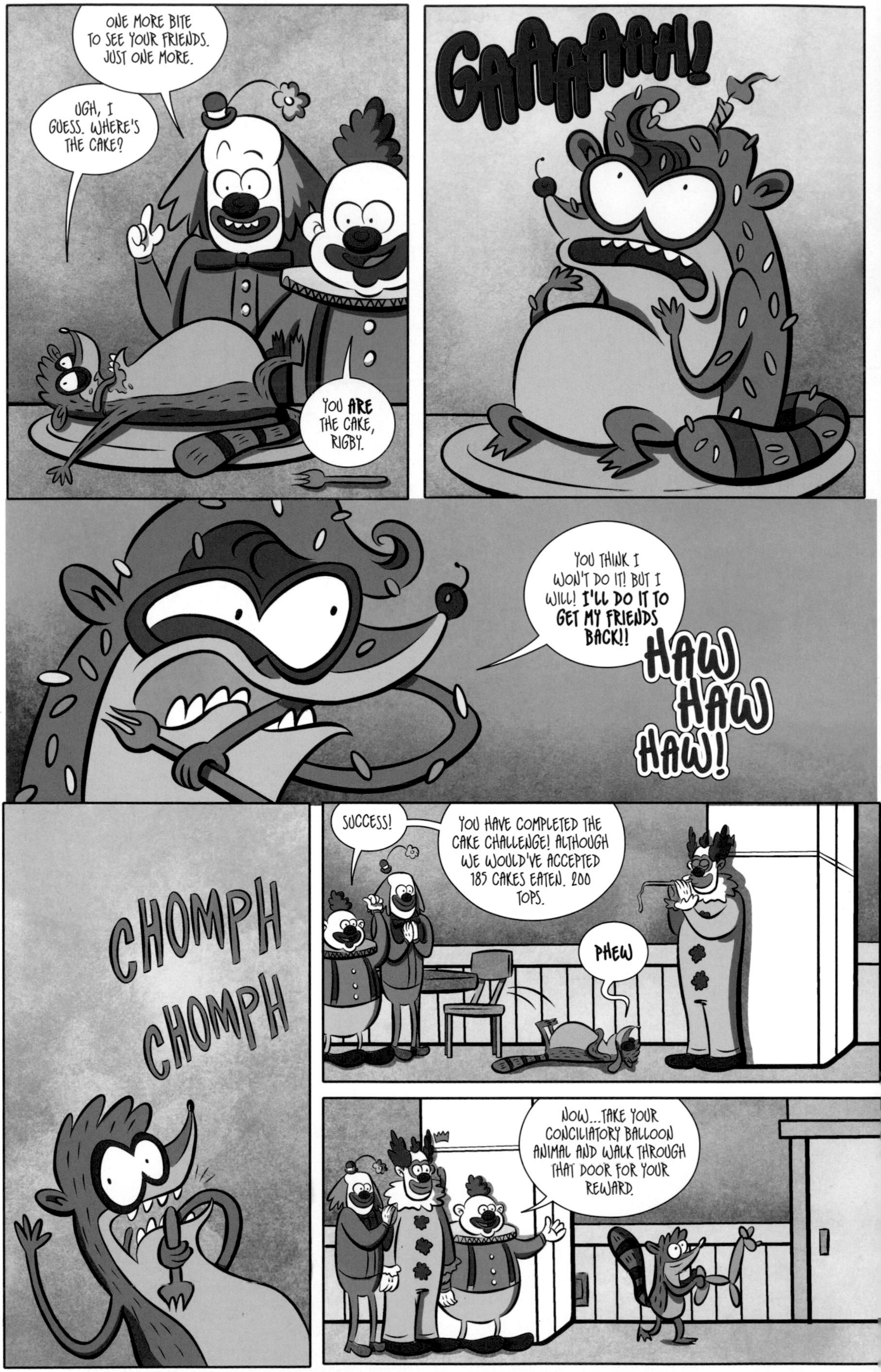
ONE MORE BITE TO SEE YOUR FRIENDS. JUST ONE MORE.
UGH, I GUESS. WHERE'S THE CAKE?
YOU **ARE** THE CAKE, RIGBY.
GAAAAAH!
YOU THINK I WON'T DO IT! BUT I WILL! **I'LL DO IT TO GET MY FRIENDS BACK!!**
HAW HAW HAW!
CHOMPH
CHOMPH
SUCCESS!
YOU HAVE COMPLETED THE CAKE CHALLENGE! ALTHOUGH WE WOULD'VE ACCEPTED 185 CAKES EATEN. 200 TOPS.
PHEW
NOW...TAKE YOUR CONCILIATORY BALLOON ANIMAL AND WALK THROUGH THAT DOOR FOR YOUR REWARD.

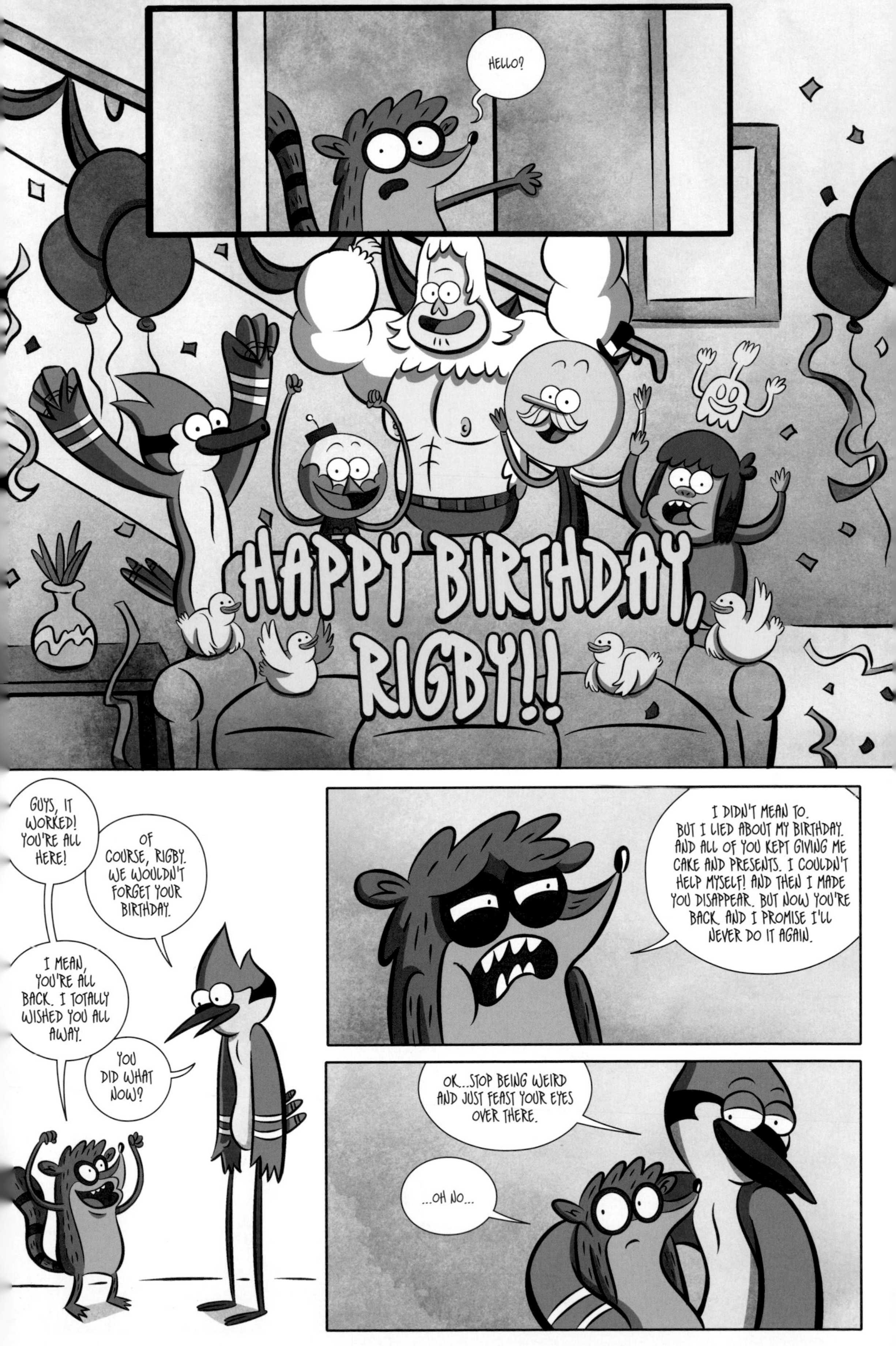

HELLO?
HAPPY BIRTHDAY, RIGBY!!
GUYS, IT WORKED! YOU'RE ALL HERE!
OF COURSE, RIGBY. WE WOULDN'T FORGET YOUR BIRTHDAY.
I MEAN, YOU'RE ALL BACK. I TOTALLY WISHED YOU ALL AWAY.
YOU DID WHAT NOW?
I DIDN'T MEAN TO. BUT I LIED ABOUT MY BIRTHDAY. AND ALL OF YOU KEPT GIVING ME CAKE AND PRESENTS. I COULDN'T HELP MYSELF! AND THEN I MADE YOU DISAPPEAR. BUT NOW YOU'RE BACK. AND I PROMISE I'LL NEVER DO IT AGAIN.
OK...STOP BEING WEIRD AND JUST FEAST YOUR EYES OVER THERE.
...OH NO...

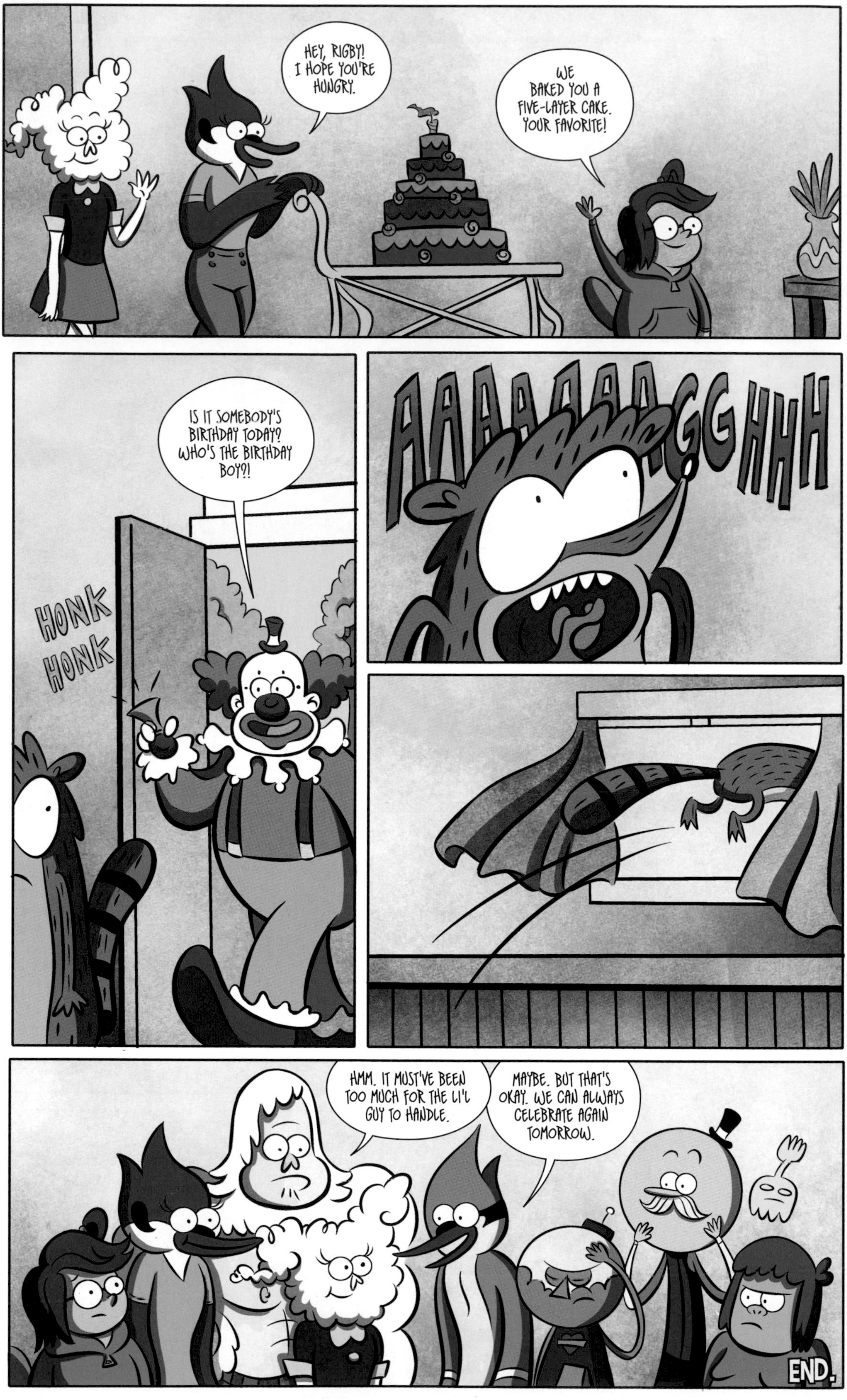
HEY, RIGBY! I HOPE YOU'RE HUNGRY.
WE BAKED YOU A FIVE-LAYER CAKE. YOUR FAVORITE!
HONK HONK
IS IT SOMEBODY'S BIRTHDAY TODAY? WHO'S THE BIRTHDAY BOY?!
AAAAAAAAGGHHH
HMM. IT MUST'VE BEEN TOO MUCH FOR THE LI'L GUY TO HANDLE.
MAYBE. BUT THAT'S OKAY. WE CAN ALWAYS CELEBRATE AGAIN TOMORROW.
END.

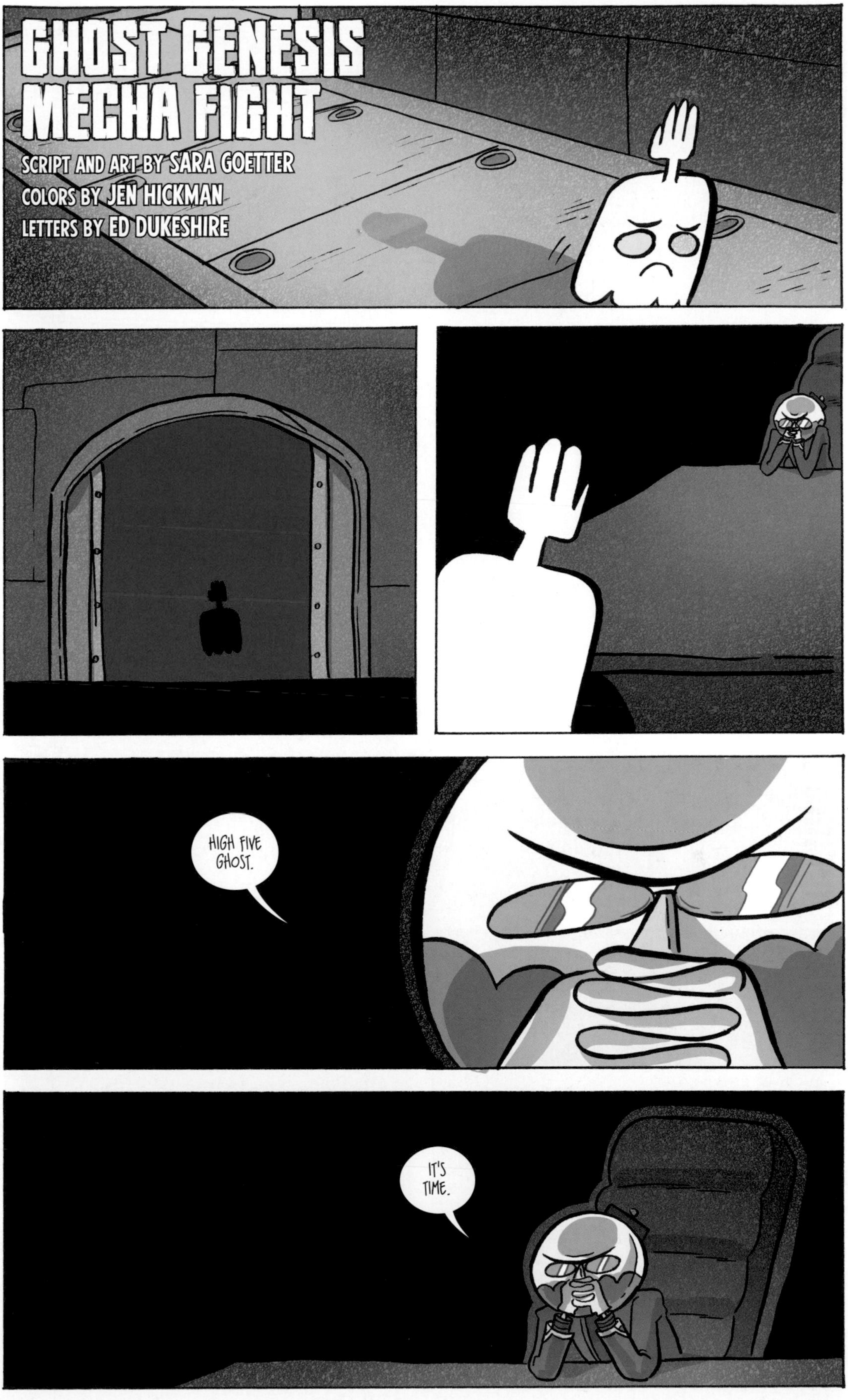
GHOST GENESIS MECHA FIGHT
SCRIPT AND ART BY SARA GOETTER
COLORS BY JEN HICKMAN
LETTERS BY ED DUKESHIRE
HIGH FIVE GHOST.
IT'S TIME.

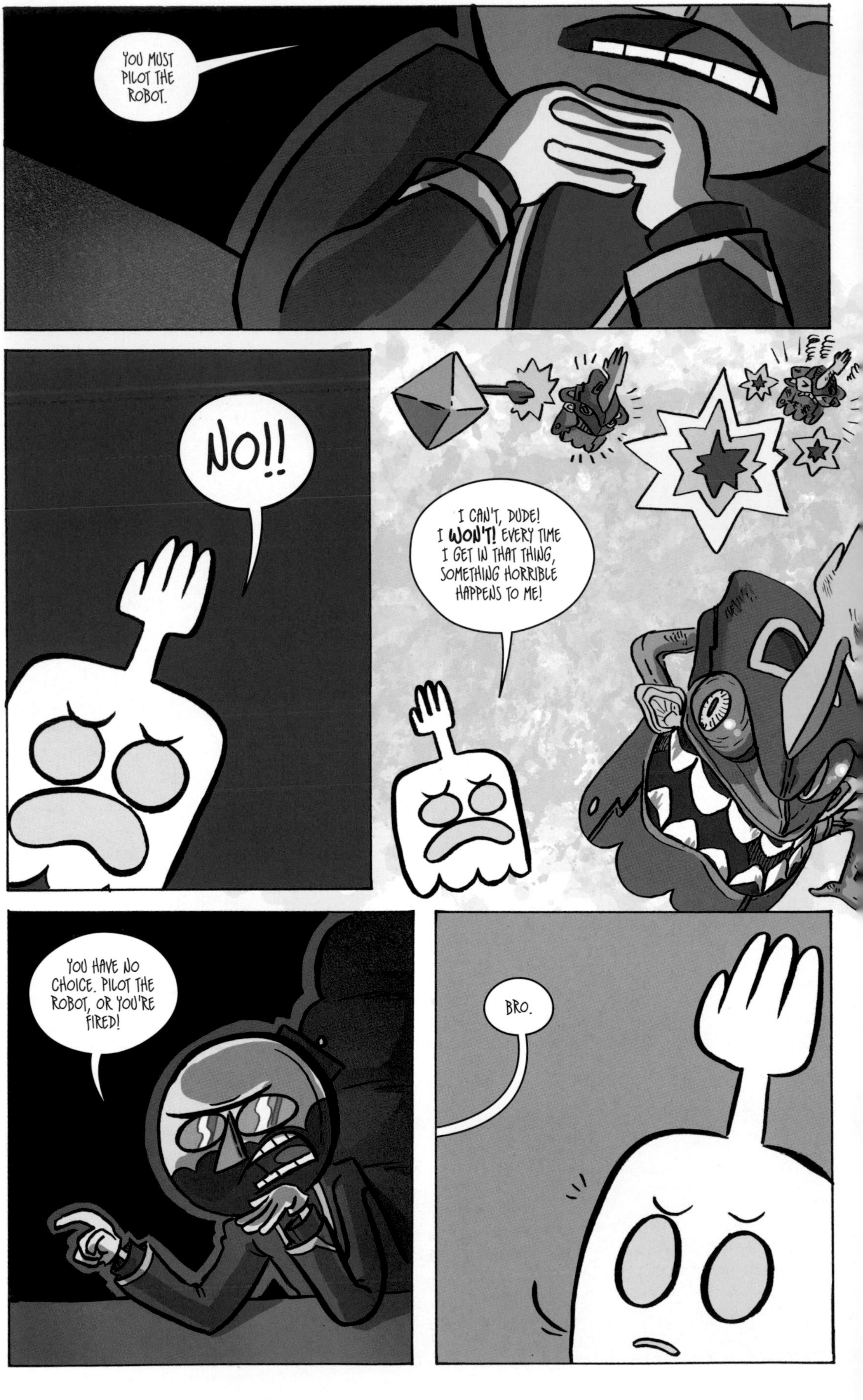
YOU MUST PILOT THE ROBOT.
NO!!
I CAN'T, DUDE! I WON'T! EVERY TIME I GET IN THAT THING, SOMETHING HORRIBLE HAPPENS TO ME!
YOU HAVE NO CHOICE. PILOT THE ROBOT, OR YOU'RE FIRED!
BRO.

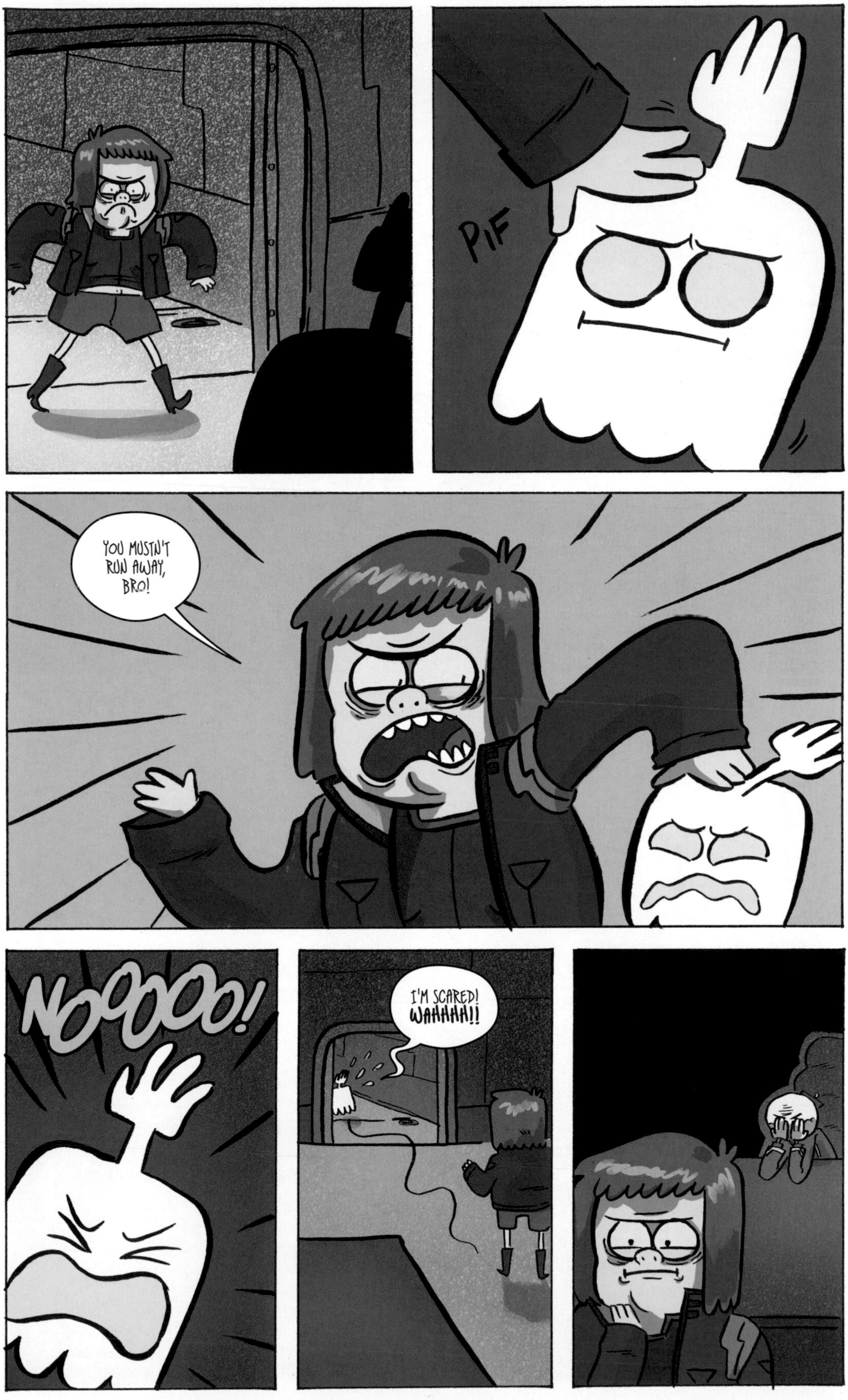
PIF
YOU MUSTN'T RUN AWAY, BRO!
NOOOOO!
I'M SCARED! WAHHHH!!

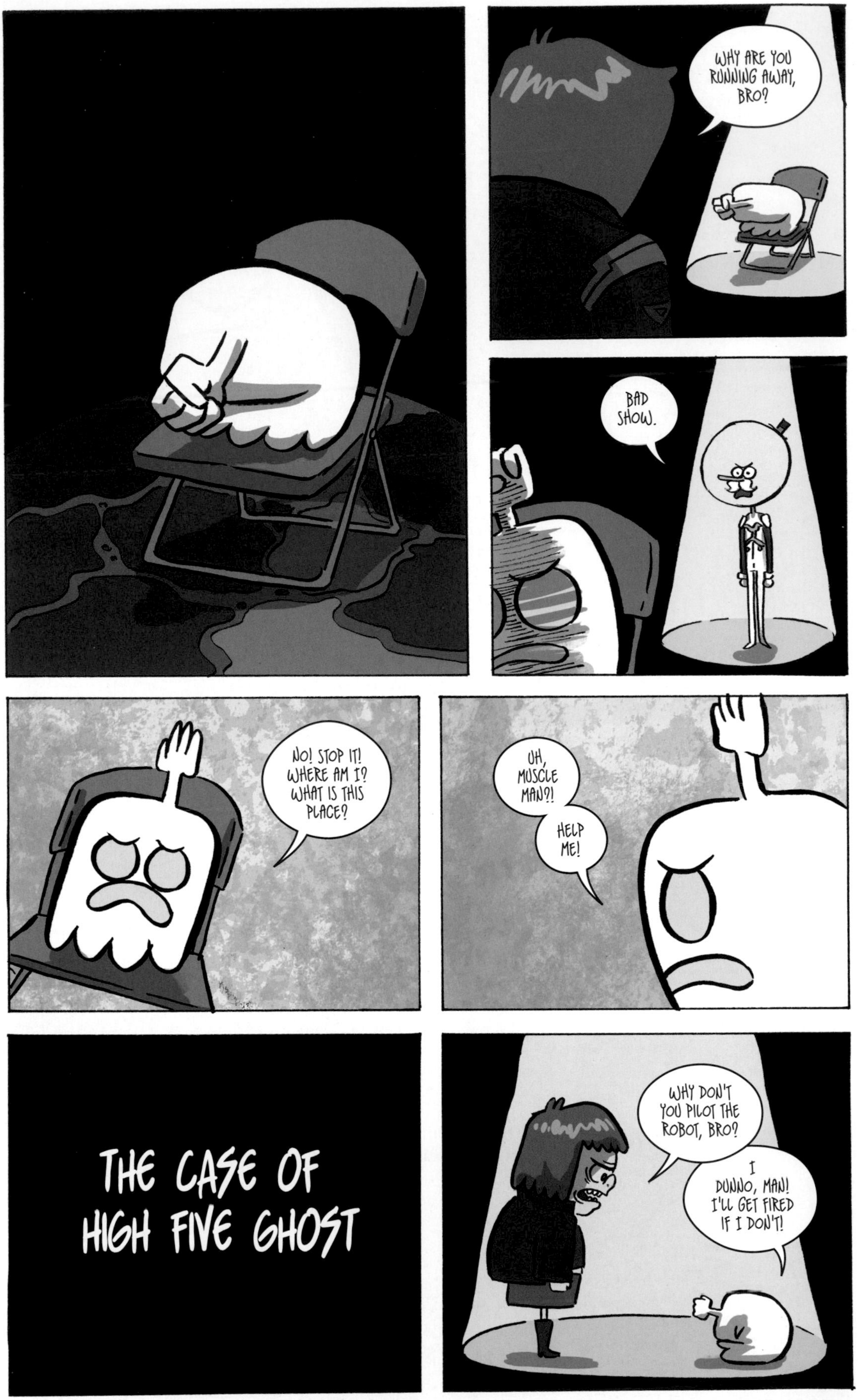
WHY ARE YOU RUNNING AWAY, BRO?
BAD SHOW.
NO! STOP IT! WHERE AM I? WHAT IS THIS PLACE?
UH, MUSCLE MAN?!
HELP ME!
THE CASE OF HIGH FIVE GHOST
WHY DON'T YOU PILOT THE ROBOT, BRO?
I DUNNO, MAN! I'LL GET FIRED IF I DON'T!

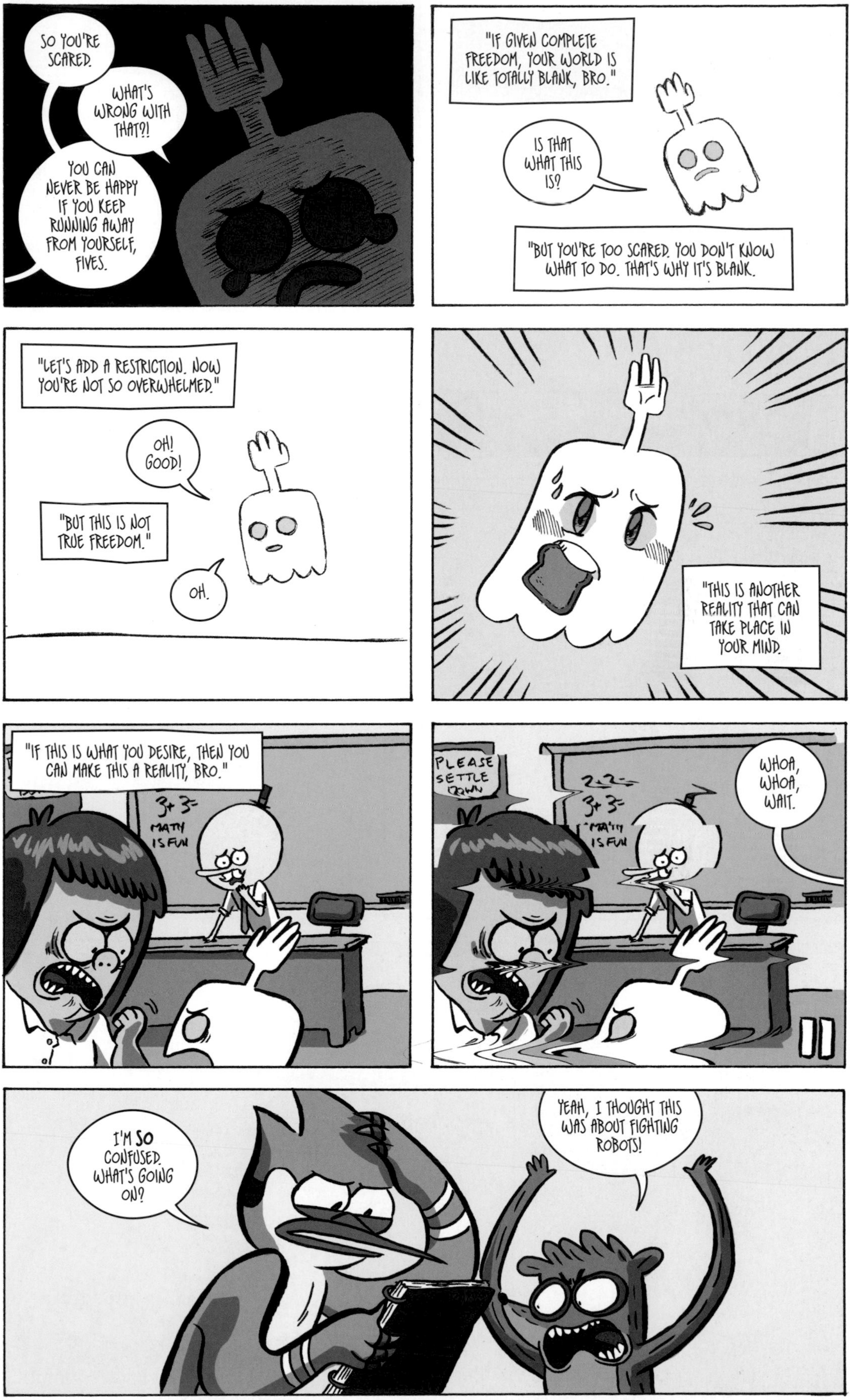
SO YOU'RE SCARED.
WHAT'S WRONG WITH THAT?!
YOU CAN NEVER BE HAPPY IF YOU KEEP RUNNING AWAY FROM YOURSELF, FIVES.
"IF GIVEN COMPLETE FREEDOM, YOUR WORLD IS LIKE TOTALLY BLANK, BRO."
IS THAT WHAT THIS IS?
"BUT YOU'RE TOO SCARED. YOU DON'T KNOW WHAT TO DO. THAT'S WHY IT'S BLANK.
"LET'S ADD A RESTRICTION. NOW YOU'RE NOT SO OVERWHELMED."
OH! GOOD!
"BUT THIS IS NOT TRUE FREEDOM."
OH.
"THIS IS ANOTHER REALITY THAT CAN TAKE PLACE IN YOUR MIND.
"IF THIS IS WHAT YOU DESIRE, THEN YOU CAN MAKE THIS A REALITY, BRO."
3+3=
MATH IS FUN
PLEASE SETTLE DOWN
WHOA, WHOA, WAIT.
I'M SO CONFUSED. WHAT'S GOING ON?
YEAH, I THOUGHT THIS WAS ABOUT FIGHTING ROBOTS!

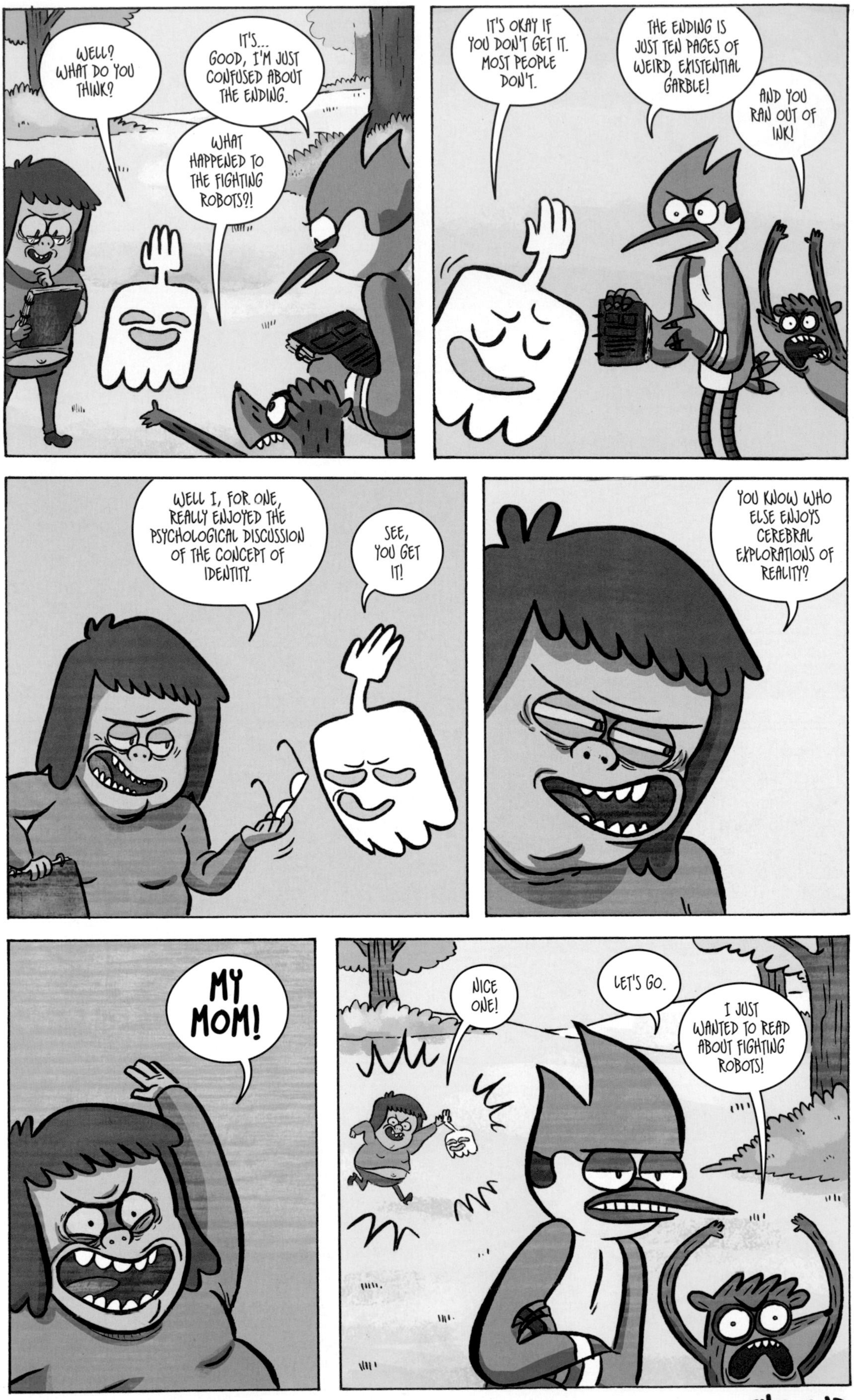
WELL? WHAT DO YOU THINK?
IT'S... GOOD, I'M JUST CONFUSED ABOUT THE ENDING.
WHAT HAPPENED TO THE FIGHTING ROBOTS?!
IT'S OKAY IF YOU DON'T GET IT. MOST PEOPLE DON'T.
THE ENDING IS JUST TEN PAGES OF WEIRD, EXISTENTIAL GARBLE!
AND YOU RAN OUT OF INK!
WELL I, FOR ONE, REALLY ENJOYED THE PSYCHOLOGICAL DISCUSSION OF THE CONCEPT OF IDENTITY.
SEE, YOU GET IT!
YOU KNOW WHO ELSE ENJOYS CEREBRAL EXPLORATIONS OF REALITY?
MY MOM!
NICE ONE!
LET'S GO.
I JUST WANTED TO READ ABOUT FIGHTING ROBOTS!

THE END

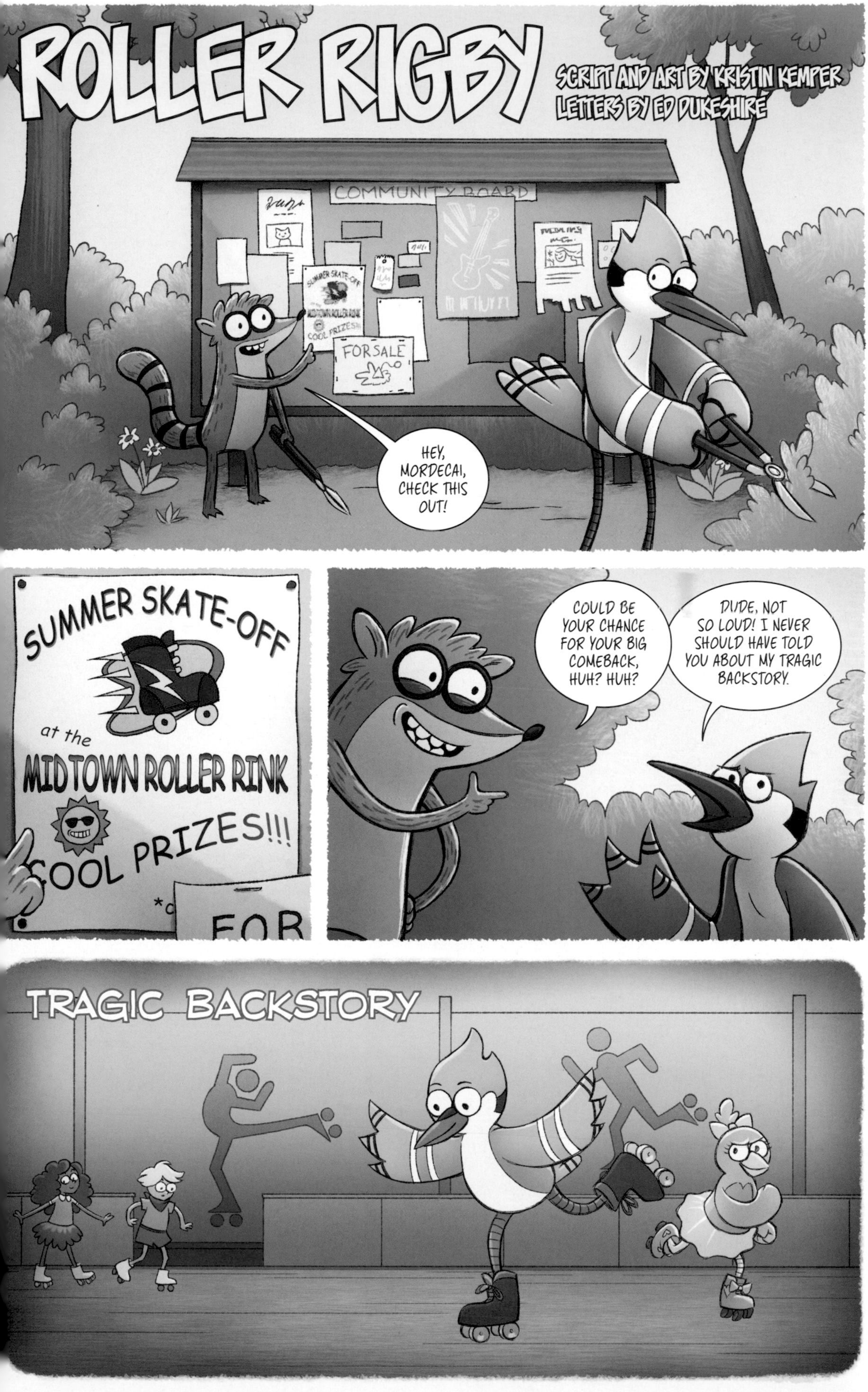
ROLLER RIGBY
SCRIPT AND ART BY KRISTIN KEMPER
LETTERS BY ED DUKESHIRE
COMMUNITY BOARD
SUMMER SKATE-OFF
MIDTOWN ROLLER RINK
COOL PRIZES!!!
FOR SALE
HEY, MORDECAI, CHECK THIS OUT!
SUMMER SKATE-OFF
at the
MIDTOWN ROLLER RINK
COOL PRIZES!!!
FOR
COULD BE YOUR CHANCE FOR YOUR BIG COMEBACK, HUH? HUH?
DUDE, NOT SO LOUD! I NEVER SHOULD HAVE TOLD YOU ABOUT MY TRAGIC BACKSTORY.
TRAGIC BACKSTORY

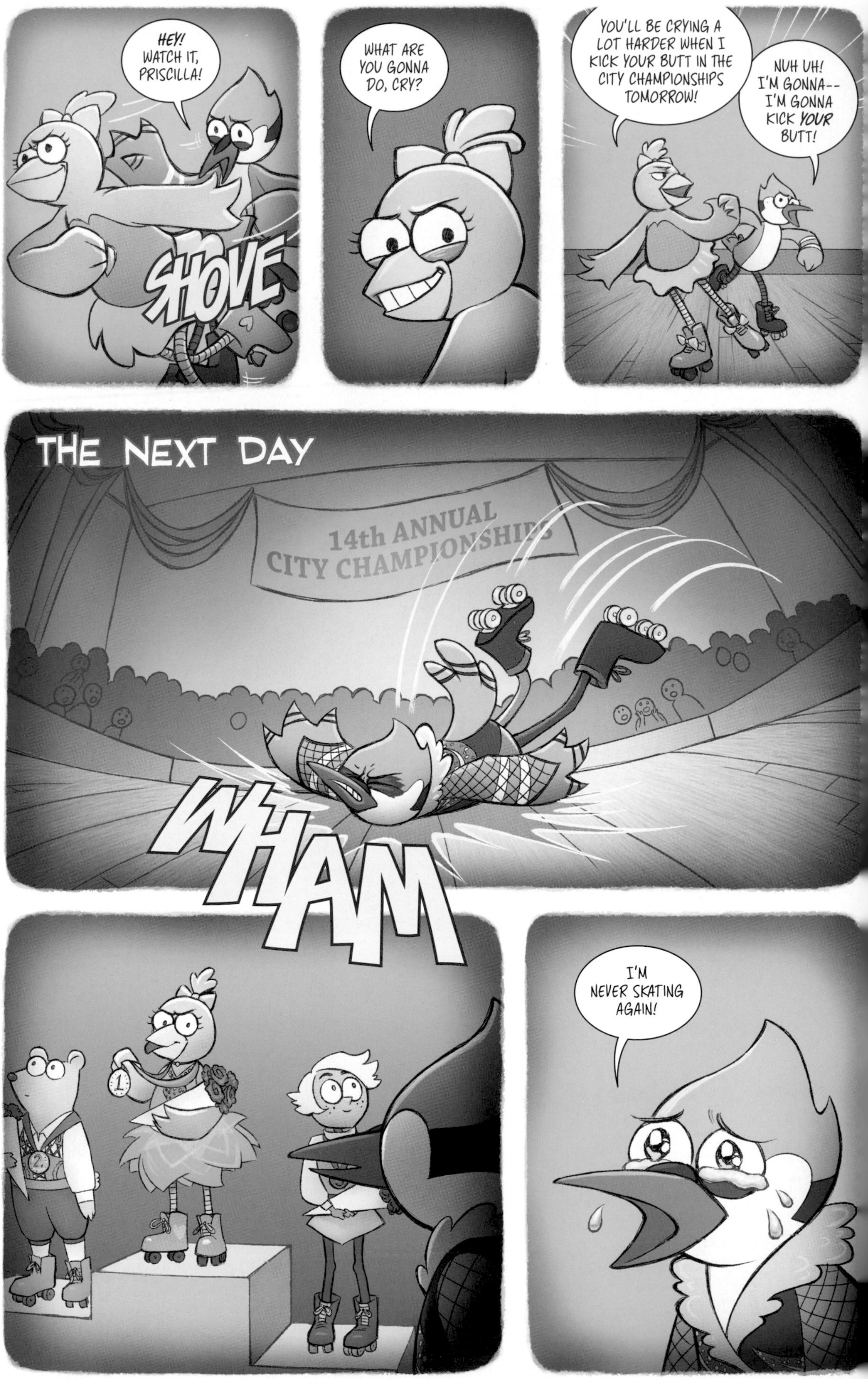
HEY! WATCH IT, PRISCILLA!
SHOVE
WHAT ARE YOU GONNA DO, CRY?
YOU'LL BE CRYING A LOT HARDER WHEN I KICK YOUR BUTT IN THE CITY CHAMPIONSHIPS TOMORROW!
NUH UH! I'M GONNA-- I'M GONNA KICK YOUR BUTT!
THE NEXT DAY
14th ANNUAL CITY CHAMPIONSHIPS
WHAM
I'M NEVER SKATING AGAIN!

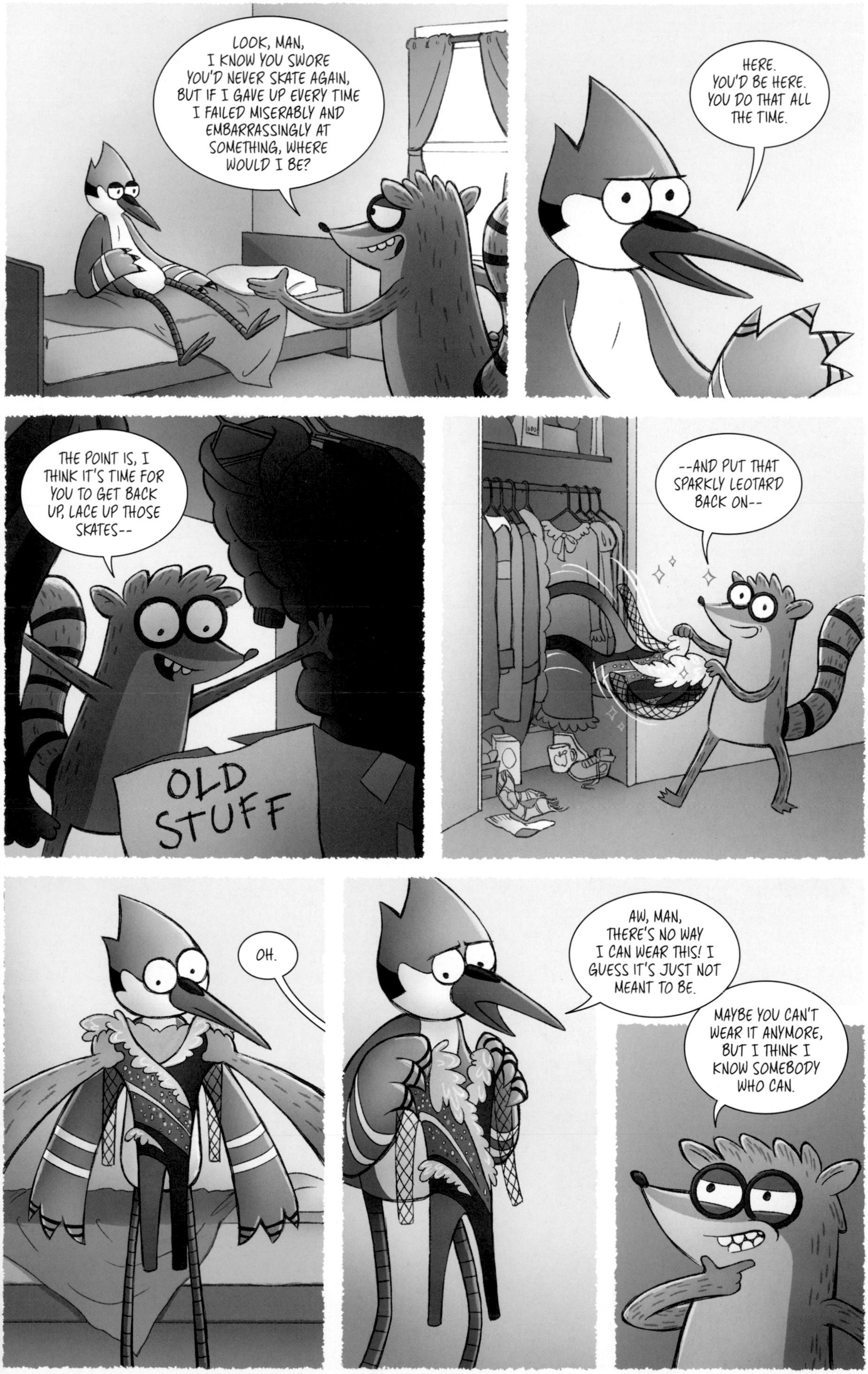
LOOK, MAN, I KNOW YOU SWORE YOU'D NEVER SKATE AGAIN, BUT IF I GAVE UP EVERY TIME I FAILED MISERABLY AND EMBARRASSINGLY AT SOMETHING, WHERE WOULD I BE?
HERE. YOU'D BE HERE. YOU DO THAT ALL THE TIME.
THE POINT IS, I THINK IT'S TIME FOR YOU TO GET BACK UP, LACE UP THOSE SKATES--
OLD STUFF
--AND PUT THAT SPARKLY LEOTARD BACK ON--
OH.
AW, MAN, THERE'S NO WAY I CAN WEAR THIS! I GUESS IT'S JUST NOT MEANT TO BE.
MAYBE YOU CAN'T WEAR IT ANYMORE, BUT I THINK I KNOW SOMEBODY WHO CAN.

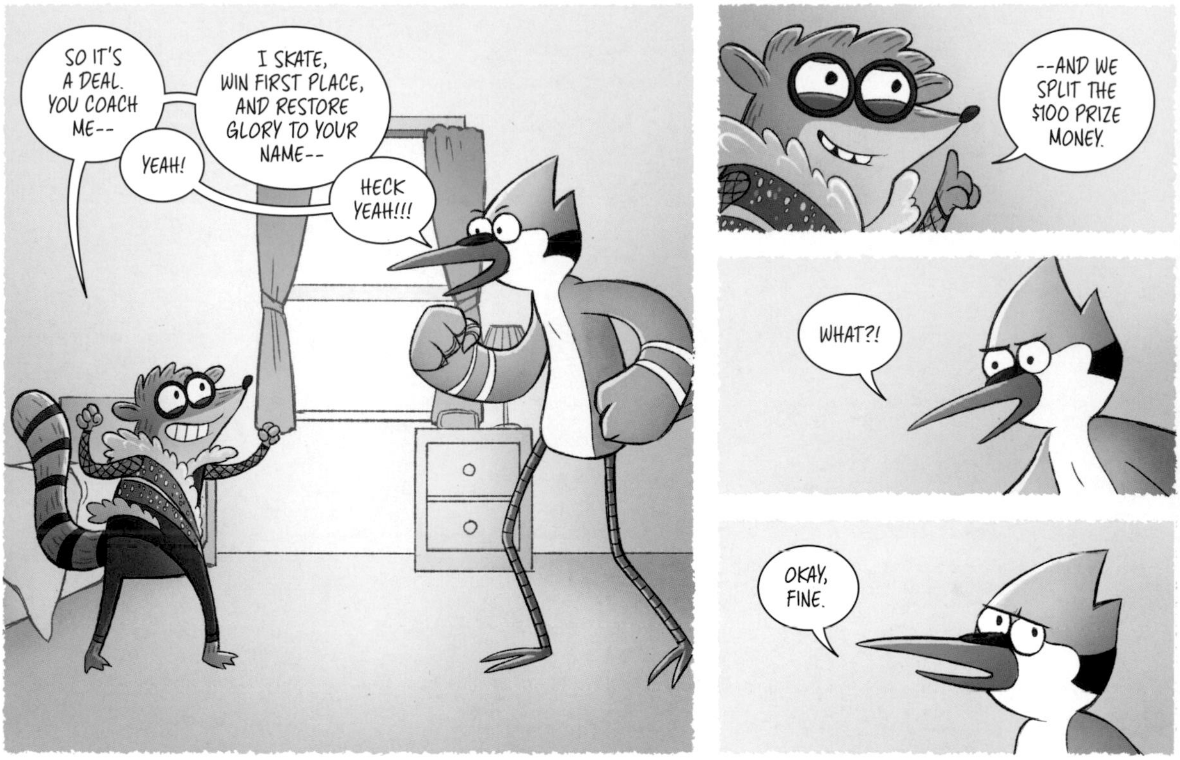

SO IT'S A DEAL. YOU COACH ME--
YEAH!
I SKATE, WIN FIRST PLACE, AND RESTORE GLORY TO YOUR NAME--
HECK YEAH!!!
--AND WE SPLIT THE $100 PRIZE MONEY.
WHAT?!
OKAY, FINE.

TIME FOR A TRAINING MONTAGE!

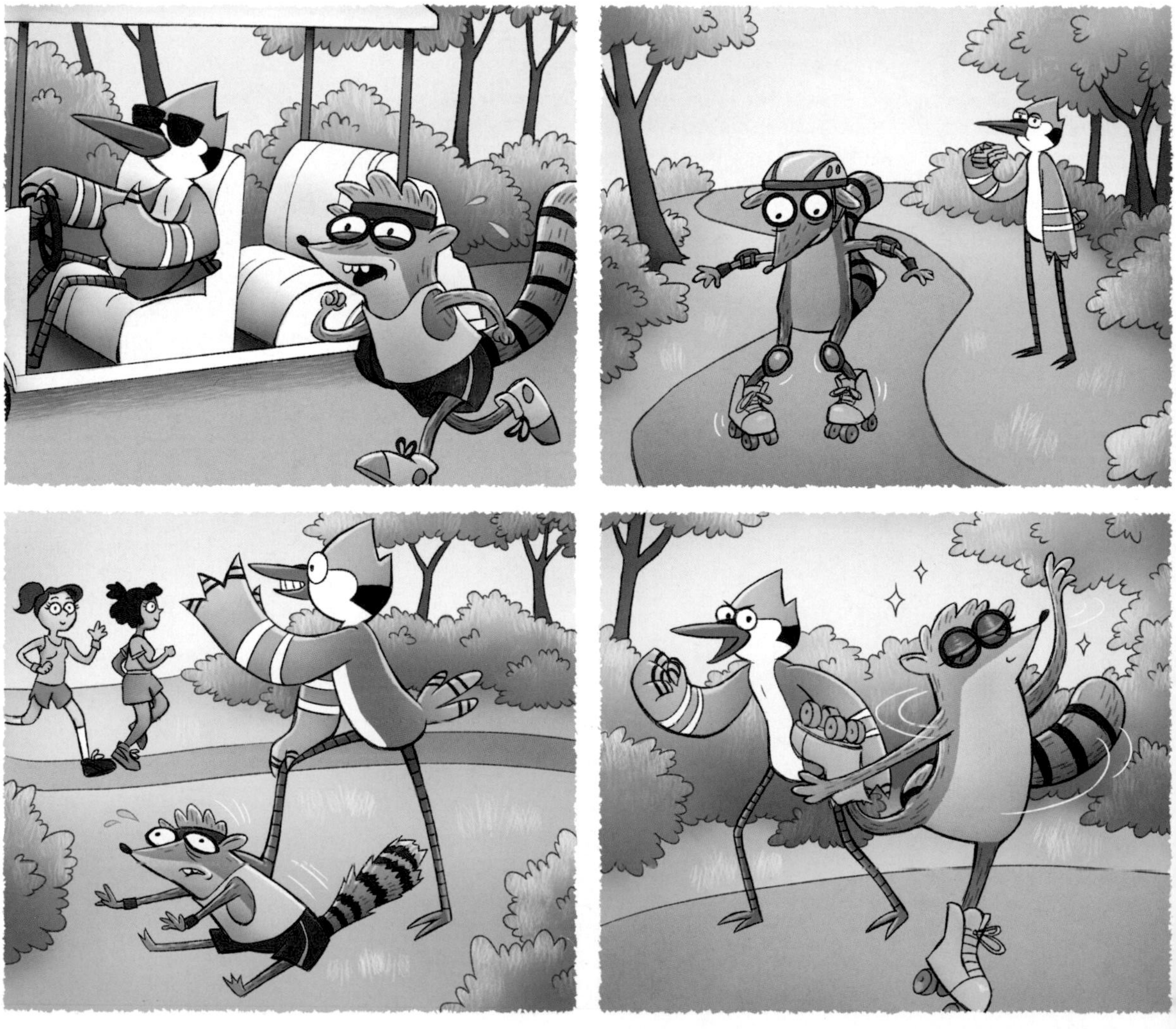

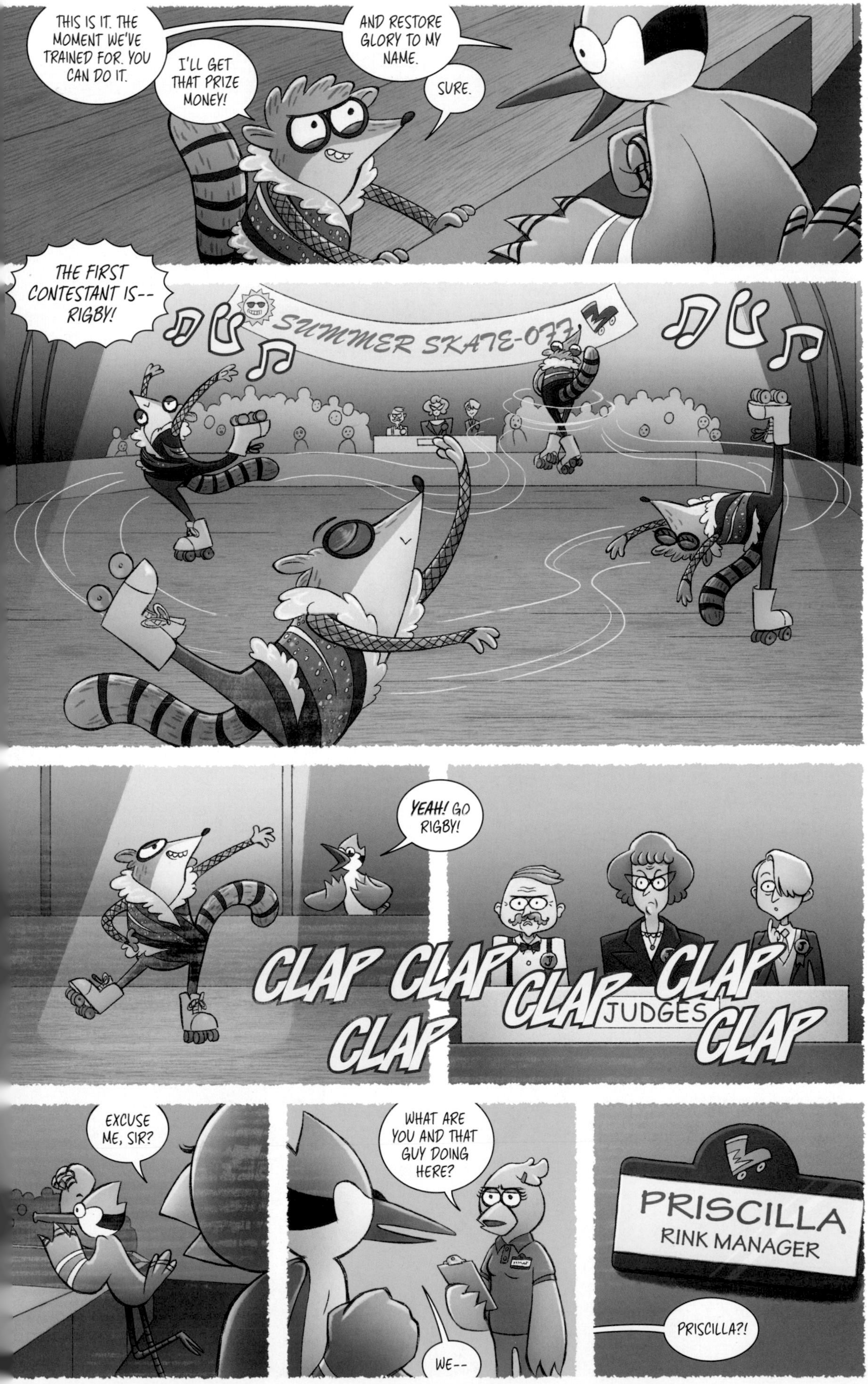
THIS IS IT. THE MOMENT WE'VE TRAINED FOR. YOU CAN DO IT.
I'LL GET THAT PRIZE MONEY!
AND RESTORE GLORY TO MY NAME.
SURE.
THE FIRST CONTESTANT IS-- RIGBY!
SUMMER SKATE-OFF
YEAH! GO RIGBY!
CLAP CLAP CLAP
CLAP CLAP CLAP
JUDGES
EXCUSE ME, SIR?
WHAT ARE YOU AND THAT GUY DOING HERE?
WE--
PRISCILLA
RINK MANAGER
PRISCILLA?!

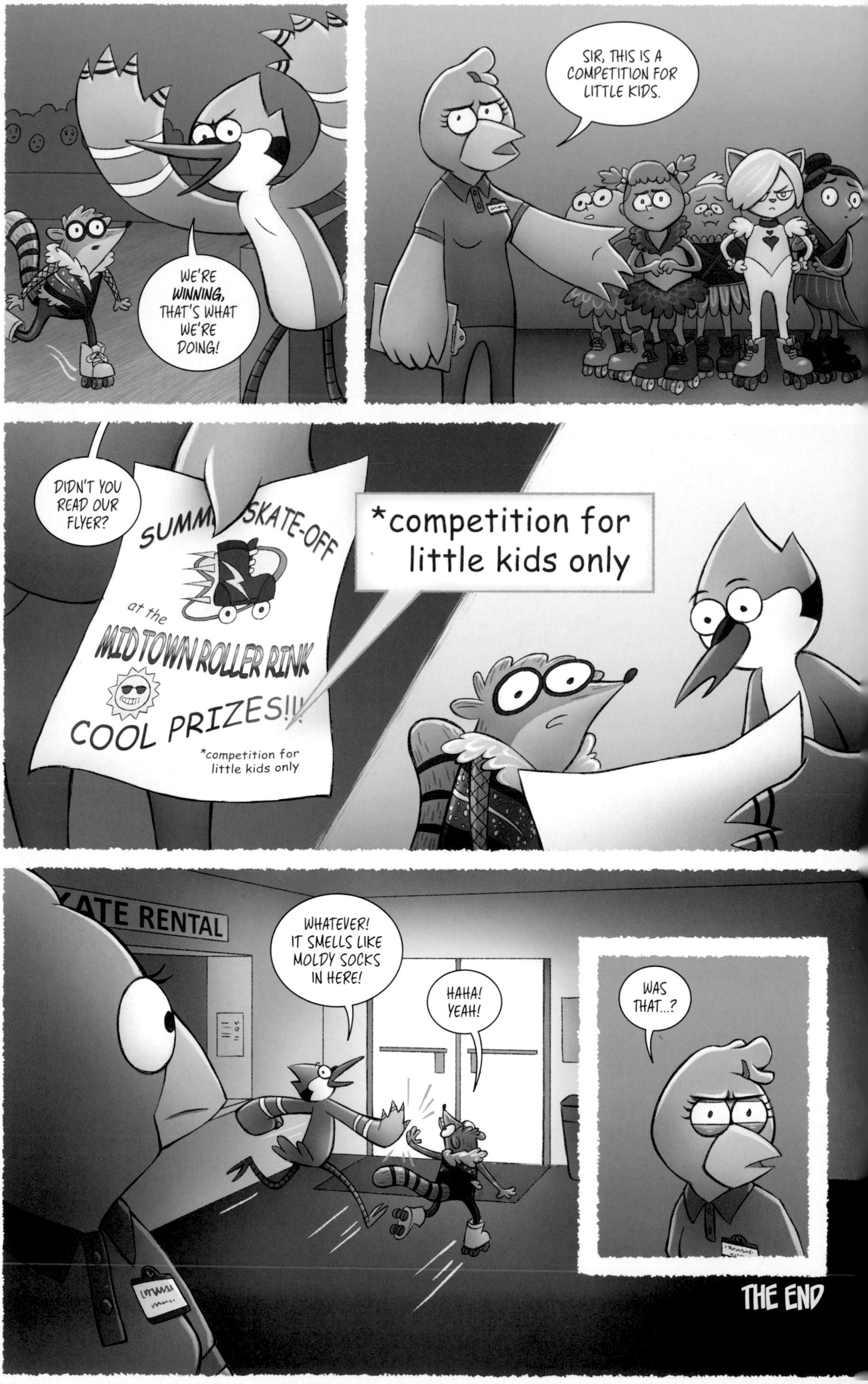
WE'RE WINNING, THAT'S WHAT WE'RE DOING!
SIR, THIS IS A COMPETITION FOR LITTLE KIDS.
DIDN'T YOU READ OUR FLYER?
SUMM SKATE-OFF
at the
MID TOWN ROLLER RINK
COOL PRIZES!!!
*competition for little kids only
*competition for little kids only
ATE RENTAL
WHATEVER! IT SMELLS LIKE MOLDY SOCKS IN HERE!
HAHA! YEAH!
WAS THAT...?
THE END

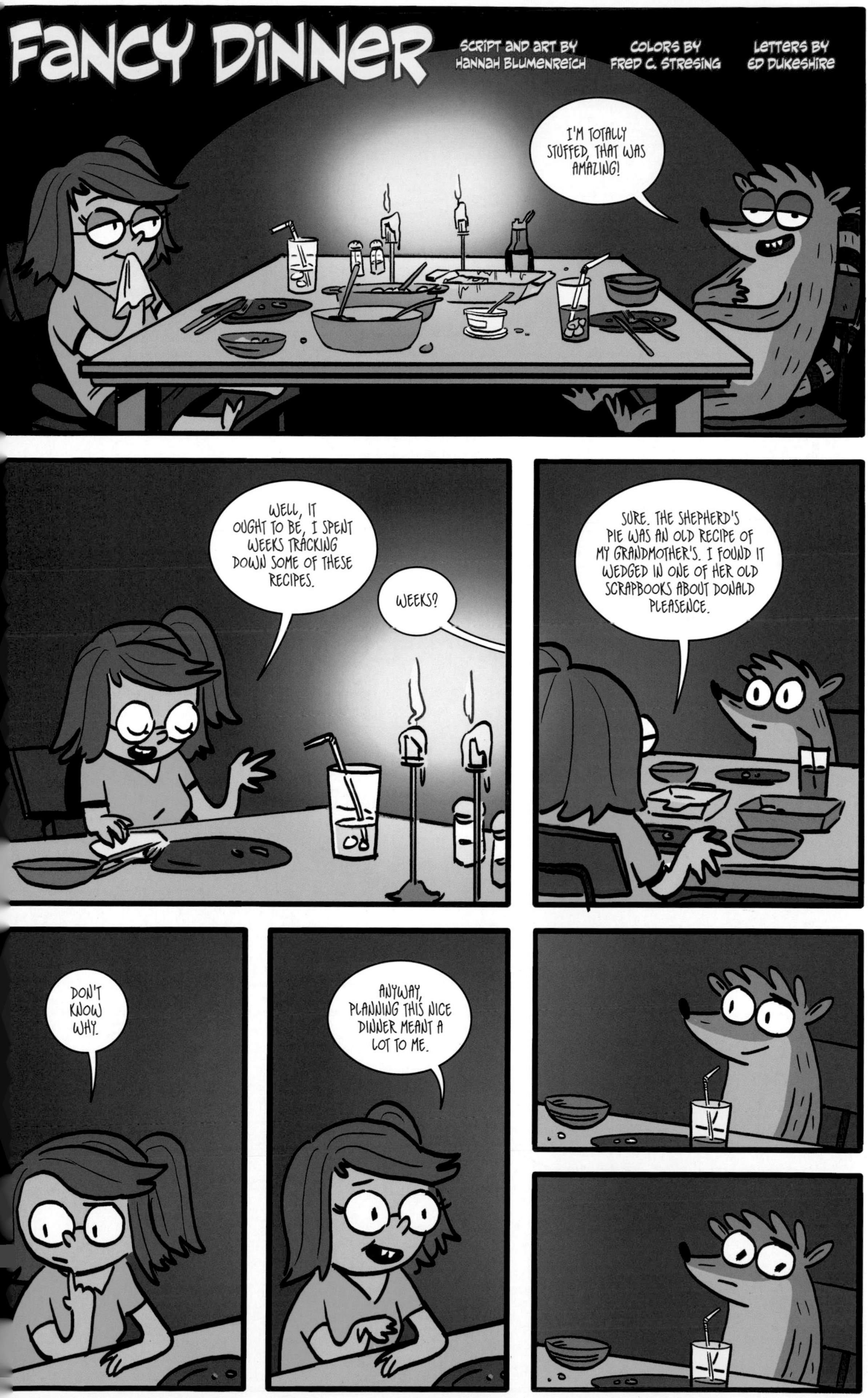
FANCY DINNER
SCRIPT AND ART BY HANNAH BLUMENREICH
COLORS BY FRED C. STRESING
LETTERS BY ED DUKESHIRE
I'M TOTALLY STUFFED, THAT WAS AMAZING!
WELL, IT OUGHT TO BE, I SPENT WEEKS TRACKING DOWN SOME OF THESE RECIPES.
WEEKS?
SURE. THE SHEPHERD'S PIE WAS AN OLD RECIPE OF MY GRANDMOTHER'S. I FOUND IT WEDGED IN ONE OF HER OLD SCRAPBOOKS ABOUT DONALD PLEASENCE.
DON'T KNOW WHY.
ANYWAY, PLANNING THIS NICE DINNER MEANT A LOT TO ME.

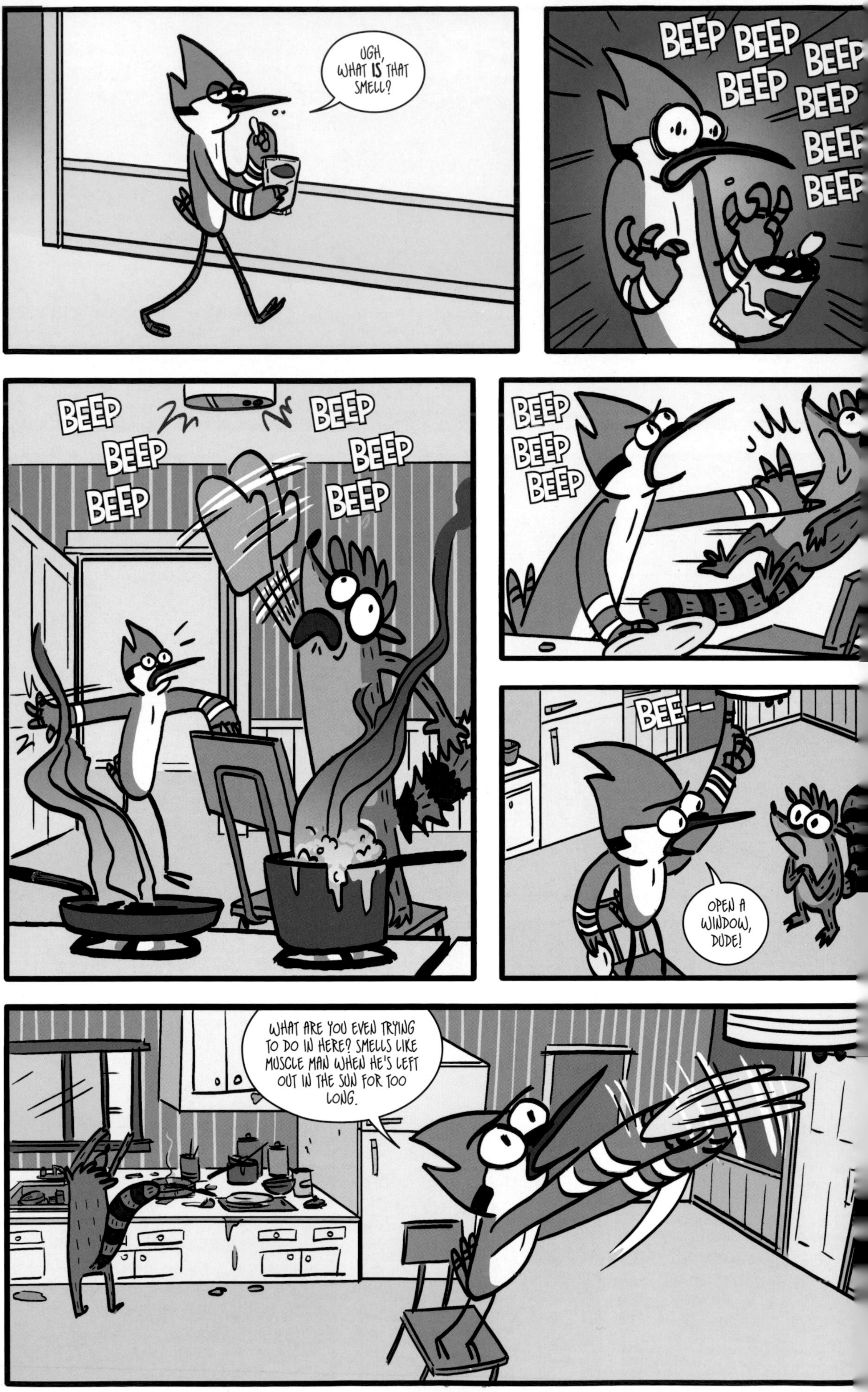
UGH, WHAT IS THAT SMELL?
BEEP BEEP BEEP BEEP BEEP BEEP BEEP
BEEP BEEP BEEP BEEP BEEP BEEP
BEEP BEEP BEEP
BEE--
OPEN A WINDOW, DUDE!
WHAT ARE YOU EVEN TRYING TO DO IN HERE? SMELLS LIKE MUSCLE MAN WHEN HE'S LEFT OUT IN THE SUN FOR TOO LONG.

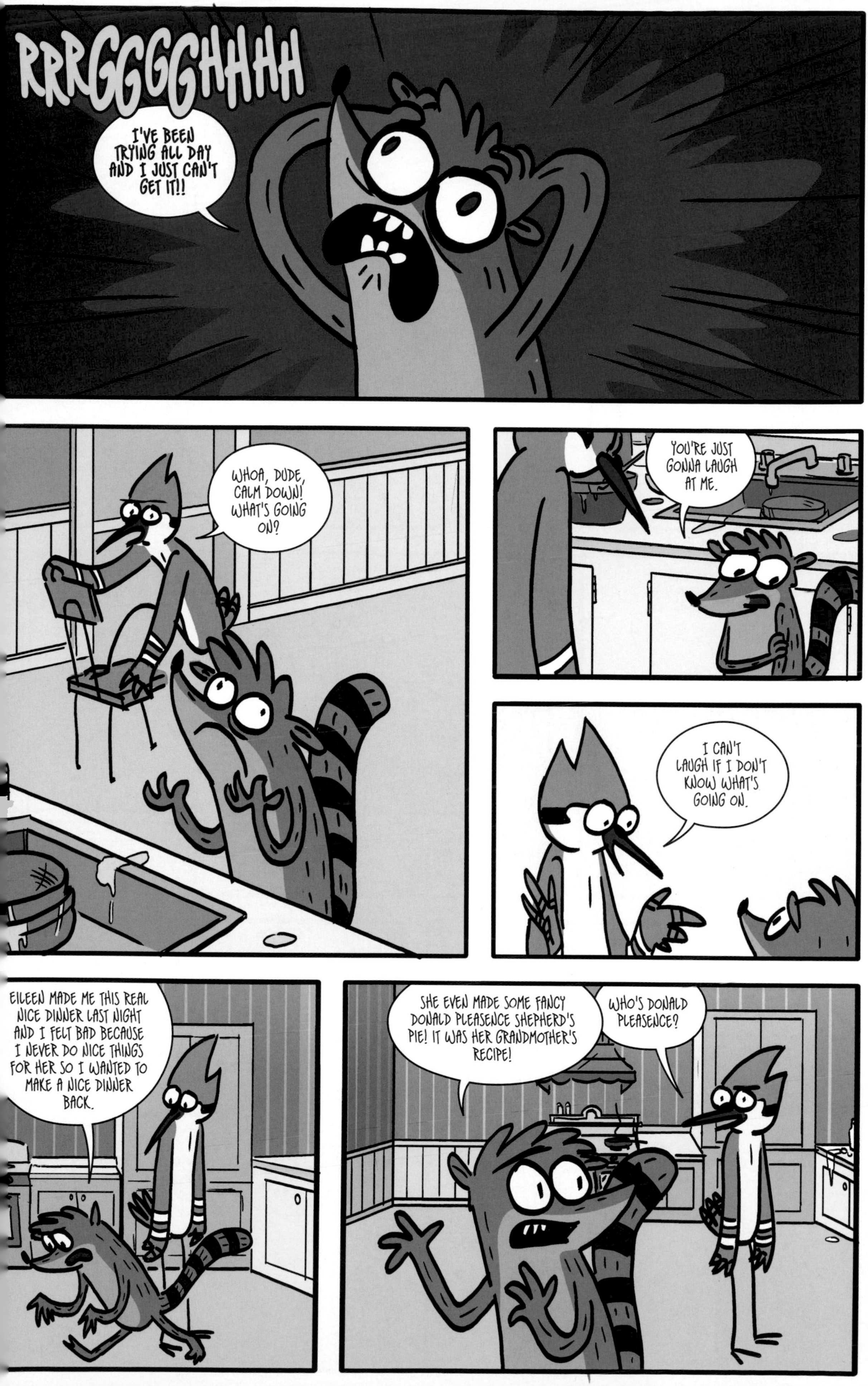
RRRGGGGHHHH
I'VE BEEN TRYING ALL DAY AND I JUST CAN'T GET IT!!
WHOA, DUDE, CALM DOWN! WHAT'S GOING ON?
YOU'RE JUST GONNA LAUGH AT ME.
I CAN'T LAUGH IF I DON'T KNOW WHAT'S GOING ON.
EILEEN MADE ME THIS REAL NICE DINNER LAST NIGHT AND I FELT BAD BECAUSE I NEVER DO NICE THINGS FOR HER SO I WANTED TO MAKE A NICE DINNER BACK.
SHE EVEN MADE SOME FANCY DONALD PLEASENCE SHEPHERD'S PIE! IT WAS HER GRANDMOTHER'S RECIPE!
WHO'S DONALD PLEASENCE?

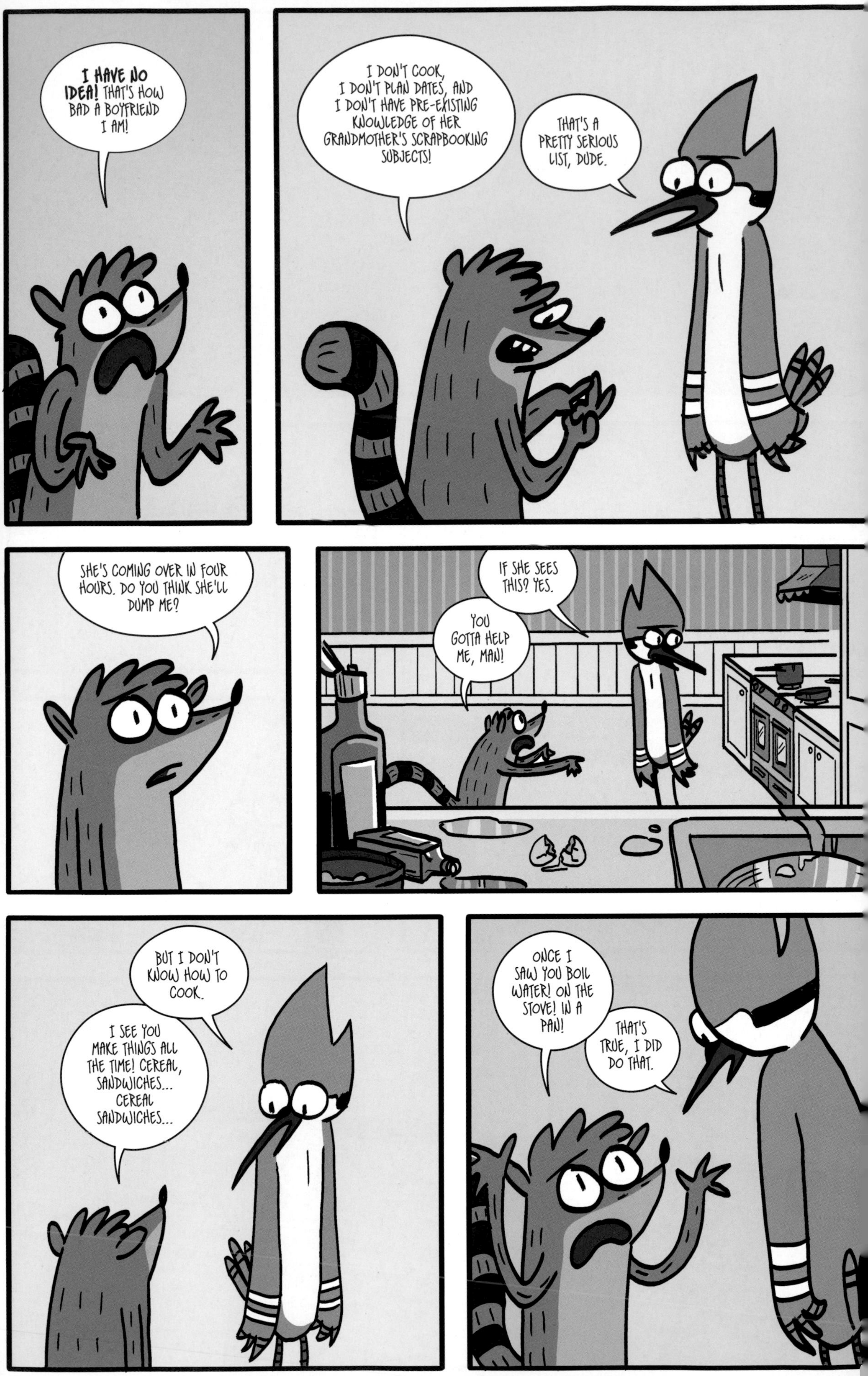
I HAVE NO IDEA! THAT'S HOW BAD A BOYFRIEND I AM!
I DON'T COOK, I DON'T PLAN DATES, AND I DON'T HAVE PRE-EXISTING KNOWLEDGE OF HER GRANDMOTHER'S SCRAPBOOKING SUBJECTS!
THAT'S A PRETTY SERIOUS LIST, DUDE.
SHE'S COMING OVER IN FOUR HOURS. DO YOU THINK SHE'LL DUMP ME?
IF SHE SEES THIS? YES.
YOU GOTTA HELP ME, MAN!
BUT I DON'T KNOW HOW TO COOK.
I SEE YOU MAKE THINGS ALL THE TIME! CEREAL, SANDWICHES... CEREAL SANDWICHES...
ONCE I SAW YOU BOIL WATER! ON THE STOVE! IN A PAN!
THAT'S TRUE, I DID DO THAT.

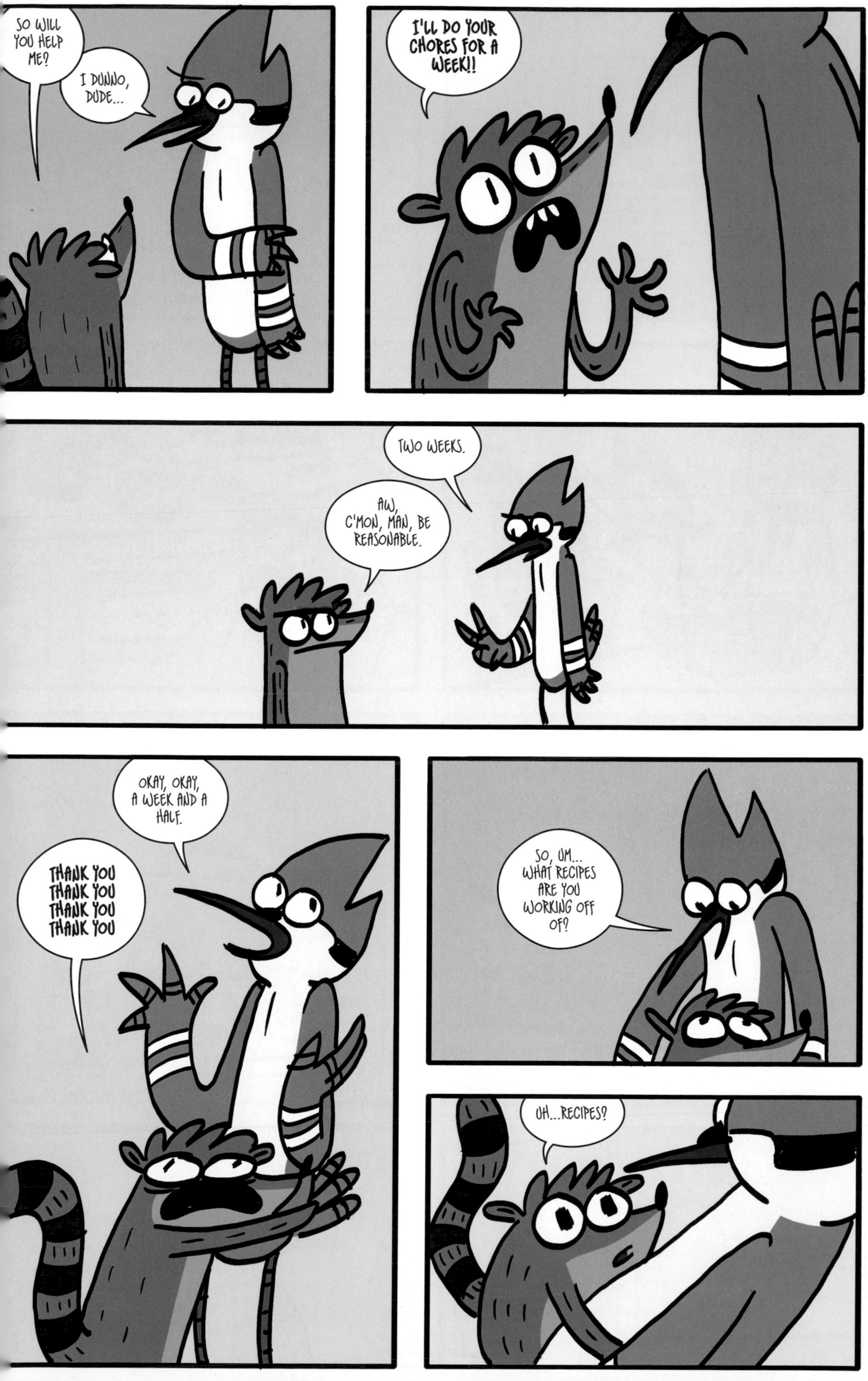
SO WILL YOU HELP ME?
I DUNNO, DUDE...
I'LL DO YOUR CHORES FOR A WEEK!!
TWO WEEKS.
AW, C'MON, MAN, BE REASONABLE.
OKAY, OKAY, A WEEK AND A HALF.
THANK YOU THANK YOU THANK YOU THANK YOU
SO, UM... WHAT RECIPES ARE YOU WORKING OFF OF?
UH...RECIPES?

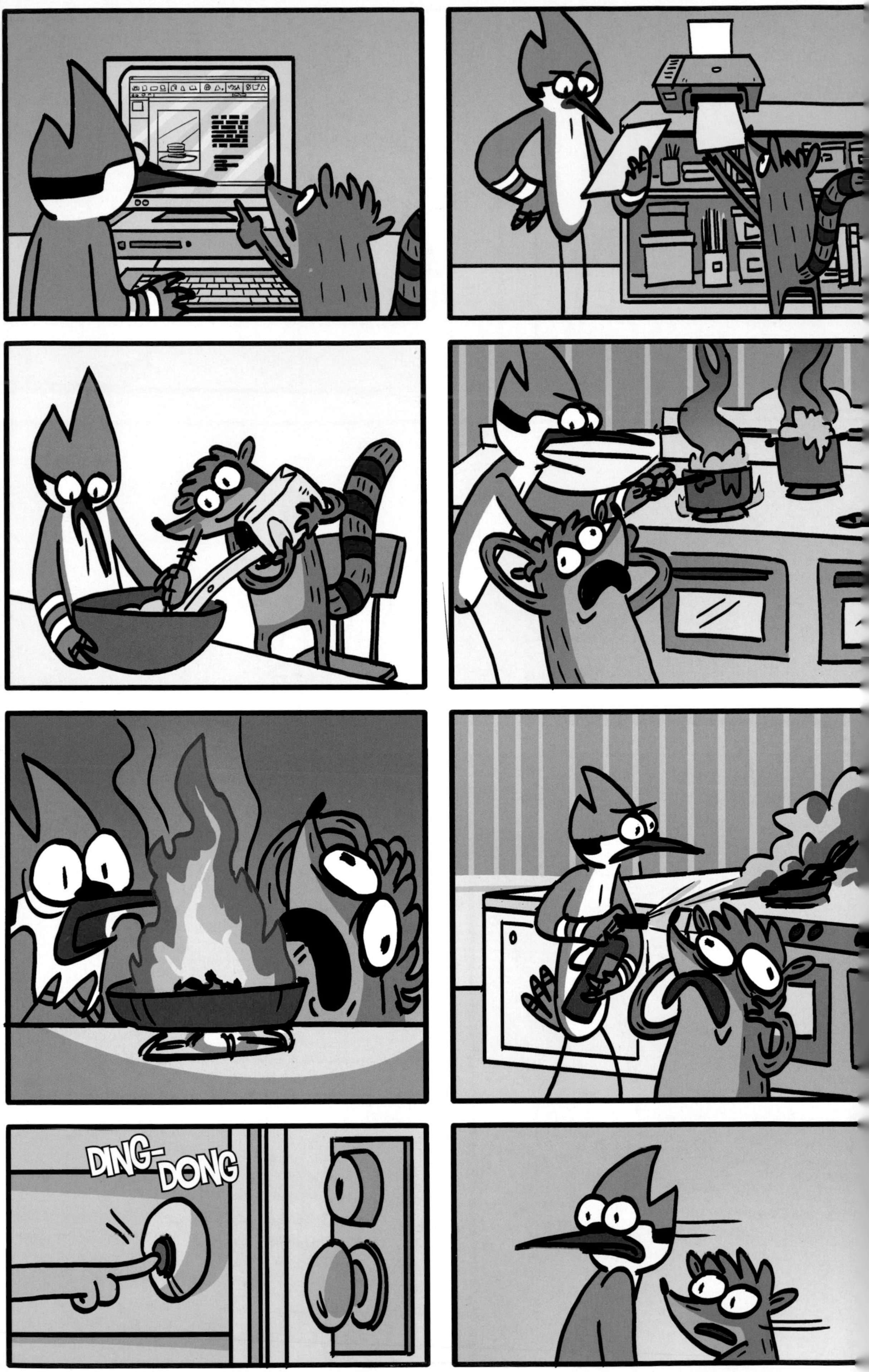
DING-DONG

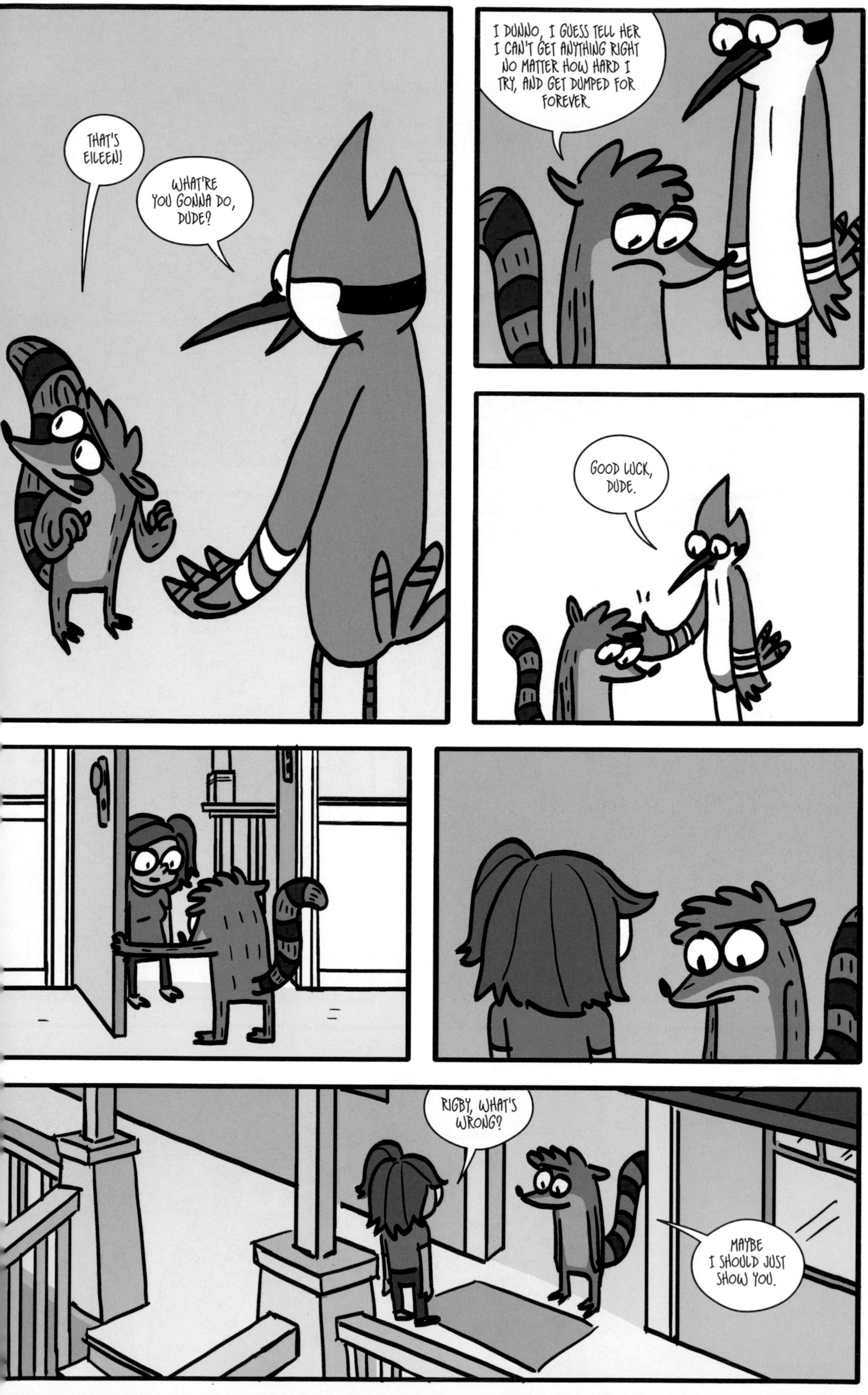
THAT'S EILEEN!
WHAT'RE YOU GONNA DO, DUDE?
I DUNNO, I GUESS TELL HER I CAN'T GET ANYTHING RIGHT NO MATTER HOW HARD I TRY, AND GET DUMPED FOR FOREVER.
GOOD LUCK, DUDE.
RIGBY, WHAT'S WRONG?
MAYBE I SHOULD JUST SHOW YOU.

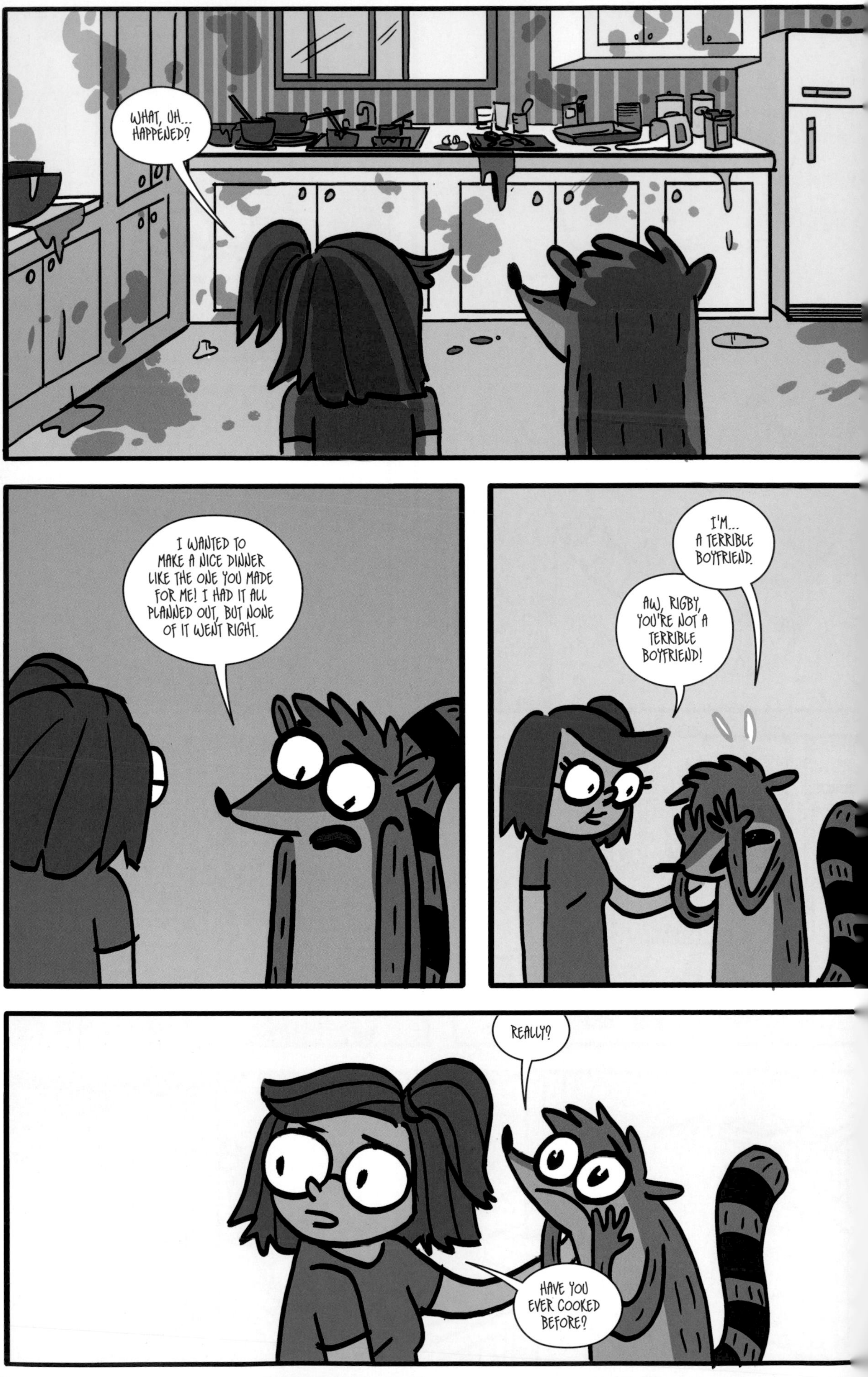
WHAT, UH... HAPPENED?
I WANTED TO MAKE A NICE DINNER LIKE THE ONE YOU MADE FOR ME! I HAD IT ALL PLANNED OUT, BUT NONE OF IT WENT RIGHT.
I'M... A TERRIBLE BOYFRIEND.
AW, RIGBY, YOU'RE NOT A TERRIBLE BOYFRIEND!
REALLY?
HAVE YOU EVER COOKED BEFORE?

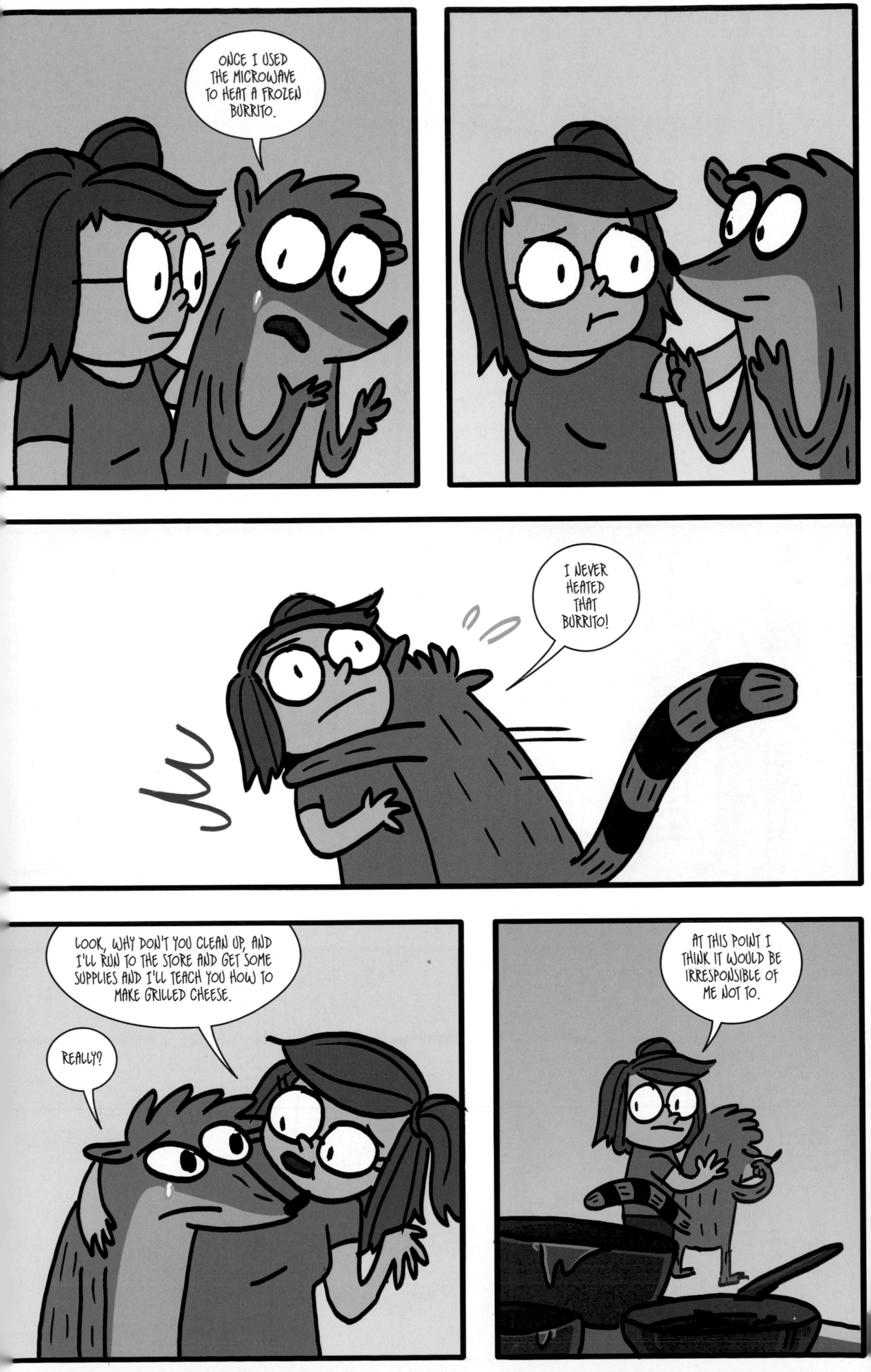
ONCE I USED THE MICROWAVE TO HEAT A FROZEN BURRITO.
I NEVER HEATED THAT BURRITO!
LOOK, WHY DON'T YOU CLEAN UP, AND I'LL RUN TO THE STORE AND GET SOME SUPPLIES AND I'LL TEACH YOU HOW TO MAKE GRILLED CHEESE.
REALLY?
AT THIS POINT I THINK IT WOULD BE IRRESPONSIBLE OF ME NOT TO.

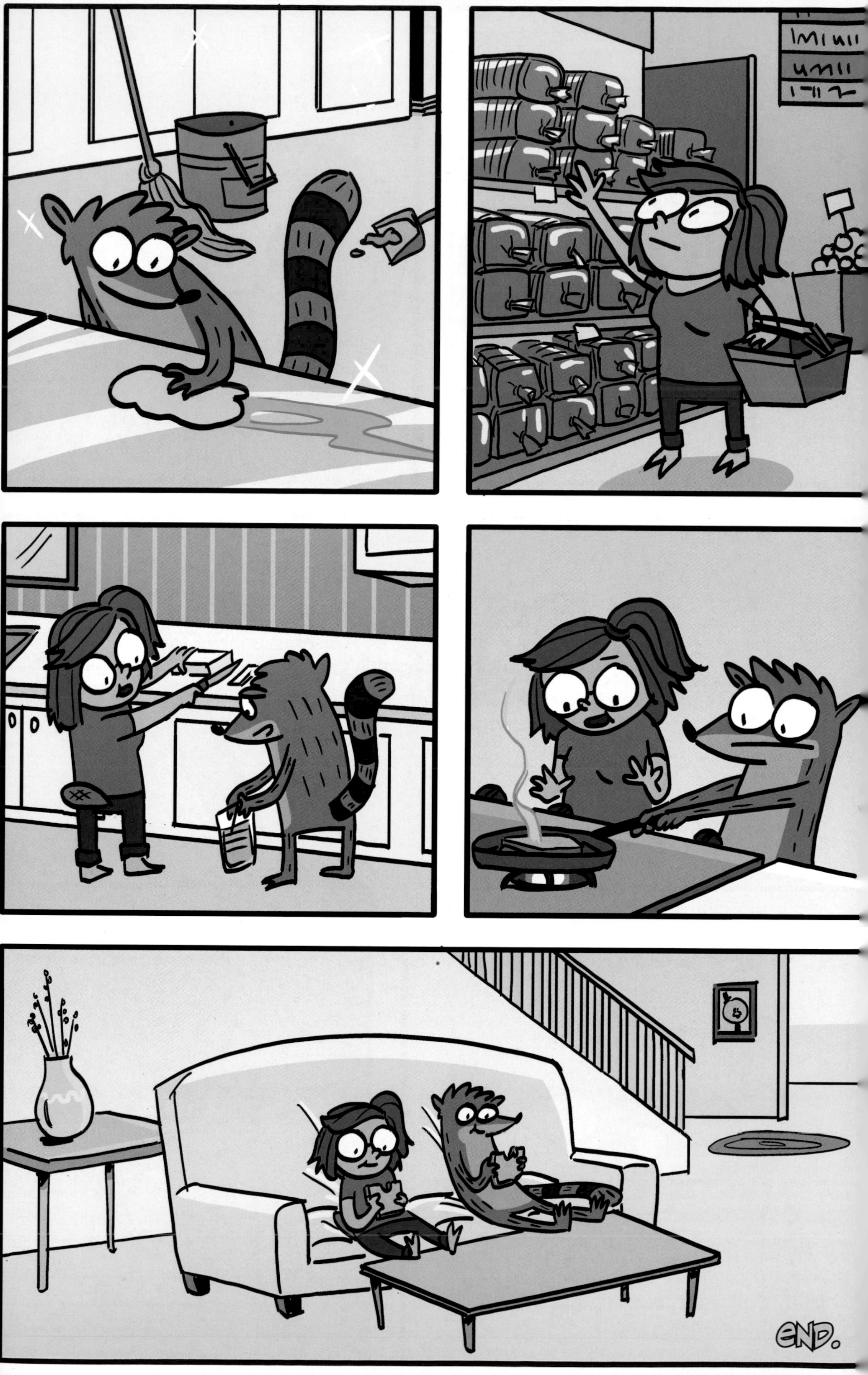
END.

"THE LAST SLICE" STORY & ART BY ALEX SOLIS

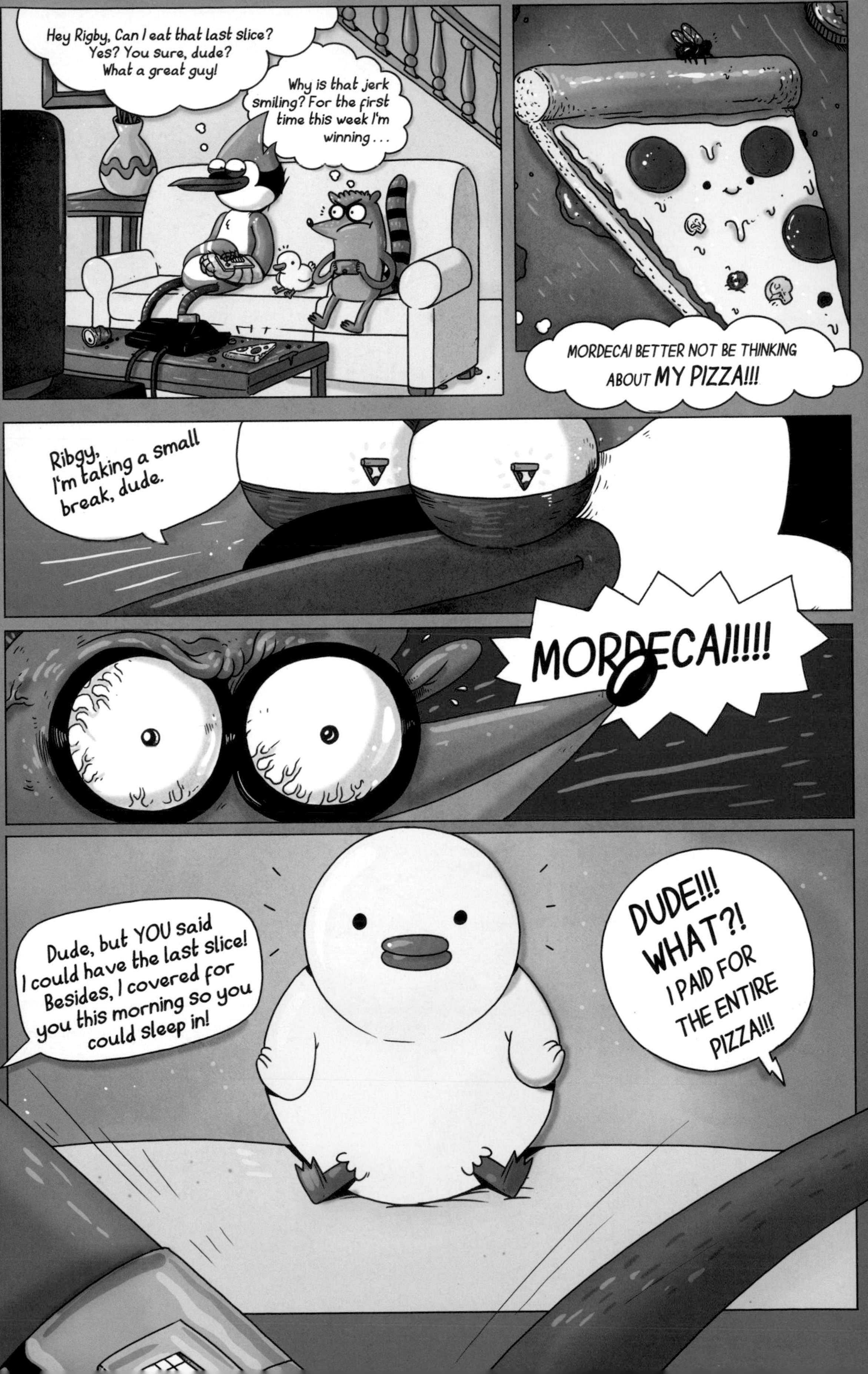
Hey Rigby, Can I eat that last slice? Yes? You sure, dude? What a great guy!
Why is that jerk smiling? For the first time this week I'm winning . . .
MORDECAI BETTER NOT BE THINKING ABOUT MY PIZZA!!!
Ribgy, I'm taking a small break, dude.
MORDECAI!!!!!
Dude, but YOU said I could have the last slice! Besides, I covered for you this morning so you could sleep in!
DUDE!!! WHAT?! I PAID FOR THE ENTIRE PIZZA!!!

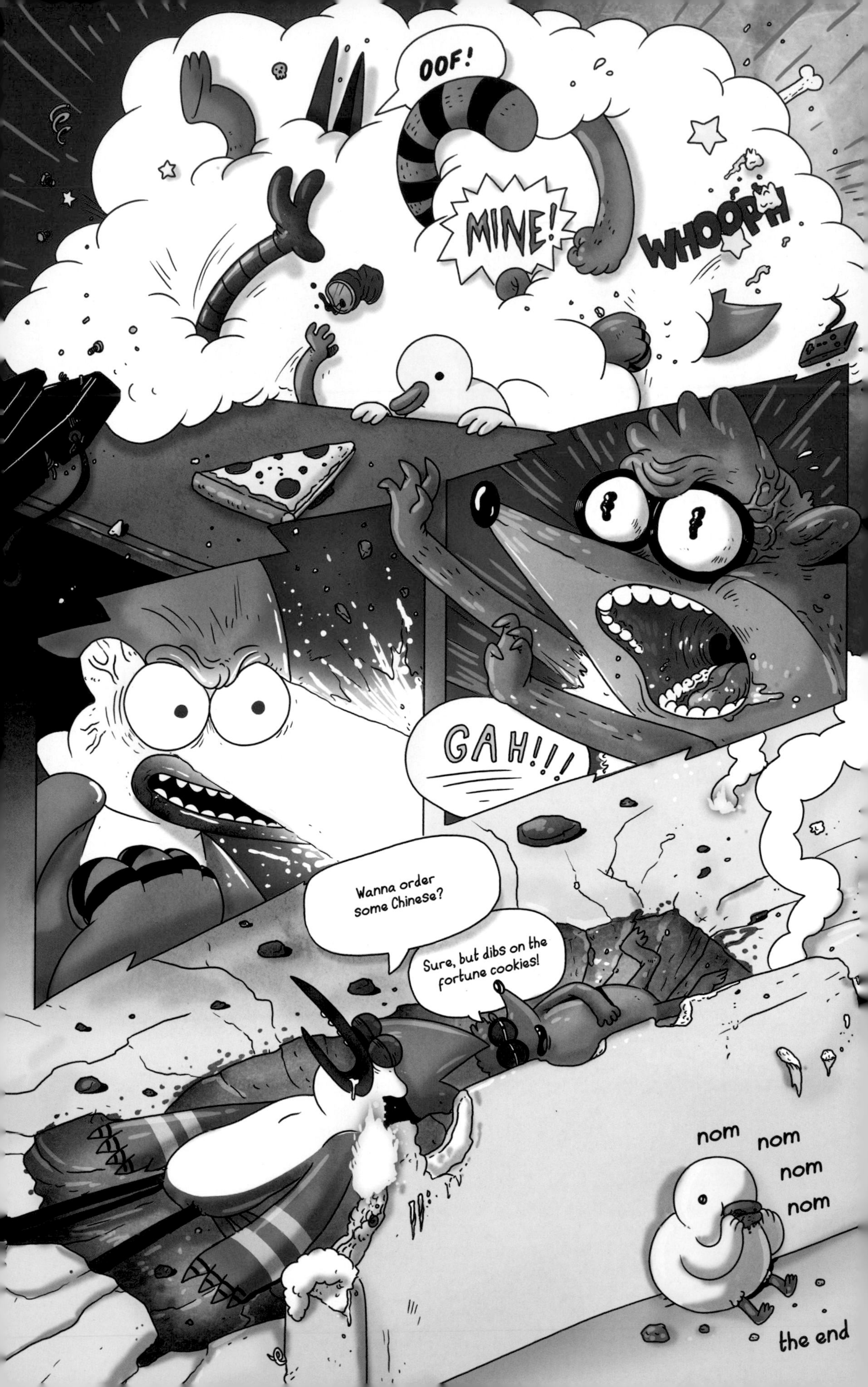
OOF!
MINE!
WHOOPH
GAH!!!
Wanna order some Chinese?
Sure, but dibs on the fortune cookies!
nom nom nom nom
the end

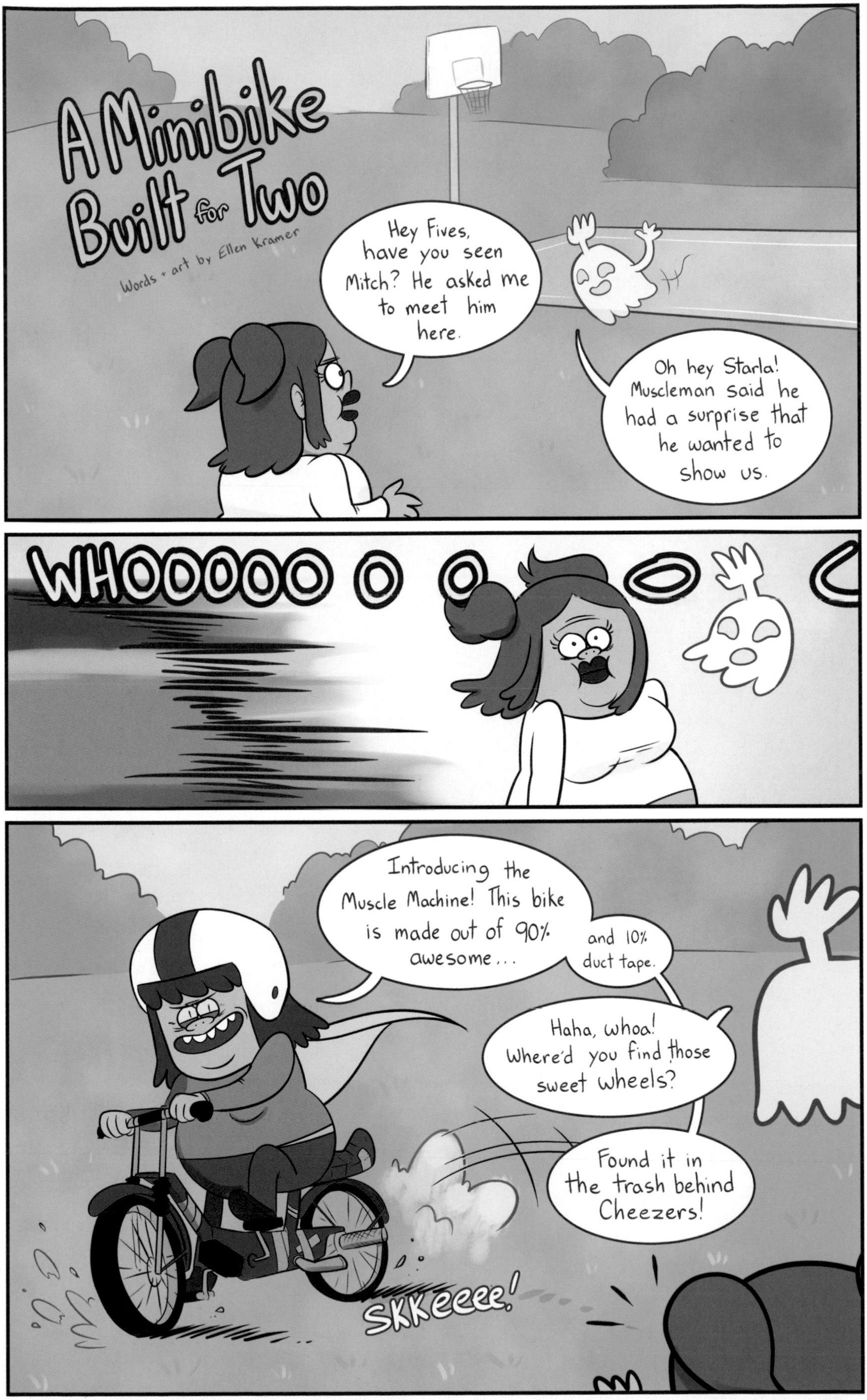

A Minibike Built for Two
Words + art by Ellen Kramer
Hey Fives, have you seen Mitch? He asked me to meet him here.
Oh hey Starla! Muscleman said he had a surprise that he wanted to show us.
WHOOOOO O O O C
Introducing the Muscle Machine! This bike is made out of 90% awesome...
and 10% duct tape.
Haha, whoa! Where'd you find those sweet wheels?
Found it in the trash behind Cheezers!
SKKeeee!

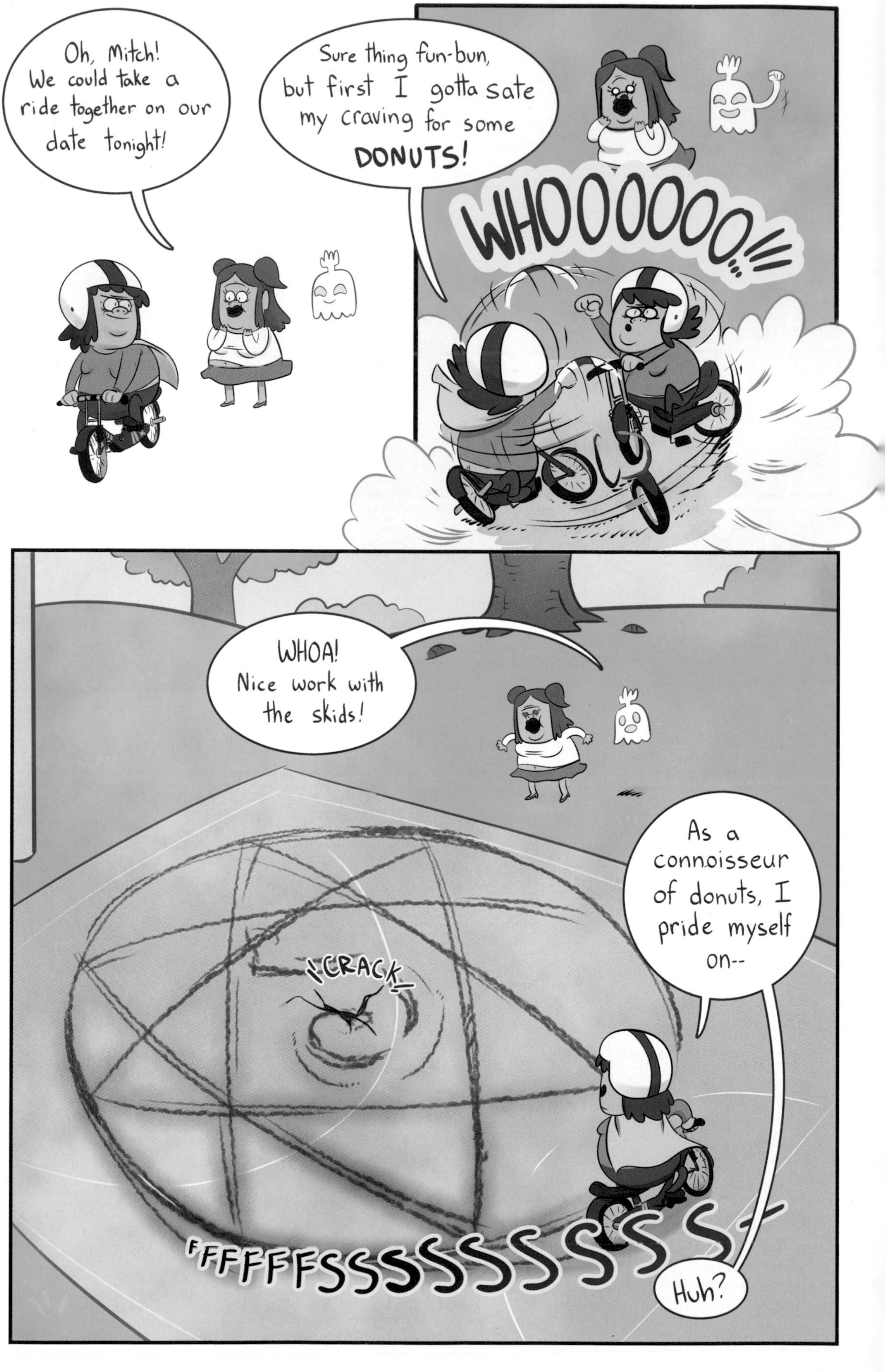
Oh, Mitch! We could take a ride together on our date tonight!
Sure thing fun-bun, but first I gotta sate my craving for some DONUTS!
WHOOOOOO!!!
WHOA! Nice work with the skids!
As a connoisseur of donuts, I pride myself on--
CRACK
FFFFFSSSSSSSSSSS
Huh?

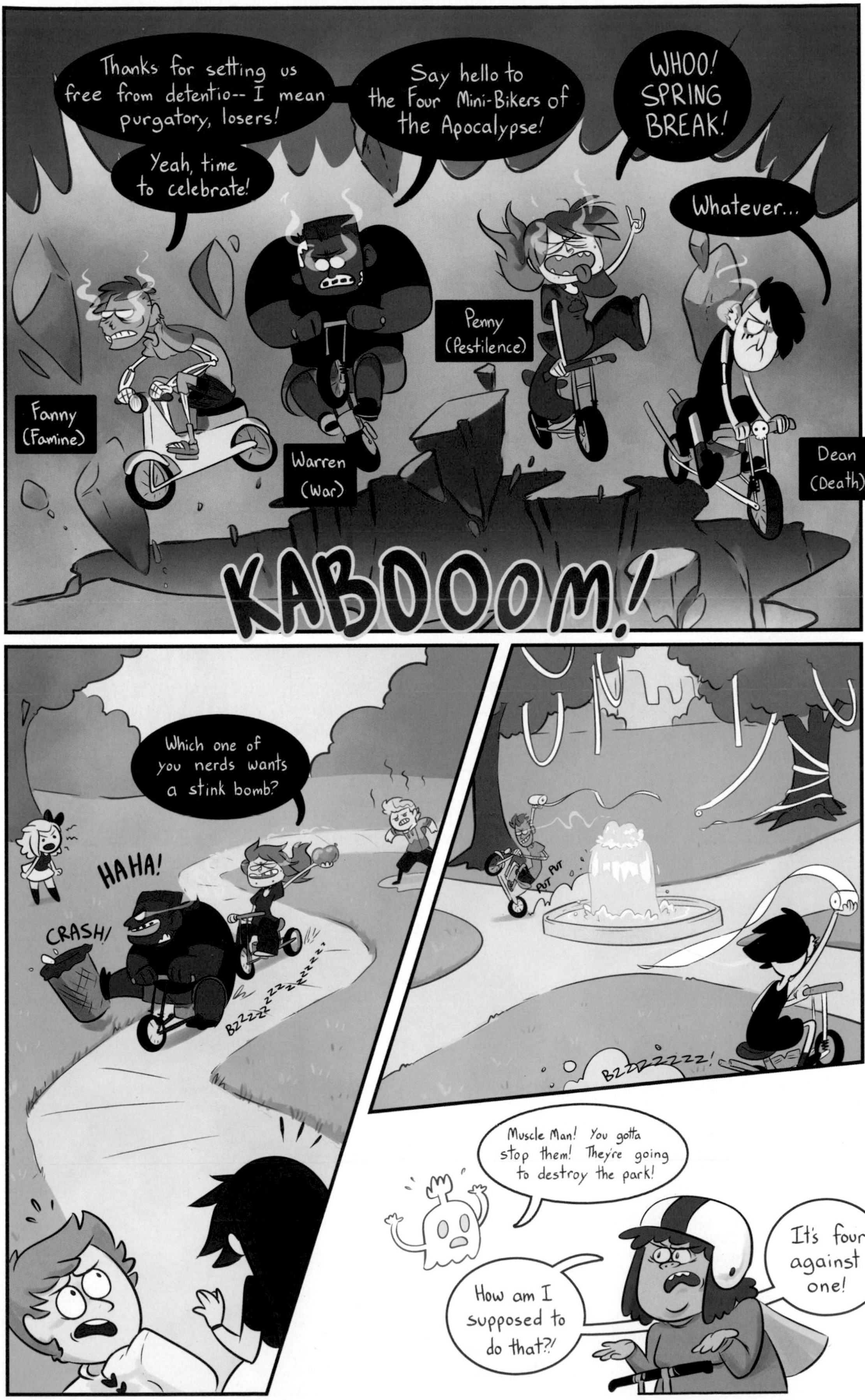
Thanks for setting us free from detentio-- I mean purgatory, losers!
Yeah, time to celebrate!
Say hello to the Four Mini-Bikers of the Apocalypse!
WHOO! SPRING BREAK!
Whatever...
Fanny (Famine)
Warren (War)
Penny (Pestilence)
Dean (Death)
KABOOOM!
Which one of you nerds wants a stink bomb?
HAHA!
CRASH!
BZZZZZ
PUT PUT
BZZZZZZZ!
Muscle Man! You gotta stop them! They're going to destroy the park!
How am I supposed to do that?!
It's four against one!

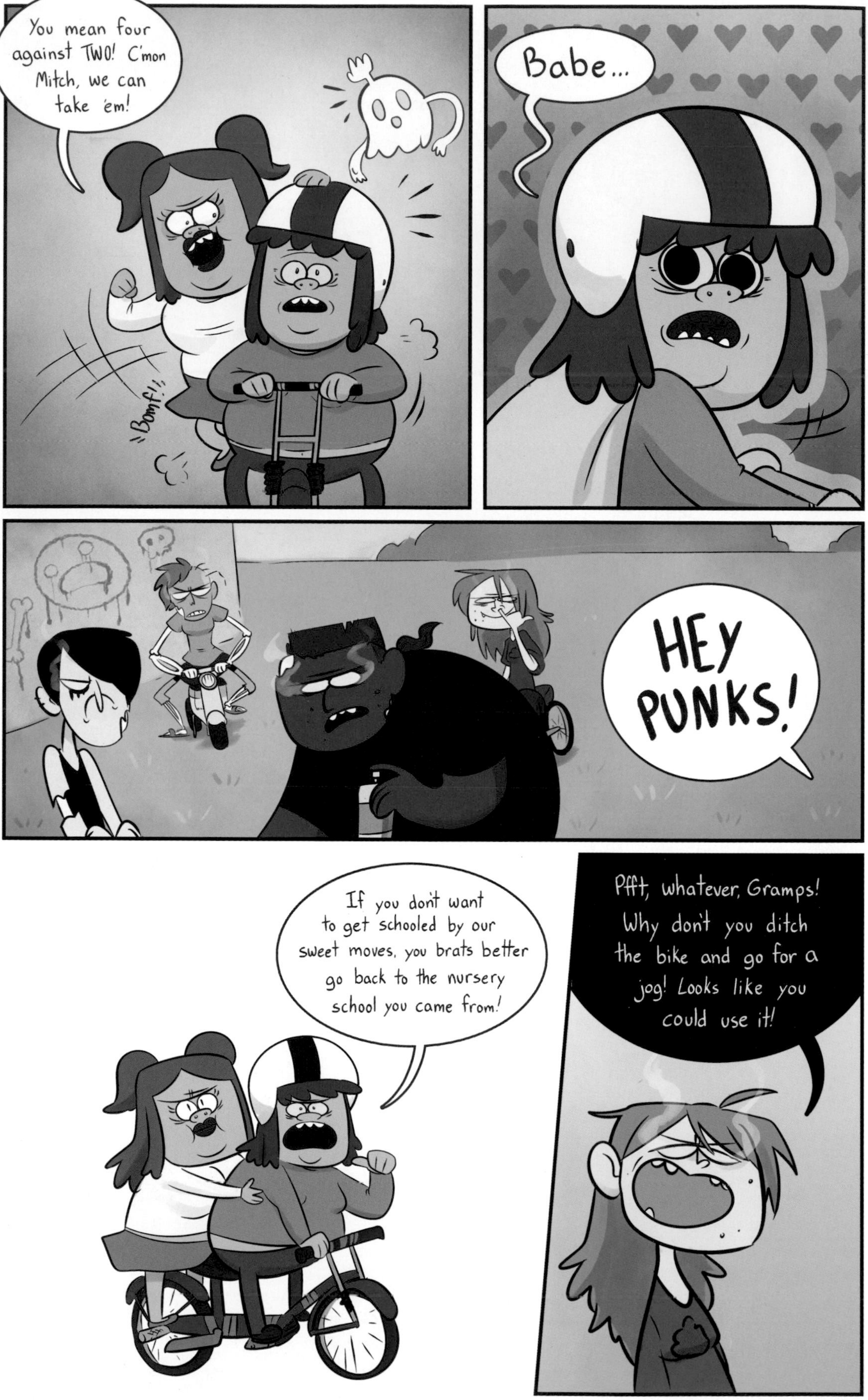

You mean four against TWO! C'mon Mitch, we can take 'em!
Bomf!
Babe...
HEY PUNKS!
If you don't want to get schooled by our sweet moves, you brats better go back to the nursery school you came from!
Pfft, whatever, Gramps! Why don't you ditch the bike and go for a jog! Looks like you could use it!

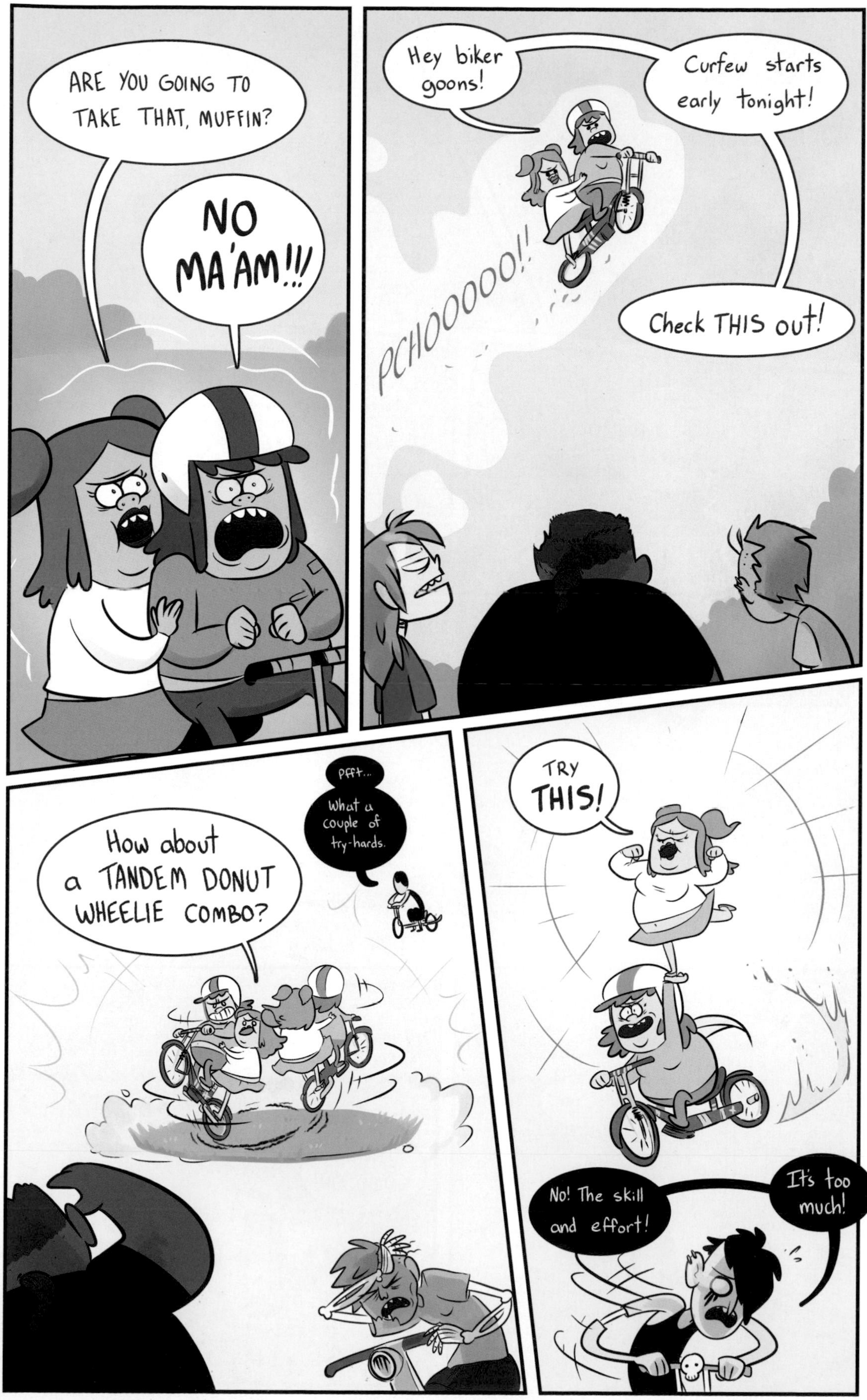
ARE YOU GOING TO TAKE THAT, MUFFIN?
NO MA'AM!!!
Hey biker goons!
Curfew starts early tonight!
PCHOOOOO!!
Check THIS out!
How about a TANDEM DONUT WHEELIE COMBO?
Pfft...
What a couple of try-hards.
TRY THIS!
No! The skill and effort!
It's too much!

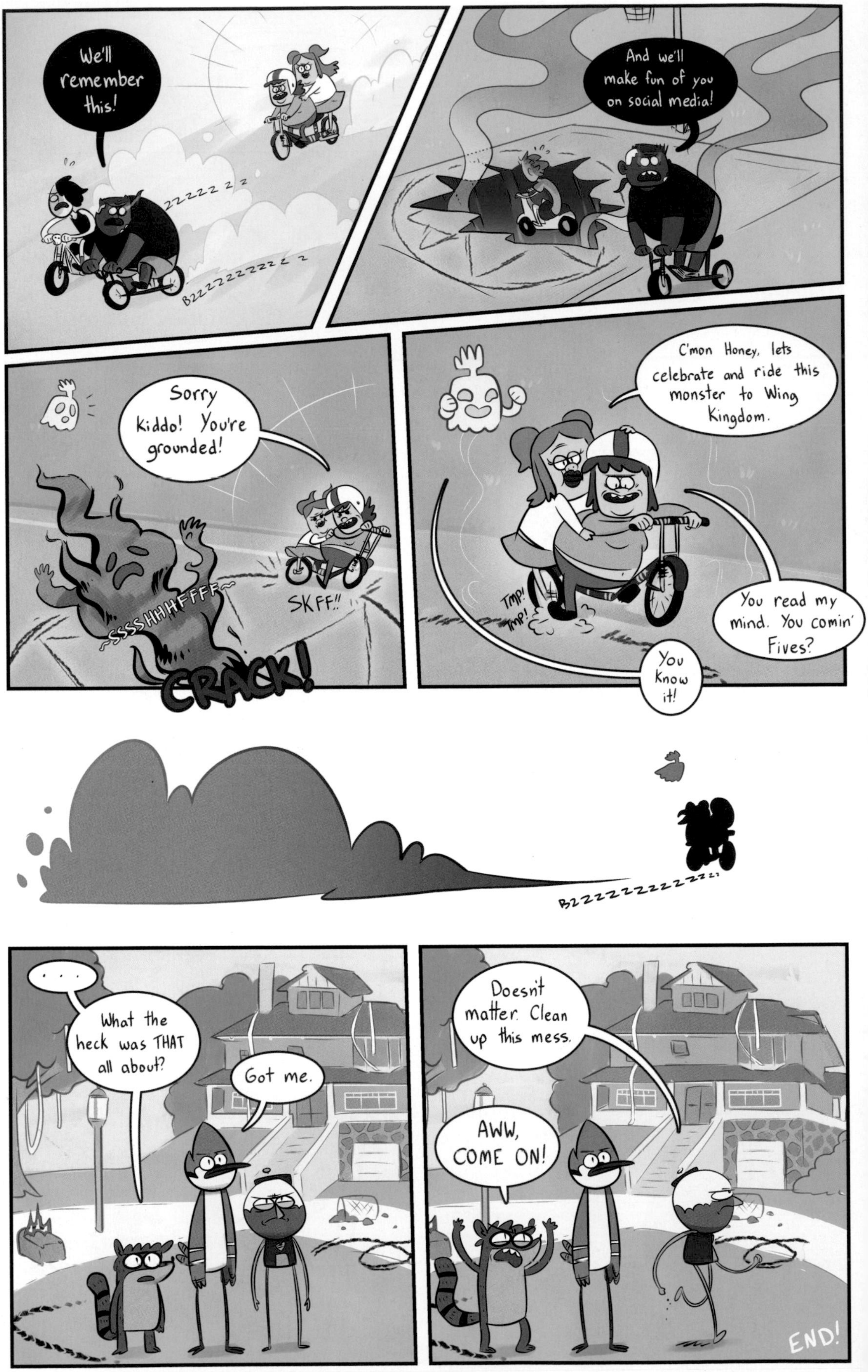
We'll remember this!
ZZZZZ Z Z
BZZZZZZZZZ Z Z
And we'll make fun of you on social media!
Sorry kiddo! You're grounded!
~SSSSHHHHFFFF~
CRACK!
SKFF!!
C'mon Honey, lets celebrate and ride this monster to Wing Kingdom.
TMP! TMP!
You read my mind. You comin' Fives?
You know it!
BZZZZZZZZZZZZZ
. . .
What the heck was THAT all about?
Got me.
Doesn't matter. Clean up this mess.
AWW, COME ON!
END!

COVER GALLERY

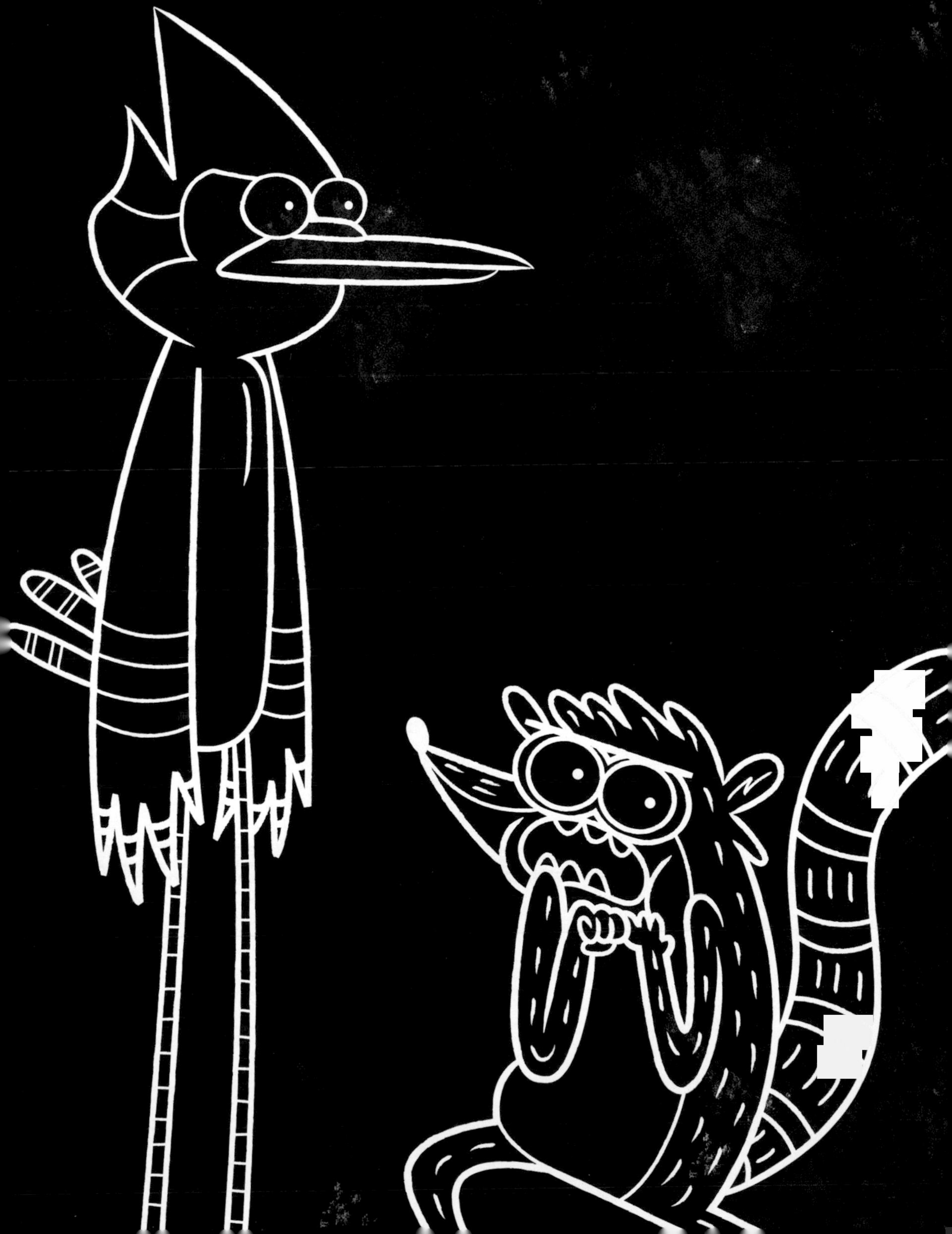

2014 ANNUAL Main Cover
ALLISON STREJLAU

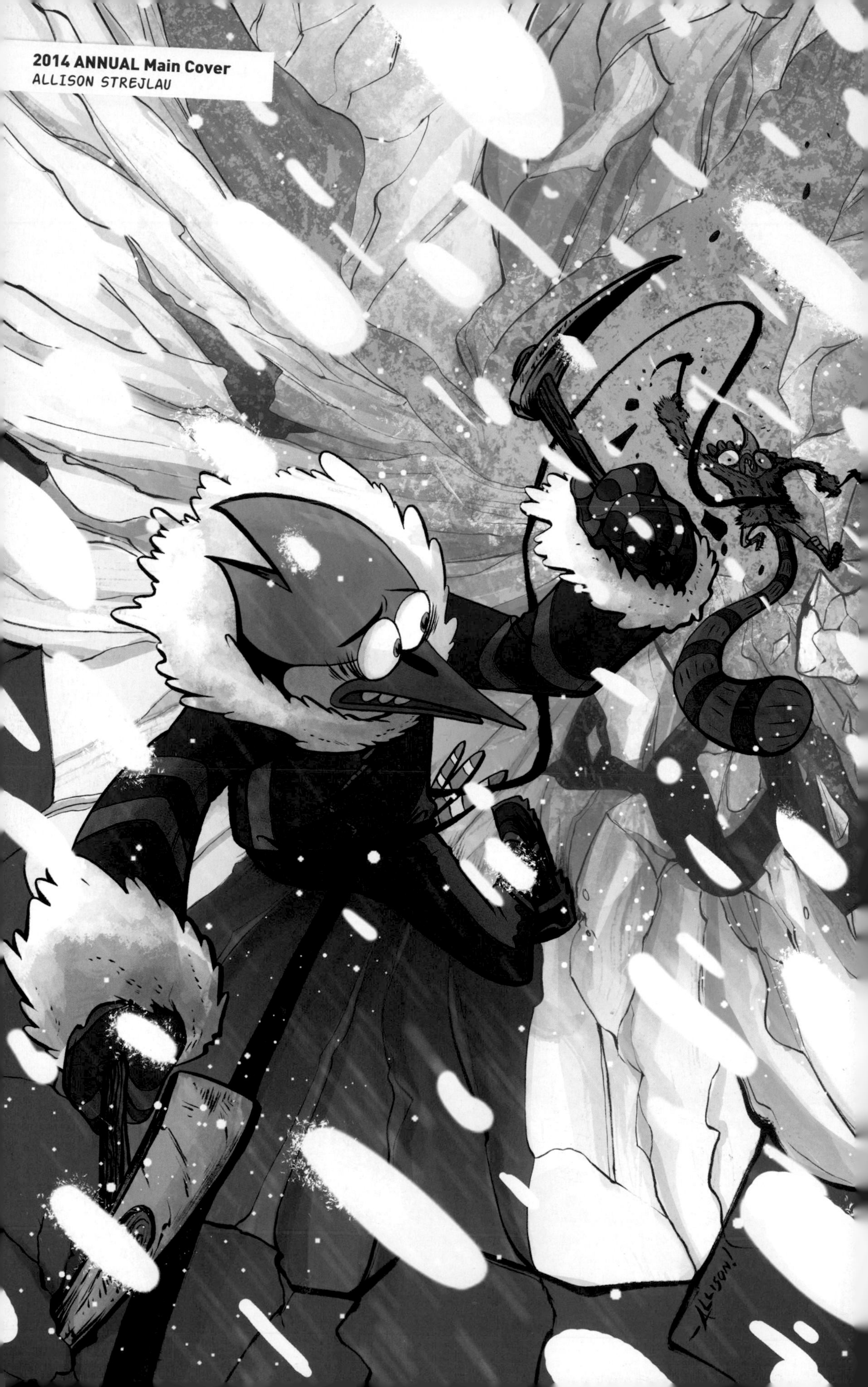
-ALLISON!

2014 ANNUAL Variant Cover
JEN LEE

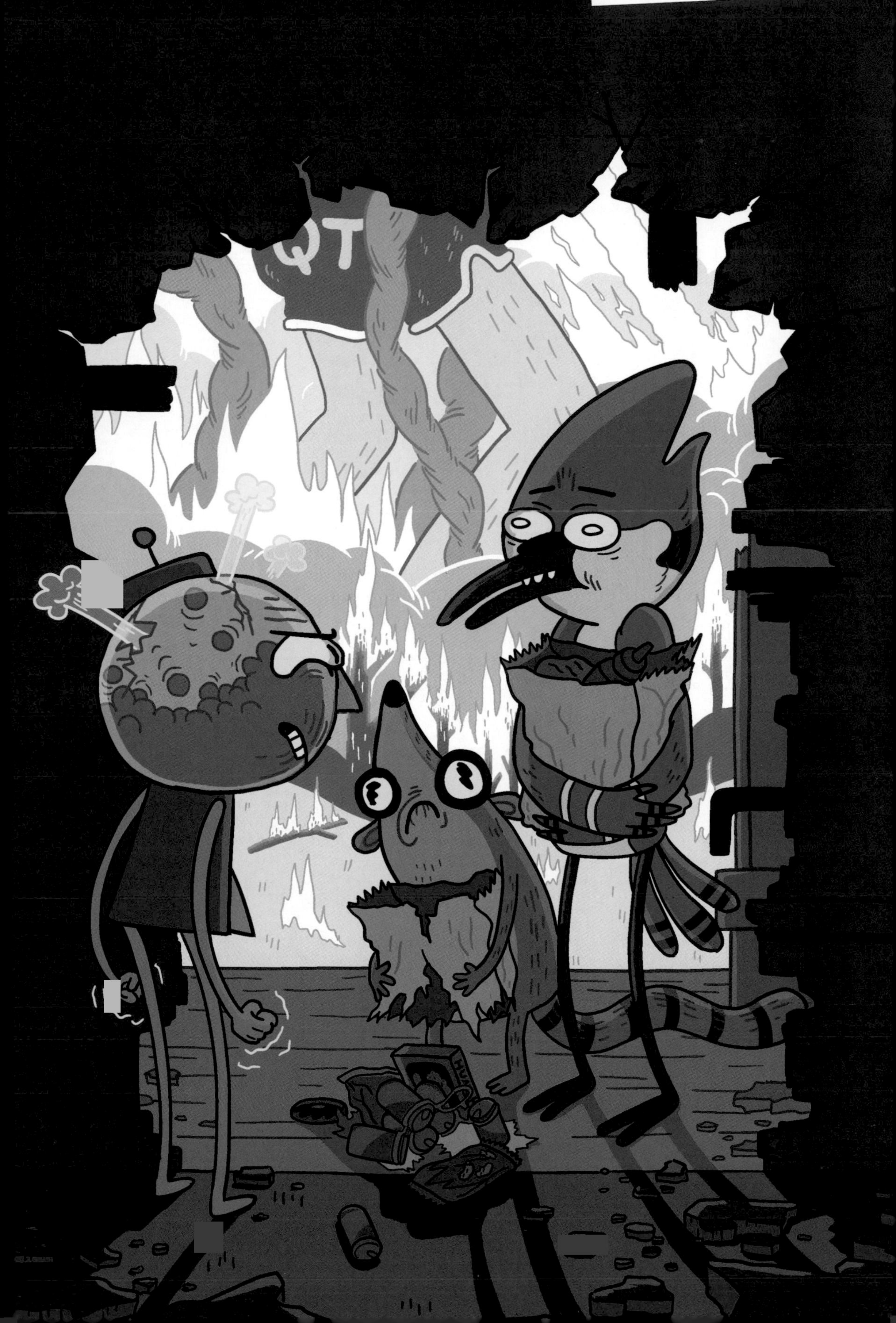
QT

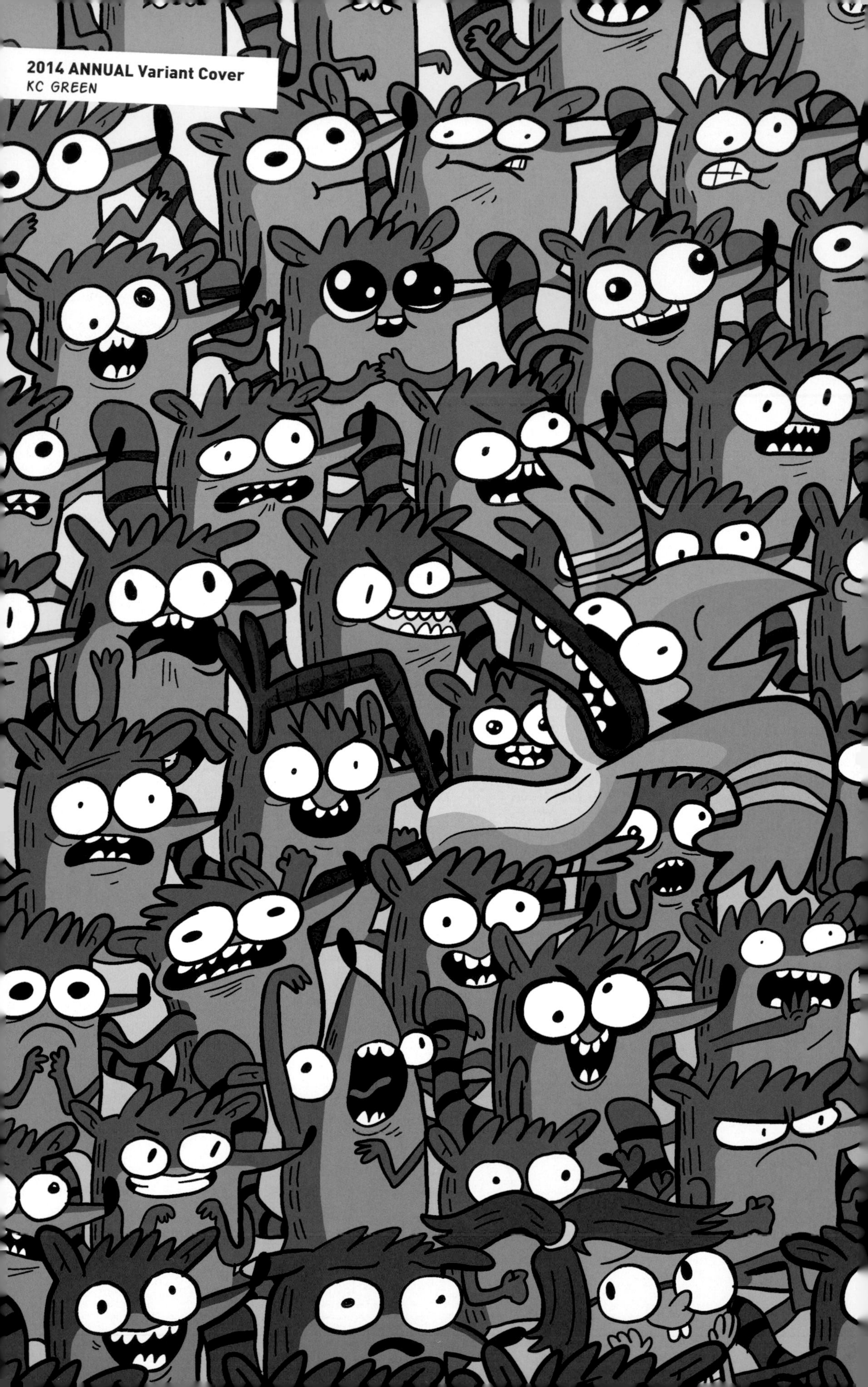

2014 ANNUAL Variant Cover
KC GREEN

2014 ANNUAL Big Wow! Comic Fest Exclusive Cover
MIKE LOWERY

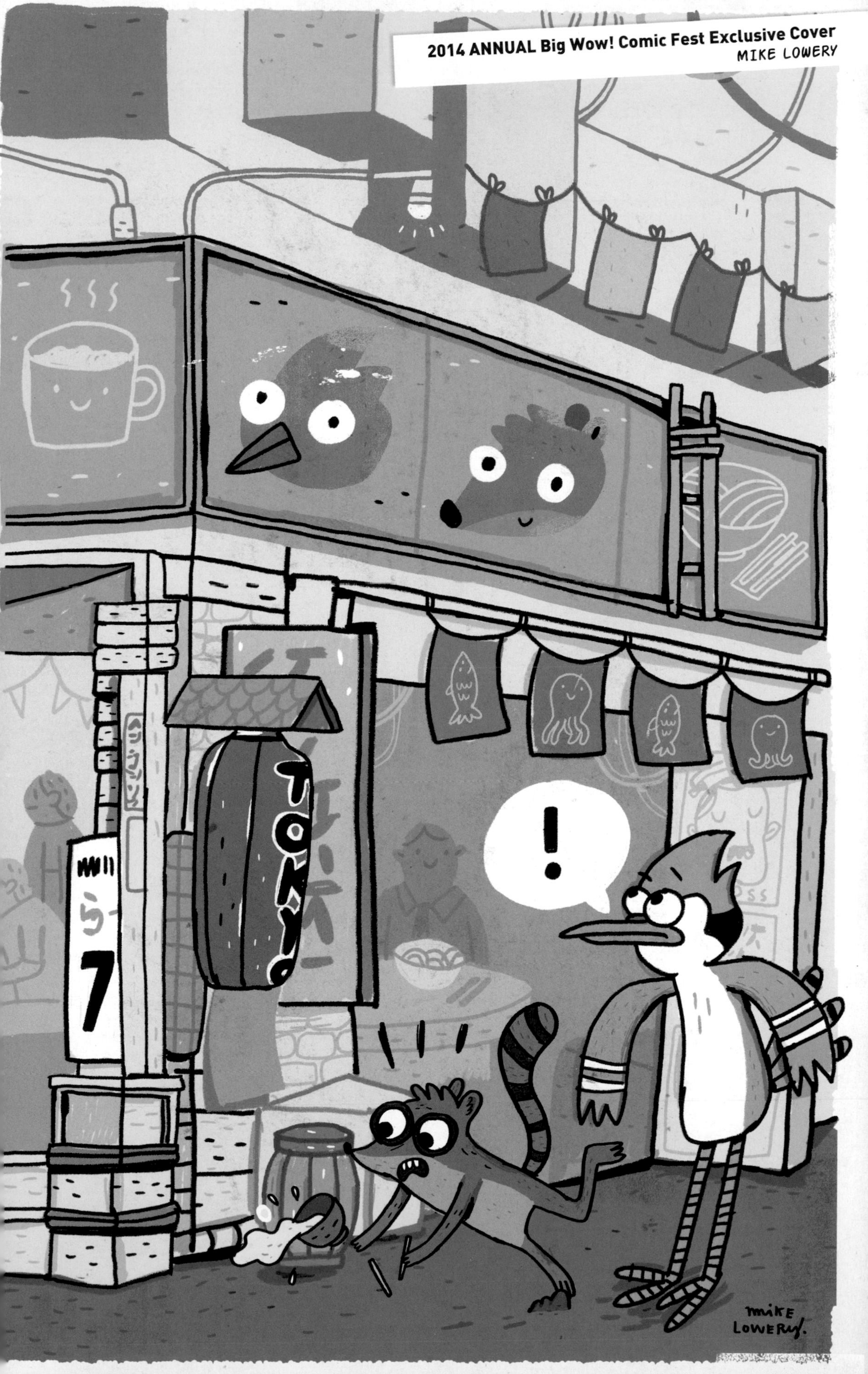
TOKYO
7
!
mike
LOWERY.

2015 SPECIAL Main Cover
RIAN SYGH

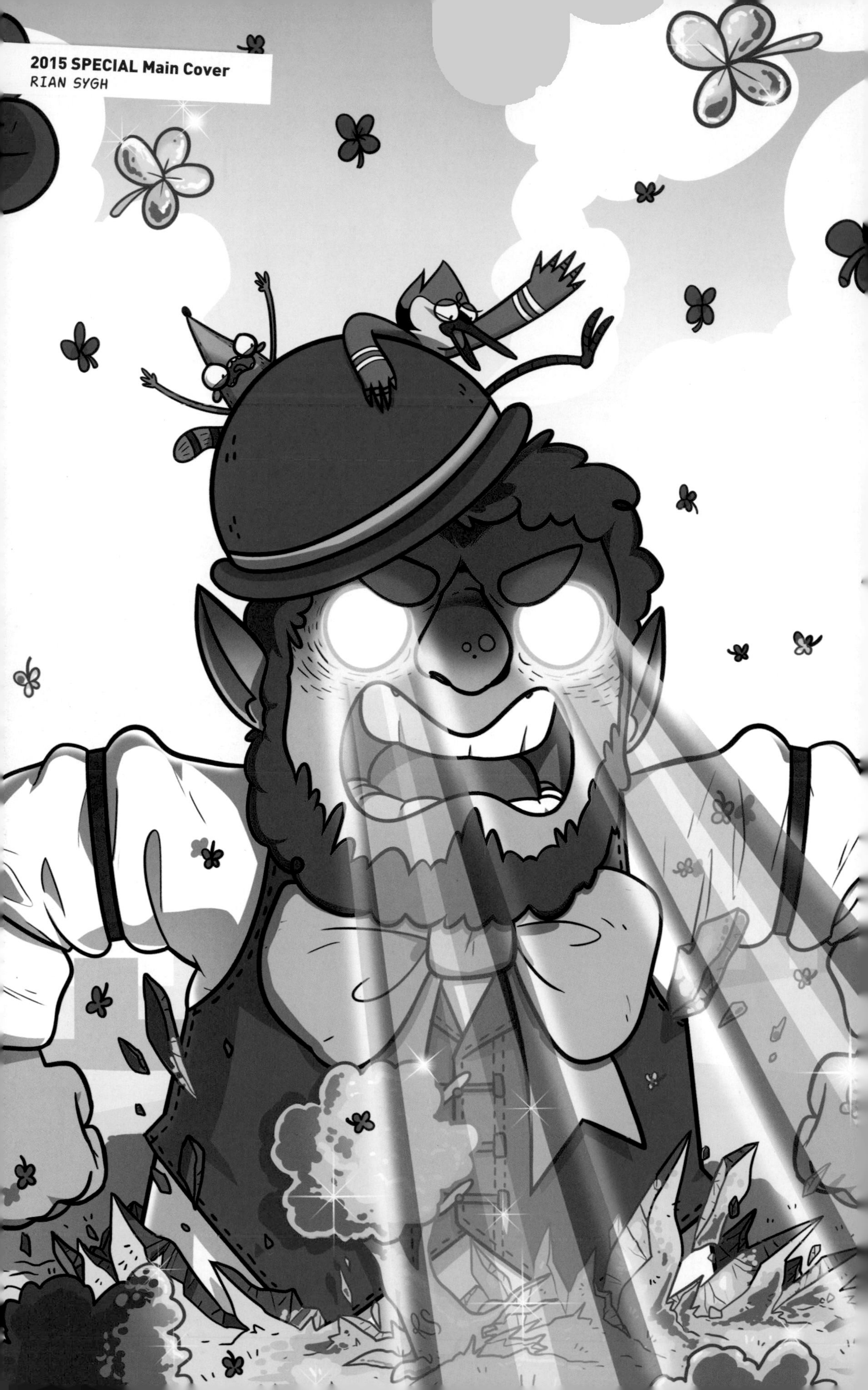

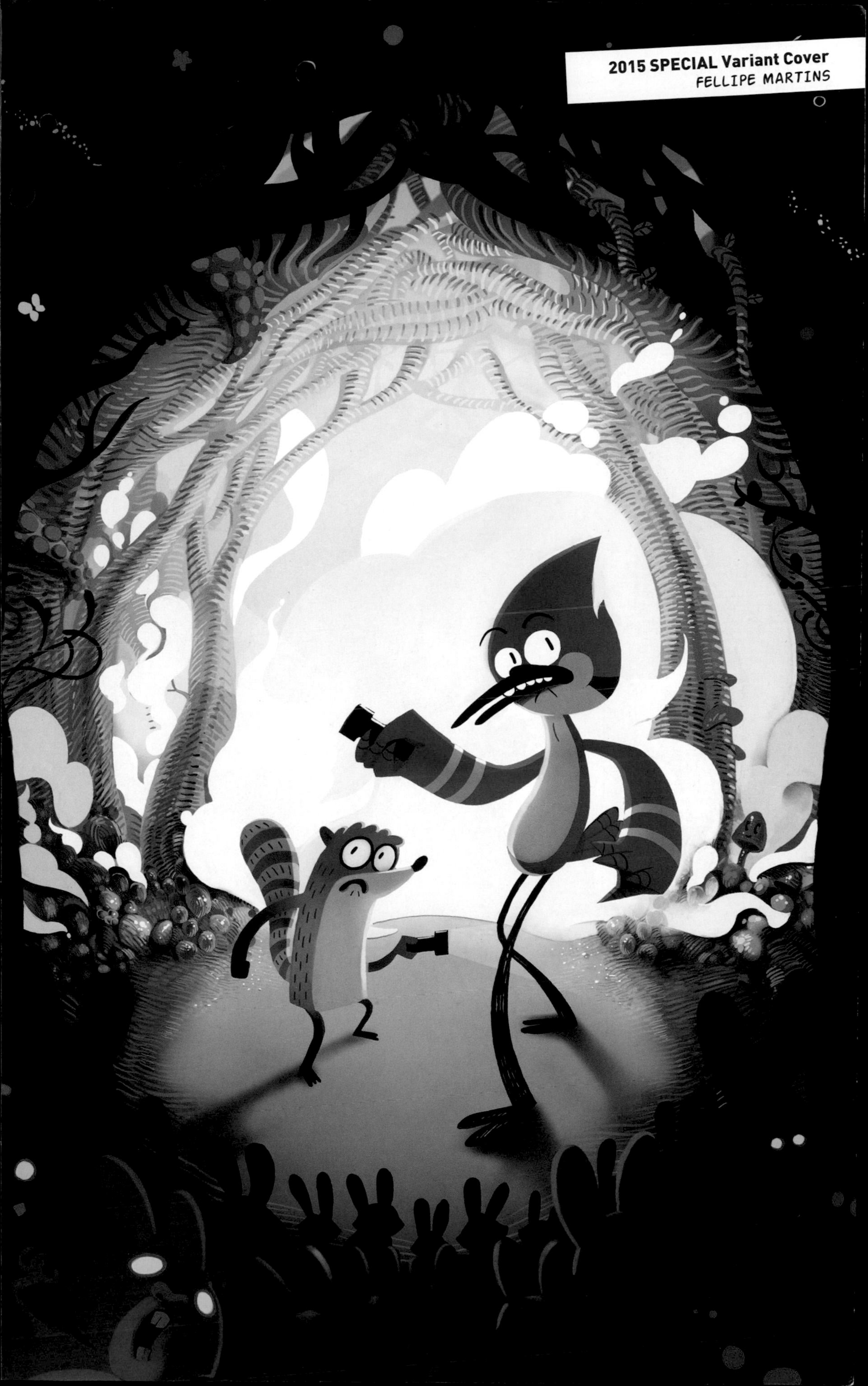

2015 SPECIAL Variant Cover
FELLIPE MARTINS

2017 SPECIAL Main Cover
DEREK FRIDOLFS
WITH COLORS BY PAMELA LOVAS

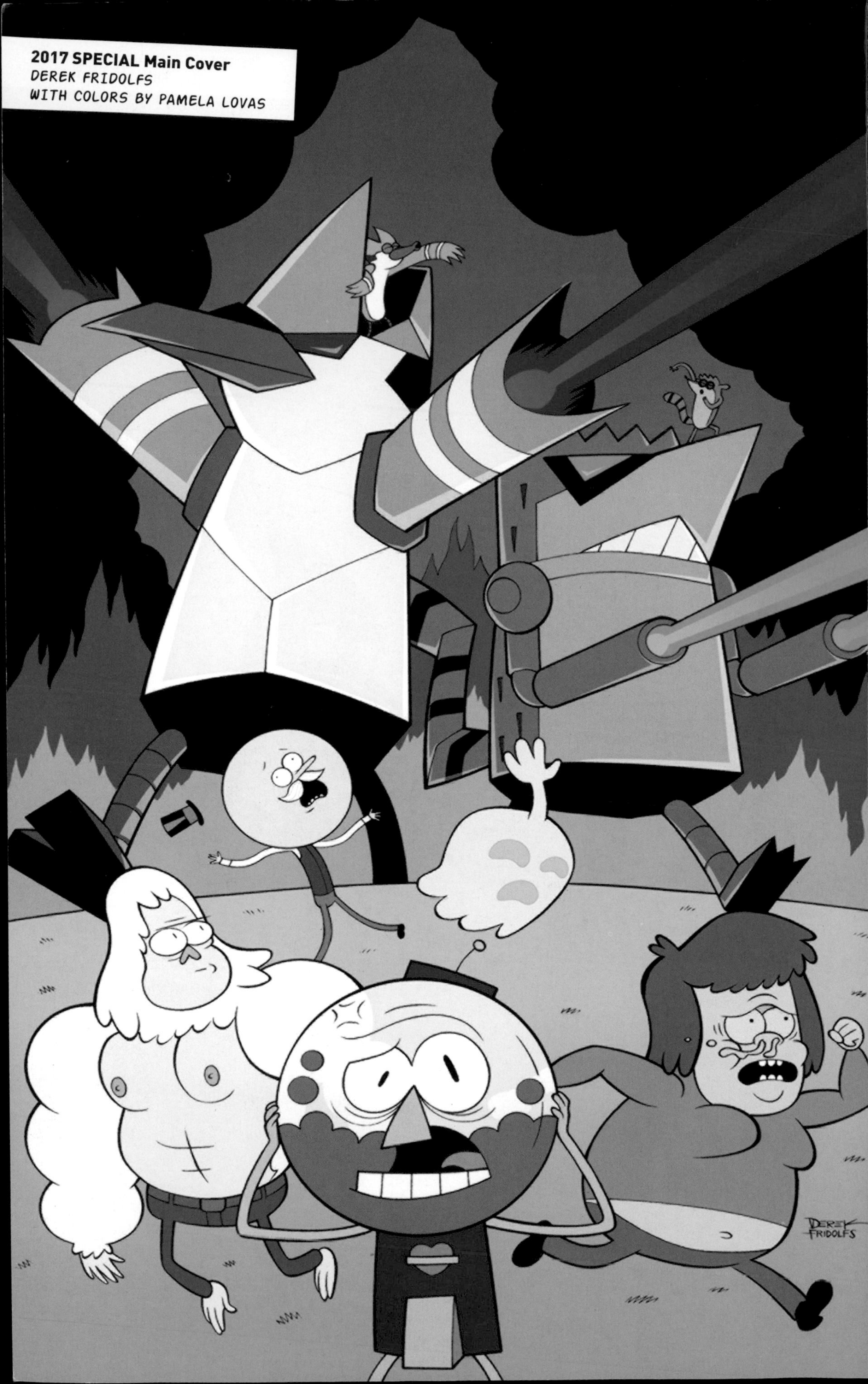
DEREK
FRIDOLFS

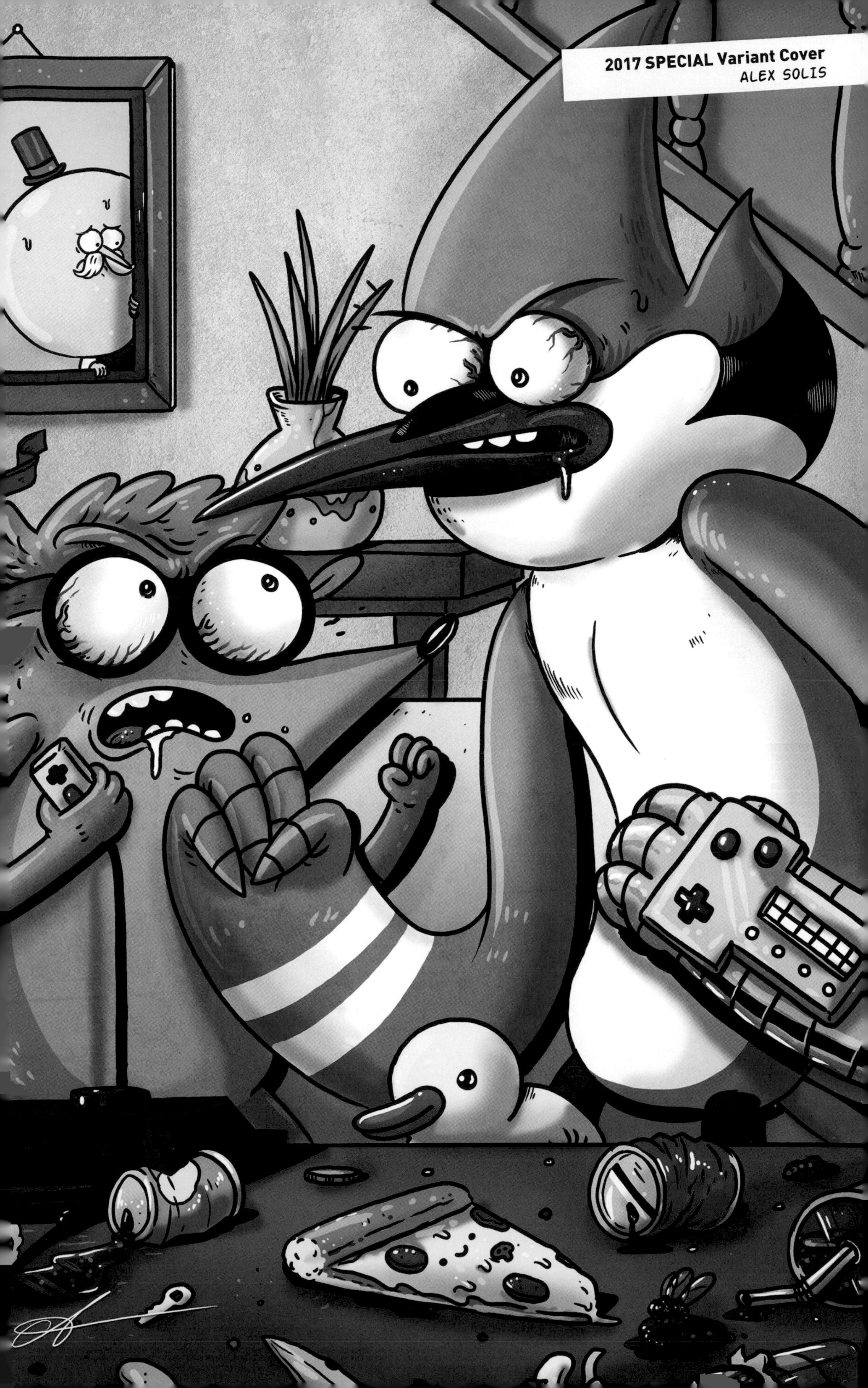

2017 SPECIAL Variant Cover
ALEX SOLIS

DISCOVER
EXPLOSIVE NEW WORLDS

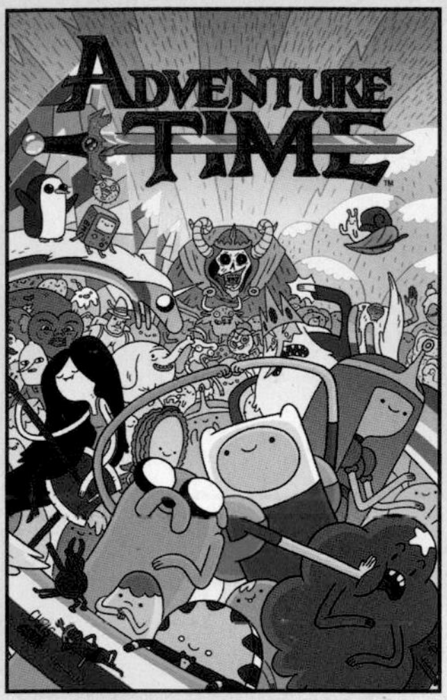
ADVENTURE TIME

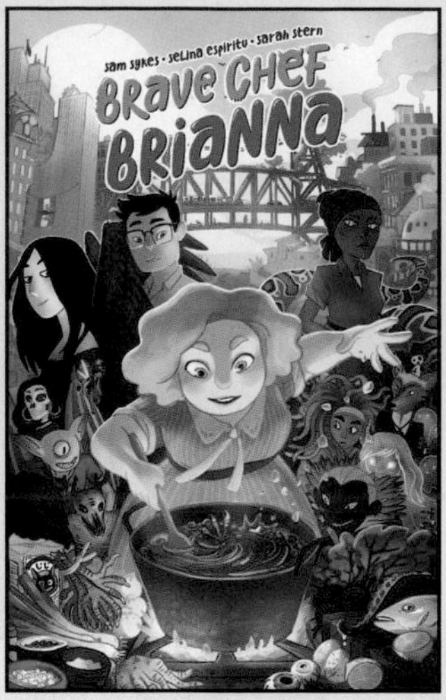
sam sykes · selina espiritu · sarah stern
BRAVE CHEF BRIANNA

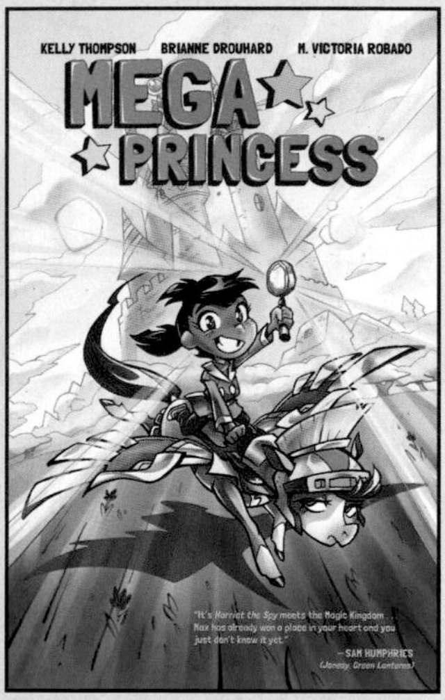
KELLY THOMPSON BRIANNE DROUHARD M. VICTORIA ROBADO
MEGA PRINCESS

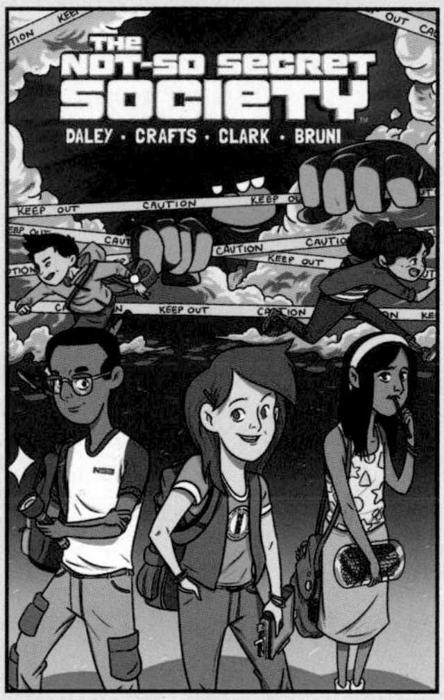
THE NOT-SO SECRET SOCIETY
DALEY · CRAFTS · CLARK · BRUNI

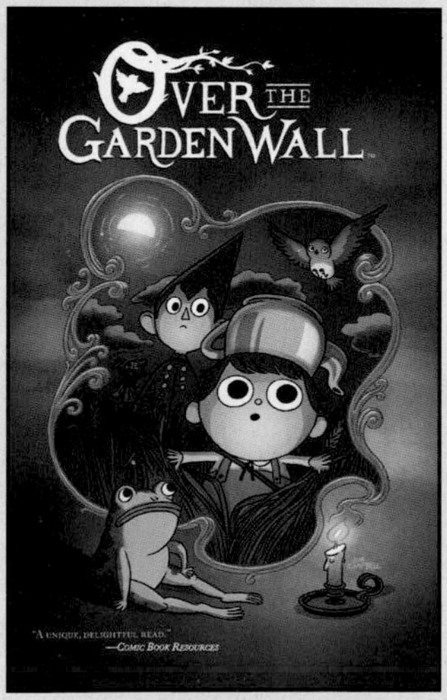
OVER THE GARDEN WALL

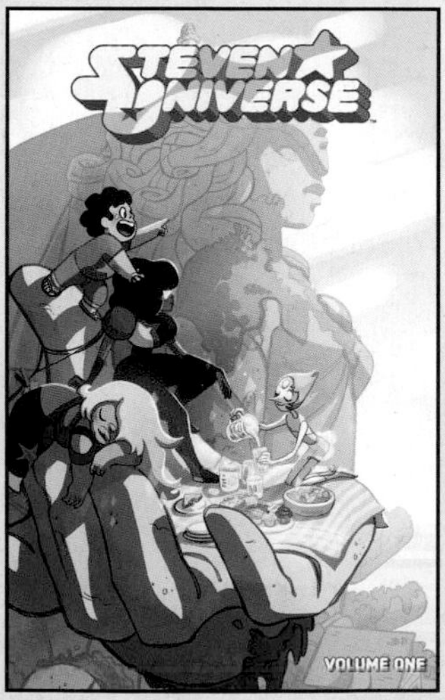
STEVEN UNIVERSE
VOLUME ONE

Adventure Time
Pendleton Ward and Others
Volume 1
ISBN: 978-1-60886-280-1 | $14.99 US
Volume 2
ISBN: 978-1-60886-323-5 | $14.99 US
Adventure Time: Islands
ISBN: 978-1-60886-972-5 | $9.99 US

The Amazing World of Gumball
Ben Bocquelet and Others
Volume 1
ISBN: 978-1-60886-488-1 | $14.99 US
Volume 2
ISBN: 978-1-60886-793-6 | $14.99 US

Brave Chef Brianna
Sam Sykes, Selina Espiritu
ISBN: 978-1-68415-050-2 | $14.99 US

Mega Princess
Kelly Thompson, Brianne Drouhard
ISBN: 978-1-68415-007-6 | $14.99 US

The Not-So Secret Society
Matthew Daley, Arlene Daley, Wook Jin Clark
ISBN: 978-1-60886-997-8 | $9.99 US

Over the Garden Wall
Patrick McHale, Jim Campbell and Others
Volume 1
ISBN: 978-1-60886-940-4 | $14.99 US
Volume 2
ISBN: 978-1-68415-006-9 | $14.99 US

Steven Universe
Rebecca Sugar and Others
Volume 1
ISBN: 978-1-60886-706-6 | $14.99 US
Volume 2
ISBN: 978-1-60886-796-7 | $14.99 US

Steven Universe & The Crystal Gems
ISBN: 978-1-60886-921-3 | $14.99 US

Steven Universe: Too Cool for School
ISBN: 978-1-60886-771-4 | $14.99 US

kaboom!™

AVAILABLE AT YOUR LOCAL COMICS SHOP AND BOOKSTORE
To find a comics shop in your area, call 1-888-266-4226
WWW.**BOOM-STUDIOS**.COM